A DANCE

⚛ WITH THE ⚛

DEVIL

A DANCE
⚜ WITH THE ⚜
DEVIL

**Rexanne Becnel
Anne Logan
Deborah Martin
Meagan McKinney**

St. Martin's Paperbacks

"The Wager" copyright © 1997 by Rexanne Becnel.
"The Haunting of Sarah" copyright © 1997 by Barbara Colley.
"Out of the Night" copyright © 1997 by Deborah Martin Gonzalez.
"The Monk" copyright © 1997 by Meagan McKinney.
Excerpt from *Dangerous to Love* copyright © 1997 by Rexanne Becnel.

A DANCE WITH THE DEVIL

ISBN: 0-312-96318-1

Printed in the United States of America

St. Martin's Paperbacks edition/October 1997

St. Martin's Paperbacks are published by St. Martin's Press, 175 Fifth Avenue, New York, NY 10010.

10 9 8 7 6 5 4 3 2 1

CONTENTS

THE WAGER

REXANNE BECNEL

CHAPTER ONE

"No. He can't be at the Devil's table!"

The young stableboy looked guiltily away. He dug his bare toes into the loose dirt and straw that made up the stable floor. "That's what he tole me, Miss Mandy. But don't you worry. Ain't nobody can beat Mr. Pierre at cards."

Amanda Chastain stared aghast at the stableboy. To hear Gerald tell it, her brother, Pierre, could do no wrong. But it was one thing to outride, outhunt and outgamble the young men of Jefferson City. It was another thing entirely to match wits with the most notorious gambler in New Orleans.

"Heavenly day!" she swore, sucking in a hard breath. She'd known it would come to this. She'd prayed it wouldn't, but a part of her had known it would. Ever since his friend Louis de Montluzin had told Pierre about the fabulous sums wagered in the imposing town house so recently purchased by Nicholas Devereaux, Pierre had become obsessed with the idea of obtaining an invitation to the exclusive card games played there. Though Pierre possessed a remarkable skill with cards, Amanda lived in dread of that one turn of a card that might ruin them. Skill would only carry her brother so far; luck was a factor far less predictable.

"Don't worry, Miss Mandy. Mr. Pierre, he's gonna whip that fancy gamblin' man. Just you see if he don't."

Amanda grimaced. "And what if Devereaux whips him? What if instead of only losing his favorite team of horses this time, Pierre loses the warehouse? Or our home?" She gestured at the stable and grounds and gracious home her parents had completed only months before their tragic deaths. "What will we do—what will *you* do without your position here at Magnolia Shade?"

Gerald had no reply to that unpleasant thought. Nor did Amanda want to consider what would happen should Pierre be so foolish as to get in over his head at the card table. But it had happened to Marcus Landry earlier this fall. He'd lost his home and small plantation. That's when she had first heard of Nicholas Devereaux, the Devil of the Tables, as he was now called. Word of him had spread far and wide, even out to quiet little Jefferson City. Devereaux was said to be a brilliant card player, possessed of uncanny luck, and utterly without a shred of mercy for his victims.

Marcus Landry had died the day after that fateful card game. Gossip held that the gunshot wound he'd sustained had been no accident, but self-inflicted in a fit of abject remorse. But Amanda did not know if that was true. Suffice it to say, the poor man was dead, and his wife and child had been forced to move downriver to live with her parents.

Unfortunately, Amanda and her brother had no one to turn to should Pierre prove as foolish as Marcus Landry. Yellow fever had claimed their parents six years previously. They had a distant cousin in Mobile, but no one else.

Pierre, however, would never take that into consideration. Of late he'd been frustrated by the steady but slow living the warehouse brought them, and his courtship of Mary Louise Delachaise only made him more so. He wanted a swifter—and easier—source of funds.

But Amanda refused to let him sacrifice their modest living to his grandiose schemes. She must stop him before he ruined both their lives.

"Saddle my mare."

Gerald's eyes widened in indignation. "Miss Mandy! You know you can't go into town on horseback."

"Yes, and I'm sure that's exactly what Pierre was thinking when he took the carriage. But nevertheless I will go, whether it be on Dolly, in the open wagon, or even on foot. Now do as I say! Saddle Dolly and bring her around while I fetch my bonnet and gloves."

Within minutes she was ready to depart. The fact that their housekeeper Effie did not scold Amanda for her scandalous plan proved to Amanda how dangerous Pierre's behavior was. The old servant, who was cook, housekeeper, and mother to Amanda and her brother, only tucked her young charge's unruly locks up into her bonnet and tied the blue grosgrain ribbon securely beneath her chin.

"Take Gerald with you. And if you see anyone you know, well, just say you lookin' for Mr. Pierre. Say that . . . say that I took sick, an' that I'm callin' for Lester, an' Lester is with Mr. Pierre. Lord, lord," she added, "I'm goin' to give that man a piece of my mind when he gits back home. Sneakin' off without tellin' me where he's goin'."

Amanda nodded as she fastened her gloves. She knew, however, that Lester wasn't the one who deserved the scolding; Pierre did. As always Pierre had sucked both Lester and Gerald into another of his outrageous schemes. But this was the last time, Amanda swore. The very last time.

She knotted a shawl over her spencer and gave Effie a tight hug. "Wish me luck that I am not too late. I promise you, though, it shall be Pierre who needs luck when I find him."

"Now, don't you go losin' your temper with him in front of his friends. That'll only make him more stubborn, child."

Again Amanda nodded. Pierre might be her older brother, but he could become as difficult as a spoiled little boy when denied what he wanted. As she hurried into the stable yard and stepped onto the mounting block, she resolved to rein in her temper no matter how provoked she became.

Still, as she urged Dolly into a brisk canter with Gerald trailing her on his pony, a part of her wished she'd brought one of her father's pistols with her. This was Nicholas Devereaux's fault. He was the one who had tempted her foolish brother to gamble beyond his means. He had ruined one man and now, without a shred of remorse, he was tempting another to the same fate. To shoot the dastardly fellow would surely be a boon to the entire community.

When Glapion, the butler, entered the smoke-filled study, Nicholas did not look up. The man should know better than to interrupt in the middle of a card game. Nicholas's man, Red, immediately signaled the butler to leave, then followed the scowling servant out. No doubt Nicholas's self-appointed bodyguard and valet would give the officious butler a quick lesson in the etiquette of gambling. A man holding two pairs did not appreciate being interrupted for any reason at all.

Marcel Robichaux threw down his cards, swearing softly in French. Nicholas turned his noncommittal stare on Nathan Soniat. The crafty banker's face was as studiously blank as was his own. But the fourth player, young Chastain, was frowning. It was faint, more a squint than an actual frown. But he did the same thing every time he had a decent hand— not a great hand that was a sure bet, but one that could go either way.

Nicholas decided to test the man's mettle. "I'll keep my cards and raise. Say a hundred."

The young man's squint turned into a full-fledged scowl. "Damn. I'm out." He slapped his cards down and looked over at Nicholas, his expression turning curious. But Nicholas had no intention of satisfying that curiosity. He had a purpose in letting Chastain play at his private table. The warehouse the youth had inherited was perfectly suited to take advantage of New Orleans's upriver growth. But it was sorely underused at the present. Properly managed it could bring in a pretty sum every month, and he was just the man to see that it did. Nicholas had already taken most of the young man's cash, as well as a thoroughbred yearling possessed of impeccable blood-lines. He meant to win the warehouse as well, and the best way to do that was to keep the eager young man guessing.

"Well, Soniat? Are you in or not?"

Sweat had begun to bead on the banker's brow. But Nicholas did not mean to fleece the man. He only wanted to keep him beholden to him, just a little in debt. After all, you could never tell when you might need a banker in your pocket.

A commotion in the hall interrupted the concentrated silence of the room. A muffled voice pierced the quiet. Was that a woman? He focused on Soniat. "In or out? Or will you raise?" he added, a hint of humor in his tone.

The banker slapped his cards down. "I'm out. And I'm leaving," he vowed, pushing to his feet. "You have the devil's own luck, Devereaux. And tonight I have none. Gentlemen, I bid you a good night."

Nicholas allowed himself a faint smile. But he was careful not to show his winning hand to the avid young Chastain. Let him wonder, he thought as he gathered up the deck. Only then did he rake in his winnings.

Something bumped against the door. Nicholas stood to see Soniat out. He also wanted to determine what was going on out in his foyer.

Then the door flew open and a disheveled young woman hurtled into the room and barreled right into his chest.

He caught her before she could fall: It was an automatic reflex. In the scant moments it took for her to regain her balance and pull out of his hold, he had the fleeting impression of soap and roses and horses. Also, of a sweetly yielding form. But she wasn't any of the several women he'd become acquainted with since moving to New Orleans. She was of the respectable sort, with her hair tucked into her bonnet and her bosom well covered by a modest gown and a knotted shawl.

"I beg your pardon," Amanda murmured breathlessly, backing away from the man who had so gallantly caught her. She'd been off-balance when that obnoxious man had tried to bar her from the room, so when the door had unexpectedly given way, she'd gone flying. Now as she straightened her jacket, tugging on the snug waist, she shot the unpleasant servant a smug look. Then she turned to her benefactor.

Though she was not short, she was only as tall as his chest—a very broad chest, that was but inches from her nose. When she tilted her head back, she found a square chin with a faint cleft in it, a pair of amused lips, soft looking and yet hard in a most distracting sort of way, and then a straight, strong nose and a pair of fathomless blue eyes set beneath slashing black brows. Amanda couldn't help but stare.

It was the face of a man who was as beautiful as an angel and as dangerous as a devil. Devereaux, she at once realized. This *must* be Nicholas Devereaux.

Faced with the very devil she'd come to protect her brother from, she could only gape at him, swallow hard, and struggle to regain her scattered wits.

"Mandy! What in God's name are you doing here!"

The sound of Pierre's voice galvanized Amanda. Relieved to have a focus other than the imposing gambler, she turned to face her wayward brother.

"What am *I* doing here? What am *I* doing here!" She planted her fists on her hips and glared at him. "What do you think I'm doing here? I've come to get you—" She broke off, remembering almost too late Effie's cautionary words, then glanced up at Devereaux. To her dismay, he was studying her with eyes far too perceptive for comfort. Wrenching her gaze away from his, she cleared her throat and again addressed Pierre. "Effie is ill. She needs Lester."

But she could tell that Pierre did not believe her, for his face had gone red with indignation. "If that's all it is, you could have sent Gerald for Lester. You didn't have to make a spectacle of yourself this way!"

Before she could think of some reply to salvage the situation, Devereaux spoke. "It appears your sweetheart is trying in her own not-so-subtle manner, to remove you from the gaming tables. Perhaps she fears you are in over your head," he added, grinning openly now.

Of all the things he could have said, that taunting suggestion strengthened Pierre's stubborn streak the most. But then, Amanda speculated, Devereaux knew that. He had not become so skilled a gambler without understanding human nature. And he had Pierre and his foolish masculine pride pegged exactly right.

"She's not my sweetheart," Pierre snapped. "She's my sis-ter. God help the poor man who marries her, for she is stubborn and willful, and she doesn't listen to a thing I say.''

"Isn't that a bit redundant?" Devereaux asked, arching one of his brows. The other two men in the room laughed, as did the feisty fellow who'd tried to keep her out. Amanda could feel her cheeks heating, but her brother's scowl only turned blacker.

"If I am redundant, it is because she's three times as hardheaded as any other woman you shall ever chance to meet." Pierre grabbed her by the arm and rudely steered her from the room. "I'll return directly," he called over his shoulder. "Just as soon as I settle with my sister."

"Take your time," Devereaux replied. "We'll refresh ourselves while you handle your domestic crisis."

If looks could have killed, the glare Amanda sent back at her brother's wicked host would have struck him down. How dare he laugh at her? But that was precisely what he was doing. Laughing at her. Dismissing her. Taunting her brother so that now she would never get him to leave here. But her hateful stare did not kill him or strike him down or have any other effect except to make him wink at her.

Wink at her!

She jerked her head around as her brother forced her down the tall stairs, across the foyer, and up to the front door. Only then did he pause, breathing hard from his angry emotion.

"What in God's name do you think you are doing, coming to this place after me? If Effie is in need of Lester—"

"This has nothing to do with Effie, which you would know if you had an ounce of common sense in your head! You have no right to risk our livelihood on a game of chance with this man!"

"I have the right to do anything I want, and no younger sister is going to stop me!" Then his expression softened and his tone became less strident. "Mandy, you have to have some faith in me. I'm good at this, much better than I am at managing the warehouse or raising racehorses. I can make a fortune for us tonight. A fortune!"

"And you can just as easily lose everything we have," she

countered. "What are you betting with, anyway? We have little enough extra cash."

He gave her a smug smile. "I've been preparing for this game. I've been saving my winnings so I'd have a large enough stake to grant me entrance here."

Amanda studied him a long moment. "And how much of that stake do you still hold?"

When his face flushed, she knew. She groaned, then took his hands in hers. "Pierre, you must stop this madness!"

But he would not listen and instead threw off her pleading hold. "I am the man of this family. I will make the decisions." Then with an angry movement, he jerked open the door and thrust her unceremoniously out onto the steps. Spying Gerald holding her horse, he called out.

"Have Lester take my sister home in the carriage, Gerald. You will wait for me with the horses. Bring them around to the courtyard." He turned back to Amanda. "Before this day is out our fortunes will have changed for the better. You will see. And you will apologize to me for this sorry display you have made." Then he closed the door right in her face.

Amanda was too outraged to think clearly. He'd put her out! And now, because she'd humiliated him in front of his decadent new friends, he would be even more reckless than before. He was that set on proving her wrong!

Helplessly, she spun around. But there was only Gerald and the two horses, and with a shrug, the boy untethered the animals and led them down the shaded carriageway into the back courtyard.

Amanda wanted to cry, but she knew that would do her no good. She wanted to knock her brother over the head and drag him home—or better yet, knock Nicholas Devereaux over the head and . . . and throw him into the river!

But neither of those was a realistic recourse. She had to satisfy herself with stomping furiously down the carriageway to find Lester and their carriage. She had no intention of leaving, however. No indeed. She would wait in the coach until the game was over.

When she strode into the lush courtyard and spied the loathsome Devereaux sauntering across the brick-paved yard heading back to the house from the privy, a desperate idea popped into her head. Though it galled her to even consider such a thing, the fact remained, she had no choice. If Pierre would not listen, then she must appeal to the devil himself.

When she came into the courtyard, he had looked over at her, and now, when she changed directions and headed his way, he paused and waited. To her dismay, his acerbic eyes studied her with a disturbing intensity, from her flushed face and disheveled hair, to her everyday dress and dusty boots, to her worn riding gloves.

She should have dressed more carefully instead of dashing out so precipitously. As she halted before him, she could not help but be aware of his impeccable dress. Even in his shirtsleeves he was the essence of masculine beauty, the form of a Greek god clad in the finest example of the tailor's art. She would wager that he had not purchased his garments in New Orleans.

Then she gave herself a stern mental shake. Neither his personal appearance nor his wardrobe were of any concern to her. She lifted her chin and tried to appear taller than she was.

"I do not approve of gambling."

He gave her a smile—a half smile, really. But it was doubly as effective as any other man's most charming grin. "That much I figured out on my own. But tell me, do you possess a name, or do you respond only to 'Pierre's sister'?" Then his smile widened to reveal a set of perfect white teeth. "But no, I recall now that he called you Mandy."

"Amanda," she corrected him.

"Amanda," he repeated. Then he took her hand and made her a short bow. "Please allow me to introduce myself to you, Amanda. I am Nicholas Devereaux, at your service."

"I know who you are!" she snapped, snatching her hand away from him.

"Do you now? And how is it that you know of me, when I'm certain we've never been introduced?" he replied, fairly burning her with the intensity of his smile.

An odd tingle of awareness swept through Amanda. Oh, but

he was every bit the devil his reputation made of him, for he could as easily entice a virtuous young woman to wayward thoughts as he tempted foolish young men to gamble away their livelihoods. But she must be stronger than Pierre—and stronger than Devereaux too. She decided to be blunt.

"Everyone knows who you are. Everyone who knows of Marcus Landry and his poor, widowed wife," she added.

That chased the smug grin from his face, much to her satisfaction. She saw a muscle flex in his jaw and felt a small spurt of self-righteousness. Maybe he would think better of flirting with her now that he knew what she thought of him.

He inclined his head as if conceding that she had reason to be suspicious of him, then gave her a questioning look. "You have sought me out for a reason?"

Amanda took a deep breath. "Yes. I . . . I would plead with you not to gamble any further with my brother."

"He is a man, is he not? And fully capable of managing his own affairs. Perhaps you underestimate his skill."

"I do not underestimate his skill," she retorted. "But I also do not underestimate yours."

"Thank you."

"It was not meant as a compliment!"

He grinned. "Nonetheless, I will take it as such. But tell me, is there no one besides you to curtail your brother's careless ways with the family money?"

"If there were I would not be forced to make my appeal to you. Had I a father or other brothers, I would have them drag him away from here, though he go kicking and screaming the whole way."

This time he laughed out loud, a deep rumble she found most disconcerting. Although she had not come here to amuse him, she could only hope that his good humor would put him in a generous mood. "So, will you end this game before he loses all to you?" she pleaded.

He cocked his head to one side as if he were giving serious consideration to her request, and Amanda allowed herself a tiny flicker of hope. But then he shook his head and even that hope vanished.

"I cannot send him away from my card table. It would not be polite, nor would it enhance my reputation among New Orleans's sporting elite."

"But . . . but . . ." Amanda wrung her hands as she searched her mind. "But what if you pleaded a . . . a headache? Then no one would know—"

He took her clenched hands in his. "Where is my incentive to do such a thing?"

"Your incentive? What about common decency?" She tore her hands from his. "You've already ruined the Landry family. Isn't that enough? Must you ruin my family too?"

She was angry; she was desperate. She was breathless with the depths of her emotion. He, meanwhile, was as cool and unfazed as ever. It quite sent her over the edge. "You dress as a gentleman and set yourself up in a gentleman's house. But you are no gentleman. No, not at all!"

He did not so much as wince. "No doubt you meant that as the vilest sort of insult, but I am afraid you aim it at the wrong man. I am a gambler, Miss Chastain. And if you would bargain with me, you'd be better served thinking as a gambler might."

That drew her up. She stared warily at him. "What do you mean?"

He again reached for her hand. "Perhaps you would enter into a side wager with me." His midnight gaze locked with hers, holding her captive. "Perhaps we can find a way for you to save your brother from his own folly. If indeed it is folly," he added, giving her the same half smile from before.

Between that potent gaze and the feel of his strong fingers encircling hers, Amanda's heart began suddenly to race. "I'm . . . I'm not certain I fully catch your meaning."

"Then let me speak more plainly. I have already won all of your brother's cash, his watch, and a fine emerald ring, as well as an exceptional thoroughbred yearling. My goal tonight is to win his warehouse along the river in Jefferson City. That is why I invited him to join me today."

Amanda gasped. He was even more ruthless than she'd thought. This was no friendly game but rather cold-blooded robbery. Except that it was legal. She tried to pull away from him, but this time he would not let her go. Instead, he forcibly drew her into a shadowed niche between the cistern and a huge camellia covered with buds.

"Listen to me, Amanda, for this is the only chance I will give you. I do not believe in charity. If I want something, I go after it. So if you would deal with me, you will have to be every bit as ruthless."

He released her hands and stepped back. "Now here is my offer. I propose a side bet between the two of us, just you and me. You can bet on who will walk away with the warehouse tonight, me or your brother. If you bet wisely, you will win back all his losses."

Though her first instinct was to flee him and the intimate setting he'd put them in, Amanda hesitated. Her mind spun. Was this a trick? "What if Pierre doesn't lose? What if he wins everything back from you?"

"Then you would be wise to bet on him to win."

"Wait a moment. Let me be sure I understand." She gnawed her lower lip. "No matter which one of you wins, if I bet on the right one, then I will win everything of ours back, whether he's actually lost it or not?"

"That's right."

"And what happens if I bet on the wrong man to win?"

"If you bet wrong . . ." His eyes held steady with hers. "If you bet wrong, then you must spend the night with me."

CHAPTER TWO

You must spend the night with me.

At first his meaning did not register with Amanda, for the implication was simply beyond her frame of reference. Even when she finally understood, she could not react—not beyond a quick intake of breath and a hot rush of color to her face.

She should have slapped him or stomped away in a huff. But instead she stupidly said the very first thing that came into her head.

"Tonight?"

He arched his brows in surprise. "If that is what you prefer. You *do* understand what I mean, don't you? By spending the night I mean—"

"I know what you mean!" she snapped. She stepped back from him, as horrified by his offer as she was by her idiotic response to it. What was she thinking? "You are even more despicable than I thought!"

He shrugged. "I did not have to make you the offer. If you do not like the terms, you have only to say no—and trust in your brother to win. It's only a warehouse, after all."

Only a warehouse. But it was also the sole source of their income. Their house was already mortgaged to the limits of its value. If they lost the warehouse, they would swiftly lose their home as well.

Amanda squashed the rising panic that realization engendered and tried to think. If she bet on Pierre to win but he lost—

Heavenly day, could she actually be contemplating such a thing?

"I need your answer, Amanda. I've already been away from my guests too long."

"If you will just let me think!"

She frowned, staring blankly at the white painted boards of the cistern. If she bet on Pierre to win but he lost, then he would have lost the warehouse and she would lose her . . . her innocence. She swallowed hard at that thought but pressed on. But if she bet on her brother to win, and he did, then they would have lost nothing, neither her nor Pierre.

But what were the odds of Pierre winning?

If, on the other hand, she bet on Nicholas Devereaux to win . . . If he were to win the warehouse from Pierre, then she would get it back, and their home would be safe. Of course, she would have to come up with some explanation for *how* she'd won it back. But she would deal with that problem if and when she had to.

But what if she bet on Devereaux to win and he lost? Their home would still be safe, for Pierre would not have lost it. But then, she'd have to submit to Devereaux.

She swallowed hard. The facts were plain: If she bet on Nicholas Devereaux to win, then she and Pierre could not possibly lose the warehouse or, therefore, their home. With that sudden understanding came a flood of relief. But did her purity as a woman have no value? Was it of less importance than their home and livelihood?

The part of her that was a proper young woman, innocent and virtuous, valued her honor and purity above all else— certainly above the price of mere property. Yet another part of her—the part that had scrimped and saved, and learned to be so careful with every penny these last seven years—that part could not bear the thought of Pierre so frivolously gambling their possessions away. Especially when she could save those possessions by simply agreeing to Devereaux's proposition, hideous though it might be.

"I must insist on an answer, Miss Chastain. My guests await."

She stared up at him, her face creased in indecision. "Is there no other way? Will you not relent?"

His smug expression was his only answer, but it was enough to dash her last vestige of hope. It had come down to her honor or her home. She gritted her teeth. "Very well then," she muttered, hoping her voice did not tremble. "I accept the terms of your wager, despicable though they are."

That half smile of his came out again. And why shouldn't it? she grimly thought. He believed he would defeat both brother and sister tonight. She had the consolation, at least, of knowing that her home was safe no matter what else she might lose.

"Very well," he said. He extended his hand to her. "Shall we shake hands on it then?"

Amanda gritted her teeth. "There is one other detail. You must agree that no one besides the two of us is ever to know of this wager we make. Not the terms nor the outcome."

"Agreed." He held his hand steadily toward her.

"Especially my brother," she continued.

"Agreed. Now come, Amanda. Give me your hand in good faith."

She did so reluctantly, mainly because he was a horrible man and she despised him. But there was a small part of her that feared the impact of his touch. There was something about him that was disturbing in a way she could not precisely explain. He was like the electrical shocking machine she'd seen at the Cotton Centennial. He sent the oddest tingle through her.

When at last she grasped his much larger hand, the tingle was distressingly strong, more so than before. Did he feel it too? she wondered.

Then he brought her hand to his lips and the tingle became a jolt of unnameable emotion.

Amanda snatched her hand back and clasped her hands at her throat. Heavenly day, what was it about this man? No wonder he was called a devil by so many!

She stared at him round-eyed as he straightened from his bow. "I regret that I must take my leave of you now. The game awaits—both the one with your brother and the one with you."

Amanda swallowed hard. "Don't you want to know whom I shall bet on?"

He arched one black brow. "I must be exceedingly distracted to have neglected that detail. By all means, reveal your favorite."

"I favor you," she stated. "I mean, I favor you to win."

"You are wagering on me to win, not your brother?"

She smiled in the face of his faint surprise. "If I bet on you, I cannot lose. Whether you win or lose the card game I shall keep the warehouse, and therefore, my home."

He smiled then, the first truly sincere smile he'd given her, and her heart gave a queer lurch. If he were only sincere all the time—

But she killed that thought before it could fairly begin. He might be as handsome as the devil, she reminded herself, but he was also just as heartless.

"Very well reasoned, Amanda. Very well indeed. I, however, believe that *I* cannot lose." So saying, he bowed, turned on his heel, and left.

Just that easily did he destroy all her confidence. Amanda watched him depart with a growing dread. What did he mean, he could not lose? No matter who won the card game, he could not hope to win the warehouse he wanted. At least that was how she had it figured. So how did he think *he* could win?

Then it struck her, and her knees grew weak beneath her. He wasn't referring to the warehouse; he was referring to her. If he would lose the warehouse even if he won the game, then he had no incentive to try to best Pierre. For if he lost to her brother, he would at least gain something: He would gain her in his bed. And though that might not be what he'd set out to win when he'd invited her brother to play, it seemed clear that he considered it adequate compensation for this day's work.

*   *   *

Nicholas splashed a generous amount of dark rum into a heavy tumbler. Behind him Robichaux and the hotheaded Chastain were settled back at the baize-covered table, impatiently awaiting his return. But he did not hurry. Better to have them anxious and overeager to bet their money—or their warehouse, as the case might be.

That was not his only reason for delaying, however. His unexpected side wager with the animated Amanda Chastain still occupied more of his thoughts than the game now at hand. What a beauty she was with flashing blue eyes and a figure made to fit a man's hands.

But she was a lady, not a woman of easy virtue. That he had proposed such a thing to her was outrageous. That she had accepted, then reasoned out a sure way to retain her family's warehouse was astonishing. But that he could be so inexplicably drawn to such an innocent and respectable young woman . . . That was beyond all comprehension.

Deflowering virgins was not his style. So why had he proposed such a ludicrous side wager?

Because he'd long passed the point of being merely a cynic, the answer came. Because the games of chance he filled his time with no longer afforded him the challenge they once had. Where once he'd had to gamble to earn his keep, that was no longer necessary. Yet still he continued in the same fashion. Long hours around the table, drinking too much, smoking too much. Spending all his time with people he didn't care anything about.

But then Amanda Chastain had come bursting into his house, and in her he'd found a new sort of challenge, one he'd not felt in too long.

He grinned to himself. She'd said she did not approve of gambling, but she'd jumped at his offer quick enough. An innocent virgin she might be, but she was also strong-willed and brave, with a passionate heart. Though he knew he should feel guilty for his despicable behavior, the fact was, all he felt was an almost embarrassing anticipation.

"Sit down, Devereaux. Sit down. You owe me the chance to recoup my losses. To delay avails you of naught."

At Robichaux's friendly challenge, Nicholas downed the smooth Jamaican spirits, then refilled his glass. Since he meant to lose, he'd better get on with it. But it was only Chastain he meant to lose to. Robichaux he meant to fleece within an inch of the man's life.

Amanda waited in the carriage. She could not bear to return to Magnolia Shade without knowing her fate. In the past she'd sent many a prayer heavenward that Pierre would give up his dangerous obsession with cards. She'd never prayed over the outcome of his games, though. That had seemed too hypocritical. Even had she done so, it would surely have been that he won. But not this day. She sat in the dim interior of the ancient coupe rockaway, aware of the passage of time, of the shadows of dusk and the cooling evening breezes, and she prayed for her brother to lose.

Please, dear God, let Pierre lose. Please make Devereaux win, though it be by some ludicrous fluke.

But it was a futile prayer, and even as she clasped her fingers together to the point of pain, she knew her fate was sealed. When Pierre's voice carried across the courtyard to her, jubilant and cocky, her heart sank.

"What? You haven't taken my sister home yet? Ah, but that may be for the best, Lester. Where is my doubting sister, my headstrong sister who cannot muster an adequate faith in her older, wiser brother?"

"She's inside here, Mr. Pierre. And she's sure gonna be glad you won tonight. She sure is."

"Perhaps she would be more satisfied hearing the news from me," another voice, deeper than her brother's, suggested.

Amanda began to tremble. Had Devereaux come to claim her here and now? He'd promised to keep their wager a secret. Could it be he had lied?

"Come, Mandy. I know you're in there," Pierre called. His voice was much changed from the biting tone it had held when he'd dragged her out of the house and ordered her home. That he could sound so indulgent and patronizing now riled her to no end. He actually believed he'd defeated Devereaux, the

Devil of the Tables. But she knew better. Only she must bite her tongue.

When he pulled the carriage door open and leaned in to see her, her face was set in a pained smile.

"I am relieved by your mood, Pierre. I gather you have won a generous sum from . . . from your host."

His smug expression faltered just a bit. "Well, I wouldn't say generous."

"He has won back all he'd lost and a small sum of cash besides." A hand pulled back the curtain, and Devereaux's handsome face filled the window opening. "He returns to you none the worse off than he arrived."

You, however, are in far less promising circumstances, his impossibly dark eyes seemed to say. They were nearly black in the fading light, the color of the midnight sky, and yet they burned her with their heat.

She looked away, suddenly short of breath. "Perhaps we should leave," she managed to say.

"Yes, perhaps so," Pierre agreed, less cocky now that it had been revealed that he'd won nothing but what he'd already lost.

"I hope we'll have another occasion to meet." Devereaux spoke this to Amanda.

She glanced sidelong at him, then down at the lace-edged handkerchief she'd twisted into knots. "Perhaps," she finally answered.

She could feel the sweep of his eyes on her downturned profile. She fancied she could hear the confident grin in his voice. "I'm certain the circumstances will be far more pleasant the next time."

This time she didn't answer at all, but only nodded curtly.

The two men made their farewells. After tying her horse behind the carriage, Pierre climbed in and they thankfully were off.

Amanda would have preferred riding alone, for her emotions were in a turmoil, and she had the foolish idea that somehow Pierre would detect her thoughts and realize what had happened.

What would he do then?

He would challenge Devereaux to a duel, she realized, shuddering. After all, the man had insulted her just by suggesting such a wager. To try to collect on it . . . A chill ran down her spine. Yes, Pierre would most assuredly challenge the man to a duel, and he might very well be killed for his efforts. The hapless handkerchief began to rip in her desperate grip. Dear God, she must never let Pierre learn of this. Never!

"You are very quiet."

She looked over at her brother. He might be rash and foolhardy, but he was her brother and she loved him dearly.

With an effort she bit back her fear. Better to express her anger than any other of her emotions. She leveled a stern gaze on him. "You came very near to ruining us this day! And for what? A few dollars?"

He shifted in the seat next to her and turned his face to stare out the window. The rockaway swayed rhythmically along the brick-paved streets of the Vieux Carre. They had an hour's ride ahead of them and she planned to make it as miserable an hour as he had ever passed.

"I did it for us," he muttered.

"Is that so? Well, I beg you to spare me such favors in the future. I would rather unload barges myself than see you ever again risk our living in so foolish a manner."

"You needn't be so dramatic about it."

"Oh, but it appears I must. For nothing else seems to pierce that thick head of yours! Did you even once consider the consequences of losing?"

"I didn't lose!"

"But you might have! Then where would we be? And where would your courtship of Mary Louise be? If her father has doubts about your finances now, how much greater would they be if you had lost our home?"

He did not have an answer to that. Nor did they speak for the rest of their journey home. It was just as well, though, for the heat of Amanda's anger was swiftly doused by the dread that hung over her. She'd made a bargain with the devil, it seemed—a bargain she'd both won and lost. She'd already collected her winnings from him. It was just a matter of time now before she must pay her debt.

When he would contact her and how, she could not predict. And though she prayed that he would forgive the debt, she knew he would not. Nothing in his demeanor suggested either kindness or generosity. As he'd said, he was no gentleman. Rather, he was the devil and she'd allowed herself to fall right into his clutches.

For three days Amanda had no word from Nicholas Devereaux. But rather than put her mind at ease, his delay set her nerves on edge. She was jumpy and distracted, not herself at all. Sunday she embarrassed herself by forgetting what she'd been speaking about with Father Clemenceau. Monday she left the gate to the kitchen garden open and one of the goats wreaked havoc with the cabbages and carrots. Tuesday she sewed a sleeve in backward. An entire sleeve! Picking the threads out of the delicate challis had been a chore she'd nearly despaired of ever finishing.

Then early Wednesday afternoon she received a note from Pierre.

"What is he thinking!" Amanda cried. She flung down the note and began to pace the length of the double parlor. "The man has come close to ruining us and yet my foolish brother would invite him into our home—and for dinner tonight!"

Effie laid down her stitching, retrieved the spurned letter, and read it. "Says here he wants to buy that yearling of Mr. Pierre's."

Amanda let out an inelegant snort. "What he wants—" She broke off and turned away from the genial housekeeper. "What he wants," she continued more carefully, "is a chance to goad Pierre into gambling with him again."

"Now, Mandy, child, I don't think your brother will be that foolish again. No, *cher,* I don't. Why, Lester, he says that Mr. Pierre learnt his lesson this time."

"If that were so, then he would have turned down that man's offer for the yearling."

Effie straightened a tatted antimacassar on the cut velvet settee. "But that's what Mr. Pierre's been wanting, isn't it? To sell that horse once he was full-grown. Lester, he says that pretty little horse is worth a pretty little penny."

Amanda had to stop herself from glaring at the innocent housekeeper. The fact that Effie's reasoning made perfect sense irritated her to no end. But she knew she must be careful not to rouse the housekeeper's curiosity. Sweet and loving Effie might be, with a heart of gold. But she was also as tenacious as an old dog with a stew bone. If she thought there was something else to Amanda's dislike of Nicholas Devereaux, she would never let the subject drop.

Taking a calming breath, Amanda smoothed the uneven tucks in her sleeve. "Well, I suppose there's no hope for it. He's coming for dinner and we will simply have to make the best of it."

"What dress should I lay out for you?"

Something funereal, Amanda wanted to say. But instead she waved one hand negligently. "You worry over the dinner. I'll take care of dressing myself. But, Effie, don't put yourself out on account of this Devereaux. I don't like him and I shouldn't want to encourage him in any way."

Effie squinted at her. "Is this Mr. Devereaux married?"

Amanda gave her an astonished look. "I'm sure I don't know."

"Well, is he young or old?"

"I . . . I wasn't really paying attention to that. Anyway, that is beside the point."

"Is that so? Well, what *is* the point?"

"Why . . . why . . . why, that's a ridiculous question. The point is, he's a ruthless gambler who thrives on other people's misfortune. Have you forgotten how he ruined Marcus Landry and made his wife a widow?"

"If you ask me, it was Marcus Landry who did the ruinin' and who made his wife a widow. Besides," Effie muttered, "from what I hear, she's better off without him."

Amanda stared at her aghast. "Better off without him? What is that supposed to mean?"

Effie took a deep breath as if debating how best to answer. Then she planted her fists on her hips. "Let's just say that not every man treats his wife as good as your daddy treated your mama. Some men . . . some men forget their own strength and they hurt the ones they're supposed to protect." She pursed her lips in a taut line. "Do you understand what I'm sayin', child? Miz Landry is probably better off a widow livin' at home with her folks than she was livin' with her own husband. But that's enough gossip. I've got work that needs doin' and so do you." So saying, she hurried down the hall, bellowing for Mavis to come inside and help her get ready for company.

But Amanda remained in the parlor another quarter hour, her face creased in thought as she pondered Effie's odd revelation. She'd not known the Landrys well. To think that the man had gambled his home away, then shot himself in shame had been awful enough. To hear now that he might also have mistreated his wife—his petite, fragile-looking wife—was incomprehensible. Gentlemen did not behave so. And yet Marcus Landry had been considered a gentleman.

She rubbed her temple where it had begun to throb. Perhaps she'd been hasty to chide Nicholas Devereaux for ruining the man. Then again, it wasn't as if he'd done the deed out of the goodness of his heart. No, he'd ruined Mr. Landry without any thought to the effect it would have upon the man's family. If it had ended up benefiting Mrs. Landry, as Effie seemed to imply, that was purely inadvertent.

Thinking of Nicholas Devereaux, however, only made her head ache worse. She must prepare for his arrival, she told herself. And she must somehow find a chance to speak to him privately. There was no telling what that brazen rogue might let slip to Pierre. And while she would give anything to avoid paying her obligation to him, she would not risk her brother's life in a duel with Devereaux. No, she must resign herself to her fate. The best she could hope for was to get the deed over with, and the sooner the better.

But it would never be over, not really, the unwelcome thought intruded. For she would be ruined for marriage, soiled forever. A gentleman expected his bride to come to him untouched.

She grimaced and pressed her fingertips against her eyes. She couldn't think about that right now. She simply couldn't. Anyway, it wasn't as if she had a special beau or anything like that. For now she must get through this evening, and then pay her debt to that terrible man. Her future beyond that she would worry about another time.

Devereaux arrived with Pierre, the two of them cantering up Peters Street just as the sun nicked the tops of the giant magnolias that fronted the house. From her place in the front parlor Amanda let the lace panel over the window fall back into place. She took a fortifying breath, then patted her new surplice-wrapped waist, smoothing it where it met with the four-gored skirt. Though simple in design, the costume flattered her very well, both in its elegant line and choice of fabric. The blue and cream striped cambric draped as well as silk did, and the colors made her eyes appear a deeper shade and her complexion seem softer and more clear.

But she hadn't picked it out tonight for that reason. No, not at all. She did not seek to impress Nicholas Devereaux. Rather, she knew that Effie would be suspicious if she did not wear it. She'd completed the garments a week ago and as of yet had found no reason to wear them. Since they rarely entertained at home, Effie would expect her to wear the new clothes and, no doubt, would question her if she did not.

Better simply to acquiesce. Nicholas Devereaux was not worth arguing over with the eagle-eyed housekeeper.

She tugged the waist down one last time, then forced herself into the central hall. She would remain calm. She would play her role as her brother's hostess and entertain their guest in a polite, if distant, manner. And she would somehow get through this farce of an evening. She would.

She heard Gerald's young voice as he collected the two horses, and also Pierre's. But it was Devereaux's deep tones that her ears seemed most attuned to. How could someone she'd met on only that one occasion impact her life so?

"You have a handsome home," he remarked as the two men mounted the wide steps.

"My father had it built right after we moved out of New Orleans. Sadly though, he did not enjoy the pleasure of it for very long. He and my mother died during the the yellow fever epidemic of 1882."

"I'm sorry to hear that—"

Amanda pushed open the muslin curtain in the doorway, putting an end to his insincere remarks. Perhaps Pierre was impressed, but she was not.

"Mr. Devereaux," she began, eschewing any need for reintroductions. "I had not expected to see you again so soon."

"Miss Chastain," he said, removing his flat-brimmed hat and making a short, very correct bow. "You and your brother are very kind to invite me into your home. I especially hope that you and I will be able to begin our acquaintance anew."

With him smiling so benignly at her, and Pierre beside him with such a hopeful expression on his face, Amanda was hard-pressed not to respond in a like manner. Though it galled her to no end, she forced as much of a smile to her face as she could manage. "Yes, I would like very much to forget our initial introduction and begin *entirely* anew." She placed subtle emphasis on the last words, hoping against logic that he might be implying the dissolution of their wager.

In response, however, he grinned and•winked at her. That damnable wink!

Her nervous glance shot to her brother, but he, thankfully, was looking at her, not at their black-hearted guest. Pierre stared hard at her and shook his head ever so slightly, and she realized why. She was frowning. Though it pained her sorely, she somehow pasted a smile back onto her face.

"Won't you come in, Mr. Devereaux? While you two refresh yourself from your hot ride, I'll summon Mavis with cooling libations. What do you prefer?"

"Have Effie make us her special julep," Pierre put in. "Before we clean up, though, we're going out to the stable. I want Nicholas to see Duke Chastain while the light is still good. We won't be long."

So saying, he led Devereaux down the long hall, toward the back door that led onto the porch and out to the stables. Amanda watched them as they went, silhouetted by the western sun sinking beyond the open door.

Next to Devereaux her brother appeared short and slight, though he was in reality neither. It was just that Devereaux was so tall and so imposing in his manner. His bold confidence sent a shiver of awareness through her. She recalled the parting look he'd given her before going off with Pierre, a look filled with promise. No, threat was a better word. He did not mean to let her out of the wager. That was clear.

She shivered again and wrapped her arms tightly about her.

"Ooh, Miss Mandy. Is that him, the one they call the Devil of the Tables?"

Amanda spied the young maid Mavis peeping out from the door to the butler's pantry. "That's him," she confirmed dryly.

"Ooh! To think that our Mr. Pierre bested the likes of him!"

Amanda chose not to respond to Mavis's comment. Better to let Mavis and anyone else who heard the tale believe the obvious rather than suspect the awful truth. "Bring a pitcher of mint julep into the front parlor. I'll serve the men when they return. Meanwhile, tell Effie that I want this meal served in as timely a fashion as she can manage. I want to be rid of that man before he can engage my brother in any more foolishness."

Mavis's brown eyes widened at Amanda's sharp tone, but she scurried off to her tasks without comment.

Amanda pressed the back of her hand to her cheeks. They were warm and she was no doubt flushed. Thank goodness the light was fading. Then she frowned. She'd better light the lamps in the dining room now. Hopefully the candles on the table would not reveal the depths of her discomfort. But she feared Nicholas Devereaux would make it a point to goad and taunt her all through the meal. Not so far as to alert Pierre, of course. But it would be a long and arduous evening, she feared. Long and arduous indeed.

*   *   *

"Play a tune for Mr. Devereaux, Amanda. She's very good,"
Pierre added, glancing at Nicholas.

"Really, Pierre. I do not think Mr. Devereaux has come all
this way to hear a country girl play her scales," Amanda protested from her perch on one of the parlor side chairs.

"Scales? Scales? You are quite better than merely scales.
And Jefferson City is no longer considered the country. We're
an important part of New Orleans now. Country, indeed. Go
on, Amanda. You must undo the negative image of your first
introduction to Mr. Devereaux, otherwise he will think you a
shrew. Would you have only your family know the true extent
of your feminine talents?"

At that, Nicholas had to stifle a grin. If looks could have
killed, Amanda's narrowed stare would have struck her brother
down. It was obvious her brother was anxious to present his
sister in a good light. But why? Though she was clearly of an
age to marry, she was hardly so old as to be considered a
spinster. And though she was not a flashy sort of woman, she
possessed a quiet, serene sort of beauty and an elegant figure
that stopped just short of being considered lush. She could not
lack for suitors—unless her headstrong ways chased them
away.

Again he had to hide a smile. Perhaps that was precisely
the reason her brother was promoting all her better qualities.
As he'd learned when he delved into the young man's affairs
before inviting him to play at his table, Chastain was currently
courting a Miss Delachaise, the youngest daughter of the cotton mill Delachaises. To have his sister out of the house and
settled elsewhere would be an advantage to him. But was the
young man so foolish as to hope to pair his sister with *him?*

"Go on, Amanda. Don't pretend to a shyness you do not
possess. Play for Mr. Devereaux."

"Yes, do," Nicholas threw in. He studied Amanda, unac-
countably pleased by her not so subtle reluctance to cooperate.
No one could ever accuse her of a lack of spirit. But she had
interfered in matters she should not have. Now she must pay
the price. It was clear she could barely endure his presence in

her home; the knowledge that she must eventually satisfy her debt to him had her as skittish as a high-strung filly.

She crossed to the second parlor and seated herself at the square grand piano that dominated the high-ceilinged room. The flickering lamplight streaked her luxuriant hair with gold and emphasized the smooth line of her cheeks. Her thick lashes cast long shadows over her eyes.

Look at me, he silently commanded. *Look up at me, Amanda.*

When she did just that, the impact of her gaze was profound. Like a beast quite out of his control, arousal struck him with painful intensity. Their gazes held until he feared his discomfiture would become obvious. When he shifted, she looked away, and the moment was gone. But he could not so easily quash his desire for her.

She bent her head and began to play a moody piece. Chopin's *Adante Spianato,* he recognized from his own childhood lessons. She played it even more slowly than it was intended to be played, so that it sounded mournful. Haunting, even. While the music filled the spacious parlors, he studied her face. What was it about her that roused his interest? A reluctant virgin—it was preposterous. And yet he would not deny that it was so. Amanda Chastain had captured his interest like no woman he could recall.

He'd finagled this invitation on the pretext of seeing the yearling, and he meant to buy it without haggling over the price. What he really wanted, of course, was to advise her privately of the circumstances by which she would pay her debt to him. Now, however, though he desired her more violently than he could have imagined, he felt a vague unease about collecting on the wager. Idiocy, he told himself as her playing flooded the night with rich, haunting music. He hadn't lost a calculated risk with a woman or a deck of cards in years.

Then the song ended and she rose from the piano bench before he and Pierre could make any further requests of her. They both stood and clapped.

"Thank you, but it was nothing," she demurred. "Nothing."

"It was as lovely as angels' voices," Pierre stated. "Wouldn't you agree, Devereaux?"

"Indeed," Nicholas responded. "Like angels' voices." Judging by her shuttered expression, however, she regretted mightily that such angelic tones had been played for his devil's ears.

His smile faded to barely restrained annoyance at the apparent depths of her dislike for him. He was a fool to hesitate about collecting his debt from her. No one had forced her to enter into the wager with him. Like every other gambler she had to learn not to wager what she could not afford to lose.

He'd come here for a reason, damn it all. Time to get on with it.

He turned to his host. "You and your lovely sister have entertained me most admirably. I fear, though, that I have overstayed my welcome."

"No, not at all. In fact, if you do not relish the long ride back to town, you are most welcome to stay the night."

"That will not be necessary," Nicholas answered. At least her brother was eager to please him, he thought.

"But we have not concluded our negotiations," Pierre persisted.

Nicholas smiled to himself. Here was his chance to get Amanda alone. "Perhaps you would like to prepare a bill of sale for the horse now."

"Now?" The young man's face split into a wide grin. "Now it is. Let us go into my office."

"Actually, I would beg another cup of coffee from your sister." He said no more, but the young man's quick glance at his sister, followed by his knowing grin, indicated that he understood: Nicholas Devereaux might be interested in his sister.

Pity the fool did not know what for.

"Very good. Very good indeed. I trust you will entertain our guest while I am away," Pierre said to Amanda. Then not allowing her the chance to object, he strode from the room.

At his departure a deafening silence fell over the room. Outside the cicadas shrilled. A dog barked in the distance; another answered from somewhere closer by. But from Amanda there came only silence and an accusing sort of stare. Though it should not, it irritated him all over again. He decided to dispense with any niceties.

"Have you any place in town you can visit, say on the pretext of a shopping trip?"

He saw her swallow hard. To her credit, however, her gaze did not falter. "My mother's dearest friend lives on St. Ann Street," she slowly began. "She has often asked me to spend some time with her."

He nodded. "Go to her, then, and once there, send word 'round to me. I believe you are acquainted with the location of my residence," he added, unable to resist goading her. "I'll pick you up at her home on the stroke of midnight, and return you to her before dawn."

"Is there no other way—" She broke off and he saw her draw a deep breath. "Is there no way you will change your mind?"

"I'm afraid not." From the moment she'd tumbled into his arms he'd wanted her. He had no intention of letting her go now when he'd finally caught her.

Then she trembled and her eyes glinted as if with gathering tears, and self-recrimination stabbed through him. Hell's bells! What was he doing here, anyway? Tormenting young innocents was surely a new low, even for him.

But before he could react to his latent guilt over his hateful proposal, she drew herself up. She lifted her chin and glared at him. "All right then. However, upon my return to her house, you and I will be quit of one another once and for all. Debt paid and silence guaranteed."

His eyes narrowed. By damn, but she had a core of steel. It was a pity *she* did not manage her family's business. No doubt she would be much better at it than her brother.

"Debt paid and silence guaranteed," he echoed. But he'd be damned if he would allow her to pay that debt in so cold and unemotional a manner as she presently wore. He crossed the room to where she stood, not stopping until she stepped back defensively. "Shall we seal our agreement?" He stuck out his right hand, a challenging light in his eyes.

He saw her hesitation, and in response he let his grin turn taunting. That got to her at once, he saw. Drawing a breath, she thrust her hand forward and took his to shake.

It was not a handshake he wanted of her, though. It never had been. Once he had her hand in his grasp, he tugged her forward. She stumbled into his chest and would have immediately pushed away. But he tangled his other hand in her silken hair, holding her head steady.

Only when it became obvious that she knew what was coming, that she knew he meant to kiss her and that she dare not cry out to her brother for help, did he finally lower his head and possess her mouth.

He possessed it, fitting his mouth to hers, and stroking the seam of her lips until she gasped for breath and granted him entrance.

He possessed it further still, pressing deep inside the warm, minty recesses of her until he felt the precise moment of her capitulation.

Then he drew her fully against him, her breasts pillowed against his chest, her belly pressed up to his raging erection. Only when he felt her melting acquiescence to the pure physical sensation of their embrace did he force himself away.

Her eyes were round with shock; her lips red and swollen from his demanding kiss. But he had the answer he sought.

Cold and unemotional she might try to be, with a core of steel. But there was also fire to temper that steel. And it would not be long before he would taste fully of that fire.

CHAPTER THREE

Amanda kept her head averted, pretending to concentrate on the embroidered fichu in her lap. "Fiona is always pleading with me to spend time with her in town. I thought, since it has become cooler, that I might like to do that." She stifled an oath when she pricked her left forefinger. "Besides," she made herself continue, "I'd like to look at some cloth for a new cloak and a winter suit. Effie needs fabric too—"

"That's a very good idea," Pierre cut in. "Very good. You can take Mavis with you."

Amanda looked up at him, then just as quickly away. She'd never lied to her brother before, and she was so consumed with guilt she feared he would read it in her face. "I don't need Mavis. After all, Fiona has Lottie and Abigail. Lester can bring me into town and then return for me the next day."

"Only one day? That's hardly time enough to conduct a proper visit, let alone shop." Pierre refilled a tumbler with his favorite whiskey. "Stay another day and I will fetch you back myself. I need to bring Duke Chastain to Devereaux anyway. Speaking of Nicholas Devereaux," he continued. "Has your opinion of him improved after last night? I thought him quite the gentleman. And unless I am mistaken, he appears very much taken with you."

Amanda's head jerked up and her face turned scarlet with embarrassment. "He . . . he is not," she stammered.

But her denial did nothing to deter Pierre's grin. "What's this? A blush? Could it be that you like him too?"

Amanda sprang to her feet. "I could never like a man like that. Never!" she exclaimed. "He is . . . he is arrogant and cruel and . . . and he doesn't give a snap for how easily he destroys other people's lives!"

Pierre's grin vanished in the face of her tirade. "If you're referring to his gambling, Mandy, well, everybody gambles. There's not a self-respecting Creole gentleman in New Orleans who hasn't won or lost a bundle at the gaming tables."

"Oh, I simply cannot talk to you about such things!" She flung her needlework down on the settee. "But on this one matter I am adamant, Pierre. Nicholas Devereaux is the most hateful and despicable man of my acquaintance. Do not bother to expound upon his good points to me. Do not ever invite him to our home and expect me to entertain him. Most especially, do not even *think* about recommending him to me, nor me to him. Do I make myself clear on this matter?"

He stared at her slack-jawed, then gave a jerky nod. She did not wait for him to make any further comment before storming from the room. But even before she burst onto the front porch, then strode furiously down the steps and into the garden, she knew she'd overreacted. Pierre would wonder at the vehemence of her emotions. He would wonder and he would speculate and he would not give up whatever idiotic imaginings he held regarding her and Nicholas Devereaux.

Oh, why had the man sent Pierre alone to his office last night, giving the distinct impression that he was interested in her?

She pushed open the cypress gate that separated the front garden from the orchard, then paused, leaning back on the rough wood and staring into the shady bower. The pecan trees had grown tall in the years since her parents had bought the land. It had been a small farm then, not the gracious country estate they had since made of it. The loquat trees had also filled out, as had the pears and persimmons.

More than the rich rewards the orchard gave them, however, Amanda loved the shady quiet of the place. Though greedy squirrels and busy birds kept it alive with sound, it nonetheless seemed quiet and peaceful. Still, it did nothing to calm her on this particular morning.

Heavenly day, but she was behaving like a fool. She was letting that horrible, wretched man completely unnerve her.

And yet, how could she not? After that kiss—

She broke off that thought with a cry of anguish. Oh, but she must never let that happen again! She must brace herself to endure his crude attentions and simply get through that hideous night she so unfortunately owed to him.

But if her wanton response to him last night was any indication . . .

"God, help me." In desperation she spoke the words out loud. But the only response she received was the scolding cry of a blue jay and the chattering disapproval of two fat gray squirrels.

The fact remained that no one could help her but herself. And the best she could do was harden her resolve and get her ordeal over with.

"Now isn't this cozy?"

Amanda smiled at Fiona Carpenter, then glanced surreptitiously at the tall clock in the corner beside the archway that led into the dining room. Eight-ten. In less than four hours she would be in his clutches. She closed her eyes and swallowed. Should she pray for time to stop, she wondered, or pray for it to speed up?

"Are you tired, my dear? Oh, of course you are," Fiona answered her question before Amanda could. "That long trip all the way into town is so wearying."

"No, no. I'm not tired," Amanda retorted.

But Fiona would hear none of that. She rang the little bell on the side table. "Lottie, be so good as to bring each of us a toddy." Then she smiled and her kindly expression reminded Amanda of a sweet little girl, albeit an aging one. "Lottie makes me a special toddy—to settle my nerves, you know. I have it every night, sometimes two, if it's been a particularly trying day. It puts a body right to sleep, and I promise you the sounds from the street will not disturb your slumber. A restful night is so good for the complexion,'' she added, patting her pale, plump cheeks.

Under Fiona's approving gaze Amanda drank down the toddy. It was more brandy than anything else, she decided, a cherry bounce flavored with a hint of almonds and mint. Quite good, and quite strong, she thought as its fiery heat spread through her veins. She felt a reassuring return of her resolve.

Nicholas Devereaux might possess her body this night, but her will remained her own. He could never possess that.

"Well, my dear. Would you have another? I can ring for Lottie."

"No, one is more than sufficient. But if you would like another, please do not hesitate on my account. Here, I will ring for Lottie myself," she insisted. Fiona's cheeks were already flushed with the warmth from the strong concoction. A second one would ensure she slept through anything, even the sound of her houseguest coming and going during the night.

Fiona beamed, her cheeks round, her eyes sparkling already with the effects of the toddy. "You are such a sweet child, Amanda. Very much the image of your dear departed mother at the same age."

By the time the second toddy had been downed, and memories of Fiona's own youth exhausted, the older woman had to lean on her maid's arm to manage the stairs to her bedchamber. Within a quarter of an hour the house had quieted. Abigail and Lottie shared a room above the kitchen. That meant no one would hear Amanda leave by the front door.

While Fiona snored peacefully in her high, curtained half-tester bed, Amanda stole into her room and borrowed the house key. Then she returned to her own room to wait and worry, and wonder how long this terrible night would last.

Maybe he wouldn't come for her. Maybe he'd had a change of heart and his conscience had gotten the better of him.

No, Amanda knew that would never happen. Nicholas Devereaux plainly did not have a conscience.

But maybe he hadn't received her note. Maybe the boy she'd given it to had taken the money she'd paid him and

gone straight to some candy counter, forgetting entirely about
delivering the slender missive to the house on Toulouse Street.
She could only pray it was so.

Still, that wouldn't save her for long. Eventually she must
pay her debt to that devil. Better to get it over with than to
have it hanging over her head like a guillotine blade.

When the tall clock finally struck the midnight hour, she let
herself out, still unsure whether she wanted Devereaux to be
waiting or not. The street lay in darkness, save for the occasional pool of light from the gas lanterns. Then she saw it, a
carriage parked down the street. It started forward when she
appeared, and though it was shadowed by darkness she recognized the driver as Devereaux's man—the one who'd tried
to prevent her from entering that gambling den. Now he stared
at her with a close, assessing look.

The vehicle halted. The door to the very smart landau
swung open, and then Devereaux himself stood before her.

"How nice to see you again, Amanda." He bowed and
extended a hand to help her up into his conveyance.

Her heart began to race. Though her mouth felt as dry as
cotton she said, "I would prefer it if you would not address
me in so intimate a manner. Only my dearest friends call me
by my given name. We are not, nor shall we ever be, that
friendly."

His face was shadowed by the sharp angle of the moonlight,
but not so much that she could not see his expression. Handsome he was, as tempting in appearance as the priests had
always warned that Satan could be. It was enough to make
even a saint despair, and heaven knew, she was no saint.

"We might never be friendly," he answered after a long
moment. "But we shall most assuredly be intimate." He
paused, then added in a lower tone, "Amanda." Again he put
out his hand to help her into the landau.

Amanda drew back, though she was not able to break the
hold of his eyes. It wasn't going to work, she thought as panic
made her knees weak. She'd never be able to best him, to
remain aloof. She'd never be able to harden her resolve when

just the way he spoke her name set her heart to hammering in panic.

She beat back her fears as best she could. "Is there . . . is there no way I can convince you to . . ."

"Convince me to what?" he asked when she trailed off.

She swallowed hard and found courage in reminding herself how much she despised him. "Convince you to reconsider what you are about to do."

He took a step nearer her. "My dear Amanda. I am a gambler. You knew that when you wagered with me, as did your brother when he sat down at my table. What sort of gambler would I be if I did not collect on my winnings? Besides, you agreed to the terms."

"Yes, but . . . but . . ." She compressed her lips to prevent them from quivering. "You know that this will ruin me. No man will ever agree to marry me, not after tonight."

"No man but myself will ever know about tonight," he countered. "Not unless you tell him. If anything, you will learn things this evening which will please your future husband very well."

A blush heated her face. He was very near her now, so near that she had to tilt her head up to meet his glittering gaze. But she refused to back away this time. "What if I will not pay this debt?"

His mouth slanted up in that wicked, one-sided grin of his. "If I cannot gain satisfaction from one who has gambled with me and lost, then I generally approach his—or her—family and demand that they make good on the debt. But I know you would not want me to have to do that in your case."

He did not say anything further, for there was no need. If Nicholas Devereaux approached her brother, it would result in a duel. They both knew it. And as he also must suspect, Amanda would not risk her brother's life for the sake of her honor. Not against the notorious Nicholas Devereaux, anyway.

She gritted her teeth. "Let us get on with it then." Avoiding his hand, she stepped unassisted up into the carriage. He climbed in after her, settling himself across from her. The door closed: The landau lurched forward. But neither of them spoke during the short drive to Toulouse Street.

Though Amanda did not look at him, but instead peered out the window at the tall, narrow houses crowding the brick banquettes, she could feel the touch of his eyes on her. By the time the vehicle turned into his carriageway and halted in the courtyard, she could have jumped right out of her skin.

He exited first, then turned to help her down. Though she tried again to avoid his touch, this time he did not allow it. As she hesitated on the carriage step, he unexpectedly grasped her about the waist and lifted her down.

"Let me go!" Amanda squealed, shoving against his arms. But she might as well have tried to shove aside an oak tree.

"No. Not until dawn's light satisfies our wager." So saying, he lifted her higher still, then abruptly flipped her so that one of his arms caught her beneath her knees while the other supported her back. Then, with her held humiliatingly secure in his arms, he kicked open one of the French doors and, two at a time, mounted the curving stairs to the upper floor, with her skirts and petticoats belling out behind them.

Only when they entered a small sitting room did he let her down. But even then he held her steady before him, resisting her frantic efforts to tear free of his hold.

"Be still. Be still, Amanda. I have no intention of hurting you."

"No intention of hurting me!" she cried. "You're hurting me now!"

"I have frightened you, not hurt you. Now, stop behaving like a child and instead show me the strong woman you were when first we met."

Those unexpected words gave her pause, and for a moment they only stared at one another. His eyes glittered in the soft golden light of the candle lamps mounted on the walls. His dark hair gleamed. That he could be so unnaturally handsome, so damnably lucky, and now, so frustratingly right, was *so* unfair. Still, he could have proposed a different sort of wager, she reminded herself as she struggled to remain calm.

"I find it perverse that you work so hard to unnerve me and then belittle me when I am unnerved."

That brought out his wicked grin, and in turn, his grin restored a modicum of her confidence. Where his hands held her, her skin began to warm.

"That's a point well taken," he admitted. "If I promise not to deliberately unnerve you, will you stop behaving like a cornered wildcat?"

Amanda closed her eyes and took a slow breath. "I will try." She opened her eyes and decided to be candid. "But I cannot promise not to become skittish again. I . . . I am frightened by . . . by what must occur between us this night."

His hands moved ever so slightly on her arms as he regarded her with eyes far too observant for her comfort. "There is nothing to fear, Amanda. I suspect, however, that you will not be convinced of that until you see for yourself. So, feel free to question me about what I do and why I do it. You will learn things from me tonight that no one of your acquaintance would ever explain to you. Now, since you have already proven to be very good at it," he said as he removed her bonnet, "why don't we begin with a kiss?"

A kiss.

A hard hammering began in her chest. A pounding fear, yes. But a small part of her—a terrible, shameful part of her—repeated his words. *You are very good at it. Very good at it.*

She stared at him entranced as he lowered his head. She could not look away, nor could she resist when he drew her nearer. Then his mouth met hers and the kiss began and she knew that somehow she'd lost much more than the wager they'd made. As his lips took possession of hers, as he coaxed all her resistance away, she knew that one little compliment of his had pried open the door to her emotions.

And now she'd never get it closed, she feared as he pressed his advantage.

When his tongue stroked her lips as he'd done that other time, she was not able to deny him entrance—nor deny herself the stirring response to that fiery, intimate invasion. And when his tongue slid provocatively between her lips, rubbing their sensitive inner surface with a throbbing regularity, she felt as if instead of hating this, she'd been waiting to kiss him all her life.

Her hands that had pushed against him now curled into fists, clutching the fine merino of his coat. His arms slipped around her, one hand splayed at her waist, the other hand cupping the back of her head, as he pressed her fully to him. She felt the full imprint of his hard male body on hers; she felt her bonnet fall away and the coil of her heavy hair falling free as his deft fingers removed her hair pins. Yet the kiss raged on through all of that, hot and frantic and voracious.

When at last they drew apart, if only to catch a breath, Amanda's plan to remain unaffected by him lay in utter ruin.

He moved his clever lips along her jaw, then down the arch of her neck. "You are very good at kissing." He whispered the hot words against her sensitive skin. "But there is more to kissing than simply lips and tongue. There are ears." He nibbled on her earlobe, letting his hot breath fan across the damp trail he left.

Amanda squirmed at the unnameable sensations generated by that subtle caress. He kissed her lips and her limbs grew weak; he teased her ear and her stomach seemed to catch fire. Heavenly day, but the devil himself could not tempt a woman half so well!

His hand had tangled in her heavy hair and now he tilted her back over his other arm and let his mouth move down her throat, to the tender hollow at its base. "I plan to kiss every portion of your body, my sweet Amanda. To taste you and nibble on your delectable flesh until you beg me never to stop."

A shiver of fear joined with the flame of excitement he'd built in her to make her weak all over.

"No," she protested, but faintly. "You can't—That's not what I thought would happen—"

Slowly he righted her. But he did not release her. "Tell me, my lovely innocent. Exactly what did you expect would occur between us?"

Amanda's face grew scarlet under his amused and watchful gaze. "I . . . well . . . you know."

"I know what *I* expected. What I'm asking is what *you* expected."

She averted her gaze, though in truth it was nearly impossible to see anything but him. Still, it was too hard to meet his astute stare. She looked at his mouth—no, not there, for looking at those well-shaped lips roused the most sinful feelings in her. She looked lower, at the cleft in his chin, and fixed her gaze there.

"I am a country girl. I know well enough the mating practices of animals."

He chuckled. She felt it in all the places where their bodies touched: chest, belly, loins. "Ah, but man is a unique animal—and woman too. We invest more than just that one brief coupling act in the ritual of our joining together. The pleasure can be intensified. And prolonged." With one finger he tilted her chin up. When their eyes met he rubbed his thumb over her lower lip, a simple movement that belied the powerful effect it had on her.

"Undress me, Amanda."

Amanda swallowed so hard she nearly choked. Undress him! "I . . . I . . . I cannot possibly do such a thing."

He smiled and rubbed his thumb over her lip again. "Of course you can." With that he loosened the brooch at her throat, then began to release the carved shell buttons that lined her bodice.

"Wait! No!" She batted his hands away.

"If you would rather do it yourself, I will not object." He gave her his most wicked and seductive smile.

"You . . . you're doing it again," she accused him, though in truth she was searching frantically for a way to divert him. "You're trying to unnerve me."

His grin turned rueful. "So I am," he conceded. "But it seems we have reached an impasse. If you will not let *me* remove your clothes, then *you* must do it. Which is it to be, sweetheart?"

In the face of his reasonable tone, Amanda felt like an un-

schooled child. But what was she to do? How was she to
behave? When he kissed her she could forget and just succumb
to the violent pleasure of it. But now he wanted more.

She stepped back. As if putting some distance between them
would help! "Perhaps . . . perhaps if we began more slowly.
You . . . you remove your jacket."

He shrugged out of it in a moment. "Your turn," he said.

"I've already removed my hat. You remove your . . . your
waistcoat."

It was gone before she could finish speaking. "Your turn,"
he repeated.

Amanda thought fast. Somehow removing her skirt seemed
safer than her bodice. She had three slips and a petticoat on
beneath her skirt. But under her bodice was only her corset
cover, the corset and then her chemise. She untied the skirt
tabs and let the sprigged muslin slither to the floor. Then she
stared nervously up at him. "Your turn," she whispered.

His eyes swept down, from her face to the tips of her toes,
and though there was little enough to see, she blushed the full
length of her body. He grinned. "With all the layers a woman
wears this could take all night. And no doubt you wish it
would. But I think, Amanda, that we are losing the mood.
Come here," he ordered in a voice grown huskier even than
before.

She swallowed hard but didn't move. "Why?"

"Since you like kissing so well, I think I will kiss you. It
will make everything else much easier. Now, come here."

It was simpler to do as he asked than not. On trembling
legs she crossed the short distance to him. "Perhaps you are
right," she murmured.

"Perhaps I am."

Then she was in his arms and he was devouring her with
his mouth and the rest took care of itself. Her bodice fell away.
The slips disappeared, and the petticoat. Her corset he removed as he walked her backward through the sitting room
and into a luxurious bedchamber. At least that's how Amanda
assumed they'd come into this new room, her nearly naked
and him yet clothed.

Then he pressed her down into a huge bed and she became acutely aware of their circumstances. Featherbed and silken coverlet beneath her; his exquisitely masculine body on top of her. In the fury of his kisses she'd let herself be consumed by him and now, as foreign and frightening as it was to be overwhelmed in such a manner, there was that part of her that seemed full to bursting with the pleasure of it. He played his erotic games with his mouth, enticing her tongue to play as well, and every other portion of her seemed to respond.

Before she even realized what she'd done, she removed his collar, then opened the front of his shirt. Together they somehow rid themselves of that garment. Then there was only her chemise between them, and his trousers, and her fingers faltered.

"We are far past the point of modesty," he told her when she would not meet his gaze.

"I . . . I do not know . . ." She didn't finish. She couldn't.

But he must have understood, for he pulled away and rose to his knees, staring down on her near naked form. He unfastened the waistband of his breeches but did not pull them down. Her legs were still parted by his knees and now he reached down and began to stroke her thighs.

"Don't be afraid of what's to come, Amanda. It's a natural thing, designed by God, though the priests would have you believe otherwise. You are a woman, an exquisite woman meant to be loved by a man who knows how." *And I know how.*

The silent promise in his eyes sent a perverse thrill through her. "I fear you are more devil than man," she confessed in a shaky voice.

His response was to laugh. "There are times to pray, but there are times to play as well. And this is one of them." He moved his hands higher up her legs, pushing her chemise up almost to the apex of her thighs. She let out a little cry; fear, dismay. Capitulation. Then he moved the wispy fabric completely aside and she knew there was no turning back.

He'd said he knew how to make love to a woman, and she was swiftly convinced of that truth. Like a dark magic, he brought every portion of her body under his spell with merely his touch. Thighs and belly, waist and breasts. He bared them to his view, then took possession of them with every stroke of his fingers. He ignited her with the erotic power he wielded, burning away her modesty and even her sense of shame.

When he circled her nipples with the pads of his thumbs, her breath turned to a shallow panting. When he finally stroked the aching tips, she gasped out loud. And when he leaned forward and let his tongue continue the fiery caress, she ceased breathing altogether.

Then she felt the stroke of his fingertips in another place, in the place she knew must be his ultimate goal, and she let out a helpless groan. Heavenly day, but she'd never imagined it could be like this! Her head tossed wildly on the silken bedclothes as her body responded in ways she did not understand. If she'd known he would make her feel this way, she never would have made that wager.

Or else she would have made it long ago.

That was her last rational thought. After that it was only sensation she responded to, sensation strengthened by the intensity of her careening emotions. He slid his fingers into her most private place and roused her entire being to a fever pitch. He stroked her with a pagan rhythm that melted her very bones.

Then far away a clock chimed, and somehow her chemise disappeared, as did his breeches. He leaned over her and kissed her mouth again, a deep kiss that demanded the same returning passion that he offered her. She wrapped her arms around him, pulling him shamelessly down onto her so that their damp bodies met without any barriers between them.

Amanda gave herself up completely to the kiss, to the embrace, and to the burning pressure of his fully aroused maleness. She felt it press against her belly and, when he nudged her legs apart, at the entrance to her feminine self.

Then it was inside her, pushing and withdrawing. Pressing in, then easing away.

She felt a quiver of panic. It was too large. She was too small. But he swallowed her panic when his palms cupped her face and he deepened their kiss. His tongue possessed her mouth, teasing her with the same erotic rhythm he played with his hips. It was frightening. It was exhilarating.

Then without warning, he made a deeper thrust and pushed much farther inside her than he had before. Amanda gasped at the sharp, tearing pain. But it was gone as swiftly as it had come. He lay still upon her then, and after a long moment it dawned on her that it must be over.

It must be over, and yet she did not want it to be over.

Sweet lord, what was she thinking? She should be relieved that that was all there was to it, and that now she could dress and be done with it. But the awful truth could not be avoided. Though he was finished, her body yet clamored for more.

"Are you all right?" he murmured.

She nodded but kept her eyes clenched shut. God forbid that he should see the terrible truth in them!

"I didn't hurt you too badly?"

She shook her head. Then she felt his thumb wiping the edge of her eyes.

"Why do you weep, then?"

She turned her head to the side. Instead of answering, however, she asked the question uppermost in her mind. "Now that you are done, am I to leave?"

"Done?" She felt him chuckle. Like before she felt the sensation from the tips of her sensitive breasts to the depths of her feminine core. It only increased the terrible desire in her. He chuckled again and in her confusion she chanced a glance up at him.

"But I thought—" She broke off when he moved within her. "Oh!" she gasped when he withdrew a little then pushed back in. "Ooh!" she groaned when he repeated the movement, only slower and deeper.

"Heavenly day," she whispered when he repeated the same movement over and over again.

"We are far from done," he murmured in her ear as he began to increase his pace. "The night is just beginning for us."

Then there were no words between them, just their harsh

breathing and the voluptuous feel of their bodies meeting in a harmony of motion and desire. He gave and she received; she offered and he accepted. Like a dark heaven the room and the bed, and both time and place shrank in on them, until with an exquisite burst, it all turned to flame, to a heaven filled with fire that consumed her.

And she wanted to be consumed by it. That was the worst part—and the best. She wanted to burn forever in the fire he'd created. But she only had one night.

CHAPTER FOUR

Not a word passed between them on the return drive to St. Ann Street. Amanda kept her gaze squarely upon her tightly laced fingers. Nicholas kept his locked upon her pale face.

He should never have put her in this position, never have made so outrageous a proposal, then backed her into a corner until she had no choice but to agree. And yet, how could he honestly regret it now? By her very innocence she'd managed to affect his jaded senses in a way no woman had in years. No, if he had to do it all over again, he would change nothing—except, perhaps, to have demanded two nights with her rather than only one.

He forced himself to look away from her. Two nights? Ha! The fact was that he wanted to make her his mistress. He wanted to shower her with flowers, jewels, gifts, and every minute of his attention.

But with a determined effort he beat back that ludicrous idea. What did he honestly think, that a woman of her reputation and standing in the community would agree to become his mistress? No. As much pleasure as she'd taken of him during the long hours they'd spent together in his bed, she would never agree to a permanent liaison between them.

Not that a position as a man's mistress held any real permanence. A wife was the only permanent woman in a man's life, and he was far too jaded to be in the market for a wife.

Nor would she be likely to agree to hold that position either, he admitted. No, this one night was all he would ever have of the delicious Amanda Chastain.

What a pity that was, he thought, shifting restlessly on the leather seat opposite her. He could not remember ever having partaken of such intense pleasure with a woman. Any woman. Even the renowned mistress to the French minister, the one he'd shared two nights and a day with, had not satisfied him so thoroughly as had the past few hours with this artless young woman.

He frowned, annoyed by that disturbing truth. To think that he found an untutored virgin more exciting than an experienced courtesan. But there was no point in denying the truth, nor any point in regretting what could never be again. Delicious she might be, with a natural passion he could never have foreseen. But he'd had all he would ever have of her. Best to remember that.

The carriage slowed, then stopped just outside the pool of light cast by a flickering gas streetlight. He opened the door, stepped out, and turned to assist her. It was an automatic gesture, one he did not even think twice about. Though she hesitated, not meeting his eyes, he waited there, hand outstretched to her.

Then she sighed and placed her hand in his. At the same time she lifted her dark lashes. Their eyes met, and in that moment every logic he'd just preached to himself fled his mind. His hand closed around her gloved fingers, but instead of helping her down, he stepped right up to her, trapping her on the landau's narrow step.

"When may I see you again?" It was not what he'd meant to say, but once said the words could not be taken back.

Her beautiful blue eyes widened with surprise, then darkened with another emotion, one he hoped was passion. She was nothing if not a passionate woman, he now knew.

When she did not answer, as if too shocked by his words to respond, he pressed on. "I enjoy your company, Amanda, as much as you did enjoy mine. Though we came together due to unlikely circumstances, I see no reason for us not to maintain a relationship from which we both derive so much pleasure.''

''That . . . that is impossible,'' she choked out. ''Impossible.''

Of course it was; he'd already decided that. But some perverse demon drove him now, and he refused to take no for an answer.

He moved his hands to her waist. With her on the step, they were eye to eye. She could not escape him, nor would she dare cry out for help. He stepped even closer so that her skirts pressed against his legs, and her lovely bosom just grazed his chest. She tried to lean away but he kept her steady.

''There is a sweetness and a fire in you that I yet hunger for, Amanda. Do not try to deny your own hunger, for it lies too near the surface to remain hidden. I see it in your beautiful eyes, and I have but to kiss you—''

He broke off and did just that. He pulled her into his arms and kissed her. It was harsh and raw and revealed every bit of his desire for her. Only when her resistance fled, yielding to that sweet ancient response he'd hoped for, did he pull breathlessly away.

''You see? There is something between us, something that is too strong to let die. I must have you again, Amanda. How long do you plan to stay in town?''

But even though her eyes were dark with passion and her breaths shallow and aroused, she shook her head. ''It cannot be. No, not ever again. You and I—'' She broke off, shaking her head again. ''It cannot be,'' she repeated in a whisper.

''I will be discreet.'' He pressed his advantage, sliding his palms up her arms, feeling the heat of her, aware of the warm feminine smell of rose water and sexual satisfaction. He grew hard all over again.

''No. Don't do that.'' She turned her face away from him. ''Haven't you done enough? Must you torture me even more?''

''What I want, sweetheart, is to ease your torture. To ease our torture.''

''I can't!'' she cried, pushing against his chest. ''You know

I can never do that.'' But Nicholas did not want to hear that. He knew she would find pleasure in continuing their association.

"You want me as much as I want you," he insisted. "I know it, Amanda, and so do you."

He thought he saw a glint of tears in her eyes, and he felt a sudden pang of guilt. But there was no other way, he told himself. He bent to kiss her, to kiss her tears and hesitance away, to use the force of his passion to defeat the moral code she clung to so desperately.

He captured her mouth with his and for a moment he felt her capitulating. Then with a cry she tore her lips from his and shoved at his chest. "I have paid my debt to you! I owe you nothing more. Nothing!" Her voice cracked. "You must let me go."

His grip tightened. "And if I do not?" Though it was madness to say such a thing, he could not prevent the words. She had made him a madman.

They stared at one another, his face determined, hers stricken by conflicting feelings. "I cannot be your *whore*."

She uttered the word with such abhorrence Nicholas stepped back from her. His grip slackened, and at once she shoved past him and hurried down the street to her door.

He watched her go. He watched her pause at the door and fumble with the key. He watched her wipe her eyes with one small gloved fist, then glance fearfully down the street to see if he was still there.

Then he watched her slip past the door and into the house, beyond his view and beyond his grasp.

He stood there a long while, just staring at the darkened town house. One of the horses stamped his foot on the brick-paved street. He heard Red shift in the driver's seat and also the distant crow of an early rising cock.

She'd paid her wager; he would have no more of her. Though he'd been a fool to broach the subject, he nonetheless felt a bitter disappointment. He wanted her again. He would want her for a long time. But she had made her position clear;

she did not want him enough to breach the bounds of society's expectations of her.

He shoved his hands deep into his pockets. That left him two choices: forget her or marry her.

Then he paused. There was a third choice, the same one that had brought her to his door the first time. He could invite her brother to his card table again. She had paid her brother's debt once before. Who knew how many times she might do so again?

"Son-of-a-bitch," he swore. He *could* invite Pierre Chastain to play cards again, but he didn't want to force her that way. Not anymore. The next time she came to him he wanted it to be because she wanted to.

Though she'd sworn she never would do that, he was not ready to concede the game they'd begun. He'd won the first round and drawn her into his bed; she seemed to have won the second, if his unquenchable desire for her was any indication. But the game was not over, he vowed. Not nearly.

Amanda sneaked into the bedchamber without mishap. In the dark she unfastened her bodice and skirt, stripped off her undergarments, and kicked off her shoes. Then she dove under the satin counterpane and burrowed into the depths of the bed.

She was safe!

She had paid off her debt and no one was the wiser. Now she just had to get back home to Magnolia Shade and somehow put this night behind her.

But as she lay there in the dark, conscious of every breath she took, every beat of her heart, she knew with a sinking despair that it would not be that easy. For the unfortunate truth was that Nicholas Devereaux, the Devil of the Tables, had done more than simply make use of her body.

She'd thought that part would be awful, that she would feel defiled and revolted. The truth, however—the shameful truth which she must somehow learn to live with—was that once he'd started kissing her, she hadn't wanted him to stop. And with every new intimacy he'd taken, she'd grown more and more aroused. She could blame it on clever manipulation and call him the devil come in the night to tempt a young innocent. But reality was that once embarked on her sinful path with him, she had not wanted it ever to end.

A tortured groan slipped out and she clenched her eyes tighter, desperate to shut out the ugly truth. But it was all too recent and all too real. What she'd begun in dread she'd ended in dread, but for entirely different reasons. What she'd feared then to undergo, she feared now never to experience again. Oh, the wonder of it! Oh, the fire!

With every caress he'd introduced her to a new realm, a new world of knowledge based not on logic but rather on feelings, on the reactions of her poor untutored body. And she, foolish girl that she was, had reveled in it. Even now, just recalling it made her body quiver with remembered passion.

"Heavenly day!" she breathed the words, throwing off the stifling coverlet. She was far too warm.

Yet the movement of the silk over her thin chemise only stoked that fire further. Her skin was so sensitive, so alive. So hot.

He'd done that. He'd touched her there—on her breasts, along her ribs. He'd awakened her to an awareness of what clever fingertips could do to her nipples—or a callused thumb, or hot damp lips.

Frustrated she rolled onto her stomach and buried her face in the lavender-scented pillows. But that only made things worse. The pressure on her breasts. The roll of coverlet between her legs.

Involuntarily she thrust her belly against the bed, then let out a cry of half-anger, half-desire. They'd done it the second time just this way—no, the third time. He'd pulled her on top of his body and made her straddle him.

He'd not had to *make* her do anything else, though. The rest she'd managed very well, all on her own. She'd sunk down upon him. Taken him into her. Then she'd made love to him like a wild woman might, like a wanton. Like the whore he wanted to make of her!

Yet even that monstrous thought could not quell the violent feelings that gripped her now. She writhed upon the deep featherbed, hot and restless and frantic for some sort of relief. But she could find none, and only when she had worked herself into a lather of frustration did she finally stop. She would not find that splendid release without him. And that meant that she would never find it at all. She was done with him. Her obligation fulfilled; her debt paid.

But even as she told herself that—as she curled into a ball and ordered herself to be glad it was over—a part of her feared it had only just begun. She'd paid her debt to him, yes. But it was not over. She would feel its lingering effects for a long time to come. For a long time.

Maybe forever.

Fiona's habit was to sleep late, then linger the rest of the morning at her breakfast and her ablutions. Amanda had always thought the woman's schedule the waste of a perfectly good morning. But not today. Today she was thankful for the time she had alone, away from Fiona's curious gaze.

She called for a bath once she heard the two older maids moving about in the courtyard, then hurriedly cleansed herself and prepared for the day. She'd not intended to hurry, especially since she had nothing to do but wait for Fiona to arise and after that go shopping or visiting or some such other diversion. But the feel of the steaming water, the slide of the soapy cloth across her skin, awakened her feelings all over again. Even the slightest touch to her flesh revived the most vivid memories of the night she'd just spent—of Nicholas Devereaux and the wondrous way he'd made her feel.

Only it wasn't supposed to feel wondrous, and that was her problem.

After a hasty and unsatisfactory bath she dressed herself in a plain gown of striped muslin. The tall clock in the stair hall chimed nine o'clock. Now, what was she to do with herself?

"I believe I should like to go to the market for you," she announced to Lottie and Abigail when she descended to the back gallery.

"Land's sake, Miss Mandy, Miz Fiona, she won't like it if we allow her special guest to do the household errands for

us.'' Lottie shook her graying head. ''No, she won't like it
a'tall.''

''She doesn't have to ever know,'' Amanda insisted. ''I'm
a country girl, remember? I'm used to being up doing chores
all morning. Fiona won't arise for hours and I'm already bored
to tears. Let me go for you. It'll save you a long walk,'' she
added, suspecting that might help to sway the two older
women.

Lottie looked at Abigail who only shrugged and cocked her
head. ''But you can't go off to the French Market all alone,''
Lottie protested. ''It wouldn't be right.''

''See if the boy across the street wants to earn a few pen-
nies. He can accompany me and carry the goods home.''

In the end Amanda had her way. But even as she headed
down St. Ann Street toward Decatur Street and the riverside
market buildings, she was not entirely pleased. This was only
a diversion, a way for the sights and sounds of the city to
distract her from her distressing thoughts. But it would not
banish them. Nor would it change anything that had happened.

She bought fresh greens and corn, a chicken and five sat-
sumas. On impulse she bought the boy, Jack, a praline and
added a still-hot sweet potato pie to his load. She'd forgotten
how busy the old market could be with vendors and shoppers
crowding the aisles, and everywhere the pungent smells of
mules and produce and oyster shells.

''D'ye want fish?'' Young Jack pointed toward North Peters
Street and the seafood market. ''My uncle has a stand there.
He knows Miz Fiona and he always gives her a good price.''

As they made their way toward the seafood stands, Amanda
thought she saw a familiar face in the crowd. She looked
again, alarmed because she'd thought it was Nicholas's driver,
the one he called Red. But if it was he, he had moved out of
sight.

And she would not think of Nicholas Devereaux as Nicholas. She would not! She must never think of him in any way
at all.

''I don't think we need fish today after all.'' She turned

abruptly, causing Jack to bump into her. "We have enough here. I think we'd better start back."

They made only one more stop, at a bakery on Dumaine Street for croissants and fresh baguettes. But as they came out, Jack with his arms filled, Amanda clutching a bag of warm breads and a bunch of yellow chrysanthemums, her heart began to thud painfully. It had been one stop too many, for there waiting in front of the bakery was a familiar looking landau. And leaning nonchalantly against it was Nicholas Devereaux himself!

Her heart sank and yet managed somehow also to lodge in her throat.

"Good morning, Miss Chastain," he began, straightening up with a smile. He doffed his flat-brimmed hat and made her a very correct bow. "I hope you will not find me too bold if I say that you are looking particularly lovely this morning."

She was too stunned to reply. Too shocked by his unexpected presence; too awed by the virile aura he projected. She glanced worriedly around. Did no one else sense it? Did no one else feel the overwhelming force of his appeal? Was she the only one he focused that dark, erotic magnetism upon?

When she still did not answer he grinned and gestured to his magnificent vehicle. "It would be my pleasure to deliver you home." Then not allowing her time to protest, he took Jack's box of groceries and placed it next to Red on the driver's seat. "Up on top," he ordered Jack.

When the boy immediately clambered up with an excited grin, Nicholas turned back to Amanda.

"Come, my sweet," he murmured for her ears only. "I promise not to be anything more than a perfect gentleman."

He reached for her packages, but she only clasped them tighter against her chest. "You . . . you cannot behave as a perfect gentleman, because . . . because you are not a gentleman. No, not at all," she answered, but breathlessly. Then gathering her scattered wits, she added, "I would rather walk."

He moved closer. "Perhaps you would, but I have no intentions of allowing you to do so, Amanda. Now, unless you wish to make a scene you will allow me to assist you up into my carriage.''

She did as he asked—as he demanded—but only because a scene would draw the attention of passersby and someone might relate everything to Pierre. She couldn't risk that. With a muffled oath she shoved the shopping bag of bread and flowers at him, then climbed into the conveyance without his aid. She sat squarely in the middle of the forward facing seat, so that he could not sit beside her. But having him directly across from her, with his long legs outstretched so that the toes of his boots disappeared beneath the hem of her skirt proved every bit as bad. She pulled her own feet back, trying to control her full skirt and petticoats, but to no avail. If he was a gentleman he would not encroach that way onto her side of the narrow space. But, of course, he was no gentleman. And that was the crux of her problem.

The landau started forward. Though Amanda knew it would be wiser to ignore him, to freeze him with her icy disdain, she was too angry to be wise. Instead she glared at him, abandoning any pretense of civility. "Have you been following me?"

He arched one dark brow consideringly. "Would I have the opportunity to speak with you otherwise?"

Amanda tilted her chin up to a pugnacious angle. "Absolutely not."

He grinned. "Then I am forced to take whatever measures I must."

That supremely confident remark roused her anger to a fever pitch. But it also deflated her. Did he mean to pursue her forever?

Would she be able to resist if he did?

She looked away, suddenly afraid of him and what he was capable of making her feel. "You should not do this," she whispered.

She heard him sigh. "No, I should not," he conceded.

"Then why?" She chanced a peek at him.

This time his smile was more honest, devoid of its usual smugness. "As you said, you will not see me otherwise. What other choice do I have?"

Though it should not have, that admission sent a curl of unbidden heat spiraling up from the vicinity of her belly. A wicked little curl. She cleared her throat and looked away. "We made a wager and . . . and now it is fulfilled."

He did not immediately respond. The steel-rimmed wheels clattered over the ballast stone pavers. The horse hooves rang in noisy rhythm. Voices carried from the outside; a dog yapped. But louder than all of those was the tattoo roaring in her ears. Though she should despise him and what he wanted of her—and she did, she really did!—there was, nonetheless, a sinful part of her that rejoiced. Rejoiced!

She swallowed hard and tried to beat down that unseemly reaction, but not with complete success. The carriage turned onto St. Ann Street and she did not know whether to be relieved or not. Only when it began to slow did he finally speak.

"Will you always rush to your brother's aid?" he asked in a quiet tone.

She looked up. "What do you mean?"

He met her gaze without blinking. Without smiling. "Should he find himself sitting across a deck of cards again, in danger of losing everything he owns, will you rescue him again, as you rescued him this time from me?"

Her eyes widened in horror. "He shall never do that again!"

"Can you be certain of that? Nathan Soniat would be happy to have that warehouse. So would any number of shrewd businessmen. Will you save your foolish brother from them as you saved him from me? Will you barter your body—"

She slapped him. Her reaction, so automatic, stung her hand and left a red place on his cheek. Though it may have pained her more than it did him, she could not take it back, nor regret it.

"You have ruined me and now you imply—Oh!" She grabbed the door and tried to get out, but he caught her by the arm.

"I imply nothing," he hissed in her ear. "But I do not trust Pierre to behave responsibly."

"You imply that I will . . . that I will *whore* for my brother!"

"No, I fear, rather, that I have opened a Pandora's box. You have a natural passion, Amanda. A passion so pure, so violent . . ."

She shuddered and pulled away from him. She did not want to be reminded of that violent passion, and yet she knew she would never be able to forget it.

"Pierre will not bet again. I will not allow it," she vowed.

The landau had stopped, and now without responding he alighted and turned to help her down. Before she could descend, however, he closed the space between them. "He can be tempted to gamble again. *I* can tempt him to do so," he warned.

Amanda caught her breath. Would he do that? After the way he'd treated her last night, as if she were a treasure to be valued, could he possibly be so cruel as to use her brother's weakness against her? But then, he was the Devil of the Tables, she reminded herself, the man with the uncanny ability to influence foolish young men, and entice sensible young women.

He'd introduced her to a side of herself she'd not known existed. He'd seduced her and thrilled her, and for a short while made her forget how devious he could be. But he was reminding her now. She'd be doubly a fool to ignore the threat he implied.

"Are you saying that you will try to lure my brother to gamble again? You will try to ruin him too?"

A muscle jumped in his jaw, and she saw the flare of anger in his dark eyes. "I don't want to ruin anybody," he bit out.

"But you will. You've already ruined me and you won't hesitate to ruin him too!" She shoved past him, leaping down from the carriage step. But he caught her by the wrist and angrily spun her around to face him.

"We made the wager, you and I. It could not have been done without both of us having agreed. I warned you that I was a gambler and that I gamble to win. It's far too late for regrets."

"It may be too late to change what has already passed between us," she retorted. "But it is not too late for me to regret ever having met you. I would rather . . . rather hire myself out as a serving girl than ever have to deal with you again!"

Then spying Jack's curious face peeping down from the roof of the landau, she clenched her teeth, spun away, and stormed up the granite steps. She didn't look back to ascertain Nicholas Devereaux's expression, nor to see whether Jack had gathered up all their packages. She had to get away before she embarrassed herself here on the street, right in front of anyone who might be passing by. Whether she exploded in anger or in tears, the last thing she wanted was to make a public spectacle of herself.

It was awful enough that she'd made a spectacle of herself in private.

Nicholas was furious. The landau rocked along St. Ann Street, then turned onto Dauphine, heading for home. And none too soon. He needed to do something physical or else explode from the force of his pent-up emotions.

God save him from virtuous women—especially hot-tempered little shrews like Amanda Chastain!

Unfortunately, the fact that she was no longer virtuous seemed to have made her more resistant to him rather than less. And while he could easily follow through on his threat to once again gamble with her brother, he did not want to resort to that.

But damn! What other choice did he have? He wanted her. He wanted her back in his bed, melting beneath him as he took his pleasure of her. And he wanted to know she took as much pleasure from him, despite all her objections to the contrary.

Most of all, he wanted to banish all her objections to him and have her come to him willingly.

He rubbed his cheek where she had slapped him. He had deserved that, and much worse. But he'd been angry and unable to stomach the idea of her ever having to bargain with another man as she'd been forced to bargain with him. Though she'd sworn she would never have to do so again, how could he be certain?

She'd been desperate when she'd made that wager with him. Who knew how desperate she might again become, so long as her fate rested in the hands of her foolhardy brother?

CHAPTER FIVE

It took every bit of Amanda's nerve to accompany Fiona that afternoon on a round of social calls. Trailing Lottie behind them, the two women made their way up Royal Street to call on two of Amanda's mother's oldest friends, Mrs. Hortense Fontanelle and her spinster sister, Eloise De Gruy. After partaking of a late luncheon of oysters en brochette with those two, they then moved on to Chartres Street to take tea with Mrs. Eleanor Vinet and her daughters, Anne and Elizabeth, in their recently refurbished apartments on the Place de Armes.

So far so good, Amanda thought once the iron gate had clanged closed behind them. Neither Nicholas Devereaux nor his loyal hound of a manservant had shown their faces. Pray God the man had taken her threat to heart and would focus his unwelcome attentions elsewhere.

Only they hadn't been entirely unwelcome, and that terrible truth continued to haunt her. As surely as her legs trembled from last night's unaccustomed activities, and her eyes burned from lack of sleep, her body yet tingled with remembered passion. Every time she thought of Nicholas Devereaux and the intimacies she'd shared with him, she fairly quivered with shameful desire. And though she tried hard not to think of him, that was proving to be an impossible task.

"... your brother as yet unmarried?"

Amanda looked up with a start. Was Mrs. Vinet addressing her? "My brother? Oh, yes. My brother. He ... he is as yet unmarried. But," she added, seeing the sudden light in the woman's eyes and in her daughters' as well, "I believe his affections are engaged and that it is merely a matter of time before he will announce a betrothal." More's the pity for Mary Louise Delachaise, Amanda thought, somewhat ungraciously. But then, perhaps a wife would be able to control Pierre's gambling more effectively than could a sister.

Pierre and his troublesome fascination with gambling remained uppermost in Amanda's mind as the visit wore down. But as she and Fiona made their farewells and descended the curving stairwell, then turned back toward Royal Street and the milliner's shop, she spied a smart black carriage and gasped. Nicholas Devereaux's?

No, it was a brougham, not a landau.

"Are you all right, my dear? Of a sudden you appear so flushed. You're not becoming ill, are you? The city air is so foul these days, and you are so unused to it—"

"No, I am quite well," Amanda cut off the little woman before she could get too wound up. Although Amanda would have preferred feigning illness and returning to Fiona's house, the resultant fuss would simply not be worth it. Fiona would insist on bed rest for her and not allow her to return home to Magnolia Shade. The stress of travel and all that. Amanda had no intention, however, of allowing anything to delay her return home.

They reached the milliner's without mishap, though Amanda could muster no enthusiasm for hats or any other such fripperies. While Fiona ordered a new winter bonnet, burgundy net and velvet trimmed with gold braid and jet beads, Amanda kept a wary eye turned toward the front window.

No black carriages in sight. Thank goodness. She spied a tall man in a flat-brimmed hat, and her heart leaped. But then he turned and she saw his heavy whiskers and knew it was not him.

"Shall I order Lottie and Abigail each a new sunbonnet for Christmas?" Fiona whispered in Amanda's ear.

Amanda smiled, though the smile was caused more of relief than anything else. "That's a wonderful idea. Shall I occupy

Lottie while you place the order with Mrs. Lapin?''

Fiona nodded, glowing with her little secret. Amanda drew Lottie aside, ostensibly to ask her opinion of a new style displayed in the window, a cloche-type bonnet that looked little more than a boy's cap made of green satin, black lace, and a small cluster of rooster feathers.

"How is the thing worn?" Lottie wondered. "You couldn't fit any amount of hair beneath it. Are you s'posed to let the hair fall free down the back while you . . .''

Amanda did not hear the rest. She could not have heard had the dear old servant shouted the words in her ear. For there, through the window and right across the street stood the very man she'd most feared to see. And beside him, heading toward the narrow milliner's shop, was none other than her traitorous brother.

The devil himself with Pierre in tow. She could not have imagined a more horrible situation!

She spun away from the window. What to do? What to do? Then her frantic gaze landed on Fiona and she made a beeline for her. "Are you nearly finished, Fiona dear? These shoes are pinching my toes and I fear I must return home straightaway to remove them.''

"Why, you poor child. You should have said something to me earlier. You know, we needn't have come here today. We could have come tomorrow, or the next day.''

Then the bell over the door jangled and Fiona looked up, and Amanda's heart sank down to the soles of her innocent leather walking shoes.

"Why, Pierre. Do you seek us out? How sweet!'' Fiona exclaimed. She placed her hand on Amanda's arm. "Look, Amanda, it's your dear brother. I certainly hope you have not come to fetch her back already. I would keep her in town with me a little longer,'' she said to Pierre, shaking a warning finger at him.

Pierre bent to kiss Fiona's cheek. "I had business in town and I thought only to call on you to see how you both fared.'' Then spying Fiona's curious glance at his companion, he smiled. "Fiona, I would like to introduce you to Mr. Nicholas

Devereaux. Nicholas, this is Mrs. Jacob Carpenter. Though she is not truly our aunt, she is the nearest thing to it we have. You have already met my sister, Amanda,'' he added, almost as if in afterthought.

In all this Pierre had not met Amanda's furious gaze, nor did he do so now. Coward, she fumed. Coward! He knew her feelings regarding Nicholas Devereaux.

Not your true feelings, an accusing little voice in her head threw in.

She immediately banished that voice. He knew she wanted nothing whatsoever to do with Nicholas Devereaux. She'd been very clear on that point. And he knew she didn't want *him* to have anything to do with the man either. Yet here he was, the rogue at his side as if they were the best of friends, accosting them in a milliner's shop!

"I am most pleased to make your acquaintance,'' Nicholas said in his smooth rumble of a voice. Fiona replied in her shrill little-girl tones. Amanda, more conscious of her own racing heart and shallow breathing, barely heard Fiona's reply. How was she to face him without revealing all? How was she to disguise her feelings and pretend to a restrained civility when she was suddenly flushed with heat and overwhelmed with erotic memories?

"I am especially pleased to see you again, Miss Chastain.'' He extended his hand, and after only the briefest hesitation, Amanda reciprocated the gesture. But at the first touch of his strong fingers an embarrassing shudder of awareness rippled through her.

Did they all see?

She looked up in alarm. Fiona was smiling sweetly at Nicholas. Assessingly. No doubt weighing his suitability as a beau for any of the various unmarried young women of her social circle.

Pierre was smiling too and staring at his sister now with an expression of obvious relief. Had he feared she would make a scene? Worse, had he already been enticed to gamble again?

Amanda sucked in a worried breath and turned her eyes finally to Nicholas. She was rewarded with a smile of such blinding male beauty and utter sincerity that for a minute she quite forgot to breathe. He held her hand firmly but without any undue pressure. Her gaze, however, he managed to hold with a force that defied description.

"I came in town to deliver the yearling," Pierre said, to fill the awkward silence when Amanda still did not respond. He looked back and forth between his sister and Devereaux.

"Oh, you have bought one of Pierre's fine horses, Mr. Devereaux?" Fiona's grip tightened pointedly on Amanda's arm. "Amanda is an excellent horsewoman. Did you know that?"

Nicholas turned his devastating half grin on the older woman. "So I have recently been given to understand. In fact, I hoped that I might entice her to ride out with me one day. I have a very fine palomino mare that I think she would enjoy. How does that sound to you, Miss Chastain?"

She pulled her hand from his with a jerk. Her eyes, however, remained riveted upon him. What was he thinking? Such an invitation was tantamount to declaring his interest in her. Was he mad?

"Perhaps it can be arranged," she finally answered, but with a decided lack of enthusiasm. Perhaps it could be arranged, but only if she had no care whatsoever for her reputation.

For a moment, though, she let herself imagine such a scenario: him coming to fetch her on some tall fine steed; her riding out beside him with a picnic hamper attached behind her saddle. They would share a meal beneath a shady oak, perhaps alongside the Mississippi.

Oh, what was she thinking?

But before she had the presence of mind to steer the conversation elsewhere, Fiona turned to Pierre and with a firm hold on his arm, drew him toward a display of feathers and artificial fruits. "I need your opinion, dear boy, about storing my hats. The heat and humidity of our lengthy summers always take such a terrible toll upon them . . ."

Amanda could not believe it. They were both abandoning her to Nicholas Devereaux. No, they were doing far worse than that. They were throwing her at him. If they knew his true intentions toward her they would never do so. But they did not know. And she had to make certain they never did.

"You are not pleased to see me."

That fast her anger turned into an infinitely darker emotion. His husky whisper—the last time delivered in her ear and followed by a heart-stopping kiss on that tender appendage—sent a shiver of fire skittering down her back. Oh, she truly was a wanton to be recalling such things here and now.

She shot one last desperate look toward Fiona and Pierre. But they were on the opposite side of the store with their backs turned. She had no other recourse but to deal directly with Nicholas.

"Why are you tormenting me so?" she asked in the barest of whispers. "What do you gain by this false-hearted attention?"

The smile faded from his handsome face. "Why do you think it false-hearted?"

Her expression turned bitter. "We do not want the same thing, you and I. No matter what you think of me now, I cannot be . . . I cannot be what you would have me be."

Their gazes held, his dark and determined, hers paler and, unfortunately, far less resolute. "Will you ride out with me some morning, Amanda? Or would you prefer a carriage drive?" he asked, ignoring her words.

"I . . . I can do neither."

"Your brother does not object to me. Why do you?"

"You know why!" she hissed, then glanced fearfully at Pierre. He was still engaged with Fiona, but Amanda managed to catch his eye. To her infinite dismay, however, he only smiled and nodded as if in encouragement.

Oh, was she the only one of them possessed of any sense at all?

"Don't you like me, Amanda? I could have sworn you enjoyed my company."

She sucked in a harsh breath when he bent nearer her. "I would swear it on my very soul." Then he caught her hand in his and brought it up to his mouth. His lips were firm when he kissed her gloved knuckles. But when he turned her hand over and kissed first her palm, then the bare place at her wrist where her glove met the hem of her sleeve, those same lips seemed to become damp and warm. Sweetly moist and devastatingly warm.

Or was that *her* reaction to him? Not only had her own hand become unnaturally hot, something deep inside her felt the exact same way. Like a fluid sort of fire, it erupted in her, surging up from her most private parts—parts she'd not known she possessed until he'd brought them to life in the most erotic fashion.

With a helpless gasp she pulled her hand away. But she was unable to hide her reaction to him. When he smiled at her she knew he'd seen it. She knew also that now he'd never relent.

To her profound relief the sound of a throat being cleared interrupted their too intimate discourse. Pierre stood there, his avid gaze moving between her and Nicholas while he worked to keep his expression stern. "You two seem to be in disagreement," he stated. Though his voice was serious, the gleam in his eyes was less so. "Perhaps we can all dine together this evening and bring about an accord. Once our business is done." He added this last to Nicholas.

"That will not be possible," Amanda stated before Nicholas could accept. "We have made other plans, haven't we, Fiona dear?" She stared pointedly at the older woman.

Fiona's round face creased in confusion. It was clear she thought the handsome Nicholas Devereaux quite a catch for Amanda. But she'd obviously heard the message in Amanda's voice.

"It's just as well," Nicholas threw in, smoothing over the awkward moment. "I have previously made plans for this evening myself, plans which I cannot change. If you're at loose ends, Chastain, you are welcome to join me. Several other men will be my guests for a friendly game of cards. My house," he added. Though he addressed Pierre, he kept his gaze steady on Amanda.

She couldn't help it. Amanda grabbed Pierre's arm and turned a pleading look on him. But she wisely held her tongue and when Pierre's face reddened slightly and he shook his head, she knew she'd done the right thing.

"Sorry, Devereaux, but I've sworn off gambling. At least for awhile," he added, subtly removing his arm from Amanda's tight grasp.

Nicholas grinned, first at Pierre, then at Amanda. "Perhaps another time," he said, holding Amanda's eyes with his own. "I regret that I must depart this lovely company now. Mrs. Carpenter. Miss Chastain." He bowed handsomely to the two women.

"I'll be off too," Pierre said.

"I shall be ready to go home tomorrow," Amanda told Pierre, staying him when he would have departed with Nicholas. "Will you come for me in the carriage?"

"Yes, yes," he answered impatiently. "And if I cannot, I'll send Lester. Now let me loose, Mandy. I'm not a child for you to keep tabs on."

So saying, he left, hurrying to catch up with Nicholas Devereaux. Amanda stared after the two men, her emotions in a turmoil. He was not done with her. Nor with Pierre, she feared.

"What a handsome man that Nicholas Devereaux is," Fiona said, breathlessly, pressing one gloved hand to her ample bosom. When Amanda did not respond she gave her a curious look. "I cannot understand why you were so rude to him, Mandy. Don't you like him? He seems awfully taken with you."

Amanda tried to calm her shattered nerves. "He's a gambler and . . . and I think he's a bad influence on Pierre."

"Pish, posh. All gentlemen gamble. Why, Mr. Carpenter used to give me fits with his card playing. But it was just his way of passing the time with his friends. He always swore he did most of his business over a deck of cards."

Amanda did not respond to that. What use was it to protest that Nicholas Devereaux did more than pass the time when he played cards? What use was it to protest that he wasn't simply doing business over a friendly game of poker? Gambling *was* his business. He earned his living that way. He destroyed other people's lives that way.

All she could do was try to avoid the man and try to keep Pierre away from him. But she feared that would prove to be a Herculean task. For the truth remained immutable: When he'd kissed her hand, then her palm and wrist, she'd practically dissolved at his feet.

"Don't take this the wrong way, Mandy dear. But you can't afford to be too particular when it comes to suitors. There's few enough men to go around these days, and even fewer who keep a good household—especially Southern gentlemen. And you know your father would never have approved of a Yankee for you, even one as rich as Croesus. If you'll take an old woman's advice, you'll not turn your nose up at a man even your brother seems to approve of."

"Perhaps I don't want a suitor. Perhaps I don't want ever to marry," Amanda muttered obstinately.

"Gracious me! What a terrible thing to say!" Fiona exclaimed.

But at least it put an end to the subject of Nicholas Devereaux. Still, as Fiona concluded her purchases and they headed back to her town house, Amanda pondered that very thought.

Maybe that was as it should be. She should never wed. How could she explain her loss of innocence to her husband? It simply wouldn't be fair to another man for her to come to him sullied as she now was.

But more than that, she did not think she could bear going to another man's bed. Not after having spent a night with Nicholas. Though there was no comprehending such a ludicrous idea, she nevertheless knew it was so. No other man would affect her as he had. To even suffer another man's touch—

She shuddered at the very thought. But to consider Nicholas touching her again, that brought a shiver of inexplicable heat and longing.

Oh, she must truly be mad to feel so. Mad, or else the most wanton creature alive!

*   *   *

"What time is the game to begin?"

Nicholas studied Pierre Chastain a long moment before answering. Just minutes ago Pierre had reassured his sister that he'd sworn off gambling. Now, in private, he seemed ready to renege on that vow.

"Around eight or nine. Whenever we have enough players to begin. Are you reconsidering joining us?"

Pierre shrugged in a boyish motion that made him look far younger than his twenty-five years. Though the younger of the two, it was clear that Amanda was by far the more mature and responsible of the siblings.

"I'm in town with no other plans. It seems as pleasant a diversion as any," he added, trying to appear off-handed about the subject.

Again Nicholas took a long time to respond. But instead of studying Chastain, this time he examined his own perverse reaction to the man's words. To his own amazement, he did not want Chastain betting at his table.

He *should* want him there, for the odds were good that he could again win the man's money, and perhaps, as a result, make the same arrangement with his sister.

But he could not do that, and he knew it. For that would make Amanda hate him even more than she already did. Incredible as it seemed, he did not want her to hate him. Even more incredible, though, was what he *did* want. He wanted to protect her. He wanted to keep her safe from her brother's recklessness.

He shook his head at his own perversity.

He'd wanted many things of women in the past, but never this. He'd been unattached for years, and unhindered by any emotions save those that drove him to gamble, to take chances. But he'd only been gambling with money, he now realized, something he could as easily lose as win. There was always more where that came from.

Now though . . . now he was faced with a far more dangerous game—but with a much greater payoff. If he wanted to walk away the winner this time, he would have to put himself on the line in a way he'd never had to do before.

But he was a gambler and he'd learned to trust his hunches. Amanda might be the biggest gamble of his life, yet he was willing to take the chance. He clapped Chastain on the shoulder. "If I were to let you join us tonight, I'm afraid your sister would never forgive me."

"My sister—"

"Has captured my heart," Nicholas threw in before Chastain could say anything derogatory about Amanda. His words stopped the younger man in his tracks.

"What? As rude as she has been to you?"

It was Nicholas's turn to shrug. "The fact is, she is completely justified in her opinion of me. If I am ever to improve that opinion, however, it will not be by gambling with her brother."

Chastain stared at him in amazement. For that matter, Nicholas was pretty amazed at himself. He'd practically declared his intentions to her brother. This was serious business.

Chastain clearly took it the same way. "Are you asking my leave to court her?"

Nicholas took a deep breath. This was it, the day he'd never expected to come. Now that it was here, however, it felt inevitable.

"Yes," he answered, no trace of doubt in his voice or his mind. "Yes, that's exactly what I'm asking."

CHAPTER SIX

Pierre came with the brougham in the early afternoon. Amanda would have preferred Lester, for she could more easily have avoided conversation during the hour-long drive. But Pierre wanted to talk to her and they had no sooner said their good-byes to Fiona and turned the corner onto Royal Street than he made that abundantly clear.

"Why are you so rude to Nicholas Devereaux?" he began without preamble.

Amanda clenched her jaw and looked away. What had Nicholas told her brother to prompt such a question? "Do I have to like every man of your acquaintance? I don't like Calvin Harrison and you do not take me to task for that."

"Calvin Harrison is a shiftless no-account and everyone knows it. Nicholas Devereaux hardly falls into the same category."

"I happen to believe that gambling is a shiftless preoccupation."

"All men gamble," he countered.

"That doesn't make it right!"

Pierre stared at her so hard her face grew hot. "There's got to be more to it than that, Amanda. I think you're attracted to him despite all your protests to the contrary. And I know he's attracted to you."

This time her face went scarlet. Yes, he was attracted to her, but not in the honorable manner Pierre believed. All Nicholas wanted was more of what he'd already had. That she wanted it too was a shameful secret she must hide forever.

"I don't wish to discuss him any further," she stated in a strangled voice. "It's clear you refuse to believe anything I say, so let's just move on to another subject. Did you find another foreman for the warehouse? Someone to replace Mr. Jenkins?"

"He's asked leave to court you."

Amanda blinked. She heard Pierre's words but they simply did not register. "Mr. . . . Mr. Jenkins?" she stupidly stammered.

"No!" Pierre exclaimed. "Blast it all, Mandy, you should be flattered that a man like Nicholas Devereaux is interested in you—especially given your unforgivable rudeness to him."

Amanda suffered her brother's temper in silence. Indeed, she hardly heard a word of it. Nicholas had asked her brother for permission to court her? To *court* her? It was quite beyond comprehension.

"I told him yes, of course. Did you hear me, Mandy? I told him he could call on you this evening." Pierre's voice had risen in anger, so much so that passersby looked up at them curiously.

Doubly embarrassed, Amanda pinched him on the arm. "Lower your voice. I can hear you plainly enough, and so can everyone on the street."

"I just don't understand your hesitation," he bit out, though at least in a less carrying tone. "He's wealthy, young, and a favorite of the ladies. You should be flattered."

Unfortunately Amanda *was* flattered, so much so that her logic and good reason faltered. After seducing her and muddling every sensible thought in her head, did he now wish to marry her?

Or could it be just part of his scheme to seduce her again? To get her alone and convince her to succumb to him, then afterward find a reason to break off the courtship?

Then an even worse thought struck. Maybe he was doing this out of guilt. He'd taken her virtue. Perhaps he possessed just enough lingering decency to be ashamed of his behavior, and so he thought to remedy things by making this belated offer for her.

Amanda pressed her lips together as too many confusing emotions crowded in on her. Longing, fear, regret, and a terrible sadness held her in their grip. She did not want anyone to marry her out of a sense of obligation, especially not Nicholas Devereaux. If only she knew why he'd chosen to do this.

"Well?" Pierre demanded once they were past Canal Street and into a less crowded part of the city. "Will you greet him with more courtesy this evening than you did yesterday at the milliner's?"

Amanda did not trust her voice to speak, so she only gave him a curt nod. That seemed sufficient for Pierre, however. For the remainder of the drive home, down tree-lined St. Charles, past the beautiful new mansions that lined the avenue, he rode contentedly in silence, only breaking it every now and again with whistled snatches of "Camp Town Ladies."

But while Pierre whistled, Amanda's thoughts tumbled madly about. As preposterous as it seemed, Nicholas Devereaux, notorious gambler and man-about-town meant to come calling on her. The man she'd wagered her home and reputation with—and both won and lost to in the process—had asked permission to court her, and would begin to do so this very day. Somehow she must keep her wits about her and determine what motivated this unlikely declaration of his.

But beyond his motivation, she must wonder at her own. By agreeing to see him, she was tacitly stating that she was amenable to a match between them. But was she? Did she dare even consider such a thing—assuming he was serious?

When they arrived home she hurried inside, throwing only a distracted greeting to Effie before she closed herself up in her room. She had to prepare for Nicholas's arrival—not so much her appearance as her nerves. She flung herself across her neatly laid bed. How ever was she to deal with him?

With honesty, the answer presented itself at once. With candor and honesty, and a demand that he deal with her in the same fashion.

She would have to demand also that he be respectful of the

proprieties, for if he touched her or tried to kiss her, she feared her planning would be completely lost in the resultant rush of violent emotion.

Worst of all, she feared that he knew it.

"Miss Chastain." Nicholas bowed but did not take her hand. That's because she did not offer it, but instead kept her hands clasped in a knot at her waist.

"Mr. Devereaux," she answered, her voice civil but not particularly warm.

She felt the annoyance in her brother's stare but she ignored it. She had much more at stake this evening than did Pierre. Her entire future might be decided during the next few hours. Pierre could just stew in silence. "Might I offer you something cool to drink?" she added in her best hostess manner.

"I would appreciate that very much. The sun was unmerciful on the ride up." Though his reply sounded as bland as her question had been, he sent an altogether different message with his eyes. Dark and smoky, they held her gaze captive and made silent promises that caused her stomach to tighten and her heart to race. She prayed he did not see how he affected her.

"Yes, well, I'm afraid I cannot linger with the two of you," Pierre threw in. "I've books to look over. On my way to my study I'll instruct Effie to bring out refreshments. Will you sit on the front porch?"

"Yes. It's cooler there," Amanda answered. Plus, she needed to be alone with Nicholas, though not for precisely the reasons Pierre suspected. She smiled at Pierre, for the first time grateful for his interference. After a moment he smiled back, clearly relieved by this, her first show of cooperation. He was trying so hard, she admitted. As her only brother he felt responsible for her future. To marry her to a well-fixed gentleman seemed to him a logical goal. That he was handling the details so awkwardly was actually rather endearing she decided.

"Yes, let us sit outside," she repeated, smiling again at Pierre, all the while avoiding Nicholas's gaze. He knew the impact he had upon her and he was shameless enough to take full advantage of it. But she did not intend to make this interview that easy for him.

Amanda led the way to the front porch, to the wicker settee and pair of rocking chairs her mother had bought for this very spot. A pair of Chinese palm plants flourished in two Nipponese bowls, and a pottery container of trailing roses bloomed unrepentantly though it was well into October. All in all a very pretty setting for a man to court a woman.

If he truly was courting her.

She positioned herself in one of the rockers, and after a moment Nicholas took the other one. Effie came out with tea and when she left, so did Pierre, but only after sending Amanda a stern look to behave.

Then it was only Amanda and Nicholas, and though the windows were open so as to discourage any improprieties on his part, the two of them were, for all intents and purposes, completely alone.

Dusk had brought the first breath of a cooling breeze. The lavender shadows increasing across the lawn, combined with the sweet fragrance of night-blooming jasmine, bathed the front garden in a dreamy, romantic mood. Amanda fought the urge to succumb to that mood.

"I gather you will resist any entreaties to join me on the settee," Nicholas murmured in a low rumbling tone that sent a disturbing shiver through her.

Amanda glanced at his handsome face and then away, staring at the magnolias and their large red-berried seed pods. "There are a few matters we need to resolve between us before we can progress to that point," she answered primly. She feared, however, that her obvious breathlessness ruined that primness.

He crossed his legs nonchalantly, resting one ankle across the other knee. "I believe the biggest issue—that of our, shall we say, suitability—has already been settled."

Amanda fought the blush that rose in her cheeks and the frisson of heat that began to coil in her stomach. She failed on both counts. "It takes more than . . . more than *that* to forge a successful union between a man and a woman.'' Be blunt, she reminded herself. Confront him with candor and demand an honest answer from him. ''Why are you doing this?'' she added, meeting his gaze despite the scarlet that still stained her cheeks.

He gave her that devastating half smile. ''I am courting you, Amanda, because I hope to convince you to marry me. I thought you understood that.''

''Yes, that is what Pierre told me. But I cannot help but wonder if that is your true purpose.''

His raised boot hit the floor and he leaned forward, his elbows on his knees as he stared intently into her eyes. ''I have not come here under false pretenses, if that is what you're thinking. I hope to win your affections and convince you to marry me. In truth, I believe that despite your resistance to me, you do feel some affection for me.'' Without warning he reached forward and caught her hands in his. ''Tell me, Amanda. Do you harbor any warm feelings for me? Any at all?''

Again her cheeks heated with color, robbing her of any opportunity to deny his accusation. ''I . . . I admit that . . . that I enjoy your company more so than I had expected to. But you avoid my question,'' she added, trying unsuccessfully to free her hand from his warm hold.

''What was the question?''

''Why? Why do you court me now when you have had . . . Well, when there is no need to?''

He opened her hand and laced his fingers with hers. Palm to palm he created an aura of sensuality that belied the otherwise completely proper appearance of their conversation. They were properly attired and seated quite properly in public view of anyone who cared to look. But the feelings seething inside her were anything but proper.

''Most people would think just the opposite, Amanda. They would feel I am obliged to marry you precisely *because* of what has already passed between us.''

This time Amanda succeeded in freeing her hand from his hold, and she lurched to her feet. ''Is that why you are doing this? Out of guilt feelings? Because if it is—''

"No. It is not." Nicholas rose as well. But his nearness on the shadowed porch, coupled with the scent of flowers and the evening hum of cicadas proved too overpowering. She wanted to believe him but she feared to do so. He was a gambler, she reminded herself, not simply for idle entertainment, but as a way of life. He was a man who lived by a different code of conduct than did the other men of her acquaintance.

"Amanda." Again his low voice stroked some unseen nerve inside her. But she refused to succumb to the seduction in it.

"Perhaps we should walk," she managed to say, sidling past him toward the wide steps that led down into the garden. More than walking, however, she needed time to think. Time to ponder what to do. How to answer him. For though she knew she should not encourage him in any way, a tiny part of her wanted to do just that. No, it was more than just a tiny part. She should send such an unreliable suitor packing. Instead she wanted to fling herself willingly into his arms.

Oh, but she was a fool to pit her lack of experience against his worldliness—more of a fool than Pierre had ever been! How could she even consider gambling so recklessly with her own future?

Then it struck her. Gambling. She'd gambled with him once before, making that wager to save her home. And she'd won. Of course, she'd lost something else in the process. It had not actually been so terrible a loss though. In fact, she'd gained much that she'd not expected from their one night together.

There had been the carnal pleasure of it, of course. The physical joy. The indescribable passion. But there had been more as well, a communion of their souls, as if they'd somehow become one, at least for a little while. To even remember that feeling made her ache to experience it again. But not with anyone else. Only with Nicholas.

Dear God, she thought as an incredible realization hit her. Could it be that she was in love with him?

Her stomach gave an odd lurch; a quiver marked its way down her spine. She loved him. Heavenly day, who could ever have predicted such a thing?

But her new knowledge seemed to give her a renewed courage. She would take the chance. She'd gambled with him once before and she would gamble with him again. Only this time *she* would propose the wager and it would be on *her* terms, not his.

Then she stopped beside a rose trellis where a scattering of single salmon-colored blooms still put on a display. Did she really dare to take such a chance?

The answer could not have been more obvious. If she did not do it she would regret it all the days of her life. All the long, lonely days of her life.

She turned abruptly, only to find him right there, just inches away.

He placed his hands on her upper arms. "I thought you wanted to walk. But if you'd rather linger with me beneath this cascade of roses—"

"I propose a wager between us," she blurted out, cutting him off before he could divert her from his purpose. "I propose another wager between us. *If* you are so inclined."

"A wager?" His brows arched in mild surprise and the half smile came out in full force. "And what would the terms of this wager be?"

Amanda swallowed hard, but she kept her eyes locked upon his. He might be amused, but she was deadly serious. How he reacted to her proposal would determine the entire course of their lives.

She took a deep breath. "I propose a game of cards."

"Cards? Poker, or some parlor game like Beggar My Neighbor or Cribbage?"

"You may choose the game," she snapped. "I don't care about that."

"You don't care?" A faint frown creased his forehead. "What exactly would we be wagering?"

This was it. "If you win the game, I will spend another night with you." She felt his fingers tighten on her arms; she saw a flame rise in his eyes. "Only one, never to be repeated again."

"And if I lose?"

"If you lose—and I win—then I will agree to marry you and you will agree to give up all gambling. *Completely*," she added so that there could be no doubt about her meaning.

She saw the quick turn of his mind as he weighed her words, and she knew his gambler's mind would swiftly understand. She was offering him the chance to have another night of passion with her, with no strings attached, or the chance to marry her, promising in the process to be a good and reliable husband. They both knew she could not best him at cards—not unless he allowed her to.

When his face creased in that cocky half grin, however, she could not be sure which prize he meant to seek. "I accept your wager, Amanda. But I would seal our wager with a kiss."

"That's . . . that's not necessary."

"Oh, but it is to me. Men shake hands as a pledge of good faith—"

"Then we can shake hands too."

"You are not a man, but instead the most delightful, delicious female I've ever had the pleasure to know."

So affecting were those unexpected words that Amanda could not react other than to stare up at him dumbfounded. He proceeded to take full advantage of her astonishment and drew her up for a kiss.

It was so sweet. It was so incredibly powerful. And it left her in no doubt of how she wanted their wager settled. When they finally pulled apart, however—she weak-kneed and breathless, he breathing harder too—she was no more certain of how the wager would turn out than she'd been before. Was this passion of his one that could be sustained over a lifetime? Or would he settle for one more fiery, erotic night?

"When shall we play this game of cards?" he asked, his breath hot against her ear. His hand splayed against the small of her back, holding her near.

"Oh, . . . now. Now seems as good a time as . . . as any," she answered, breaking off each time he nibbled at her earlobe. She pulled away from him.

"This seems a better time for kissing than for playing cards," he murmured, pulling her back and devastating her senses with a line of bold kisses down her neck to the lacy edge of her scoop-necked bodice. When had he bent her back in his arms? When had all her good sense fled?

She shoved at him and this time he relented. But though he allowed her to straighten up, he did not let her go.

"Are you having second thoughts?" His vivid eyes bored into hers, compelling her thoughts in the most wicked direction. But it was those wicked, wanton thoughts which made her plan seem all the more rational. Whichever way the wager went, she would learn his feelings for her. She would also learn the true substance of the man, beyond his attractive exterior and mesmerizing personality.

She shook her head. "No, I have not changed my mind. I'll fetch a deck of cards now. Wait for me there." She pointed to the cutting garden where two benches and a low table sat surrounded by lilies, irises, azaleas, and camellias. Though little bloomed there now, soon enough the cycle of winter, spring, and summer flowers would begin.

So would the fertile blooming of her own life take root there, she hoped. If she were lucky.

Pierre came into the hall when he heard her footsteps. "Where is Devereaux? You have not insulted him or sent him away, have you?"

"He's waiting for me outside," she retorted, not even looking up from the bow-front commode she rummaged through. "Go back to your office and your papers, Pierre. You've done all you can to throw us together. The rest is up to us." Then clutching the slightly ragged deck of cards her father had so often played Patience with, and grabbing an oil lamp from the hall table, she hurried from the house, toward Nicholas and whatever future she was to have with him.

He was sitting on one of the benches, his arms stretched wide across the back and his legs splayed in typical male fashion. But his bemused expression was obvious even in the shadows of dusk, and it did not alter as he watched her approach.

He straightened when she sat on the bench opposite him. "Are you certain this is what you want to do, Amanda?"

She set the deck of cards down on the marble-topped table

and slid it toward him. "Yes. What game shall we play?"

"The wager need not be so dramatic. We can take our courtship slower if you are not sure of me."

But Amanda knew that taking it slower would solve nothing. "It is far too late for us to go slow. Why don't we play Poker, as you did with Pierre?"

He didn't respond but instead reached slowly for the deck of cards. His hands were strong and well-formed, sprinkled with dark hair. His fingers were long and slender with neatly clipped nails. Capable hands. Clever hands. They could manipulate a deck of cards or a woman's untried body with equal expertise. What she needed to know, however, was if he could handle her heart with the same level of skill and caring.

How she prayed he could, for whether he knew it or not, she'd already given it over into his keeping.

"All right, Amanda," he said, no longer smiling. "If this is how you want it to be."

He picked up the deck and began to shuffle. Only it was not the simple shuffling that she knew. No, it was like a dance performed between his hands and the fifty-two cards. He flipped them one way and then, with only a slight shifting of his wrists, flipped them in just the opposite direction. The cards fanned together in a rush, then immediately ruffled in another pattern.

Amanda watched, mesmerized by the magic he created. But at the same time her heart sank. She was asking him to give up his entire life, she realized, a lifetime spent perfecting the skill he displayed to her now. She was asking him to abandon that life, and for what? For her? Why should he do that when any number of other women would not demand so great a sacrifice from him?

He leaned forward, his expression noncommittal, his eyes focused on her. "I'm going to deal five cards to each of us. You may keep them all or exchange any number of them for new cards. Since the wager is already on the table with no room to raise and no opportunity to fold, we'll show our cards then. Do you know Poker, how the hands are ranked?"

Amanda nodded, all at once terrified. She was going for all or none, trusting on blind luck to win.

No, not luck. She was trusting Nicholas Devereaux. If he was being honest and truly meant to make a life with her and be a good husband to her, he would lose this game.

He dealt the cards in a slow, steady pattern. One, two, three, four, five. She stared at them, at the five identical images that lay on the table before her. Then she reached for the cards, gathered them up, and turned them to see what hand fate had dealt her.

Nicholas lifted his cards and fanned them open with only one hand, a move he often used to intimidate other players. But that was not his purpose now. He did it more from habit than anything else. Hell, if anyone in this game was intimidated, it was him.

What did this wager of hers mean?

Did she want to marry him or not?

Was she counting on him to win—and give her another thrilling night with no strings attached and, as a result, a minimum of guilt feelings? Or did she really expect him to lose to her and give up his entire livelihood in the process? Were those the only terms by which she would marry him—or had she devised them so that she would *not* have to marry him?

He studied her face, but that didn't help. She was flushed with emotion, but which emotions he could not tell. Her thick lashes shielded her expressive eyes and she stared fixedly at the cards she clutched in her white-knuckled hands.

Why was she doing this? How was he supposed to play?

Did she want to marry him or not?

He stared at the cards he held, but without really seeing them. He'd gambled many a fortune in his time. He'd won more than he'd lost and he'd amassed money, property, and a stable full of exquisite horseflesh in the process, not to mention caches of jewelry, and even partial ownership in a steamship. But what lay on the table in this game was his entire future.

He wanted to marry Amanda. Though it went against every logic, the truth remained immutable. He wanted to marry this

woman he'd known for so short a time. She was passionate
and daring, and loyal to those she loved.

But did she love him? Did she want to marry him? Did she
want him to lose this game?

He simply could not tell.

She pulled two of her cards out of her hand and threw them
facedown on the marble tabletop. "I'll take two cards,
please."

For an instant their eyes met before she lowered her lashes
again. Nicholas dealt her the two cards, but his mind focused
entirely on that one brief glimpse of her startlingly blue eyes.
She was terrified, but of what? Him winning, or him losing?

He didn't realize she was waiting for him to play until she
cleared her throat. "Are you going to keep the cards you
have?"

He shook his head. This was it. He had to play.

He forced himself to see the cards he held. A pair of jacks,
the ten of spades, seven of diamonds, and two of hearts. He
started automatically to throw away the seven and the two,
then paused.

The two of hearts.

He looked up at her but she was staring resolutely at her
cards. She was not going to make this easy, was she? No doubt
she would not make any part of their lives together easy. What
had Pierre said of her, that she was more willful than any three
women? And yet it was precisely that will, that spirit, which
drew Nicholas to her.

With a decisive movement he snatched the jacks, ten, and
seven and threw them down. "Dealer takes four cards."

They were a six, another ten, another jack, and a five. And
as Nicholas stared at them, a slow grin lifted one side of his
mouth. "It's time to show your cards," he said, eager to be
done with this farce. He meant to marry her, whether it was
what she wanted or not. And if it was not what she wanted,
well then, he'd change her mind. He'd show her that he could
be more than a good gambler, he could be a good husband
too. He would be a *great* husband. He would abandon his
bachelor ways and it would be no hardship at all. Giving up

evenings at the gambling tables would be easy, for he would have his beautiful bride, his deliciously wanton wife to wile away the hours with.

"What do you have?" he prompted her again.

He saw her take a deep breath. Her shapely bosom filled out the soft fabric of her bodice and he felt his loins tighten in response.

She spread out her hand. She held nothing, no pairs, not even a face card. When she looked up at him her face had gone pale. Her eyes were huge and in them he saw something she'd kept hidden before. It was the deep, melting look she'd revealed only when they'd lain naked together, in the soft aftermath of their lovemaking. She'd been his in that moment, his in every way. And now, in her eyes, he recognized that she wanted to be his again. Only this time forever.

He threw his cards facedown on the table. "Your hand beats mine."

She did not move, but only kept her gaze fixed disbelievingly on him. "Are . . . are you sure? You don't have even one card higher than mine?"

It was easy to lie, but he vowed to himself it would be the last lie he'd ever tell her. And once they were safely wed, he'd confess the truth about the jack he'd held. But for now he was taking no chances.

He picked up one of his cards and turned it over. "This is the only card of value I have in my hand." He pushed the two of hearts toward her. "My only hope is that it will win me the woman I love."

Amanda heard his words. She saw the raw sincerity on his unsmiling face. But only when she stared down at the card did she allow herself to believe. The two of hearts. The two of hearts!

She'd won the wager! She'd won the man she'd so unwisely fallen in love with!

She reached out for the card and their hands met. First their fingers tangled together, then their hands pressed palm to palm. Then he rounded the table, and pulled her up and into his arms.

"You have won, my sweet Amanda. You've won the game, but more, you've won my heart. I love you and I promise I will be the husband you need."

Clasped against his solid chest, wrapped in the welcome heat of his powerful embrace, Amanda answered him in the only way she could. She pulled his head down to hers and kissed him.

It was not the kiss of an innocent maiden, but then she wasn't that and never wanted to be again. She kissed him with all the love and passion of a woman who knew what she wanted and was willing to risk all to have it. She kissed him there in the garden with moonlight flooding over them, sealing their wager in the same way he'd demanded once before.

"A bargain's a bargain," he said, when the need for air forced them slightly apart.

"Yes, it is," she breathlessly agreed.

"We will have to be wed as soon as possible," he warned. His torrid gaze made the reason plain.

"Sooner than that," she replied, her body quivering with desire while her eyes shone with love.

"And I will gladly give up gambling. Except with my wife," he added with that wicked half grin of his.

His wife. How wonderful that sounded. Still, Amanda was not quite certain what he meant. "What reasons shall you and I have to gamble in the future?"

His grin grew downright devilish. One of his hands loosened the pins in her coiffure, allowing her heavy hair to tumble down her back. The other moved in a deliberately arousing fashion across her derriere.

"I see all sorts of reasons. We might place a wager on whether it will rain. Or whether the next bird to land on our windowsill will be a dove or a mocking bird."

"But . . . but why should we wager with one another over such things? I don't understand."

"Because, Amanda, if we wager on them, then one of us must win and one of us must lòse." He started kissing her ear and that simple caress so distracted her she could barely keep her thoughts straight. Still, she began to have an idea of what he was getting at.

She arched her neck and smiled into the warm darkness. "And what shall we wager with? Surely not coins."

"I expect you to be far more creative than that," he murmured, his breath so hot she squirmed against him. At once he groaned and the realization of how she affected him emboldened her. Creative. Yes, she would have to be quite creative if she were to keep up with this very clever man she'd won.

She squirmed against him again, but this time on purpose. "I'll make a wager with you now," she teased him when he pressed her suggestively to him.

"Now? What sort of wager?"

"I bet I can find a much better use for that table in your study than for playing cards."

He stared at her in such surprise that she feared she'd gone too far. Then he began to laugh, and without warning she found herself flat on her back across the marble garden table, with him leaning down over her.

"You know, I just bet you can. And I'll make you a wager," he added, lowering his head to seal their bet with another long, delicious kiss. "I wager that you, my beautiful, wicked bride, shall prove to be the true Devil of the Tables."

Amanda smiled against his hungry kiss, then circled his neck with her arms and pulled him down upon her. The Devil of the Tables. Yes, she rather liked the sound of that.

THE HAUNTING OF SARAH

ANNE LOGAN

CHAPTER PROLOGUE

S arah Bonvillain shivered and pulled her shawl tighter as a cool breeze from the Mississippi River blew across the veranda. In the shadowy twilight, she could barely see the needlework she had been working on to pass the time, and since she had little patience for the intricate stitches required anyway, she pushed aside the frame holding the tapestry and stared at the winding road that led to the house.

Jason was coming. Just the thought of seeing her handsome, dashing fiancé set her heart to fluttering beneath her breasts. He'd sent word earlier that he would call on her after supper, but he had yet to arrive. Sarah wasn't worried though. The trip from New Orleans to her family's plantation took a good hour and a half of hard riding.

She still couldn't believe that in less than a week she would become Mrs. Jason Dubuisson. From the first moment she had laid eyes on him at her coming-out party, he'd captured her heart. When he had held her in his arms as they danced, all the other men who were in attendance had paled in comparison. She had known then that Jason was the one she wanted to spend the rest of her life with.

A smile played at her lips. Wedding preparations had been going on for weeks. The last alterations had been made to her gown, and Sarah couldn't wait to see Jason's expression when he saw her wearing it. And after the wedding . . . Sarah felt her cheeks grow warm just thinking about the moment she would finally be alone with him without a chaperon.

Out of the quiet evening, a voice shouted, "Rider coming."

Sarah squinted her eyes and strained to see the lone rider approaching at a gallop. At the sight of the tall, dark-haired man, she felt dizzy with anticipation. The moment he dismounted, she wanted to run and throw her arms around him. She wanted him to sweep her into his strong embrace and kiss her until she fainted.

Sarah glanced sideways where her mother sat and she sighed. Her mother would be scandalized if she even suspected Sarah had such thoughts. Proper Southern ladies never did such things, so Sarah stood and waited patiently while he briefly paid his respects to her mother first.

Finally, he turned and approached her. "Could we walk a bit?" he asked curtly.

Nothing in his voice gave her a clue to his reasons for calling. She had just assumed that he had wanted to be with her like she wanted to be with him, but when she noticed that he couldn't quite bring himself to look directly into her eyes, some of the excitement and anticipation she'd felt waned.

Sarah nodded, and taking his arm, she followed as he led her down the veranda steps. His muscles beneath her fingers were stiff, almost as if her touch were repugnant to him, and a tinge of unease seeped through her veins as a feeling of foreboding washed over her.

Still well within sight of her mother, but out of earshot, he stopped beneath one of the many ancient live oaks that lined the road leading to the house.

Sarah squeezed his arm. "Jason, what's wrong?" When he pulled his arm loose from her grasp with a jerk, the unease she'd felt grew.

He lifted his chin at a haughty angle, and for a fleeting moment, there was a coldness in his expression that she had never seen before, a coldness that almost reminded her of Jason's twin brother, Jared, the few times she'd been around him.

Jason's dark blue eyes bored into hers. "There's no other way to say this but straight-out," he said in a low, terse voice. "I've had second thoughts about our engagement and decided that I'm not ready to be burdened with a wife, especially with one whose family comes with such dire financial needs as yours, so I'm calling off the wedding."

Burdened? The word roared through her head like a wounded bull. It was true that when her father died he'd left the family with tremendous debts. Although her mother was depending on Sarah's future husband to help them, that wasn't the reason Sarah had accepted Jason's proposal. Debt or no debt, Sarah loved him with all of her heart.

Sarah opened her mouth to speak, but no words would come. Almost from the first day they had met, he'd claimed he loved her. He'd told her so not just once, but many, many times. He'd said it would be an honor and a privilege to help the mother and sisters of the woman he loved. Not once in actions or words had he ever indicated that marrying her would be a *burden* . . . until now. What could have happened to change his mind?

"I'm sure you won't have a problem finding another man suitable for your needs."

Sarah gasped as the cruel implications of his words stung her ears.

"Well? Don't you have anything to say?" For a moment more, he stood there, staring at her, waiting.

There was plenty she wanted to say. She wanted to beg, to plead with him, to demand to know why he was doing this, but pride and years of ingrained manners kept her silent as she fought to hold back the humiliating tears that were stinging her eyes.

Then with a snort of disgust, Jason abruptly turned and stalked off toward the hitching post where his horse was tethered. And as he galloped away into the fast-approaching darkness, Sarah could do nothing but stand there and watch while her heart shattered into a thousand tiny pieces.

CHAPTER ONE

J ared Dubuisson lay in bed, propped against a stack of pillows. His broad chest was bare except for the bandages covering the wound he'd received in battle when Sherman marched on Atlanta.

"Jason's dead," he sneered. There was no mistaking his smug tone or the look of pure malice in his expression.

Spots suddenly danced before Sarah's eyes and her vision blurred as she stared down at her husband. The last time she had seen Jason, had spoken to him, was the night he'd broken off their engagement. She'd heard later that he'd left New Orleans to join the war effort.

"You hear me, woman?" Jared's voice rose to almost a shout. "Dead! Shot by a firing squad."

His malicious words reverberated through Sarah's head. Not possible, she kept telling herself. Jason, the dashing, handsome man she had once loved just couldn't be dead. This had to be yet another of Jared's vicious lies designed to torture her because of his insane jealousy of his brother.

Even though Jared was feverish and in pain, Sarah was well aware of her husband's cruel intentions toward her and also well aware that he wasn't the least bit remorseful about the fate of his brother, Jason.

Once Jared and Sarah had wed, Jared had made his feelings

toward Jason painfully clear and had taken every possible opportunity to let her know how much he loathed his brother.

Sarah willed herself to ignore the trembling weakness in her knees and the cold sweat that trickled between her breasts. Though every fiber of her being demanded that she argue with Jared, that she scream, cry and deny what he had just told her, she gave no outward indication of the devastating effect his news was having on her. To do so would give her sadistic husband too much pleasure. And to do so would put her at grave personal risk.

Finally, when Sarah was sure that her legs wouldn't buckle, she turned and walked to the door, her eyes trained straight ahead so he wouldn't see the tears escaping down her cheeks.

"Don't you want to know why he was shot?"

Sarah paused, but she didn't trust herself to speak, so she remained silent.

"Spying for the Union." He threw the words at her, his voice cold and vicious. "My brother was a dirty traitor, an embarrassment to our company, the Confederacy and to the Dubuisson name."

Sarah would never believe that Jason had purposely betrayed the Confederacy. While it was true that he hadn't agreed with most of his compatriots on the issue of slavery, he was a loyal Southerner.

Swallowing the lump that threatened to choke her and praying that her voice wouldn't betray her, Sarah cleared her throat. She'd learned the hard way how to handle Jared's peculiar moods, and how, in small measures, to get back at him for his cruelties.

She lifted her chin and took a deep breath. "You have my deepest sympathies, sir," she taunted softly, knowing that her sympathies for the death of his brother were the last thing her husband wanted to hear.

"I don't want your goddamn sympathies!" he shouted, enraged. "Get out of here! Get out of my sight!"

Sarah fled the room immediately and headed straight down the hallway to her own bedroom. But even with the distance between them, she could still hear Jared raving and swearing at her.

Once inside her bedroom, she slammed the heavy wooden door shut, collapsed against it, and slid in a heap of petticoats and skirts onto the bare floor. With her hand covering her mouth to muffle her sobs, she finally gave in to the shock and grief that was ripping her apart.

Jason had betrayed her and broken her heart, but even in her darkest moment after he'd jilted her, she hadn't been able to hate him for long. Since that awful night, she'd had plenty of time to think about why he'd done it, and she had concluded that there had to be reasons other than the one he had given her. Nothing else made sense.

As Sarah wept uncontrollably, all she could think of was that Jason, the man she had once loved more than life itself, was gone forever, and now she would never have the opportunity to find out the real reasons he'd thrown their love away.

Two weeks later, Sarah awoke with a start. Her bedroom was dark and still, lit only by the faint glow of the smoldering coals in the fireplace and the wan light from the half-moon outside the window.

Still groggy from sleep and wondering what had awakened her, she propped herself up on one elbow and absently stared through the gauzy mosquito netting that surrounded her bed. But the open doorway to her bedroom was empty.

Downstairs the tall case clock chimed. Its melodic tones echoed throughout the house, and as she automatically counted each note, she wondered how much longer they would be able to keep the heirloom before it—like other valuables they'd owned—would be confiscated by some Yankee officer.

"Twelve," she whispered, and just as the clock struck its final chime, from out of nowhere a shadowy figure suddenly materialized in the midst of the doorway.

Sarah smothered a gasp with her hand.

The dark shape was large and appeared to be a man. Time slowed to a crawl. Numb terror held Sarah hostage and a scream clawed in her throat for release. *Don't move or make a sound,* a silent voice of reason cried out from within her.

Then, within the blink of an eye, as suddenly as the shadow appeared, it vanished. For long, torturous moments afterward, Sarah remained frozen, unable to move as she waited for any telltale sound that would confirm that she hadn't simply imagined what she'd just seen. But the house remained ominously silent and the doorway empty.

Was there really someone there, an intruder, or had her fear of the hated Yankees who had occupied New Orleans for the past two years finally unnerved her to the point that her imagination had begun to play tricks on her?

Then a terrifying thought struck her. Could the shadow have possibly been Jared? Had her husband finally regained consciousness from his death sleep?

A shiver of fear crawled along her spine even as she told herself that such a thing was impossible, that he was too far gone to recover.

Despite her devoted, albeit reluctant care, the chest wound he had received in battle had begun to fester a few days after he'd been brought home on medical leave. When his raging fever had finally broken, her husband had fallen into a deep coma, a state of sleep so near death that at times it was hard to determine if he was still breathing.

Sarah frowned and curled her hands into fists. Even if by some miracle he had regained consciousness, surely he would be too weak to get out of bed by himself.

Familiar guilt gripped her as she recalled all the times during the past weeks she had wished for his death, had even prayed he would die. And it was that guilt weighing heavily on her conscience that finally prodded Sarah into action.

There was only one way to know for sure if the shadow she had seen was truly Jared, an intruder, or simply the results of an overactive imagination, she decided. With her eyes still trained toward the doorway and her nerves stretched to the breaking point, she quietly slid to the edge of the bed and parted the mosquito netting.

The wooden floor was cold under her bare feet and Sarah shivered from the cold as well as fright. Glancing quickly around for something she could use to defend herself if the shadow was indeed an intruder, her gaze landed on the iron fireplace poker. She'd never hit another person in her life, and even the notion of striking another human being repulsed her, but she didn't fancy being the victim of someone else's brutality either. She'd received enough of that at Jared's hand to last her a lifetime.

Expecting the intruder to return at any moment, Sarah kept a watchful eye on the door as she tiptoed across the room. Grasping the poker firmly in hand, she took a deep breath for courage. As she cautiously eased out into the dark hallway, she was careful to keep her back flat against the doorjamb.

For endless, nerve-racking moments, Sarah stood there, peering into the darkness, waiting and listening for the slightest sound. But as far as she could determine, the hallway was empty.

Trembling with fear and dread of what she might find, she raised the poker, ready to strike anything that moved, and made her way toward the doorway of her husband's bedroom.

If by some cruel miracle Jared had recovered, what would she do then? she wondered, as she stealthily approached her husband's bedroom door. Would she be able once again to survive his savage attentions as she had before he'd gone off to war?

Sarah's grip tightened on the poker, and she shuddered just thinking about the things he'd done to her on their wedding night, unspeakable things no woman should have to endure. He'd brutally taken her like a wild animal who had finally cornered his prey, and when she had cried out from the pain he'd inflicted, he'd used his fists to silence her cries.

Inside her husband's bedroom, the fireplace of banked coals cast an eerie glow. Sarah quietly approached the bed and pulled back the netting. Jared seemed the same as she had left him earlier. She stared down at the pale face of the man that lay in the bed, a face identical in every way to another man, the man she had once loved with every ounce of her being.

As far as she could tell, there had been no miraculous cure. But instead of being disappointed or saddened by the realization that her husband was no better but the same, Sarah felt nothing but relief . . . relief, quickly followed by familiar guilt for feeling that way.

How could fate be so cruel? she wondered as a sudden, sharp pain of sorrow pierced her heart and she lowered her arm that wielded the poker. How could two men look so much alike yet be as different as day and night, good and evil? If only she had known just how different Jared was before she'd married him, she thought, once again recalling the fiendish pleasure he had taken in telling her of Jason's execution.

Sarah turned away, and as quietly as she'd entered, she left her husband's bedroom.

Jason . . .

As always, each time she thought of Jason lately, Sarah became hopelessly distracted and completely oblivious to everything around her. And for the moment, she forgot about her fears of an intruder as memories of another time and place engulfed her, memories of the last time she had seen Jason alive.

Not even the two years that had passed since that night had eased the pain she'd suffered when he'd called off their wedding. Hurt and humiliated, she had shut herself up in her room for days.

Then Jared had come along, and under the pretext of upholding the family honor, he had offered to marry her instead. Sarah hadn't wanted to accept and had been honest from the beginning about her feelings. Even the fact that Sarah didn't love Jared hadn't seemed to matter to him. He'd claimed that honor was more important.

For Sarah, it was either marry Jared or see her mother and sisters put out of the only home they had ever known. She had been grateful for Jared's offer of marriage at the time and desperate enough ultimately to accept his proposal. After all, she reminded herself, he had been the perfect Southern gentleman, right up until their wedding night when they were finally alone.

Even now Sarah shivered just thinking about that night. It

was during that night and the days that followed that she had
learned just how evil a man's soul could be.

Back in her bedroom, Sarah carefully propped the poker
beside her bed. It was then that she thought of the shadowy
specter once again. Was it possible that Sam had been prowl-
ing upstairs, checking on Jared? Possible, she supposed, but
highly unlikely, since the servant usually stayed as far away
from Jared as he could get. Of course there was always the
likelihood that she'd simply imagined it all, she thought.

Yes, Sarah decided with a sigh as she climbed back in bed
and snuggled beneath the covers. She had simply let her fear
of the Yankees and her imagination get the best of her. But
no matter how many times she told herself that or tried to
rationalize what she had seen, for the remainder of the night,
she tossed and turned, unable to shake the eerie feeling that
there was another presence in the house, a threatening presence
that didn't belong.

The following morning, Sarah was changing Jared's bandages
when a loud commotion downstairs suddenly erupted. She immediately identified the raised voices as belonging to Marie
and Sam. They were fighting . . . again.

Marie and Sam had been part of her life since she was a
child, and when she'd married Jared, they had come with her.
The day Jared left for war, she'd freed them. Many times,
especially during the past two weeks, Sarah had often thought
she would have been better off if she hadn't encouraged the
two former slaves to stay with her instead of leaving to go
north. Thanks to the Yankees, food and necessities were so
scarce that no one ever seemed to get enough to eat, and tem-
pers were short.

Sarah's hand shook, and she sighed as she tied off the last
bandage around Jared's arm wound. Even on the best of days,
she loathed having to touch her husband. Tending to him had
been like living in hell on earth, and Sam and Marie's constant
bickering only made matters worse. Maybe today, she would
find the courage to send the two servants packing.

A smile played at Sarah's lips as she imagined the looks on

the two servants' faces if she were to order them to leave. More than likely, they would laugh at her.

Besides, she thought as she made her way down the stairs, who was she trying to fool? Without Sam and Marie, she couldn't have managed all these weeks and probably would have starved long before now. What little food and supplies they had were due to the chickens that Sam faithfully cared for, the small garden he tended, and the generosity of Marie's free Negro friends who lived in the nearby bayous and often shared whatever game they killed.

Jared had left her stacks of Confederate notes and a small cache of gold when he'd ridden off to war. But with the Yankee invasion and occupation, the Confederate money was worthless and the small cache of gold hadn't lasted long at all, no matter how careful Sarah had tried to be.

When Sarah entered the kitchen, it was just as she'd suspected. Marie, brandishing a stick of firewood, had cornered Sam near the fireplace.

"What's going on here?" she demanded.

Both servants froze at the sound of her voice, then, inch by inch, Marie lowered the stick of firewood.

Sam was the first to speak. "This woman—" He shook a beefy finger at Marie. "She's done gone crazy, Miz Sarah. It ain't bad enough she's been stickin' those foolish voodoo charms all 'round the house, but now, she's hanging them on *my* bed." Sam immediately crossed himself. "I'm a Christian and I don't hold with such nonsense anymore."

"You fool!" Marie glared at Sam. "Being a Christian don't have nothing to do with this. I'm a Christian too, but I figure we can use all the help we can get."

"Help for what?" Sarah asked, becoming more confused and frustrated by the moment.

With her question, both Sam and Marie ducked their heads and stared at the floor. Sarah normally had the patience of a saint, but the last days of nursing Jared combined with her sleepless night had taken their toll, and she had no tolerance left for such nonsense. Placing her hands on her hips, she marched over to the two servants.

"Out with it. Help for what?"

Marie slowly raised her head. Her dark eyes were round with some unknown fear. "There's been some strange goings-on at night in this house lately. I don't mean no disrespect, Miz Sarah, but I figure that since Mr. Jared is closer to dying than living, his spirit is already restless . . ." She crossed herself, then ducked her head and stared at the floor again. "Probably 'cause he knows the devil will soon be coming to claim it," she finished in a whisper.

The last of what Marie said almost made Sarah smile since she'd often thought that Jared was a spawn of the devil anyway. But thoughts of her own experience the night before intruded, and she shuddered instead.

Was it possible that she hadn't imagined the shadowy specter after all? Had Marie seen something too? One way or another, she intended to find out, but first things first, she decided. So for the moment, Sarah ignored Marie and rounded on Sam instead. "Did you check on Mr. Jared during the night?"

Sam shook his head. "Oh, no, ma'am. You know I wouldn't go upstairs at night without asking you about it first."

A whisper of unease slid beneath Sarah's skin as she turned back to Marie. She was sorely tempted to out and out ask the older woman if she had seen the shadowy figure during the night, but knowing how superstitious Marie was anyway, and too tired to cope with the servant's mumbo jumbo, Sarah decided it was best not to encourage her. "Just what kind of strange goings-on are you talking about?" she asked instead.

Marie shrugged. "Noises that shouldn't ought to be and stuff moved around, 'specially in the kitchen and library."

The stroke of midnight. The devil's dancing-hour. The old superstition popped into Sarah's head, and the hairs on the back of her neck prickled. Nonsense, she thought. Pure nonsense. Although she'd heard of such things all of her life, Sarah didn't believe in ghosts, demons, voodoo and such. She'd lived at Dubuisson Manor for the past two years, and unlike many other homes in New Orleans, there had never been even a whisper of hauntings or evil curses connected with the house.

"There has to be a reasonable explanation for what is happening," she finally said. "Either that or you're imagining things, Marie."

"Oh, no, ma'am." Marie shook her head. "I've been to see my godmother, and she agrees with me. Even told me what kind of charms to use."

In spite of herself, Sarah shivered. Marie's godmother, the woman Marie had been named after, was Marie Laveau, the most famous of all New Orleans voodooists. And since Marie Laveau had been dead for three years by all accounts, the only way the servant could have possibly visited the Voodoo Queen was at the St. Louis Cemetery. Despite the rumors surrounding Marie Laveau, Sarah didn't believe for a moment that dead people could talk back.

Sarah straightened to her full height of five feet and looked Marie straight in the eyes. "There will be no more arguing and no more voodoo charms hung in this house. I've got enough on my mind tending to Mr. Jared and worrying about the Yankees without this kind of nonsense. You know I don't hold with such things."

With that said, Sarah whirled around and stomped out of the kitchen. But at the doorway, she paused. "And another thing," she said over her shoulder. "There will be no more of that devil talk about Mr. Jared's soul. He isn't dead yet."

CHAPTER TWO

B y the time she entered her bedroom that evening, Sarah was exhausted, both in mind and body. She'd sat with Jared almost all day, waiting, wondering if each breath he took would be his last. For the first time since he had lapsed into a coma, she hadn't been able to get any food or drink down him that day, and his breathing seemed more labored than before.

She'd debated whether to send Sam for Dr. Deville, but finally decided against doing so, since the last time the doctor had come, he'd told her there was no hope and all she could do was make Jared as comfortable as possible.

When the doctor had first told her there was no hope, she hadn't thought it would be so hard to watch such a cruel, mean-spirited man die. But lately, each time she looked at Jared, thoughts of Jason filled her mind. And watching Jared die was like watching Jason die.

Would Jared last the night? she wondered as she began to undress in preparation for bed. If by some miracle he survived the night, would tomorrow be the day he would draw his last breath? And once he died, would his soul be claimed by the devil as Marie predicted?

With a grimace of distaste, Sarah walked over to the window. She was letting her own imagination as well as Marie's superstitious mumbo jumbo affect her entirely too much, she thought. And that's all it was, a lot of mumbo jumbo.

Sarah pulled aside the heavy brocade cloth of the drapery and peered out into the dark night. Storm clouds had been building all day, and the air inside the house was humid and oppressive. She was sorely tempted to tie back the drapery and open the window. But to open up the window would be an invitation to all manner of night critters, including the pesky mosquitos.

Suddenly, without warning, a streak of jagged lightning split the sky and a clap of thunder rent the air with the force of a hundred exploding cannons. Sarah cried out, and releasing the drapery as if it had caught fire, she jumped back a step. Squeezing her eyes shut, she threw up her hands to cover her ears as the horrendous rumbling of the thunder continued.

Then, almost as abruptly as it had begun, the lightning disappeared and the thunder ceased. Sarah sighed and lowered her arms. It was during the chilling silence that followed when something creaked loudly in the hall.

Sarah whirled around to face the open doorway. "Marie?" she called out. "Is that you?"

For agonizing seconds, she stood, frozen to the spot, listening. But no one answered. Unbidden, more of what Marie had said earlier that morning came to mind. *Noises that shouldn't ought to be.*

Had it been just such a noise that had awakened her the night before? She didn't remember hearing any noises. One minute she'd been asleep, and the next, awake, staring at the shadowy apparition hovering in her doorway.

Sarah shivered. When she'd searched the night before, she'd found nothing.

The creaking noise in the hall came again, this time louder. "Who's there?" she cried, her voice shaking with terror. Suddenly, a shadow moved past the open doorway. One second it was visible, and the next, it was gone.

Sarah screamed. Her vision blurred, then a great gulf of darkness closed in around her.

When Sarah came to, she was lying on the bed, and Marie was standing over her, alternately chafing her hands and shaking Sarah's shoulder. The servant's eyes were wide with worry and fear. Just behind Marie stood Sam, holding a candle and looking just as concerned and frightened as Marie.

"Wh-what happened?" Sarah whispered. "What's going on?"

"Oh, Lordy, Miz Sarah." Marie stepped back and began wringing her hands. "You screamed loud enough to wake the dead and you're askin' me what happened?" The older woman shrugged. "Had to be the granddaddy of all nightmares for you to end up on the floor like you did."

"Nightmare?" The murky fog in Sarah's head was lifting and suddenly she began to remember. Sarah shook her head. "That was no nightmare, and the reason I was on the floor was because I hadn't gone to bed yet," she whispered. "No!" Her voice rose and she shook her head again. "I was awake and there was someone in the hallway. I—I saw something there and I must have fainted."

"Now, Miz Sarah." Marie leaned forward and took hold of her hands. "Don't go gettin' yourself all worked up. It's possible you fainted seeing as how hard you been working and what with you near 'bout starving yourself lately. But I still think it was just a nightmare, nothing more than just a bad dream. Sam and me came straightaway and we didn't see no one. And there's only one way up and down them stairs."

"I wasn't dreaming," Sarah insisted. "And I want this house searched. Search every corner of it right now, starting with Mr. Jared's room."

Marie shook her head. "No use in Sam searching," she said patiently, as if humoring a child. "He ain't gonna find what you're looking for. No one can find the devil unless he wants to be found, and there ain't no one else around." Marie patted Sarah's hand. "Now you just go on back to sleep. I'll sit here with you till you do, and Sam will check on Mr. Jared."

Sarah closed her eyes and tried to think. Was it possible that Marie was right? Was it possible that she'd had a nightmare? But how could that be when she didn't remember going to bed to begin with?

Ever since Jared had told her about Jason's death, Sarah hadn't been quite herself. She had been more tired than usual, yet restless at night. And of late, it seemed that she was forever on the verge of tears. She still couldn't believe that Jason was dead or that she would never see him again.

It was true he'd jilted her and broken her heart, and it was equally true she was his brother's wife now, but regardless, she could no more stop loving Jason or grieving for him than she could stop the sun from shining.

Then real fear struck at her heart. Sarah looked up at Marie and clutched her hand. "Am I going insane?" she whispered.

Marie smiled sadly. "Honey, if you're going crazy, then the rest of us are too. No." She shook her head. "You're not crazy. Just tired and plum worn-out from tending to that man in the other room down the hall. Now you go on to sleep."

What Marie said made sense, a lot more sense than seeing something that obviously wasn't there. Sarah felt drained, and her body felt leaden as if weighted down by some unseen force. Even the effort of talking seemed beyond her. Sleep might be the best thing after all, she silently reasoned as she closed her eyes. Then tomorrow, after she'd rested, she could think more clearly. "No more of that devil talk," she mumbled as she finally drifted off.

The following night, Sarah felt weary to the bone, and she took her time undressing, equally dreading and looking forward to climbing into her bed.

Jared had rallied somewhat during the day, and she'd spent what seemed like hour upon hour trying to get just a few swallows of broth and water down his throat without him choking.

If only she could get one good night's sleep without being awakened, she thought, feeling even more exhausted than she had the day before and recalling the disturbing episode during the previous night.

No matter how many times Marie had insisted that she'd had a nightmare, Sarah still wasn't certain. Yet, there seemed to be no other logical explanation.

Noticing that the drapery and netting behind it were askew, Sarah walked over to the window to pull it closed again.

How strange, she thought, fingering the heavy brocade. The drapery looked almost as if someone had pushed it aside. Sarah shrugged. She supposed it was possible that Marie had aired out the room at some point during the day, but she didn't remember the servant doing so.

The night outside was shrouded in darkness with no hopes of relief. Ordinarily, the streets would have been lit by street lamps, but the Yankees had begun shutting off the gas each evening. And now, with the moon and stars hidden by the heavy clouds left over from the storm, the utter darkness outside made her even more uneasy.

Once she extinguished the small candle on the dresser, there would be no light at all, inside or outside, she thought. "As if a light would ward off ghosts or spirits," she muttered, instantly disgusted with herself for acting like such a coward and thinking such hogwash.

Sarah pulled the drapery closed and turned away from the window. As she glanced around the room one last time, her gaze lingered on a rosary that lay next to the candle on the dresser. What was it that Marie had said? *We can use all the help we can get.*

Telling herself that her actions had nothing to do with Marie's irrational fears, Sarah picked up the chain of wooden beads. The only reason she was taking the rosary to bed was because she needed to say her prayers, she reassured herself, a ritual she had neglected of late.

The second Sarah leaned over and blew out the candle, the room was plunged into darkness, and the temptation to relight it was almost too strong to ignore. But burning a candle all night was not just silly but foolhardy, she reasoned as her grip tightened on the rosary and she quickly climbed onto the bed. Their store of candles was running low and there was little hope of getting more since most of the supplies to the city had been cut off by blockades.

Pulling the covers to her chin, she stared into the yawning blackness of the room and held her breath, waiting . . . listening and wishing she'd built a fire in the fireplace. At least with a fire, there would be burning coals left to give off some light.

"Ridiculous," she whispered, releasing her pent-up breath with a sigh. "You're letting your imagination and Marie's mumbo jumbo get the best of you again." Having said that and feeling somewhat better for having done so, she began fingering the beads as she murmured the familiar prayer ritual. At the end of the ritual, as she had done the night she'd heard of his death, Sarah added a prayer for Jason's soul. Wondering where the Yankees had buried him, she finally gave in to the sleep her exhausted body demanded.

Sarah didn't want to awaken, but in a far corner of her sleep-drugged mind, she could hear the tall case clock downstairs chiming, as if taunting her to count its melodic notes.

One . . . two . . . three . . .

More than anything, she wanted to return to her dream.

Four . . . five . . .

In her dream, Jason had been there, very much alive, standing by her bed.

Six . . . seven . . . eight . . .

And in her dream his hand was warm and gentle as he'd smoothed her hair.

Nine . . . ten . . .

The skin on her cheek still tingled from his caress, and her lips still ached from the touch of his lips against hers. He'd whispered something in her ear, and she could have sworn that he'd whispered words of his undying love and devotion, but she couldn't be sure.

Eleven . . . twelve . . .

Twelve! Midnight! Suddenly Sarah was wide-awake, her heart pounding beneath her breasts as a feeling of dread chased away the last remnants of her beautiful dream. She didn't want to wake up. Waking up meant having to face the reality of Jason's death all over again. Every moment that she was awake was a constant reminder that there was absolutely nothing she could do to change the fact that he'd died. Just more moments of grief and hopelessness.

"Oh, God," she cried out. Gasping for breath, she sat straight up and peered into the yawning darkness. She wanted to scream and throw things, somehow release all of her pent-up frustration and longing.

If only she could go back and change things, she thought. When Jason had told her he was calling the marriage off, at first she'd been too stunned to react. Then after the first initial shock, pride and years of ingrained teachings of how a lady should conduct herself had held her back, and she'd calmly stood there without uttering a word of protest while Jason had mounted his horse and ridden off into the night.

If she had known then what she knew now, she would have never let him leave without a fight. She would have begged, pleaded, done anything and everything within her power to change his mind.

"Just one last time," she groaned, recalling her wonderful dream and how his lips had felt against hers. There had been passion, but gentleness. Even now, she fancied she could still taste him on her lips.

Sarah curled her hand into a fist, and with a start, realized that she still clutched the rosary. She gripped the rosary tighter and the wooden beads bit into her flesh. All of her life she had believed, had kept all the rules. She'd gone to her marriage bed a virgin, and what had it gotten her? What had been her reward?

Nothing but pain, terror and fear, she answered silently. She'd never lied to Jared, never claimed to love him. So why was she being punished so? Why was the man she'd loved dead, and the evil man she'd married still breathing in a room down the hallway?

In a sudden fit of anger, she jerked aside the netting, drew back her arm and flung the beads across the room. The rosary bounced off the wall and hit the floor with a clatter that sounded like a gunshot in the quiet room, and with that gesture, something wild and uncontrollable inside Sarah tore loose.

She raised her fist and shook it into the darkness. "If I could have just one night with Jason, I'd sell my soul to the devil and gladly risk eternal damnation," she cried out. "You hear me?" Her voice rose. "Just one night!" she cried out again.

The room remained forebodingly silent, the darkness, menacingly complete. There was no one to answer her or acknowledge her impassioned vow.

Finally, realizing the futility of her gesture, Sarah lowered her arm and bowed her head. She felt drained of everything . . . everything but the guilt of what she'd just done. "Just one night," she whispered longingly as tears streamed down her cheeks. "One night to last me an eternity. Is that too much to ask?"

CHAPTER THREE

During the two days and nights that followed, Sarah was reminded constantly of the night she cursed God and swore a vow to the devil. At times, she began to think she was truly going mad, regardless of what Marie had said to the contrary.

Tending to Jared was becoming more of a chore the closer to death he came, and except for that one day, she was unable to get any sustenance down him.

More than once she recalled an old saying she'd heard all of her life. *They always get better before they die.* And with each labored breath he drew, she was sure it had to be his last. Yet he continued to hang on tenaciously to a thin thread of life.

Each night she continued to take her rosary to bed, but before she would get halfway through her prayers, she always fell asleep.

And each night, she had the same recurring dream where Jason would come to her, whispering words of love. But Jason was dead, she kept reminding herself, gone forever, and no amount of cursing, wishing or longing would bring him back or change her circumstances.

On the morning of All Hallows' Eve, Sarah awoke to shouts coming from downstairs.

"Now what?" she grumbled and threw back the covers.

Wondering what Sam and Marie were fighting about this time, she grabbed her shawl and rushed out of the room.

As she approached the kitchen, she could hear snatches of their heated argument.

"Miz Sarah's been sleeping poorly enough lately, and there ain't no use in bothering her with such—"

"She has to know," Sam roared. "And besides, who do you think you are, tellin' me what I can and can't do?"

When Sarah stepped inside the kitchen, Marie was nose to nose with Sam, each trying to outyell the other.

"Marie! Sam! Stop that shouting immediately." Sarah glared at both of the servants.

Marie turned to face her. "Now, Miz Sarah, this ain't nothing you have to bother yourself with." She turned back to Sam and gave him a threatening look. "Right, Sam?"

Completely ignoring her, Sam shouldered past Marie. "Please, Miz Sarah. I need to talk to you. I—"

"Don't listen to him." Marie grabbed Sam's shirtsleeve.

"Stop it!" Sarah pulled on Marie's hand until she finally let go.

Marie backed away, a mutinous look on her face. "Just don't say I didn't warn you." Then she whirled around, and muttering beneath her breath with every step she took, the servant stomped out of the room.

Sarah faced Sam. "Now what's this all about?"

"I done seen the devil, Miz Sarah." Sam crossed himself. "Right here in this house, he was."

He started to cross himself again, but Sarah grabbed his arm. "Stop that and calm down."

Sam dropped his head and stared at the floor. Not for one second did Sarah believe that Sam had actually seen the devil, but sweat had popped out on his forehead and from the way he was nervously shifting from foot to foot, she knew that something had truly frightened the man.

"Out with it, Sam."

"It . . . it was last night. I . . . I was thinkin' I should check on Mr. Jared when I heard a noise—someone comin' down the stairs. So I hid and watched, thinkin' it might be one of them Yankees done broke in the house. But, oh, Lordy, me. Wasn't no Yankee.'' Sam started to cross himself again, but glanced up at Sarah and dropped his hand instead. ''Sorry,'' he whispered, his eyes wide with fear.

''It's okay, Sam.'' Sarah patted the servant's arm. ''Go on now.''

Sam swallowed so hard that Sarah saw his Adam's apple bob. ''''Twas the devil,'' he whispered. ''Carrying Mr. Jared off.''

Sarah shook her head in denial and started to speak, but Sam interrupted. ''I swear it, Miz Sarah. On everything that's holy, I swear that's what I saw.''

Sarah wasn't quite sure why she continued standing there, listening to Sam's wild story, except that Sam wasn't given to tall tales and superstitions, and he'd never outright lied to her before. ''You sure you weren't simply dreaming . . . or maybe you had a little too much of that red-eye again?''

He shook his head fiercely. ''Oh, no, ma'am. I was as wide-awake as you are, and I haven't touched nary a drop of whiskey, not since that last time when I was so sickly.''

Sarah held up her hands. ''Very well. But what on earth makes you think what you saw was the devil?''

'' 'Twas him all right. Had on one of them long black cloaks with the hood. I couldn't rightly see his face, but there he was, all dressed in black, carrying Mr. Jared as if Mr. Jared was no heavier than a feather. And so I followed him, followed him right to the cemetery. He took Mr. Jared straight to the family tomb, broke open the vault and put Mr. Jared inside.''

Sarah found herself actually picturing the scene in her mind—a sinister, dark-cloaked figure making his way through the aboveground tombs in the creepy, old cemetery. ''Sam!''

''I swear it.'' He crossed himself again. ''I swear I'm tellin' the God's truth. And Jesus help us, he done gone and put Mr. Jared in that tomb backward, with his feet facin' west, 'stead of east, a sure sign the devil already took his soul to hell.''

Sam began to moan, a sound that sent chills dancing up Sarah's arms. ''And that's when I knew for certain he was the devil.'' He shuddered. '' 'Cause the second he sealed that tomb, he whipped off his cape, and just like a flash of lightning, he done changed hisself to look just like Mr. Jared.''

Sarah stiffened. ''This is ridiculous, and I've heard enough.''

Sam suddenly fell to his knees, and when he looked up at Sarah, tears filled his eyes. ''I know you don't believe me, but—''

''Oh, Sam, for pity's sake.'' Sarah grabbed the man's arm. ''Get up off the floor.''

Sam stood, but he was shaking his head and his eyes were so wide with fright that his irises looked like tiny dots lost in a sea of white. ''That devil's up there, right now,'' he said. ''He's pretendin' to be Mr. Jared. I swear it, Miz Sarah.''

Sarah sighed, wondering what she could say to allay the servant's fears. ''Sam, do you remember three nights ago when you and Marie heard me scream and you found me on the floor?''

Sam nodded gravely.

''I was just like you. I too thought what had happened was real. But later, after I had time to reason it out, I decided it must have been simply a nightmare after all. Just like Marie said.''

Sarah hoped she'd be forgiven for telling such a lie, since she still wasn't completely convinced that her terrifying incident was a nightmare. But Sam's story, unlike her own experience, was simply too outrageous to be true.

''All I'm trying to tell you is . . .'' She paused and took a deep breath. ''All I'm trying to say is that sometimes nightmares can seem so real that we think they truly happened.''

Sam's face took on a stubborn look. ''What I saw last night wasn't no nightmare. He's up there all right, just as sure as I'm standin' here.''

Now what? Sarah wondered. How on earth was she going to convince Sam that he had simply had a dream? Until she did, there would be no peace in the house.

Sarah put her hands on her hips and cleared her throat. ''There's only one way to settle this.'' She spun around. ''They say that seeing is believing, so come with me.'' She walked briskly out of the room and was almost to the staircase when she realized that Sam hadn't followed. "Sam," she called out over her shoulder, but there was no answer.

Sarah retraced her steps back to the kitchen where she found Sam still standing in the same spot. He was wringing his huge, work-worn hands, and there was a look of pure horror on his face as fat tears streamed down his cheeks.

She grabbed hold of his arm and tugged. "Whether you like it or not, you're coming with me and we're going to settle this matter."

Sam pulled away. "Oh, please, Miz Sarah. Don't make me go up there. That devil, he done come back for a reason. He ain't just satisfied with Mr. Jared's soul and body. Now he's after another one too."

"Enough of this, Sam!" Sarah shouted. "You're coming with me if I have to drag you every step of the way." Since the servant was almost twice her size, Sarah was well aware that Sam knew her threat was empty, but she had to try something, and threats were all she had.

Sam held up his hands as if to ward her off, and Sarah noted they were both trembling. "I'll come," he said. "But just to the door. I ain't settin' foot inside that room. What's in there is pure evil."

How right you are, Sarah thought. But the only devil in that room was Jared Dubuisson himself.

With Sam muttering every step of the way, Sarah and the servant trudged up the stairs, and in spite of her convictions that Sam had either been hallucinating or having a nightmare, Sarah felt a whisper of unease run through her the closer to the top they came. There had been too many strange occurrences happening lately to completely dismiss them all. And even stranger, the only time an incident seemed to occur was in the middle of the night.

At Jared's door, Sam held back.

"Oh, for pity's sake," Sarah muttered. Still glaring at the servant, she boldly stepped inside the room, marched over to the bed and jerked the netting aside.

"There—" Sarah threw out her hand, motioning toward the

man lying in the bed, her gaze following her gesture. But the moment she looked at her husband's face, she went still as a statue. Blood roared in her ears and her heart thundered beneath her breasts.

Not possible, a voice cried within her. God surely wouldn't be so cruel. "Jared?" she gasped, her voice conveying her disbelief.

Instead of closed eyes and the lifeless face she'd grown accustomed to, his blue eyes were wide-open, blinking and staring back at her. Instead of the death pallor skin tone she'd come to expect, his cheeks above the white sheet and dark shadow of his beard were tinged with the pink of health.

"Miz Sarah?" Sam poked his head around the door frame.

For a moment, it was as if time stood still, the silence was so eerily complete. Then Sam screamed a guttural cry of sheer terror that shattered the unearthly moment.

It was the servant's scream of terror along with the sound of his footsteps thundering down the hallway and stairs that finally jolted Sarah back to reality.

Like Sam, Sarah wanted to turn and run too. All she could think about was that once again she would be forced to endure days of torture and nights of terror as she had before Jared finally left to fight the Yankees. At the time, she'd hoped he would never come back. And for days afterward she'd wrestled with her guilty conscience for wishing such a thing.

But Sarah had no place to run. In spite of the sacrifices she'd made for her family, her mother and sisters had died from an isolated outbreak of yellow fever just after her marriage, and their plantation had been burned to the ground by invading Yankees. Dubuisson Manor was the only home she had now.

Gathering every bit of courage she could muster, Sarah fumbled with the ties that held back the netting. Jared's fixed expression never changed and he'd yet to utter a sound as his eyes followed her movement.

Sarah swallowed the lump in her throat and hoped her voice wouldn't betray her trepidation. "I—I see you're much better today. You'll have to forgive me for being so surprised, but the doctor had given us little hope that you would recover at all.''

There was nothing in Jared's expression to indicate his feelings one way or another, or for that matter, that he'd even heard what she'd said, as he continued staring at her with his penetrating blue eyes.

At first Sarah thought it a bit strange that he hadn't attempted to respond, then it suddenly occurred to her why he hadn't, and backing up just short of touching distance, she paused. Was it possible that the fever and coma had affected him to such an extent that he couldn't respond? Such fevers had been known to render their victims completely helpless, or worse, crazy as a Bessie bug.

Sarah didn't believe for one moment that Jared was crazy. His eyes were too lucid, but the possibility that he might be unable to respond in a normal way any longer was certainly something to consider.

Then again, Sarah knew her husband too well to trust anything he said or didn't say. Unease and suspicion began to take root and spread like cholera as another thought occurred to her, a thought that sent her blood sliding through her veins like cold needles.

What if Jared had never been as ill as she had thought? What if he had been playacting all along? If he had, then that would at least explain some of the strange noises and goings-on in the house at night.

But what about his wounds? a voice taunted. There was no way he could fake the severity of his wounds, was there? *With a doctor's help, he could,* that same voice answered.

Sarah shivered. Dr. Deville was a longtime family friend of the Dubuisson family, a man they trusted completely. But why would Jared embark on such a charade to begin with?

Almost before the question formed in her mind, the answer came to her. As long as the Yankees thought Jared, a high-ranking officer in the Confederacy, was near dead, they didn't bother him, didn't insist that he either take an oath of loyalty to the Union or go to prison like the others who had refused.

Sarah's new revelation was so logical and so daunting that

her knees grew weak. This was something she needed to think through more thoroughly, but for the moment, the way he kept staring at her made it impossible to concentrate on anything. It was almost as if he could read her mind and knew exactly what she was thinking, and it was enough to make her flesh creep.

Sarah inched backward toward the door, and using the first excuse to leave that came to mind, she said, "I-I'm sure you must be hungry."

Jared didn't respond and his expression remained unchanged. Then, from out of nowhere, a vision of Jared rising up from the bed and coming after her danced in her head. At that moment, all she knew was that she had to get out of that room immediately.

"I'll get you something right away," she whispered just before she turned and fled the room.

In her bedroom, Sarah tried to make sense out of what was happening as she hurriedly dressed. The more she thought about Sam's wild devil tale, Jared's miraculous improvement and her newest revelation, the more confused she became.

Was it possible that even now she was experiencing a nightmare of some kind? Would she awaken and find that everything had been simply a bad dream?

Deep in thought with her eyes cast downward, Sarah stepped over to the washbasin, bent down and splashed her face with water. She reached for the towel folded neatly next to the basin, and as she straightened, she patted her face dry. When she lowered the towel and stared into the mirror, she gasped, not recognizing the strange woman staring back at her.

Her once healthy, glorious head of blond hair was now limp and hung in wild tangles. She reached up and traced the dark circles beneath her eyes, eyes that used to shine with life but were now dull and bleak, filled with fear and uncertainty. Her once peaches-and-cream complexion had turned sallow, and not even pinching her cheeks seemed to make a difference.

Unbidden, tears filled her eyes and spilled down her cheeks. Jason had once compared her eyes to rare, sparkling emeralds,

and her hair to the finest of silks. He was forever telling her
how beautiful she was.

What would he say if he could see her now? A sob caught
in her throat, and Sarah squeezed her eyes tightly shut then
leaned over the basin to splash more water on her face. Jason
would say nothing, could say nothing . . .

Jason was dead, truly dead.

And even though it hurt like a knife plunging into her heart,
Sarah knew she could have eventually borne the pain of Jason's death more easily if Jared hadn't been there to remind
her of Jason—Jared who was Jason's spitting image.

Sarah raised her head and stared once again at her reflection.
Water dripped and mingled with her tears.

For weeks now she'd been fooling herself, playing a dangerous game of pretend. It had been so easy to confuse the
two men in her mind, especially once Jared had lapsed into
the coma that had rendered him speechless and helpless. There
had been many days when pretending that Jared was Jason
had been the only way she'd been able to touch her husband
while tending to his wounds.

But now the game was over. Now Jared was conscious
again. . . .

Sarah closed her eyes and clenched her fists. "Oh, God!"
she cried. No matter what Marie said to the contrary, a sane
woman wouldn't have played such a dangerous game. "You
foolish, foolish woman," she sobbed.

Sarah would have liked to stay holed up in her room all day
with the door bolted shut, but a mere bolted door wouldn't
keep reality at bay forever, she finally decided. So once again
she wiped her face dry. Then gathering her strength, she ventured down to the kitchen.

There she found Marie stirring a pot of simmering liquid
that smelled suspiciously like gumbo, gumbo with honest-to-
God meat in it. "Is that chicken I smell?"

Marie glanced over her shoulder. "Now don't go fussin'
and worrying. Now that Mr. Jared's on the mend"—the servant winked and a secretive smile pulled at her mouth—"he'll

be needin' somethin' that will stick to his innards instead of that stuff we been eatin'.''

Marie's knowledge of Jared's condition as well as her attitude left Sarah momentarily stunned. It was almost as if the servant thought Jared's recovery was something to celebrate.

Sarah frowned. "But how—" The half-formed question came out a mere whisper.

"Why, child, don't nothing go on in this house that I don't know about or find out about sooner or later." Marie's smile broadened into a smug grin. "God works in mysterious ways, and the devil gets his due," she added with another wink.

Sarah's insides quivered, and she got the funniest feeling that Marie was hiding something. She narrowed her eyes. She was tempted to question the servant further, to demand that Marie explain exactly *how* she knew Jared was better, but more superstitious mumbo jumbo was likely all she'd get out of the woman, she decided.

But the chickens were another matter. "Sam's going to be upset when he finds out you killed one of his chickens."

"Sam's always upset about somethin'. Besides, wasn't one of his chickens," Marie said, a smirk on her face and a sly look in her eyes. "It's what you might call a gift from God." The servant chuckled and fingered the voodoo charm she wore around her neck.

A queasy feeling spread in Sarah's stomach. She'd heard stories before of voodoo rituals, animal sacrifices and such, and although they never spoke of it, she knew that Marie often participated.

"Besides," Marie continued. "Tomorrow is All Saints' Day, so I thought it fittin' that we have a decent meal."

"Tomorrow?" Sarah closed her eyes and groaned. "With everything else that's happened, I completely forgot."

Marie spooned some of the broth of the gumbo into a bowl. "I figured you did, so I took care of things. Promised them boys down the street workin' for Miz Lemonte a bowl of this gumbo if they would scrub the tomb and pull out all the weeds around it. I even traded some eggs for extra candles"—she motioned toward the small cache of candles on top of the table—"and flowers for tomorrow."

Just thinking about the cemetery and the once-a-year ritual of lighting candles on the family tombs on the eve of All Saints' Day, Sarah couldn't suppress a shudder. The cemetery represented death and was just one more reminder that her beloved Jason had been shot by a firing squad. The last thing she wanted was another reminder that Jason was dead, especially after Sam's tall tale of seeing the devil put Jared in the vault backward—Jared, a man who looked exactly like Jason.

Still, it was an old, longtime tradition she couldn't ignore, not unless she was willing to be the center of neighborhood gossip for weeks to come. And Sarah took consolation in the fact that she wouldn't be alone in the cemetery. Despite the curfew the Yankees had established, the whole neighborhood would turn out for the ritual.

"Thank you, Marie," she whispered, truly grateful that the servant had taken care of all the arrangements.

Marie grinned. "Can't have the neighbors lookin' down their noses at the Dubuissons for not properly tending to their kin. Now you go on to market, and I'll see to Mr. Jared today." She held up the bowl of broth. "This is just about cool enough, and it will do you good to get out of this house and into the sunlight."

Sarah was overwhelmed by relief, but a bit puzzled. After all of Marie's talk of strange goings-on at night and Sam's tale of the devil turning into Jared, she would have thought that the last thing Marie would do was offer to go near Jared. Even before he'd left to fight the Yankees, Jared and Marie hadn't gotten along. Whatever Marie's reason for her change of heart, Sarah decided against questioning the servant for now. She'd dreaded the moment she would have to face Jared again, and though she knew she would still have to do so eventually, she was grateful for the small reprieve Marie was offering.

Impulsively, Sarah stepped over and hugged the servant. "Ah, Marie, what would I do without you?" she whispered. "And Sam," she added, frowning as she pulled away.

"Now don't you go worrying about Sam. Once he gets ahold of hisself, he'll be back."

That evening, Sam still hadn't returned by the time Sarah was ready to leave for the cemetery. As she and some of her neighbors set out on foot, she wondered if she would ever see the servant again. Marie had assured her he would show up, sooner or later, but Sarah could still hear his scream of terror and could only hope and pray that Marie knew what she was talking about. To Sarah, Marie and Sam were family, the only family she had left . . . besides Jared.

The evening was cool, and the ever-present dampness that chilled bone-deep permeated the air, leaving a thin layer of fog to hover near the ground. Above, only an ethereal light shone through the mist from the shadowy full moon.

At the cemetery gate, Sarah's group joined others already gathered there and listened as the priest said the Mass in his droning voice and performed the ancient rituals for the souls of the departed. With a heart heavy from grief, Sarah added her own prayer for Jason. And as she had other times, she wondered again where the Yankees had buried him.

Once Sarah's candles had been blessed, she slowly made her way among the aboveground tombs to the back corner of the cemetery where the Dubuisson family plot was located.

The drooping, moss-laden boughs of an ancient live oak tree shaded that part of the cemetery from the dim light of the moon, and the flickering candles on the surrounding tombs cast grotesque, unworldly shadows.

An unexpected feeling of impending danger took root and spread within Sarah, and she hesitated as she approached the family vault.

I done seen the devil, Miz Sarah. Sam's words chased through her head as she stared at the sepulcher. *He took Mr. Jared straight to the family tomb, broke open the vault and put Mr. Jared inside.*

"Not true," Sarah whispered, as if saying it out loud would help her believe it wasn't so. Jared was home in bed, she reassured herself. Alive. Not dead . . . unlike her beloved Jason. She had always been cursed with a vivid imagination, and now she was letting Sam's wild tale of devils and such get to her. The sooner she lit the candles and finished her duty, the sooner she could leave.

Sarah braced herself and stepped forward. The moment she came within touching distance of the tomb, the already cool air suddenly grew markedly colder. She pulled her shawl closer as a body-shaking shiver seized her, and she clutched the candles tightly.

Was her mind playing tricks on her . . . again? she wondered. Stretching up on her tiptoes, she quickly placed one candle on top of the tomb. Then she bent down and set another candle at the shadowy base just below the door of the vault.

The first match she struck flared, then immediately died. Two more times she tried with the same results. When the last match she'd brought with her died too, Sarah was at a loss as to what she should do next.

All around her, candles flickered in the dark, and it was then that she realized that she was all alone. Unlike years past when families would sometimes sit by the tombs throughout the entire night, everyone had quickly performed the ritual and left. Just one more thing to thank the Yankees and their cursed curfew for, she thought sarcastically.

With one last uneasy glance around her, Sarah walked to the nearest tomb and quickly removed the candle that was burning on top. Using the flame of the borrowed candle, she lit the one she had placed on top of the Dubuisson tomb first. Then she stooped down to light the other one. The second that the wick caught and the flame flared, Sarah gasped in disbelief at what she saw.

''Noooo,'' she moaned as she dropped the borrowed candle and scrambled to her feet. With her gaze riveted to what should have been the sealed door of the vault, she backed away. The seal had been broken, the vault tampered with, and every word that Sam had uttered earlier that morning roared in her head.

Sarah turned to run, and almost as if an icy hand had reached up out of the earth and grabbed her, she tripped on a root. With a shriek of terror, she stumbled and fell. She heard a rip and a sharp pain shot from her knee up her leg. Ignoring the pain, she struggled to her feet, hiked up her skirts and ran.

By the time she burst through the front door of Dubuisson Manor, she was gasping for breath. The sight of Marie's worried frown was the last straw, and unable to help herself, Sarah burst into tears.

"What on earth has happened to you, child? Saints preserve us! You look a sight."

Sarah could only shake her head and continue sobbing.

"Now, now," Marie soothed as she removed Sarah's bonnet and placed her arm firmly around Sarah's shoulders. "Let's just get you upstairs and cleaned up. Maybe then you can tell me all 'bout it."

Marie helped Sarah out of her soiled and torn dress. Then clucking like a mother hen at the sight of Sarah's scraped and bleeding knee, she gently cleansed the wound and wrapped it with a clean bandage. Sarah's sobs had finally subsided into sniffles and hiccups, and she was relieved that Marie hadn't asked a lot of questions yet.

"I'm gonna make you a nice cup of tea to warm you up," the servant said as she slipped a clean nightgown over Sarah's head. "It won't take but a minute." Marie urged her toward the bed. "Now just get yourself up in that bed and I'll be back in two shakes of a coon's tail."

On her way out, Marie paused by the dresser, picked up Sarah's rosary then retraced her steps. "Here." She placed the rosary in Sarah's hands. "This should make you feel better."

Sarah clutched the rosary and watched Marie disappear through the doorway. Downstairs, the tall case clock began chiming out the hour, and unconsciously, Sarah counted the chimes, noting that it was already eleven P.M.

It seemed an eternity before Marie finally returned, and when the servant entered Sarah's bedroom, Sarah was still clutching the rosary and staring down at her hands. Marie had been right. She did feel better just holding it.

"Here's that tea I promised you."

Sarah wound the rosary around her wrist, then took the cup.

"I expect you to drink every drop. It's a special brew that should help you sleep."

Sarah sipped the tea, and though she thought it tasted a bit bitter, the warm liquid helped chase away the chill she still felt as a result of her harrowing experience in the cemetery.

"Sam was right, you know," Sarah whispered in between sips. "The seal on the vault was broken."

"Hmp! Sam's scared of his own shadow. Could have been done any time," Marie said matter-of-factly. "And don't say I didn't warn you. He should have knowed better than to fill your head with his nonsense, 'specially with you in the state you been in lately, bein' so tired and all." Marie took the empty cup from Sarah's hand. She set the cup on the dresser then returned to stand by the bed. "Now you just lie down there and go to sleep. I'll stay right here till you do."

Even as Sarah snuggled under the covers, she could feel her eyelids as well as her body growing heavier and her muscles relaxing. Finally it became too much of an effort to keep her eyes open, so she closed them. "I'll be better tomorrow," she mumbled. "Just need to rest, to sleep. Just need—"

Sarah wanted to say that she just needed to see Jason one more time, even if the only way she could do so was in her dreams. But she caught herself just in time. Thinking such a thing, much less saying it out loud just wouldn't be proper, especially now that it looked as if her husband might recover.

After all, she had vowed to honor and obey her husband before God and a priest.

And what about your other vow? a voice taunted, *The one you made to the devil?*

CHAPTER FOUR

Sarah was certain that she was still in bed, but she felt as if she were floating on a warm cloud through a hazy mist of peace and tranquillity. Was she dreaming or was she awake? she wondered. Once before she'd thought she was awake but later discovered that she'd probably been dreaming, so how could she know for sure this time?

Whether dreaming or awake, she decided she didn't care, as long as the blissful feeling continued.

Then a sound caught her attention, and Sarah turned her head and strained to see through the mist. A man slowly materialized out of the haze and walked toward her. He seemed familiar . . . his body . . . the way he moved . . . even the clothes he wore, but his face was still hidden by the mist.

Sarah waited. Her heart pounded with fright, but there was anticipation as well. She wanted to cry out to him, to demand to know who he was, but her tongue felt thick and heavy, and she couldn't seem to speak.

Then the mist cleared, and she could see his face. Sarah gasped. It was a face she had both loved and hated. But was he Jason or Jared? They looked so much alike that until one of them spoke, she was never sure which one she was talking with, and even then, one could sound like the other, if he chose to do so. They had often played such games when they were growing up, Jason had once told her.

But Jason was dead, she suddenly remembered, gone forever. Only in her heart and in her dreams was he still alive, so she must be awake, and the man approaching her bed had to be Jared. Sarah was vaguely aware that there was something wrong with her reasoning, but she couldn't seem to concentrate long enough to figure out what it was.

"Sarah," he called out. Even though he was standing by her bedside, he sounded far away and sounded like neither Jared or Jason. "I've missed you so," he said.

"Jared?" she whispered in a faint, fearful voice.

When he neither confirmed nor denied who he was, she wasn't sure he'd heard her. "I'm sorry, so sorry for everything," he said instead, his tone grave and sincere.

Always before, even the thought of Jared coming into her bedroom terrified her, but this time was different. This time she sensed that *he* was different, that he meant her no harm, and she felt peculiarly at ease.

He leaned toward her and reached out, and for reasons she didn't understand, she didn't have the urge to cringe or run. When his finger slid along her cheek, her skin didn't crawl with repulsion as it had so many times before. His touch was soft and gentle, loving . . .

Tingles of awareness rippled through her. She wanted him to touch her . . . and even more incredible, she felt an overwhelming desire to touch him.

Then before she had time to protest, he pulled her into his arms and kissed her. His lips were firm but moist and tender with explosive passion, and Sarah felt as if she were drowning in a sea of conflicting emotion. This was the way she'd felt in her dreams when Jason had kissed her. But this man wasn't Jason. This was the man she'd hated since her wedding night, the man who had abused her in the worst way. Yet . . . she felt no fear, no hatred or loathing. Only longing.

How could that be? she wondered, more confused than ever. Yet again, she was unwilling, unable, to question the rationale too deeply, not when everything within her cried out for more of his earth-shattering kisses.

He ended the kiss, pulling away almost reluctantly it seemed, and he stared deeply into her eyes. "Ah, Sarah, I love you," he groaned. "I've always loved you." He leaned over her again and whispered in her ear. "Please say you love me too. Please say it's not too late for us."

Sarah had to wonder once again whether she was dreaming or awake. Only in a dream would Jared Dubuisson beg for anything.

But people can change, can't they? a voice whispered within.

Was it possible that Jared had changed, that his brush with death had somehow transformed him? Or, once again, was she confusing Jared with Jason as she had during the past weeks when she had tended her husband's wounds?

Sarah didn't have the answer, and at the moment, the answer didn't seem important. All she knew was that she wanted him to continue the exquisite things he was doing with his lips and tongue as he moved from the soft skin behind her ear to her neck.

With the flick of his wrist, he loosened the ribbons of her nightgown, and though she seemed to be on fire inside, a draft of damp, night air made her shiver with anticipation when he slid the gown lower, over her shoulders.

Nothing in her previous experience had come close to preparing her for the onslaught of yearning that surged within her when his lips touched the beginning swell of her breasts and slid lower to claim her nipple.

The only intimacy with a man—with this man—that she'd experienced had been terrifying, filled with pain and degradation. But as inexperienced as she'd been, she'd somehow known even then that making love with the right man could be different, could be wonderful. Still, nothing in her wildest dreams had prepared her for just how wonderful it could be as he suckled at her breasts.

Sarah groaned, pulled his head closer and buried her face in his dark hair. She wanted to freeze the moment in time, wanted it to last forever, yet there still remained an ache, a restless urge that cried out for something more.

Jared seemed to sense what she needed as he reached beneath her gown, found her secret place and slipped his fingers inside her. Shock waves rippled through her yet what he was doing still wasn't enough to assuage the powerful ache building within her.

"So sweet, so beautiful," he whispered in her ear before he released her. Then he pulled away, and within what seemed like mere seconds, he'd torn off his clothes.

As he hovered over her, with nothing on but the sheen of the soft glow reflecting from the fireplace, she suddenly realized that something about his smooth, flawless body wasn't quite as it should be. But the urgent need building within her was too powerful for her to think about anything beyond satisfying the cravings of her body.

When he finally entered her with a single, bold thrust, Sarah cried out with joy. She wrapped her legs around him, and for a moment, she was allowed to savor the sensation of being joined with him. But only for a moment.

With a groan, he suddenly withdrew, and when he thrust again, his mouth covered hers in a searing kiss that matched his fiery possession. From that moment on, she was so caught up in the storm of his lovemaking that she couldn't think of anything else but the driving force of emotion that was building within her like wildfire. And when the pinnacle of her desire peaked at the same moment as his, stars seemed to burst behind her eyelids as if the whole universe had split in two.

Moments later, Sarah was vaguely aware that Jared had separated from her, but by then, she was floating again, surrounded by a peaceful, tranquil mist of pure contentment. The last thing she remembered were his whispers of love and devotion.

Sarah awakened with a start the following morning. Feeling vaguely disoriented, she tried to open her eyes and groaned when a sharp pain shot through her head. The drapes had been tied back and bright sunlight streamed into the room.

Marie must have come in earlier, she thought, squinting in an effort to see. But the light hurt, and with another groan, she threw her arm over her eyes. A dull ache throbbed at her temples, and her mouth felt as if it had been stuffed with cotton.

As she lay there, trying to work up courage to open her eyes again, bits and pieces of the night before began coming back to her. The cemetery . . . the broken seal to the vault . . . her flight home . . . and finally, the wonderful yet absurd dream she'd had. At the time she'd thought she was awake, but now, in the harsh light of day, she knew better.

Suddenly, Sarah felt her cheeks grow hot just thinking about what she'd experienced in the erotic dream.

"Ridiculous," she muttered. "Utterly ridiculous." Why on earth would she have dreamed such a thing—especially about Jared, of all people?

Bracing herself against the pain she knew was inevitable, Sarah opened first one eye, then the other. It was time to get up and time to stop dwelling on a ludicrous dream that had nothing to do with reality. Past time, she figured, if the heat building from the sunlight pouring through the window was any gauge to measure by.

With yet another groan, she threw back the covers. The second that the warm air hit her body, Sarah knew something was wrong. When she looked down, her eyes widened in disbelief.

She was as naked as the day she was born.

Memories of the strange dream swirled through her mind again. Ignoring the dull ache in her head, she scrambled to her knees and searched frantically for her nightgown. The strange dream was just that, a dream. There had to be another explanation why she was naked.

When she finally spied the nightgown, it was wadded into a ball beneath the sheet. The moment she snatched up the nightgown, she gasped when she saw what had been hidden beneath it.

"Not possible," she whispered, growing more frantic with each passing second. But even as she said the words out loud, an inner voice cried that the evidence was there in plain sight. Not only was she naked, but there was a suspicious stain on the sheet where she'd slept.

For long moments, she stared at the stain as a moan of horror and denial welled up within her. She hadn't been dreaming. Someone had been in her bedroom during the night. Someone *had* made love to her.

But had that someone been her husband? The man had looked like Jared . . . except . . .

Sarah closed her eyes and wrapped her arms around her middle, and as an image of the man came back to her, she shivered. But something was wrong with the image, the same something she vaguely recalled being confused about when he'd made love to her.

Sarah suddenly went still, and like the rush of an icy waterfall, the reason she'd been confused hit her. Jared had been wounded, in his arm and in his chest. She'd tended those wounds. But the body of the man who had made love to her was perfect. No wounds or even scars.

So who had made love to her? She wondered, as cold fingers of fear squeezed her heart.

. . . he done changed hisself to look just like Mr. Jared.

"No," she moaned, shaking her head from side to side as she recalled Sam's words. At the time, she'd thought the servant's story was too ridiculous to even consider, but now . . .

Sarah began to shake. Her heart pounded so hard that she could hear blood rushing through her head with each frantic beat.

Madness, she thought. *It's all madness.* With one last horrified glance at the sheet, Sarah yanked the nightgown over her head. "Marie!" she screamed, scrambling off the bed as if the hounds of hell were chasing her.

Numb horror spread throughout her body as she backed toward the door. "Marie!" she screamed again.

"What on earth?" Marie burst through the doorway.

Sarah whirled to face her then threw herself at the servant. "Sam was right," she sobbed, her voice shrill with terror as she clung to Marie with a death grip. "He was right. That man in the other bedroom is . . . is the . . . the devil, and he's out to claim my soul too."

Marie tried to pry Sarah loose. "Calm down, now. Just calm yourself down."

"Calm? Calm!" she screeched. "How can I be calm when th-that man, that devil came into my room last night, and I let him . . . let him . . ."

Suddenly Sarah stiffened, and shaking her head, she pulled away. "He's not really sick you know," she whispered in an eerie conspiratorial voice she barely recognized as her own. "Jared's been fooling us all along."

Marie grabbed Sarah by both arms with a grip of iron and shook her hard. "Stop it, you hear? Stop it! You're not making sense. No one was in this room last night but you, and Mr. Jared ain't the devil."

Marie's eyes burned with determination. "You hear me, girl?" She shook Sarah again. "And he ain't been faking all this time either. Nobody came in here last night," she repeated again. "You was just hallucinatin'."

Sarah shook her head violently. "No, no, I wasn't—"

Marie's grip tightened like vices around Sarah's arms. "Yes, ma'am, you was. I put some Valerian root in your tea last night to help you to sleep. It's a root good for the nerves. Most folks just sleep like babies, but some folks—like you—have these strange kind of dreams."

Everything within Sarah cried out that Marie was mistaken, that what she'd experienced had been real, not just a dream. She wanted to point out that she'd awakened naked, that there was a stain on the sheet, but one look at the servant's fearful but stubborn expression changed her mind.

What was the use? Sarah decided, suddenly feeling even more weary than she had when she'd gone to bed the night before. Knowing Marie the way she did, she figured that the servant would probably have explanations for all of her so-called proof.

To continue insisting would only make Marie suspicious of the very thing that Sarah had feared for days now—that she was truly going insane, that God was punishing her for all of her blasphemous thoughts and deeds.

With a shudder, Sarah drew in a deep breath. There was no

known treatment or cure for the insane, and she had no intention of being locked away like some animal for the rest of her life.

Calling on what little strength she had left, she pulled away from Marie's grasp. "You're probably right," she said, surprised at how calm her voice sounded. "I . . . I apologize for being so unreasonable and causing such a ruckus."

At first Marie narrowed her eyes as if she weren't quite sure whether to trust Sarah's sudden transformation. Then, seemingly satisfied, she reached out and patted Sarah's shoulder.

" 'Course I'm right," she said. "And I don't want you worrying your pretty head another minute 'bout such things. Mr. Jared's on the mend and everything' gonna be just fine, just you wait and see. Even Sam finally came back last night just like I said he would."

Marie smiled and backed toward the door. "Yes, sirree, everything' gonna be just fine. I promise. You just need some rest and sunshine. I can take care of Mr. Jared now that he's better, so you go on and get dressed and go visitin' today. I hear that Miz Lemonte has been feelin' poorly lately, and I'm sure she'd appreciate some company."

The moment Marie closed the door, Sarah finally gave in to the weakness that was spreading throughout her limbs, and sank to the floor. Holding herself tightly, she rocked back and forth and tried to control the silent sobs that shook her body.

When she was spent and could cry no more, she dragged herself up to the basin where she splashed cold water in her face. There was nothing left to do but to try and carry on as if everything were normal. To do otherwise would land her locked away in the attic, branded as a crazy woman.

Later that morning, as she sat on the settee in Mrs. Lemonte's parlor and listened while her neighbor complained about her rheumatism, Sarah tried to concentrate on what the older lady was saying, but she couldn't stop thinking about everything that had taken place earlier, especially the way Marie had acted.

Then, out of the clear blue, Sarah suddenly realized what

was bothering her. It was Marie's changed attitude toward Jared.

From the first day they'd moved into Dubuisson Manor, Marie had never gotten along with Jared, and when he'd been brought back home wounded and dying, she'd had even less to do with him, had in fact avoided Jared's sickroom at every opportunity . . . until he'd awakened from the coma.

Since then, there had been a dramatic change in the servant's attitude. Why was she so willing, even eager, to tend to Jared all of a sudden? Sarah wondered.

Strange, she decided. Very strange.

Night came all too soon for Sarah. As she undressed in preparation for bed, all she could think of were the other terrifying nights of tossing and turning, nights of dreams that seemed so real that she still didn't know if she had been truly asleep or awake.

But not tonight, she thought, as she picked up her rosary and climbed into the bed. Tonight, she had no intention of falling asleep. If she had to stay awake till sunrise, she was determined to find out, once and for all, just what was going on in the Dubuisson household.

Once Sarah was in bed, she slipped her hand beneath the pillow and searched until she found the thick handle of the carving knife she'd placed there earlier. Tonight she also intended to find out, one way or another, just who her phantom lover was, if he was truly flesh and blood, a spirit, or simply the result of being under the influence of Marie's powerful tea.

Satisfied she could reach the knife if need be, she eyed the netting secured at the bed post as she laid her head down and pulled the covers up to her chin. She'd already decided against loosening the netting, since she didn't want anything in the way that would hamper her vision.

Turning her head, she stared at the flames leaping and licking the bricks that lined the fireplace. It wasn't cold enough to warrant a fire, and she felt a bit guilty for using the precious firewood, but this evening was different, she thought. She needed the light that the fire gave off if she was going to learn the truth.

At first the flames in the fireplace danced and burned brightly, flooding the room with a warm, comforting glow. But as the hours dragged by, the flames died, leaving only the burning embers to cast their eerie shadows.

The time between the tall case clock's hourly chimes seemed to grow longer and longer. With each passing minute Sarah found her eyelids growing heavier, so heavy, that it was becoming almost impossible to keep them open.

Finally the temptation proved to be too much. Telling herself that she would only close them for a moment, she gave in and let her eyes drift shut.

It could have been hours that passed or merely seconds—she wasn't sure—but suddenly, as if she'd taken a plunge into an icy lake, Sarah was wide-awake, her heart racing like a runaway horse. Every muscle tensed and her nerves jumped with alarm as she slowly turned her head and stared at the doorway of her bedroom. Beneath the sheet she clutched the rosary so tightly that the wooden beads dug painfully into her palms.

But pain was good, she thought. If she felt pain then she was definitely awake, not dreaming, wasn't she?

The noise was ever so slight when it came again, but Sarah heard it and identified it as the loose board creaking just outside her doorway in the hall. He—whoever or whatever *he* was—was coming.

Without a sound she slipped her free hand beneath the pillow and took a firm hold on the handle of the knife. Bit by bit, she pushed herself up then eased onto her knees. Sarah inched back as close to the headboard as she could get. Still clutching the rosary, she tightened the fingers of her other hand around the knife handle in a death grip, raised her arm in readiness and waited . . . and listened, her eyes straining in the dim light for any movement.

Time dragged to a slow crawl, and the fine hairs on the back of her neck prickled. One second the doorway was empty. The next, it was filled with the shadowy figure of a man.

"Sarah?" he called out.

Sarah swallowed the lump of fear that had lodged in her throat. "Who are you?" she demanded, unable to control the quiver in her voice.

For what seemed an eternity, he didn't move and didn't answer. Then he stretched his arms out in an imploring gesture. "Ah, Sarah, don't you know me by now?" he drawled. "I've come back to claim what is rightfully mine."

CHAPTER FIVE

Ah, Sarah, don't you know me by now? The words seemed to echo around her, growing louder and louder, until they penetrated the very heart of her soul.

Sarah whimpered as suddenly, recognition hit her with the force of an exploding cannon.

The shadowy figure standing in the doorway wasn't a phantom of her imagination come to drive her mad. It wasn't the devil in disguise come to claim her soul, and it wasn't her husband rising up from his sickbed to torture her again as she had feared.

Joy burst within her and spread like wildfire through her veins. "Jason, oh, Jason!" she cried out as she dropped the knife and the rosary and reached out toward him.

As if by magic, he was beside her. He gathered her hands between his, lifted them to his lips and kissed them, sending a fierce wave of heat coursing through every nerve in her body.

"But how?" she whispered, still unable to believe he was real flesh and blood and not some phantom of her imagination. "Jared told me you were dead, shot for being a traitor."

Jason's grip on her hands tightened. "He lied," he said, his tone turning harsh. "Just as he lied about so many other things."

Jason dragged her into his arms, and Sarah came willingly, relishing the warm solidity of his chest. Her senses throbbed with the strength and the feel and woodsy scent of him. This was the man she'd loved, the man she'd thought was lost to her forever.

"Just let me hold you, my love," he whispered.

Sarah trembled. There was nothing in the world that she wanted more than to stay safe and secure in Jason's warm, tender embrace. She wanted to forget everything and everyone around them, and for a few precious moments, she was able to block everything else from her mind.

Heart-stopping seconds passed, but all too soon, reality intruded, rearing its ugly head to taunt her. She was a married woman, married to Jason's brother who lay gravely ill just down the hallway, and no matter how much she wished things were different, she wasn't free to indulge herself or her dreams and fantasies.

She had already risked the fires of eternal damnation once in a weak moment of frustration and grief the night she'd railed against God and fate. As punishment, she'd come close to losing her mind and her soul. She dared not tempt fate or the devil again. And there were still questions that needed answering.

Sarah wedged her hands between them and shoved against Jason's chest. "No," she whispered fervently. "Please. I . . . I can't. We mustn't."

"Why mustn't we?" Jason countered, refusing to loosen his hold on her. "We've both been duped. Everything that has happened has been based on the lies of a jealous, evil man. He's hated me since we were children, hated the idea of having to share everything equally with me. Jared was the firstborn—just by minutes—but he felt he should have been favored. Then when our father died and my brother found that we had inherited equally, he set out to destroy me."

For a moment, Sarah almost relented. No one knew better than she how much Jared had despised Jason. To be with Jason was what she truly wanted, what she'd dreamed of, and she was tempted, oh so tempted, but . . .

She shoved against him again in earnest. For a moment

more he held onto her, then, with a great sigh, he finally released her.

Sarah scooted backward. "Don't you understand?" she cried. "None of that matters. None of that changes the fact that I am Jared's wife. I took sacred vows before God and my family."

For endless seconds, Jason simply stared at her with an odd expression. "Vows till death do you part?" he asked softly.

"Yes," she whispered, tears now streaming down her cheeks.

He reached up, and with a gentleness that made her want to weep even more, he wiped away her tears. "Then unless I'm gravely mistaken, my love, your vows have been fulfilled."

Everything within Sarah froze in disbelief. "Fulfilled?" she stammered. "Wh-what do you mean?"

Jason's expression turned hard and relentless. "Your husband is gone—dead. As well he should be," he added harshly.

"Dead?" Sarah frowned, totally confused. "But how can that be? When Sam and I looked in on him two days ago, he was better. He'd even come out of his coma. And Marie has been tending him. She would have told me if he'd grown worse."

"Sarah, my love, the man you saw in Jared's bed wasn't my brother. That was me."

"You?"

Jason nodded. "Yes, me."

Sarah shivered.

"I hadn't slept for two days," he explained, "and I was exhausted."

. . . there he was, all dressed in black, carrying Mr. Jared as if Mr. Jared was no heavier than a feather.

Sarah shivered again and blinked several times as the memory of Sam's strange devil tale came back to her. Jared hadn't been carried to the graveyard by the devil, as Sam had thought. Just as she'd suspected all along, there had been a logical explanation. He had been taken there by Jason.

But why hadn't Jason come forward as soon as Jared died?

she wondered. And Marie? The servant had been supposedly tending to Jared for two days now. Surely she must have known something was amiss.

Sarah tried to voice her question, but by this time she was shivering so hard that her teeth chattered.

"Oh, God, Sarah, I'm sorry! Here—" Jason pushed her down onto the bed and pulled the covers over her. "You've had a shock." He sat down next to her. "Let's get you warm." He tucked the covers snugly around her, then began rubbing his hands up and down along her shoulders and arms.

Beneath the covers, Sarah curled into a tight ball. She knew she should feel remorse or at least sadness about Jared's demise, but all she felt was relief. Even though she'd expected him to die, it was almost impossible to comprehend that she was finally free, that she was no longer bound to Jared by man's law or God's law and would never have to endure his cruelties again.

Jared had been an evil man who took pleasure in causing pain and degradation. Still, he was a member of the human race, and she only hoped that God could forgive her and that she could forgive herself for wishing for the death of another human being.

"There now." Jason slid one of his hands up her shoulder then caressed her cheek. "That's much better."

His touch was like a soothing, calming balm, and as she slowly warmed, her shivers lessened to only an occasional shudder. Then his gaze locked with hers, and in his eyes, she saw tenderness, naked love and compassion, all the things that had been missing in her marriage and in her life for so long. But there were still questions that needed answering.

"Tell me," she prompted. "I . . . I don't understand how any of this came to be."

He smoothed a strand of hair back from her face, his touch now gentle, almost reverent. "I know you don't." His hand lingered for a moment at her temple before he withdrew it. He glanced away to stare into the dying embers of the fireplace, and when he next spoke, his voice was almost harsh.

"I'll try and explain, but first I have to know. Did you love my brother?"

Jason's question took her by surprise, rendering her speechless.

When she didn't answer straightaway, he uttered an oath beneath his breath, turned and glared at her. "He said you did. Said you'd changed your mind and had chosen him over me."

Yet another of Jared's lies, she thought, and though a protest was fast on the tip of Sarah's tongue, she bit her bottom lip to keep from uttering it. How would Jason feel about her if she told him the truth?

Suddenly, a spark of anger flared inside her. After the humiliation and heartbreak she'd endured when Jason had jilted her, she shouldn't care what he thought.

Then as quickly as the spark had ignited, it died. She couldn't deny the truth no matter how much he'd hurt her, and the truth was that she did care, cared so much that she was afraid to risk losing him again.

Would he think less of her if he knew she'd married his brother strictly for convenience's sake, out of duty to her family . . . and yes, partly out of defiance because Jason, the man she truly loved, had broken her heart?

Unable to bear his penetrating scrutiny, she lowered her gaze, and instead of answering his question outright, she asked one of her own, the one that had tortured her every day of her life since the night she'd watched Jason ride away for the last time.

"Why did you break off our engagement?" Her pulse pounded in her ears as she waited, hoping and praying his answer wouldn't crush her heart all over again. "At the time, the only reason you gave me was that you'd simply changed your mind," she reminded him. "But even now—as I did then—I believe there had to be more reason than you gave."

"Did you love my brother?" Jason repeated doggedly.

The raw intensity of his voice drew her gaze upward again, and this time Sarah couldn't sidestep his question. "No," she answered. "God forgive me, but I never loved him. And later, I . . . I grew to fear him. And loathe him," she added in a whisper. More tears seeped from the corners of her eyes. "He was a cruel, selfish man who preyed on the weak and help-less."

Jason's expression turned murderous and he swore an oath. "I should have known he lied. Sarah, the man who came to you and broke off our engagement was Jared, pretending to be me."

Sarah gasped. No wonder she'd thought Jason had acted strangely that night.

"Oh, yes." He nodded. "Just before the first battle our company fought, he bragged to me about how he'd duped you. He said that after he'd married you, he'd told you about the pretense, and you said you were glad he'd done it, since you'd always loved him the best anyway."

"But that's not true," Sarah cried. "It was you I loved. Always you."

Jason's eyes blazed with fury. "I should never have be-lieved him. I knew better than to trust anything he said, and the only thing that has kept me going all of this time was the thought of coming back and hearing the truth from your lips.

"On the night he came to you, pretending to be me, he'd sent me upriver on some trumped-up family business. Along the way, I was waylaid and held hostage by a group of thugs. You have to remember that before the war, the Dubuissons were quite wealthy, so at first I thought I was being held for ransom.

"When the scalawags finally released me days later, it was too late. Jared had already married you. But marrying you wasn't the extent of his treachery. Recently I found out more . . . much more.

"I've spent the last four hellish months in a Yankee prison—yet another treachery I have my brother to thank for. But what he didn't foresee was that one of the thugs he'd paid to kidnap me landed in the same prison. It was from him that I finally learned the truth, that he'd been paid by Jared to hold me for a certain length of time."

With Jason's words, any lingering guilt Sarah felt about wishing for Jared's death disappeared. The man who had been

her husband couldn't have been human after all, she decided.
Only a spawn of the devil could plan and carry out such a
despicable, diabolical scheme.

Suddenly a strange, self-satisfied smile pulled at Jason's
lips. "Would you believe that the same man who told me the
truth risked his life to help me escape that Yankee prison?—
something else my dear, departed brother never counted on,"
he added sarcastically.

Abruptly, Jason sobered. "But by that time, it was too
late," he continued, his tone once again angry and harsh. "Jared hadn't been content to take you from me. He set out to
completely destroy me by spreading vicious lies throughout
our company that I was a Yankee spy. Since I didn't know
who to trust and didn't want to be shot for being a traitor, I
made my way back to New Orleans once I'd escaped.

"For the past two weeks, I've been hiding out in this house,
staying holed up in the attic and only coming out at night
when everyone was asleep."

"Then that explains it!" Sarah exclaimed, feeling as if a
burdensome weight had suddenly been lifted.

"Explains what?" Jason frowned as a look of bewilderment
spread over his face.

"I've never been one to believe in superstitions, but I'd
almost begun to think that Dubuisson Manor was haunted,"
she answered, "what with the strange noises and different
items being moved about at night."

Understanding chased away his confusion and amusement
danced in his eyes. "Marie almost caught me a time or two,
but you have to remember, I grew up in this house, and I
know all of the secret passages."

"What secret passages?" she demanded.

Jason grinned. "If I tell, then they won't be secret," he
teased.

Sarah tilted her head and narrowed her eyes.

"Okay, okay," he relented. "I'll tell you—No, I'll show
you, but later." He paused. "Now where was I? Oh, yes . . .
anyway, when I first came home, I wanted to kill Jared, but
once I saw how ill he was, I decided to bide my time. I'd seen

wounds like his before and knew there was little chance of his recovery.

"I had even considered the possibility that if and when he did die, I could take his place, pretend to be him. Other than leaving the country, I didn't think I had much choice. Because of the lies he spread, the Confederates think I'm a traitor, and if the Yankees catch me, I'll be sent back to prison."

Jason glanced away and stared once again into the embers. "It was the terror on your face the morning that you and Sam came to the room that changed my mind about taking Jared's place. That particular incident confirmed what I'd long suspected, that my brother had used you badly. Then that afternoon, Marie confirmed my suspicions and—"

Sarah stiffened. "Marie knew about you?"

Jason turned back and nodded gravely. "Don't be angry with her. I was able to avoid her for the first few days I was here, but then one night the inevitable happened and she finally caught me. I made her promise to keep my secret until I felt ready to reveal myself."

The look in Jason's eyes suddenly softened, and Sarah soon forgot about Marie, forgot everything but the love and compassion glowing in the depths of his gaze. It was as if he could see all the pain and suffering she'd endured at his brother's hand.

"I couldn't bear it," he said. "No matter what happens to me, I decided I couldn't pretend to be Jared without telling you. I couldn't bear the thought of you being as terrified of me as you were of him." He paused as if carefully choosing his next words. "I intended to tell you last night. Then when I came to you, and you . . . I thought I might have been mistaken after all about your feelings for my brother and I—"

Sarah bolted straight up. "Then I wasn't dreaming?"

Jason shook his head slowly, and though she couldn't be sure in the dim light, she thought a flush of embarrassment stole across his face. "I suppose I should apologize, but seeing you again, having you in my arms was like a dream come true, even if you did think I was Jared. That's why I had to ask if you loved him. I had to know if you were too drunk on

Marie's tea to know what you were doing, or if you—''

Sarah quickly placed her hand over Jason's mouth. ''Don't—'' She shook her head. ''I've already·told you I never loved Jared, and I'm not sure I'll ever understand or be able to explain last night completely.

''I knew what I was doing, yet I didn't. The drugged tea made me confuse my dreams of you with the reality of being Jared's wife. I already felt tremendous guilt for . . . for . . .'' Sarah swallowed hard. ''For so many things, and even though I thought Jared was whom I was making love to, my heart and my soul must have recognized you or else I never could have responded in such a way. When I first awakened, I was sure I'd had another one of my strange dreams. Then, when I discovered that I was naked, I was terrified. I thought I must be truly insane.''

Jason covered Sarah's hand with his own and held it to his lips as he kissed her palm. Then he lifted his head, and placing his hands on her upper arms, he pulled her close. As he stared deeply into her eyes, she could feel his warm breath caress her lips.

''I love you, Sarah,'' he whispered in a voice rough with emotion. ''I've never stopped loving you and won't until the last breath leaves my body.'' He pulled her into his arms and held her so tightly that she could feel his heart keeping rhythm with her own.

''Oh, Jason.'' His name was like a whispered prayer on her lips, and something painful twisted inside her. Up until that moment she hadn't realized that Jared's abuse had left scars on the inside as well as the outside.

Tears of joy filled her eyes when Sarah suddenly realized what was happening. With Jason's avowal of love, the scars left by Jared were already beginning to disappear.

''I love you too,'' she cried out. ''With all of my heart and soul—''

The rest of what she'd wanted to say was swallowed up in the sudden, burning kiss he gave her. His mouth possessed hers, his lips moving sensually against her lips, and a wave of warmth spread throughout her veins. Then his tongue slipped between her lips to meet and mate with her own, and sparks of excitement shot through her.

All too soon he broke off the kiss, and with a firm grip on her upper arms, he held her away from him. "Who am I, Sarah?" he gasped, his breath coming in short spurts as if he'd run miles and miles.

As she stared into his eyes, at first she didn't understand. Then slowly, bit by bit, it came to her and she realized what he was asking and why.

"I know who you are, my love," she whispered as she reached up between them and caressed his firm jaw. He was in dire need of a shave but she relished the rough feel of his beard against her fingertips. "I'm not drugged," she continued. "I'm not delusional and I'm not dreaming." She lightly ran her forefinger back and forth over his lips which were still wet and slick from their kiss. At first he didn't move, didn't seem to breathe. Only when the muscle in his jaw tightened was she finally satisfied that she was having her desired effect on him. "You're my other half, my soul mate, my heart of hearts," she whispered.

Jason nipped her finger with his teeth. "Then say my name," he insisted, his voice rough with desire. "This time I don't want there to be any doubts as to whom you're making love to."

Even though his words sent a thrill of anticipation racing through her veins, there was a tiny part of her, some perverse part of her, she decided, that wanted to punish him for all the nights he'd crept around Dubuisson Manor like some shadowy ghost without making himself known.

Sarah slid her hands down to his chest and toyed with the buttons on his shirt. "Maybe you truly are a ghost or the devil in disguise," she taunted as she unfastened the first and second button. "Or maybe I've finally crossed over that line that distinguishes the sane from the insane." She slid her fingers inside his shirt and rubbed the taut skin on his chest.

"Sarah—"

His tone was a warning that his patience was at an end and though an imp of mischief urged her to prolong the game,

Sarah hadn't counted on the erotic effect her wanton teasing would have on her own body. It was as if every nerve had suddenly caught fire, a fire that only Jason had the power to extinguish.

Sarah reached up and pulled his head close to her lips. "Jason," she whispered in his ear. "You're Jason. *My* Jason."

She was rewarded when he swiftly turned his head then kissed her with renewed passion, and for the following moments, the only sounds in the dim, quiet room were the rustling of clothing being quickly stripped and groans of urgency and need.

For Sarah it was *déjà vu,* as he hovered over her, with nothing on but the sheen from the soft glow reflected by the dying embers of the fireplace. But this time there was no dreamy haze of confusion as there had been the night before. This time she was wide-awake and very much aware of what was happening and who it was happening with.

The man above her was her beloved Jason. And as he rained kisses from her lips down her neck, and lower, to her breasts, Sarah was fully conscious of each heart-stopping, earth-shattering moment.

Then, without warning, he grabbed hold of her, rolled to the side and switched their positions. Sarah found herself lying on top on him. His body beneath her was slick and hot, her breasts were flattened against his hard chest, and his equally hard manhood pressed against the apex of her thighs.

With his hands beneath her armpits, Jason lifted her upper body and began to feast on first one breast then the other. His lips and mouth suckled and pulled at her nipples. Her belly tightened and the center of her desire convulsed, setting off a tremble of longing so strong that it shook her very being. Even more than she needed the air that she breathed, Sarah needed Jason inside her, filling her.

Maybe he truly was a devil of sorts after all, she decided. Surely only the devil could elicit such a wicked yet wonderful feeling.

But Jason didn't give her time to think too much about anything. "Sarah, I need you. I need you now," he groaned.

And before she realized what had happened, she found herself sitting upright, straddling him, his hands cupping her hips and lifting her until she felt the urgent presence of his arousal probe against her.

Sarah's insides fluttered with excitement. "Yes, oh, yes," she cried out, and without a qualm, she eagerly sank down on him, taking the whole of him inside her. The feeling was exquisite. It was as if time and motion were suspended, and neither of them moved as they savored the wonder of being joined as one.

Then Jason reached up and drew her head downward. "Kiss me," he murmured.

And Sarah kissed him. Using her lips, her mouth and her teeth, she feasted on him like a starved woman who had just been offered a sumptuous banquet.

For a while, he allowed it, relished it, and seemed to enjoy every second, but before long, he began to quiver beneath her, and she realized that he had reached the limitation of his endurance. And so had she.

"Make love to me," she whispered as she rocked against him, moving her hips suggestively. "Please, Jason, now."

Jason needed no further encouragement. He gripped her hips and surged upward. The sensations Sarah felt were overpowering and like nothing she'd ever experienced. With each thrust, together they hurled higher and higher. And as the tension within her steadily grew, all she could do was hold onto Jason as he took her to the edge of the universe and beyond.

Much later, Sarah awakened slowly.

The embers in the fireplace had died and the light of the new day was just beginning to filter through the draperies inside her bedroom.

With her bare back against his equally bare chest, she was securely cocooned within Jason's arms, and she let out a sigh of pure contentment as she snuggled even closer to him.

She'd lost count of the times and ways they had made love during the night, and she truly regretted that it had to end.

But with the light of day came reality. Decisions and adjustments had to be made. Since Marie already knew about Jason's presence, Sarah wondered if they should also tell Sam.

Suddenly Sarah giggled. Poor, terrified Sam. Of course they would have to tell him, if for no other reason than to put his tortured mind at rest about what he thought he'd seen.

Jared stirred and his arms around her tightened. "And just what do you find so amusing this early in the morning, madam?"

Sarah smiled, loving the way Jason's breath tickled her ear. "I was thinking how relieved Sam will be to find out that you aren't the devil come to claim his soul."

"What?"

"I said that Sam will be relieved to find out that you aren't the devil," she repeated.

"Maybe you'd better explain that statement a bit more."

Sarah twisted around until she was facing Jason. They were nose to nose, belly to belly, and when he reached down and pulled her hips more firmly against his own, it didn't surprise her in the least to find that he was aroused once again. Already she could feel her own passions stirring in response, and she wondered if there would ever come a day when they would get enough of each other. Not in this lifetime, she decided.

"Well?" he prompted.

Sarah sighed. There would be other nights, all the nights of the rest of their lives. "It all started on the night before All Hallows' Eve," she began. And as Sarah told Jason the story about Sam's run-in with the devil, she became so caught up in the tale that she failed to note the growing tension in the man lying so still next to her.

"So you see," she said when she'd finished her story, "once Sam knows that you were the one who carried Jared to the cemetery, he'll stop worrying about devils and such."

For long moments, Jason didn't utter a word, and it was only then that she noticed the strange look in his eyes and the even stranger expression on his face.

Sarah frowned. "You do intend to tell Sam that you're back, don't you?" When he still didn't answer, a chill of unease danced along her spine. "Jason, what's wrong?"

He reached up and placed his hands on either side of her face. "Sarah, I'm not quite sure yet what's going on here, but it wasn't me who carried Jared to the cemetery."

At first Sarah thought he was joking, but the grave look in his eyes soon belied that impression.

"While it's true that I was with Jared when he died, as soon as he drew his last breath, I left to find Marie so that she could make the necessary arrangements to bury him. When I didn't find her in her room, I figured she was either at one of her voodoo rituals or at the cemetery, visiting her godmother.

"I took a chance and went to the cemetery first. And sure enough, I found her there. But it took us a lot longer to return to the house than I'd figured, since we had to keep dodging Yankee patrols."

Jason's thumbs softly caressed her temples as if he were trying to soothe her. "When we returned," he continued, "Jared's bed was empty, so we both assumed that Sam had found him and had already moved him. Marie knew I hadn't slept in two days and knew how exhausted I was, so she offered to find Sam and take care of things. Once she'd stripped the bed and made it up with clean sheets, she insisted that I get some sleep, so I climbed in it. I only intended to rest for a little while, but the next thing I knew, it was daylight, and you and Sam were staring at me as if I'd suddenly grown horns. I was still debating as to whether I would take Jared's place, so I wasn't ready to make myself known yet. That's why I didn't say anything."

With the end of Jason's explanation, Sarah was seized by a chill, and even though she was snuggled close to him, the air around her suddenly grew much colder, reminding her of the night she'd visited the cemetery.

For long moments, she couldn't utter a sound, and as her mind raced frantically for a possible explanation for what Sam had seen that night, the room grew ominously dark and still.

If I could have just one night with Jason, I'd sell my soul to the devil and gladly risk eternal damnation.

'Twas the devil . . . Carrying Mr. Jared off . . . He ain't just

satisfied with Mr. Jared's soul and body. Now he's after another one too.

The jolt of the memory set off a seizure of shivering that Sarah couldn't control. "Oh, God, what have I done?" she cried, as her blasphemous words and Sam's declaration screamed through her mind.

"Sarah!"

She heard the alarmed concern in Jason's voice, but Sarah was beyond reason. "It's my fault," she sobbed. "All my fault. I-I've condemned us both." And as tears of torment spilled onto her cheeks, Sarah haltingly explained about the night she'd cursed God and entreated the help of Satan. By the time she'd finished her story, she was weeping uncontrollably. "Oh, Jason, can you ever forgive me?"

"Sarah, stop it!" Jason grabbed her by the shoulders and shook her. "There is nothing to forgive, because none of what you said or did has any bearing on anything that has happened. And even if for one second I thought it did—and I don't—I would gladly risk the fires of hell to be with you." His eased his grip on her shoulders and slid his hands down to gently caress her arms. "I love you," he added softly, tenderly.

With Jason's avowal of love, the cold draft that chilled the air suddenly dissipated. And with its disappearance, Sarah's mind slowly began to clear. Jason was real, flesh and blood, not some apparition she'd conjured up. There had to be another explanation for what Sam thought he'd seen. But what?

Sarah stared deeply into Jason's eyes, eyes that were the color of the sky on a bright, cloudless day, eyes that were now troubled and concerned but reflected the same fierce love that she felt for him.

And it was there, in the depths of his eyes that she found her answer.

A gentle peace settled over her like a warm, spring day full of sunshine and promise. It no longer mattered how or why Jason was there. And it no longer mattered who had spirited Jared away during the night.

All that mattered was the love she and Jason shared, the kind of pure love that could defy death and eternity if need be. And deep within her heart of hearts, Sarah knew that a love such as theirs could only have been born and nurtured by a being who was pure and holy, never one who was corrupt and evil.

"It's okay," she whispered as she reached out and caressed Jason's jaw in an attempt to smooth away the frown of concern on his face. "I'm okay now." She wrapped her arms around him and held him close. "Now and forever," she added in a whisper, "as long as I have you. As long as we have our love."

OUT OF THE NIGHT

DEBORAH MARTIN

CHAPTER ONE

It was the time of Lent in New Orleans, that period of limbo between the licentious excesses of Carnival and Easter's holy promise of spring. Devotion was the order of the day, and because the coldness of winter had passed and the hot, fever-ridden nights of summer hadn't yet ensued, disease had less of a hold on the populace than usual.

Or so it had seemed to Doctor Victor Drouet until now. After spending three torturous days and nights at the Capuchin Asylum for Orphan Boys, he wasn't so sure. He stood beside Father Tomas, surveying the cramped infirmary's four beds. Each bed held a child. Most had two. In all, there were seven boys between the ages of five and eight. They slept fitfully, their cherubic faces flushed with fever and their necks held stiff and straight. Occasionally, one would reach for the chamber pot placed by his bed and would empty his stomach's contents.

Every time Victor saw it, frustration gripped him. He slammed his fist against the wall next to the medicine cabinet. "They're not getting any better," he told Father Tomas, the priest in charge of the orphanage.

Victor was familiar with the ailment that had seized them. He'd seen it often in the Paris hospital where he'd been trained. Sometimes the ailment passed without doing harm.

More often, however, it resulted in death or permanent paralysis. There was no cure, no treatment other than to keep the fever low and the nausea at bay.

He'd met with little success in either, despite giving the children countless infusions of meadowsweet, white willow, and ginger tea. "I've tried everything. Nothing seems to work. I don't know what else to do, how to help them."

Father Tomas, an old man whose papery skin was crosscut with a mesh of wrinkles, shook his head and crossed himself. "They are in God's hands, my son. All we can do now is pray."

Victor bit back a curse. Although he'd been raised a good Catholic in a small town outside of Paris, the events of the Revolution and the later nonsensical bloodbaths that had driven him from France had also soured him on religion. What kind of God allowed such misery? What kind of God punished innocent children with an illness like this?

A rational man couldn't believe in such a God. "Your prayers haven't done much good to date, Father, have they?" he said in a low rumble. "These children are still motherless, and they're still dying."

The priest shrugged. "If they die, they go to Heaven. Maybe that is God's plan."

"A damnable plan, if you ask me."

Father Tomas shot him a keen glance. "It's not for us to question God's will. It shows a lack of faith, my dear doctor."

"There's a reason for that. I lost my faith in God long ago."

"Oh, my son." Father Tomas's voice filled with pity. "If you don't believe, how can you expect God to intercede on the children's behalf?"

Victor surveyed the children he seemed helpless to cure. He, too, had been an orphan raised in a priest-run orphanage. Only through a rabid determination to wrest himself from poverty had he changed the course of his unpromising future. But he hadn't been given the added complication of a death-dealing illness.

It wasn't fair that children given so little in life already should be visited with this, too. If God had done this, then He was no God Victor could believe in.

Victor strode to one of the beds and reached for the hand of the oldest child, Claude. Then he caught himself. He was already becoming far too attached to the children. He mustn't nurture the attachment, for they were most certainly dying. And when they did, it would destroy him if he weren't careful.

Ah, but it was unfair that they should die. "I'll tell you truthfully," he said, turning to face Father Tomas with fists clenched at his sides, "if I thought that believing in God would save these children I'd do it in an instant. For that matter, if I thought believing in the Devil would do it, I'd willingly sell my soul to him as well—"

"For shame!" the priest interjected, making a quick sign of the cross. His rheumy eyes widened in outrage. "You don't think any such thing! Surely you are not such a blasphemous fool as to call upon the Devil—"

"I'm not calling upon the Devil. I merely said. . . . Damn it, forget what I said." There was no point in arguing with him, for their views would never coincide. With a frown, Victor walked to the cot they'd made up for him near the window and sat down on the edge of it. He scrubbed his hands over his face. "I'm tired, Father. I don't know what I'm saying."

That seemed to mollify the priest somewhat, for he moved up beside Victor and laid a hand on his shoulder. "I know, my son. You've had little more than one good night's sleep altogether in the last three nights. You must rest. The children are sleeping now, and you can do naught else for them but wait. I'll watch over them, and if there's a change, I'll awaken you."

Although Victor knew Father Tomas was right, he hesitated to follow his suggestion. The man was nearly seventy and liable to fall asleep on his watch. Victor would never forgive himself if there was a change in one of the children's condition, and he slept through it. On the other hand, he'd be of damned little use to anyone if he didn't get some sleep.

"Go on," the priest urged. "Sleep. 'Tis the best thing for you now."

Victor needed no more encouragement than that. Drawing off his boots, he lay down on the moss-stuffed mattress and stretched out his long legs. Father Tomas took a seat in a chair beside one of the children's beds, then began to pray.

Knowing that the priest meant his show of devotion to be an admonition to Victor for his words, Victor gritted his teeth, then turned his head toward the closed window above the cot. He stared out at the night, at the star-laden heavens and the radiant moon that was nearly full as it dropped to earth.

Usually it comforted him to watch the moon, to note its position and size each night. The rhythm of its waxing and waning reminded him of the cycle of life, of birth and death. It helped him keep his perspective and not be overwhelmed by the pain and suffering he witnessed every day.

Tonight, however, the moon gave him no comfort, for it also reminded him how he'd wished on it as a boy, wished naively to someday have parents. It had taken him the course of a very painful childhood to discover that no supernatural talisman—be it God or the Devil or even the inconstant moon—could change the immutable facts of life.

Nor could they change the fate of these children. No matter how much he prayed or cursed or even wished on the moon, he feared the children would soon be dead. And there wasn't a damned thing he could do about it.

Victor stood in the midst of a desert. Above him was the moon; before him yawned a huge pit. Fire skittered up its sides, stretching hot fingers toward him. And Satan himself, resplendent in robes of hot coals and wearing a strangely familiar face, beckoned to him from beneath the earth.

He tried to stand very still, to ignore the gesturing hand. But he was so cold and the fire looked so warm. His feet moved forward against his will. They edged nearer to the pit, nearer to the fire that would bring relief from the icy cold seizing his body. Nearer he crept against his will, nearer . . . nearer . . .

Victor bolted up in bed, his body drenched in a cold sweat. He shook his head violently, trying to clear it. It was only a dream, he repeated to himself. That damned priest's blathering had addled his brains and caused the dream.

But he *was* cold. He glanced at the window. No wonder he was cold. It was open, the window and the door as well, letting in the cool night air. Who had opened them? His gaze swung to the priest, but just as Victor had expected, Father Tomas was asleep in his chair.

Suddenly, a movement behind the bed nearest him arrested his attention, and he lifted his gaze to stare into the face of a young woman he didn't know. Was he still dreaming? He'd never seen a woman quite like her. Draped in a shawl of jet-black lace, she wore a fawn homespun skirt and a tight-fitting jacket of the same color, only in plaid, with carved bone buttons. It was the kind of clothing he'd seen Indian women wear at the market.

But despite her dark skin, which was the creamy color of cafe au lait, she didn't look like an Indian. Her hair was fire itself, a curtain of shimmering copper that fell nearly to her hips. And her face . . . ah, such a face he'd never beheld, either in France or New Orleans. Her lips were round and full, her cheeks russet and growing even more russet as he stared. And her eyes were a solemn brown beneath a fringe of long lashes a shade darker than her hair.

"Who are you?" He swung his legs over the edge of the cot. Then he noticed that she was bathing the forehead of one of the boys with a damp cloth, and his tone sharpened. "Who are you? What are you doing with my patient?"

She stopped her motion. With a glance at the sleeping priest, she said, "My name is Lilith McCurtain. I'm a healer."

"Ah." Understanding came over him at once. Wearily, he rubbed his stubbled chin. "I suppose Father Tomas called for you."

She looked startled. Then she ducked her head and continued bathing the boy's brow. "I came because I was called, yes."

Victor groaned. Father Tomas had obviously lost faith in Victor's ability to heal the children, and who could blame him? That the priest had called a native healer for the children while Victor slept didn't surprise him at all.

It did worry him, however. Healers were unpredictable. Some of them dispensed useful advice about herbal remedies, but others offered only nonsense with it. For the latter, magic and superstition were as much a part of their work as healing, and he wanted none of that here.

It also bothered him that he hadn't heard her name before. Usually, doctors heard about the healers and midwives in the area almost as soon as they arrived. Then again, this woman looked far too young to have been working as a healer very long. She couldn't be older than twenty, a good seven years younger than he.

Leaving the damp cloth on the boy's forehead, she turned to where a rough-hewn wooden bowl of what looked like tea sat on the bedside table. She dipped a spoon in the bowl, then dribbled a few drops between the lips of the barely conscious patient. She watched until she saw the boy swallow. Then she filled the spoon again and repeated the process.

"What is it you're giving him to drink?" Victor asked as he rose from the cot.

"An infusion of bayberry and bread mold."

"Bayberry for fever, yes. I think this fever may be too high for bayberry to do much good, although it's worth a try, I suppose. But bread mold?" He raised one eyebrow. "Of what good is bread mold?"

Expecting her to spout some nonsense about mold being connected with the earth or having the power to drive out demons, he was surprised by her answer.

"I've found that the mold that forms on brandy-soaked bread can be very effective in curing ills nothing else will cure," she said.

It was a bizarre treatment at best, and a dangerous one at worst. "I don't know if you should experiment with such a thing on these children," he said firmly, moving toward her to stay her hand.

But before he could, she fixed him with a contemptuous glance and moved away from the bed to stand beside him. She lowered her voice to a murmur. "They are dying. You know that, don't you?"

He glared at her. Though he wanted to deny it, he couldn't.

Taking his silence for a yes, she glanced at the sleeping child before going on. "They're dying, and you can't help them. So why not let me try?"

"You think *you* can cure them?"

"It's possible, yes. Isn't it worth it to let me try?"

He scanned the room, noting the frail, weak bodies and the stillness that was a harbinger of death's approach. Much as he hated to admit it, she had a point. It wasn't as if the children had any other chance of survival. If they died of her remedies, it would be no worse than dying of the illness. It might even spare them some pain.

"All right. Do what you can, though I doubt it will make any difference. They are too far gone already."

"Perhaps. Perhaps not." With a little twist of her pretty head, she went back to the bed and began feeding the child the tea once more.

A cold breeze swept through the room, making him shudder. "Were you the one who opened the windows?"

"Yes."

"You shouldn't have done that," he grumbled as he headed back to the open window. "The children have fever and the night air isn't going to help that any."

"Leave it open!" she cried as he put his hands on the edge of the window. When he turned to look at her, she tilted her chin up. "Answer me this. Do you extinguish smoldering coals with a burning log? Of course not. Nor should you further inflame a fever with heat, but cool it with water and night air."

He hesitated with his hands on the window. His colleagues had always debated the proper method of treating a fever. Drive it up until it broke? Or cool it down? He had tried driving it up, but it hadn't broken. Perhaps it wouldn't hurt to try something different.

He left the window open. Returning to the bed that held the child she was feeding, he laid his hand on the boy's forehead.

The fever did seem lower, although only a little. Still, it was more improvement than he'd seen since he'd come here.

He started to smooth back a lock of the child's thick dark hair, but stopped himself, turning away from the bed.

"Why did you do that?" she asked. "Why did you hesitate to touch him?"

"I didn't hesitate to touch him," he muttered, irritated that she should have noticed his gesture.

"Yes, you did. It's because you're wary of him, isn't it? Wary of letting him into your heart when he is so near to death."

He covered his astonishment at her perception with a sharp look. "And what would you know of it? How many children have you watched die?"

She paled. "I have . . . watched a child die, I assure you."

"What, you weren't able to save him?" His tone was too derisive, but he couldn't help it. Her confidence in her ability to succeed where he'd failed had sorely roused his temper.

Averting her gaze from his, she whispered, "It was a baby girl. And no. I couldn't save her. But at least I gave her comfort as she died. The soul needs comfort in such an hour."

The soul. She was as bad as Father Tomas. That was probably why the priest had sent for her. "I give my patients comfort."

"You give your patients help for their bodies, but I doubt you give them much comfort."

He scowled at her. Who was this woman, this purveyor of dubious cures, to come in here and tell him such nonsense? He was as good a doctor as he could be under the circumstances. "What do you know of me or my patients?"

"Don't misunderstand me. I've heard that you're a competent physician." Lifting her head, she stared at him in a way that made him think she could see into his very soul. It was extremely unsettling. "You don't do foolish things like bleed the life from your patients or cup them to add to their pain. You dispense excellent medicines and you're generally very good at assessing what ails them."

"Generally?" he said with a good deal of sarcasm.

She shrugged. "Not all ailments are of the body. Some are of the heart or mind. Those you aren't so good at assessing."

The heart and the mind indeed! What did she want of him? That he read palms and divine illnesses from the stars? "You have a very strange image of me indeed, which is amazing, considering that I've never laid eyes on you before."

She fed the child more tea. "I know all about you, Dr. Drouet. Gossip about the new doctor spreads quickly in such a small place. I know you came to New Orleans from Paris two months ago, and I know you have a vast education."

"An education sorely lacking in some areas, if I'm to believe you."

"Education is more than books and experiments. You still have much to learn about healing the sick."

He bristled at that. "And you plan to teach me."

The solemn glance she shot him made him catch his breath. Once again, it was as if she laid bare his every thought, hope, and feeling. He groaned. He was letting the moon and the priest's superstitious words get to him. She was only a woman. A woman with strange ideas and a vastly inflated view of her abilities.

Then she returned her attention to her patient. "I will teach you if you wish. If you're ready to learn."

He gave a harsh laugh. "It'll be a lifetime before I'm ready to learn your particular sort of nonsense."

"As you wish." Then she lifted her even gaze to him. "Do you think, however, you could put aside your contempt for my 'nonsense' long enough to help me dispense this tea? The quicker it is in their bellies, the sooner it can work."

He started to refuse her, but caught himself. He'd already allowed her to administer her tea to the children. What difference did it make if he helped her? "Damn it, it's probably pointless, but I'll help you."

"Good. The tea is in there." She gestured to a pot on the table near the door. "Don't wake Father Tomas, however. He needs his rest."

That was one thing on which they agreed. Wondering if he were insane or simply desperate, Victor filled a bowl at the pot, then carried it and a spoon to one of the beds.

None of this had been in here before he fell asleep . . . the pot, the bowls, the spoons. And it would have taken her time to make the tea. She'd obviously made it at the orphanage kitchen, judging from its warmth.

"How long have you been here anyway?" he asked.

"A few hours."

At her words, he glanced out the window and realized that the sky was lightening. It must be near dawn already. "I didn't mean to sleep so long. You must have been very quiet not to have awakened me."

For the first time since he'd found her here, she smiled, a smile so soft and delicate, it reminded him of moonlight. It took him entirely by surprise.

"I could tell that you needed to sleep. I'm only sorry you couldn't sleep longer."

He dipped the spoon in the bowl of tea and held it to Claude's lips. "Sleep was impossible. I had a bad dream." He regretted the words at once. He didn't want her questioning him about his dream. With her bent, she would see it as a frightening portent. And if she told Father Tomas of it, the old priest would only worry more about Victor's soul.

But whether she would have said anything or not, he never found out, for Elias, the child she was with, suddenly stirred and cried out, "Mama! Mama, where are you?"

"Shh," she crooned in a soft voice. Then she cupped Elias's cheek and began to hum a low tune, something haunting and deep that seemed to satisfy him, for he sighed and lapsed back into sleep, the worry on his brow smoothing out as she stroked his hair.

A sudden sharp pain clutched Victor's heart as he watched her. How many times as a child had he awakened in the orphanage, crying out for his mother? In those days, he would have given anything to have someone touch his cheek and sing to him. But the priests had been no more inclined to coddle children than Father Tomas. They'd only been concerned with his moral and physical well-being.

This was what she'd meant when she'd spoken of giving

comfort, wasn't it? And she was right about him. He'd never sought to give his patients comfort as she was doing. He didn't even know how.

She seemed to feel him watching her, for she lifted her head and met his gaze with her own, although she continued humming to the child. In that instant, something shifted inside him. With a shock he realized that he desired her.

He desired her in the most primeval way, despite her brazen assessment of his doctoring and despite her strange looks and even stranger manner of healing. He wanted to lay her down on the cot and lose himself inside her. He wanted to find out why her shining eyes set all his senses on fire.

It was a sobering and disturbing revelation. With an inward curse, he wrenched his gaze from her, returning it to the child before him. Obviously, he hadn't had enough sleep. Otherwise, how could he be standing amidst these dying children and lusting after a woman whom he didn't even know?

But he was, and there was no changing that fact. The only cure for it was to turn his attention elsewhere, to the child in front of him.

For the next hour, he did just that. He didn't speak to her, and she didn't speak to him, although she crooned and sang to the children. She had a lovely voice, full and round like a viol's hum. When she sang of the river, he heard the rushing current, and when she sang of the stars, the notes were as delicate and airy as starlight itself. He tried not to listen, but it was impossible, for her voice captivated him.

Unfortunately, her voice did something else as well. It awakened Father Tomas from his sound sleep. Victor didn't realize it, however, until the priest let out a cry that was half-angry, half-fearful.

Victor whirled around, shocked to see the priest staring at Lilith and making the sign of the cross. "What in God's name—" Victor began.

"Dr. Drouet!" the priest exclaimed as he shot out of his chair. "What is she doing here? That . . . that woman! Why is she touching my children?"

"She's the healer you called." Victor glanced at Lilith, who seemed to be waiting in stoic silence, though her hands trembled.

"*I* called?" The priest's voice rose to a high-pitched cry. "That *I* called? I didn't call this . . . this creature here!"

"But she told me that her name is Lilith McCurtain and that you—" He broke off, remembering her exact words— *Yes, I was called.* By whom or what she hadn't said. His voice hardened. "Isn't she a healer? Did she lie?"

"A healer? Mayhap some call her that." The priest's eyes were full of venom as he stared at Lilith. "But that isn't what she is." He faced Victor, his posture rigid. "Don't you remember the woman I told you of, the one who lives on the edge of the swamp, the one who murdered young Sophie Jourdan a year ago?" He thrust one bony finger in Lilith's direction. "This is she! Lilith McCurtain!"

Father Tomas dropped his voice to a whisper, but his words seemed louder than a shout. "She is the one we call 'the Witch.' "

CHAPTER TWO

Trying to remain calm, Lilith watched the young doctor. What would he do? No doubt he'd heard of the Witch, for people gossiped about her a great deal. They never called her by her true name, however, which was probably why he'd shown no sign of recognizing it when she'd spoken it to him.

He did seem to have heard of her. But she noticed that although he now regarded her with suspicion, he didn't seem to share the priest's fear.

"Is the father speaking the truth about you?" he asked.

She tilted her chin up. "That I am a witch?"

"No, damn it! I don't believe in witches. Is it true you murdered a child?"

She chose her words carefully. "If arriving too late to save a child is murdering it, then I did. Otherwise, I'm blameless of Sophie's death."

"Blameless?" the priest exploded. "Why, you cursed Sophie Jourdan! Henry heard you speak the curse just before his daughter died!"

Ignoring the priest, she turned to Dr. Drouet. "I told the child's mother exactly what I was doing." But Henry had been set against her. Only she knew why, though she could never tell. "I didn't curse Sophie. I only said a chant that *alikchi*—medicine men—use to ease the dying as they journey into the next life."

"Medicine men!" the priest protested, but Dr. Drouet held

his hand up, his eyes never wavering from hers. ''Are you an Indian then?''

She bristled at the general term for her people. ''My mother was Choctaw and one of the *alikchi*. My father was a Scottish trapper. I am what your people call a half-breed.''

''You see?'' Father Tomas cried. ''She's a pagan, full of witchery and potions! I don't want her anywhere near my boys!''

The doctor scowled as he turned to the priest. ''Is she a good healer? Has she cured anyone you know?''

The question seemed to confuse Father Tomas. Apparently, he didn't find it relevant. ''Some claim to benefit from her remedies, and the trappers give her food for them but . . .'' He sniffed. ''None of that matters. Don't you see? If she saves their bodies, but takes their souls, they are lost!''

Dr. Drouet raked his hand through his golden hair. '' 'Tis not their souls I'm concerned with, Father Tomas. I care for their bodies. And right now, I could use the help of a healer with a good reputation.'' To her surprise, he turned a wan smile on her. ''Even if she is a witch.''

''God have mercy on your soul!'' The priest was so full of outrage, it boiled over into his reddening countenance. ''You must send this woman away at once, before you sink more into blasphemy! Don't you see, my son? You called upon the Devil last night, and he sent the Witch! Don't you know that Lilith is the name of Satan's wife and the demon who murders children? And this Lilith before you has no husband or children of her own. That's why she preys on other people's children. If you harbor her, she'll murder the children and take their souls! She may take your soul as well!''

Lilith struggled to contain her anger. It would do no good to rail against the priest, but she hated hearing him speak such lies of her. And all unfounded! She'd never done anything to harm the priest in her life! Why must he attack her?

What if the doctor believed him? What if he remembered her evasive words—*I was called*—and believed her a demon, too?

Dr. Drouet searched her face, as if he sought for answers

there. But when he spoke, it was clear he'd decided he didn't need them. "*I* am the doctor here, Father Tomas, and you know quite well you're lucky to find one who'll treat the children for free. I'll be the one to decide who helps me with the children. At the moment, Miss McCurtain's help is welcome."

Relief swamped Lilith. So the cold-eyed doctor had taken her side, had he, despite all her criticism of him? It certainly wasn't because he believed in her remedies. No, he was merely contemptuous of the priest's fears and superstitions, just as he'd been contemptuous of her ideas about healing the mind and heart. He only believed in what he could see. More was the pity, for he seemed a good healer otherwise.

"And suppose I tell Monsieur Marigny of this outrage," the priest hissed.

The mention of the man who was the most powerful in the territory struck a shiver through Lilith. Marigny, of all people, would disapprove of her involvement.

But the doctor merely shrugged. "I don't care what you do. Go to Marigny if you wish."

"If you won't make the woman leave, then I *will* go to Marigny!" the priest retorted. "He won't tolerate this! He'll make you see sense, even if I cannot!"

With those words, the priest hurried from the room. They heard him outside in the courtyard, calling for his mule and rousing half the household. But they both remained silent until he was gone. Then Dr. Drouet muttered a curse and went to stand by the window, staring out at the early dawn.

The dull orange light caught on his bright hair, making it shine. It reminded her of a long-forgotten tale from her childhood, about the sky warrior who dragged the moon up from the earth into the heavens every night, then back down before morn. With his hair like starlight and eyes the cool blue of sky, Dr. Drouet even fit her image of the sky warrior.

But he was obviously a very tired sky warrior. He wore no coat, his shirt and sober black waistcoat were wrinkled, and he'd dispensed with a cravat entirely. The dark smudges under his eyes attested to several days with little sleep. How long had the poor man been here anyway?

Suddenly he slammed his fist against the windowsill, making her start.

"Dr. Drouet, are you all right?" she asked timidly.

He ignored her question. "Damn that foolish priest! He had to go to Marigny, blast him! I hope Marigny throws him out on his ear!"

Twisting a hank of her shawl about her hand, she crept closer to the window. "Why did he think Monsieur Marigny would have a say in what you do?"

His fingers formed a fist. "Marigny is my patron."

"Patron?" She came up to stand beside him at the window.

"He pays me a fee to care for his family . . . and those he enslaves." His voice held a hint of self-deprecation. "You might say that I work for him. In a way."

His profile showed him to be a strong man, the jaw tough and unyielding beneath the three days' crust of blond beard and the mouth set with determination. This wasn't a man who bent his will easily to another. So why had he bent it to Monsieur Marigny? "I don't understand. If you don't wish to be his doctor—"

A harsh laugh guttered up from his throat. "Wishing has nothing to do with it, not if I want to eat. When I arrived here, I had no money. Building a practice takes time, and I needed funds to carry me through until I could survive on my own. Then Marigny, after receiving a letter of recommendation for me from a friend in France, asked me to be his physician. At first I hesitated, for I abhor the practice of slavery, and Marigny has many slaves." He sighed. "But one cannot eat moral principles. So when he offered me a substantial fee, gave me a horse, and promised to help me establish my practice, I accepted."

"I see." He wasn't the only doctor who made such arrangements. New doctors often agreed to be a planter's only doctor in exchange for a yearly fee. It didn't prevent the doctor from treating other people, but part of the agreement specified that the planter's family and slaves took priority. "Then you can't afford to lose Monsieur Marigny's patronage."

"I shan't lose Monsieur Marigny's patronage over this.

He's more enlightened than Father Tomas.'' The morning sun now lit his face, showing every line etched there by worry and lack of sleep. "But Marigny also doesn't like trouble. He likes to keep up the appearance of being a devout man. It won't do to have Father Tomas accuse me of blasphemy.''

"Perhaps you would prefer that I leave, after all.''

"Nay.'' He swung around to face her, his crystalline blue eyes softening. "I'm sorry. I didn't mean to concern you with my troubles. You must stay. You're the only one so far who's helped these children.''

He led her to the bedside of the nearest child. Placing her hand on the boy's forehead, he said, "You see? His fever is already lower. I've been unable to accomplish that. How can I ask you to leave when you seem to be their only hope?'' He smiled and she felt the warmth of it to the tips of her toes. "Besides,'' he added, "you give them comfort.''

She smiled back at him, pleased that he'd taken her earlier words to heart. After a moment, she realized that his callused hand still covered hers. Then he began to trace each of her fingers with his thumb.

Her smile disappeared as she remembered the last time a man had touched her. Her instinct was to jerk her hand away, but she hesitated to do so. She couldn't afford to anger him, not if she wanted to stay and care for the boys.

He's not hurting you, she assured herself. *Let him touch your hand if he wishes. It means nothing.*

But she knew better. He was staring at her hand now, and there was something very disturbing in his eyes. Nor was he the only one affected. A faint fluttery feeling had begun in her belly and it frightened her.

He turned her hand over and stroked her palm. "Your skin is so soft. Not at all what I would have expected.'' He looked up at her, and she froze. There was desire in his eyes. Most assuredly.

She snatched her hand away, but regretted her panicky reaction almost at once. *Never let them see your fear,* she told herself. *Never let them know.*

"Why shouldn't my hands be soft?'' she managed to say.

"Am I not a woman like other women? Or have you decided that I am indeed a witch?"

Crossing his arms over his chest, he leaned back against the wall between the beds. "I didn't mean that. But Father Tomas said you had no husband, and thus no one to do the hard labor of a household. Women forced to do such things for themselves generally have roughened hands."

"Perhaps you think my hands stay soft by magic."

"Ah, but then I'd have to believe you a witch, wouldn't I?"

She had the feeling he was teasing her, but she couldn't be sure. Few men ever teased her. "Don't you believe I'm a witch?"

"I don't know. Are you?"

Dropping her gaze from him, she hesitated. Though he'd said earlier that he didn't believe in witches, surely some part of him did. Everyone believed in witches. Even her mother's people believed in the *stahullo*, who cursed people unto death. But she was not *stahullo*, and though part of her wanted to lie and tell him she was, to make him fear her, another part didn't want him to think her evil. Or regard her with contempt either.

She sighed. "I practice the ways of my ancestors—both Choctaw and Scottish. I believe in the powers of the earth and the moon, in rituals more ancient than the people of this land. If you and your priest think that makes me a witch, then I am one." Her expression grew fierce. "But I'm not *stahullo*. I'm not an evil, malevolent woman who curses children."

"I didn't think you were."

At that, her gaze shot to his, and she was shocked by the intensity she found in his glittering ice eyes. He looked at her as if he wished to stop staring but couldn't, as if he found something in her that both steadied and alarmed him.

Men had looked at her like that before, but it had never affected her like this. The panic in her wanted him not to stare so. But the woman in her reveled in it. It made no sense. He was a man like other men, and not to be trusted. Yet she found herself wanting to trust him.

"I have a question for you." His voice seemed loud in the

stillness of the early morning. "Who called you here?"

"What?"

"You said that you were called here. Who called you? Why did you come?"

She shrugged. "Why do you wish to know? Do you think the Devil sent me here to take your soul?"

"I don't really care if he did or not, although if he did, he certainly chose well." Before she could question that strange statement, he added, "But you did say you were called, and I wish to know by whom." When she hesitated, he taunted her. "Unless that was just a lie to lull me into letting you treat the children when you knew Father Tomas wouldn't approve."

"It wasn't a lie." She paused, bending her head to the sleeping child. As she drew the covers over his little shoulders, she debated what to say. "But if I tell you who called me, you'll think I'm peculiar."

"I already think you're peculiar."

Her head shot up at that, but his smile took the sting from his words.

She glanced around the room. The children were sleeping, but that didn't mean they couldn't hear. She didn't want them thinking she was peculiar, too, or they would shrink from her. "Come outside with me, and I will tell you."

He said nothing, but followed her when she headed for the door.

Once they were in the courtyard, she said bluntly, "The children called me."

He gave her a blank stare. "I don't understand."

"I . . . I often hear the voices of those who need my help. Their spirits summon me in the night. And when I hear them, I go to them. If I can."

A look of profound skepticism crossed his face. "You hear voices?"

She held her head up proudly. "You shouldn't find that so strange. Your religion has Saint Joan, who heard God's voice commanding her to lead her country in battle."

"You're not Saint Joan. And you're not pretending to hear

God's voice either. Or did I misunderstand you?"

"I'm not pretending anything," she snapped. "I told you that you'd find it peculiar. You don't believe anything you can't see."

"That's true." Her observation didn't seem to disturb him in the least. "But I still want to hear about these voices of yours. Do they whisper in your head? Or do they come out of the darkness and shout at you?"

He was mocking her. She could tell. She moved a few feet away and stared across the courtyard to the closed wooden gate as she hugged herself in the cool night air. "I'm not insane, Dr. Drouet, no matter what you think."

"I'm sorry." His voice was softer now. "I shouldn't have teased you. But I do want to know about the voices."

Turning to look back at him, she saw he was in earnest. "I say the word *voices* because I have no other way of describing the summons. But it's not really voices so much as a steady clamoring." She pressed her hand to her heart. "Here, inside. I feel someone needing me, pulling at me as a babe's anxious cry pulls at its mother. Sometimes, the 'voice' is so demanding, it claws at me until I heed it. Sometimes, as with Sophie, it's a plaintive whisper that haunts me when I sleep. And occasionally, as with Sophie, I answer the call too late."

There had been other reasons for that, shameful reasons she couldn't reveal to him, much less remind herself of. Her voice cracked as she turned away. "When I come too late, there's nothing left but to ease the patient's way into the next world."

"And you're blamed for it when the patient dies, aren't you?"

Somehow she managed a nod.

Coming up beside her, he laid his hand on her arm. "Believe it or not, I know what that's like. I've lost a few patients myself. The doctor is nearly always blamed." His voice gentled. "Sometimes the doctor blames himself."

She was so lost in memory she scarcely felt the touch of his hand on her arm. Twisting the edges of her shawl, she saw again that terrible night . . . Rosemarie Jourdan keening over her daughter's bed, and Sophie . . . poor delicate Sophie coughing up blood. "Sophie was so little, and the illness so far along that—" She broke off with a sigh. "I should have saved her. If I'd come sooner, I could have."

"You can't blame yourself for that."

Yes, she could. She had only herself to blame.

"Is that why I haven't heard much about you as a healer?" he asked. "Because of what happened with the child?"

A shudder racked her. "Probably. Many people believed Henry Jourdan's story that I cursed Sophie. There was grumbling against me . . . and . . . and some even came to my house to burn it down."

"Superstitious fools," he bit out.

"In my anger and grief, I made it even worse. I threatened to put a curse on them all if they didn't leave. They were afraid enough of me to do so, but after that no one would . . . call for me when they had sick ones."

That hadn't put an end to the voices, however. They'd been just as insistent. Only she'd ignored them. For nearly a year now, she'd ignored them. She'd been afraid to help anyone, afraid and just a little too proud.

That had been foolish. Now she understood just how foolish.

"But how have you survived?" he asked. "If you can't work as a healer, and you have no husband—"

"I don't need a husband to survive." Drawing her shawl more tightly about her shoulders, she faced him. "I have a garden. I weave my own cloth. The trappers give me meat in exchange for my remedies and my homespun. I live very well by taking what I need from the earth, as my people have always done."

"But it must be lonely." He stepped closer, until she could feel his breath on her face. "Surely you miss human companionship."

His nearness unsettled her. He gave off a potent force that scattered her thoughts and jangled her emotions. She had sworn never to let another man this close, and yet here she was, incapable of moving away. "I . . . I never had much human companionship anyway. No one wants to keep company with a witch.''

''Surely when she is as beautiful as you, there are some who would want to keep company with a witch. Some men, in any case.''

His words roused a tumult of emotion in her. Yes, there'd been some . . . and one in particular. But none like Dr. Drouet.

She looked up at him, both fascinated and terrified by his gaze on her. Hot, wanton need emanated from him, and to her shock, an answering need spread within her. Like the sun rising over the swamp, it burned off the cold mist that had settled in her soul for more than a year.

He drew her toward him with the lightest touch of his hand on her arm. Then he lowered his head. He was going to kiss her. Some female instinct told her that.

She mustn't let him. Terrible things happened when a man kissed a woman. ''Wise men steer clear of women who might put a curse on them,'' she warned in a desperate attempt to frighten him away.

''Wise men?'' His lips were now a breath away from hers. ''Nay, such men are fools.'' And before she could protest further, his mouth was on hers.

If he had kissed her with force, she would have balked at once, but he confused her by kissing her gently. He swept his lips along hers like a vintner sampling wine, like a man who was only tasting, not devouring. His mouth was soft and coaxing, full of tenderness. He played upon her lips like the river plays upon rock. She was so absorbed in the unreal sensation that she scarcely noticed him drawing her into his arms, pulling her body against his.

But when the tenor of his kiss changed, became more demanding, more needy, she realized how close he held her. She wrenched her mouth from his and stared at him wide-eyed.

''Please don't, Dr. Drouet,'' she whispered.

''Victor.'' He kissed her cheek, then laid a trail of kisses along her hairline to her ear. ''Call me Victor,'' he whispered, his warm breath tickling her ear.

''Victor, you mustn't—'' she gasped, but he murmured a

few soothing words, gentling her, making her heart race. His tender words so lulled her fears that when he took her mouth again, she let him drink from it freely.

He ran his tongue along the seam of her lips, and it was so silky and soft that she opened her mouth to him. When he slipped his tongue between her lips, she moaned low in her throat, shocked to find that she liked it. His hands swept down her sides, along her ribs, over her hips, as if he sought to know her through touch. And all the while his kiss possessed her, his tongue finding hers and playing with it, teasing it until she thought she'd go mad.

The sensations he conjured up were like nothing she'd ever known. Her breath seemed to have stopped completely, and her heart beat like the wings of a bird caught in the trapper's snares. The pulse of the earth itself seemed to pour through her veins, an ancient rhythm so insistent she lost herself in it.

Then he brought his hands up over her breasts, and she was jolted from the web of pleasure he'd woven around her. It was happening all over again . . . he was going to hurt her . . . he would hurt her . . .

She tore her lips from him, but when she tried to pull away, he tightened his arms about her waist. Now his real purpose was clear, she thought. He would hurt her! She pushed at his chest, frantic to get away. "You must . . . let go of me!"

"I don't want to let go of you." He nuzzled her hair, his breath coming hard and fast. "Not yet."

"Let go!" She shoved him hard, breaking free as he stumbled back a step.

He stared at her in astonishment, seeming to notice for the first time the full extent of her distress. "My God, what did I do?"

She backed away, wild-eyed. *Don't let him see you're afraid,* she told herself. *That's when men hurt you, when they see you're afraid.*

"Lilith? What—"

"You can't just paw me and put your hands on me any time you want!"

A change came over his face, a deadening of his expression

that was worse than any anger. "I'm sorry. You seemed to want—I didn't realize you regarded my touch as pawing."

She felt a tiny bit of shame. He hadn't hurt her. He hadn't even tried to force her. But that didn't mean he wouldn't have. "I'm not what everyone thinks I am!" Her voice dropped to a whisper. "I'm not a whore to be taken at will—"

"For God's sake, I don't think you're a whore." He ran his fingers through his hair. His eyes were slashes of ice in his rigid face. "I'm sorry. It was a mistake. I shouldn't have touched you. I only wanted. . . ." He trailed off, his mouth a grim line. "I just shouldn't have touched you."

That he was giving up so easily confused her. But she wouldn't back down until she was sure he wouldn't harm her. "Aye, you shouldn't have touched me! I have cursed men unto death for doing less!" It was a lie, of course, but it was the only weapon she had.

And the wrong weapon for a skeptic like him. Anger flared in his eyes as he advanced on her. "I'm not afraid of your curses, Lilith. And when I refrain from touching you in the future, it certainly won't be out of fear that some demon will crawl up from hell to carry me off at your bidding!"

She shrank back from him and came up hard against the wall.

He stopped short of her, his eyes blazing in his face. "Don't assume I'm as stupid and superstitious as the other fools who cower at your curses. I'm not a fool." Taking her chin in his hand, he lifted her head, though she tried to turn away. "If you don't want me touching you, then say so, and I'll refrain. Just don't insult my intelligence with parlor tricks!"

She braced herself for what would come next, for how he would punish her for spurning his kiss. But when he didn't, when he just muttered an oath and spun away from her to go back inside the infirmary, she felt ashamed that she'd acted like such a fool. She slid down the wall until she was crouching beside it.

And the curse she whispered then was not for him. It was for herself.

CHAPTER THREE

Wearing the same scowl he'd worn all morning, ever since he'd kissed Lilith, Victor poured some of Lilith's fragrant tea into a bowl. Every time he thought of how she'd gone from melting in his arms to placing curses on him, he saw red.

He wasn't so much angry at her as at himself. What had come over him? Why had he kissed the woman? He still didn't know all the details of Sophie Jourdan's death, and Lilith might have been lying about it besides.

Even if she was innocent of the child's death, however, he shouldn't have kissed her . . . or fondled her. For God's sake, he'd fondled her right there in the courtyard where anyone could have seen them! He didn't blame her for being outraged. Any other woman would have slapped his face.

Still, it infuriated him to be treated like all the other superstitious dolts—to have her throw curses at him, trying to scare him. No wonder Father Tomas feared her. If she were always so quick to play on people's fears, she had probably put half the town in terror of her.

Father Tomas. That fool. He glanced out at the bright day. It was midmorning, and still the priest hadn't appeared. Then again, he had a long ride to Marigny's plantation by mule. Once there, Father Tomas might be asked to stay and break his fast, thus delaying him further. Then the ride back. It might be noon before the man returned.

When he did return, however, he'd be shocked by the change wrought in the infirmary. Victor hated to admit it, but Lilith's infusions and her soothing touch seemed to have wrought a miracle. Four of the seven boys had rallied enough to drink the tea without help, and the other three had at least stopped vomiting. They all had a touch of fever still, but it wasn't life-threatening anymore. Though he was afraid to hope too much too soon, he believed they might recover fully.

And if they did, it would all be due to her.

Maybe she is a witch indeed, he thought sourly. *She certainly has an uncanny ability to snatch the living out of the arms of Death.*

"Dr. Drouet," croaked a young voice from a nearby bed. It was Elias.

Victor looked around for Lilith, but she was with another of the children. Taking the bowl of tea with him, he moved to Elias's side. "How are you feeling?" He laid his hand on Elias's forehead. It was warm, but not hot, a good sign.

Despite his lips cracked from fever, Elias managed a pout. "My neck hurts."

"I know." He helped Elias sit up, then handed him the bowl of tea. "But if you'll sip this tea and rest, it will stop hurting soon." Or he hoped so, anyway.

Elias pushed the bowl away. "I don't like that tea. It tastes like piss."

Despite his own foul mood, Victor smiled. From what Father Tomas had told him, Elias was a relatively new addition to the orphanage. Before dying of yellow fever, his American mother had been a prostitute to the Spanish soldiers. That would explain his frankness. And his vocabulary.

"How would you know what piss tastes like? Unless you've been drinking it, which would explain why you got sick in the first place."

"I ain't been drinking piss," Elias answered in a sullen tone. "But I bet it tastes like this."

"Perhaps." Victor held the bowl of tea out again. "But the tea is what's making you feel better, so you'd best be a good boy and drink it all down."

Although Elias took the bowl from Victor, he obviously wasn't happy about it, for he scowled in that peevish way only sick five-year-old boys could. Then he stared across the room to where Lilith was singing to Claude. "I'll drink my tea if *she* gives it to me."

Victor started to tell Elias that he'd best drink that tea or find it poured down his throat, but one look at the little boy's hopeful face scotched that. "I'll see if she can come over here."

"And tell her to sing me a song," Elias added as Victor moved away from the bed. "I kinda like her singin'. She sings real pretty."

A peculiar tightness gripped Victor as he slid around the edge of the bed. Yes, she sang "real pretty," prettier than anything Victor had ever heard. And damned if he didn't wish it was him she sang for. Chastising himself for being such a fool, he crossed the room to her.

He waited while she finished singing to Claude, whose face was rapt as he listened. Victor scanned the room and realized that all the boys wore the same expression. She'd bewitched the lot of them, hadn't she? They were half in love with their angel of mercy already.

How could they not be? Look at what she'd done for them. More than he'd done, that was for sure.

As Lilith finished her song and bent to kiss Claude's forehead, the tightness in his chest grew almost painful. Claude was a fortunate little boy, Victor thought. To be gifted with one of Lilith's kisses . . .

"What's wrong?" Lilith asked, looking up at him.

What's wrong, he thought, *is that I want you beyond reason.* But all he said was, "Elias won't drink his tea unless you give it to him. And sing him a song."

She bit back a smile. "Of course. I'll be right there, as soon as I go to the kitchen and put on another pot of water to boil."

"I'll tell him."

He watched as she went out the door, her beautiful hair swinging about her lithe hips. Then feeling even more disgruntled, he returned to Elias.

"Miss McCurtain will be here in a moment. I tell you what. Since she's promised me that she'll sing a song for you, why don't you go ahead and drink your tea? That way you'll be ready when she comes."

Elias cast Victor a distrustful look. "I ain't drinking it until she sings a song."

"Fine." Victor took the bowl from Elias and set it down on the bedside table. "Then let me examine you while we're waiting for her."

He drew back the covers and began to press Elias's abdomen, checking the internal organs, but his thoughts went once more to the kiss he'd shared with Lilith.

It wasn't as if she'd deliberately enticed him. She hadn't given him the coy looks of the prostitutes in the old quarter or the sly ones of the Spanish wives at the few public balls he'd attended. She'd just been herself, and that had been enough.

Worse yet, her rebuff hadn't dampened his desire. Not one whit. He wished it had. It would have made the morning less uncomfortable. Even now, after several backbreaking hours of feeding the children her tea and bathing their foreheads, he wanted her with an intensity he'd never felt for any other woman.

Not that he'd never lain with a woman. He'd had his share of sexual encounters, both in France and in New Orleans. But none of them had ever been anything more than a mutual satisfaction of physical urges.

What he felt for Lilith was different. Though sexual attraction played a part in it—who could not be entranced by her hair of spun copper and her bewitching eyes?—there was something else about her that captivated him. For one thing, she had the strength of character not to buckle under Father Tomas's absurd insults. Another woman might have burst into tears and fled the room at being called Satan's wife. Not Lilith. Her purpose was to heal, and that's what she did, no matter what obstacles were placed in her path.

Yet he also sensed an incredible fragility beneath her

strength. Someone had wounded her deeply once, and so she protected herself with her curses.

He gave a bitter smile. Or was he merely telling himself that because he was angry over her rebuff? Perhaps she wasn't fragile at all. Perhaps she merely disliked him.

"Ouch!" Elias cried, and Victor jerked.

Damn! He was certainly letting the woman get to him. "Sorry," he mumbled.

Someone came up beside him and he knew it was Lilith by the scent of bayberry. "Is everything all right?" she asked.

"He's poking me," Elias said crossly.

"I'm sorry, poppet, but he has to poke you a little," Lilith answered. "How else can he make sure your insides aren't loose and rolling around in your belly?"

Little Elias's eyes went wide. "Oh. I guess that's all right then."

Victor looked at her with one eyebrow raised, and she grinned. He finished examining Elias, then pulled the covers up to the boy's waist.

"Don't you think it's time for a break, Dr. Drouet?" she asked as he handed her the bowl of tea.

"It's Victor, remember?"

A becoming blush stained her cheeks. "Yes. Victor." She dropped her gaze. "Father Tomas's servants have brewed coffee in the kitchen, and I thought you might like some. After I've taken care of Elias, we could get it and come right back, if you wish."

He ran his fingers through his already disheveled hair. Casting a glance at Elias, he lowered his voice. "Won't they mind giving coffee to 'the Witch'?"

His sarcastic words made her color again. "They aren't as ... superstitious as Father Tomas."

"In that case, I could use some coffee." Victor waited while she sang Elias a song and watched the boy drink the bowl of tea. Then he offered her his arm, feeling an absurd pleasure when after a moment's hesitation she took it.

In silence, they went out into the courtyard and crossed to the small building that held the orphanage's kitchen and dining room. When they entered, an old Creole with wiry black hair and weathered brown skin was waiting with a pot of coffee he'd kept heating on the stove. After he'd poured them each a cup, Victor added a generous dollop of sugar and milk to his. Coffee in France had never been as strong as it was in New Orleans, where the Creoles often claimed that their coffee was "black as the Devil, hot as hell, sweet as love, strong as death."

He noticed, however, that Lilith drank hers as black as it had been brewed. "How can you drink it like that?" he murmured.

She shrugged. "Black coffee has more power to it."

He smiled. Some doctors claimed that coffee was restorative, even medicinal. And maybe for her, it was.

They lapsed into an awkward silence as they walked back from the kitchen with their cups. Only when they'd neared the infirmary door did she speak. "Tell me something, Dr. Drouet. Why did you leave Paris, a doctor like you, with great education and skill? Surely you would have been better appreciated in a place where great lords and ladies could make use of your services."

An acid smile crossed his face as they reentered the infirmary. "I'm afraid all the great lords and ladies were too busy having their heads cut off to spend much time visiting physicians."

When she looked confused, he realized she couldn't possibly know about the Revolution. She had no traffic with the sort of people who discussed French affairs. And he didn't want to tell her about it either. The memories of that horrible time were still too painful. He racked his brain for a simpler answer, and finally decided on what was mostly the truth. "I left Paris because I had nothing to keep me there."

"What of your family?"

"I have no family. My mother died when I was only four, and my father . . . didn't wish to care for me." Trying to hide the pain that always hit him at the thought of his father, he gestured to the boys around them. "I grew up in an orphanage like these urchins."

A soft sympathy spread over her face. "It must have been hard for you to lose both parents at once. I suffered greatly when my parents died of the fever three years ago."

"You were lucky to have them for so long." He took a long sip of his heavily sweetened coffee. "In these difficult times, it seems rare indeed for someone to have two parents. Look at these children. Most of them are here because their parents abandoned them. Like my father abandoned me."

"That is why you're so afraid to give the children your heart, isn't it?" she said, almost to herself. "I suspect you don't trust anyone with your heart, because it was too badly broken when you were a boy."

He stiffened, wishing she were less frank. And less perceptive. "Then we make quite a pair, don't we?" he growled. "I won't trust anyone with my heart. And you won't trust anyone with your body."

The minute he said the words, he regretted them. He didn't want her knowing how much her earlier rebuff had affected him.

But she didn't react with the anger he expected. She halted, staring down into her now empty cup. "How right you are." Her voice was wistful, almost mournful. " 'Tis a sad thing when you can't trust anyone. A very sad thing indeed."

He would have pressed her then, but one of the children called to her and that put an end to their conversation.

What she'd said stayed with him, however. It was true he trusted no one. Then again, he'd never seen the need before. Besides, he had trusted her by letting her stay, hadn't he?

Nay, that wasn't quite true. He hadn't trusted her. He'd merely been desperate. A desperate man will grasp at any straw, even when he thinks the straw might break. It had nothing to do with trust, nothing whatsoever.

As for her, it was clear she trusted no one at all. But why? Because so many people treated her with fear and contempt? Or was there another reason? He hadn't treated her that way, yet she seemed even more reluctant to trust him.

He found himself watching her at odd moments, trying to delve beneath the impenetrable veil of mystery surrounding

her. And his interest in her was only heightened by their tight
quarters. In the cramped infirmary, he often had to squeeze
past her to reach one of the other patients. Many were the
accidental brushes of his hand against hers, and as the hours
wore on, he was pleased to see that she stopped flinching when
it happened. Once when he laid his hand on her waist to steady
her as he passed, she even smiled at him.

Before long she was all he could think of. Part of him was
engaged in dealing with the children, of course, but another
part of him was constantly wondering about her . . . while se-
cretly craving those furtive touches.

Thus the return of Father Tomas a little after noon came as
an unwelcome surprise, especially when the priest was accompanied by two stalwart slaves.

"Dr. Drouet," the priest announced in a superior tone as
soon as he and his companions had squeezed into the tiny
room. "I have spoken to Monsieur Marigny, and he has instructed me to tell you to send the Wi— . . . to send Miss
McCurtain home at once. We have no more need of her."

As Lilith went pale, Victor strode up to the priest. "Do we
not? Take a look around this room, Father Tomas. What do
you see?"

The priest scanned the room, blinking a few times. "I see
an infirmary full of sick children." His voice was unsteady.
"I see a room of souls to be saved."

Victor balled his hands into fists. "You see a room of *re-
covering* children. You see life where there was death! I wish
I could take credit for this miracle, but I can't. It's all because
of her." He pointed to Lilith. "Her! Lilith McCurtain!"

He moved up to the priest until he towered over the man.
"How dare you say we don't need her! It's thanks to her that
these children have a chance at life!"

Father Tomas's shoulders began to shake, but not with fear.
That was obvious at once. It was rage. "They may be better,
but at what cost? The loss of your soul? The loss of theirs?"

"You damned—" He caught himself before he could make
matters even worse. "She isn't a demon, and she hasn't come
to steal our souls! She's a healer! Like me! No, I take that

back . . . a healer *better* than me! And I won't have her cast from here just as the children are beginning to improve!''

The priest grabbed Victor's hands. ''Listen to what you're saying! You're putting this half-breed witch above yourself! Don't you see, my son? You've fallen into her trap! I know how it can happen, for the flesh is weak. But you must fight it!''

Victor snatched his hands away. ''You don't know what you're talking about! And I can't believe that Marigny would condone all of this superstition—''

'' 'Tis he who sent these men with me, to take her from here. We knew that you would not give her up easily.''

''Marigny sent these men?'' Victor went white. ''He means to have her taken from here by force?''

Behind him, he heard Lilith gasp, but Father Tomas ignored it. ''Monsieur Marigny understands the depths of her powers. He doesn't blame you for allowing her here. He knows how she bewitches men with her face, but—''

''That isn't what this is about!'' Victor shouted. ''And I won't let you—''

''I will go,'' Lilith interrupted. ''I shan't cause any more trouble for you, Dr. Drouet. You can give the children the tea yourself and—''

''No!'' Victor whirled to face her, feeling as if everything were crumbling around him. ''You mustn't leave them. They need you!''

''You can take care of them,'' she whispered, her eyes hollow in their anguish. ''It is best this way.''

The priest murmured some command to the two burly slaves, and they went to Lilith's side, each taking one of her arms.

''You can't do this! The children need her!'' Victor followed the men as they escorted her to the door. ''*I* need her!''

The words were out before he could stop them, and at once he felt Father Tomas's hand on his arm. ''You see how far you've fallen under her spell, my son? You must let her go. For the sake of your soul and the children's.''

Victor watched as Lilith shot him one last look, her face

filled with regret. And something much softer. Then the two men swept her through the door and to the wagon waiting outside.

For a moment, Victor was at a loss what to do. Even if he could fight the two men for her and succeed in bringing her back, Father Tomas would simply bring more men to take her next time. No, there was only one way to settle this.

He glanced around the room. The children had all just had their dose of tea, which Lilith had said to give them every three hours. In three hours, he could be to Marigny's and back.

Striding to the door, he snatched up his coat.

"Where are you going?" Father Tomas queried in a high-pitched voice.

"To Marigny's. I'll be back as soon as I can."

"Your place is here, my son. You mustn't let her possess you to the point that you'd abandon your patients."

Victor shot the priest a dire frown as he jerked on his coat. "If I let you take her from them, then I *am* abandoning my patients. And I refuse to watch them die after they have come so far."

CHAPTER FOUR

With growing impatience, Victor paced the drawing room. Upon his arrival, he'd been instructed that Marigny was at dinner and ordered to wait in the drawing room. He knew why he was kept waiting—as a reminder of who he was—a mere physician. But knowing it didn't ease his frustration. Nor did standing in the most lavish room in Marigny's spacious mansion, with its parqueted floors, imported French furniture, and priceless porcelain vases. The room was meant to impress visitors with Marigny's power and wealth, and despite himself, he felt its force.

Pierre Enguerrand Philippe de Marigny de Mandeville was New Orleans's most prominent citizen. Brother-in-law to a former governor of Louisiana and an intimate friend of the current Spanish governor, Marigny owned a vast amount of property and was the city's most powerful man. No one ever questioned his judgment on any matter.

And here Victor was, fully determined to do so. But he felt sure that Marigny would listen to him. Once the man heard a less tainted version of the events at the orphanage and was apprised of how the children were faring, Marigny would surely see Victor's side of things and order Father Tomas to accept Lilith's help.

The door swung open, and the great man himself entered the room, cane in hand. He walked toward Victor, wreathed in smiles, as if this were a social visit and he hadn't just made Victor wait for over an hour.

Pasting a smile on his face, Victor took Marigny's hand in greeting. As usual, Marigny was the very picture of the elderly statesman with his regal air and gold-tipped cane. He had a soft, wrinkled face that always wore an amiable expression, but Victor had learned early on that Marigny could be hard as steel when he wanted.

Taking a seat on one of the settees, Marigny gestured to Victor to sit, and Victor did so, then waited until they had exchanged the usual pleasantries and inquiries for one another's health before he launched into his business.

"Monsieur Marigny," he began, "I understand that Father Tomas was here earlier to discuss my accepting the help of a local healer—"

"Lilith McCurtain, you mean," Marigny interjected.

"Yes. Lilith McCurtain." He paused, choosing his words carefully. "I'm not sure what Father Tomas told you about what she was doing at the orphanage, but I thought you should hear of the good she has accomplished. Perhaps then you might convince Father Tomas to allow her return."

Marigny's countenance still wore its benevolent expression, but his eyes had darkened just a shade during Victor's speech. "Go on, Dr. Drouet," he said, his tone colder than before.

Victor leaned forward. "Last night I thought for certain I would be burying seven children today. Indeed, the father and I had already resigned ourselves to the fact that none of the boys would probably live. Their fevers were so high and they were so weak that all we could do was wait for them to die."

His voice deepened as he remembered waking up to find Lilith standing over Claude's bed. "We fell asleep, Father Tomas and I, and while we were sleeping, Lilith McCurtain came. She gave them a special tea, and she sang to them and coddled them and gave them a mother's tender care. When I left them two hours ago, they were so improved that four of them were sitting up and talking, and the other three were at least out of danger."

Victor looked for some change in Marigny's expression,

something that showed that he understood the significance of Victor's words. But Marigny simply continued to watch him with hard eyes, his smile now grown more forced.

"If it weren't for her, those children would be dead now." Anger sharpened Victor's tone. "No matter what Father Tomas claims, she is necessary to their improvement."

"That is not the issue," Monsieur Marigny said calmly.

Victor sat back against his chair with an oath. "Then what is? I'm a doctor, Monsieur Marigny, not a priest. My duty is to make sure my patients live, and since Lilith McCurtain has enabled me to do so, I'm not about to send her away simply because some superstitious priest thinks she's doing the work of the Devil!"

"This has nothing to do with superstition either," Marigny stood and went to the door of the drawing room. Opening it, he called for one of the servants, gave him a message in a low-voiced tone, then closed the door and returned to the settee. This time, however, instead of sitting, he moved past Victor to a small table where sat a decanter of red liquor.

He poured a glass, then held it up. "Some wine, Dr. Drouet?"

"No, thank you," Victor said through gritted teeth. Had nothing he'd said penetrated Marigny's thick head? He rose and rounded his chair to stand near Marigny at the fire. "What do you mean, this has nothing to do with superstition? It has everything to do with it! Father Tomas's foolish belief that Lilith is a witch is what's making him refuse to let her stay."

Marigny shot him a cool glance. "Think you that I share his superstitions?"

"I don't know," Victor snapped. "Do you?"

For the first time since Victor had arrived, anger showed in Marigny's face. "We aren't all the 'provincials' you take us for, Dr. Drouet. Father Tomas is indeed a foolish man, but I am not. Do you truly think I would have sent my men to aid him merely out of superstition? I assure you I didn't acquire my wealth by believing in witches and goblins, nor am I one to countenance such beliefs in others."

"Then why are you sending Lilith McCurtain away?"

"Because I know the woman better than you, sir."

A knock came at the door then, and Marigny called out, "Come in." When a burly man streaked with dirt and sweat entered the room, Marigny said, "Henry Jourdan, meet Dr. Drouet. Dr. Drouet, this is Henry Jourdan, my overseer."

Victor acknowledged the humbly dressed man with a nod of his head. He'd heard the name Jourdan before, but where? Then it dawned on him. Sophie Jourdan. Of course.

He surveyed Henry Jourdan, curious about the man who'd brought about Lilith's exile from society. Despite his size, the man looked harmless enough, clutching a straw hat and lowering his eyes as subordinates often did. He was younger than Victor would have expected, and handsome in a vacuous sort of way. But there was something scary about his eyes, something that reminded Victor of the fanaticism he'd seen in France.

"I asked Henry in here," Marigny said, "because he knows a great deal about Miss McCurtain. I think you'll find what he has to say most illuminating."

Victor forced a civil tone to his voice, though it was difficult. "If you're talking about the death of Monsieur Jourdan's little girl last year, then I already know about it. Father Tomas was only too quick to relate the tale."

Marigny nodded, as if he'd already been apprised of that. "Did the good father also tell you why Miss McCurtain went to that house, even though Monsieur Jourdan and his wife did not call her to come?"

Victor hesitated. He could hardly say that Lilith had gone there because of her mysterious voices. "No, but perhaps if they *had* called her in time, she might have saved the child." Then conscious of how that must sound to Monsieur Jourdan, he added to the overseer, "Begging your pardon, sir, but that is how I see it."

Marigny swirled the wine in his glass. "For a man who has lived here only a few months, you seem to think you know a great deal about what happened that night." He set the glass down, a muscle working in his jaw. "But the fact of the matter is, Dr. Drouet, Lilith didn't go to the Jourdan house out of some worthy desire to save their child. She went there to see Henry Jourdan.''

When Henry began to nod, Victor went very still. ''What do you mean?''

''It seems that Miss McCurtain, half-breed that she is, had once tried to seduce Henry.''

''What?'' Victor exclaimed.

''This was before you were my doctor,'' Marigny went on in that clever, cold voice of his. ''Henry had called her to look at one of the slaves, and she had come here for that purpose. When she was done with her work, Henry invited her to his house to meet his wife.'' Marigny turned to the overseer. ''But perhaps you should tell it, Henry.''

''As you wish, sir.'' Henry shifted from one foot to the other. ''I didn't know she was a witch when I called her here. I thought she was just a healer. So I didn't think anything of asking her to come in and meet my wife. But Rosemarie wasn't there, so I invited her to come back another time.''

He gave a heavy sigh. ''She wouldn't go. She got a strange look in those witchy eyes of hers. Then she came up to me, putting her hands all over me. I could tell what she wanted. That was plain as day.''

A chill shook Victor. He couldn't believe it. Lilith, a seductress? When she'd reacted so violently against his own kiss?

''I'm a godfearing man, Dr. Drouet,'' Henry went on, ''but it's hard to be a saint when a woman like that starts taking off her clothes and draping herself all over a man's body.''

''Lilith took off her clothes for you?'' Victor said, skepticism in his voice.

But Henry Jourdan didn't seem to notice it. ''Yes, sir. And she kept rubbing her body up against me till I couldn't think. Next thing I knew, we were in the bed together.''

Victor tried not to imagine Lilith in bed with the virile-looking Henry, but the image seeped through his mind like an insidious poison. He gave an inward curse. Men always boasted that women tried to seduce them. It meant nothing.

Henry looked embarrassed now. ''If my wife hadn't happened upon us then, who knows what sin I might have committed?''

Victor was stunned. ''Your wife saw you?''

''Yes, sir, and in a terribly compromising position, too.'' He blushed, giving credence to his tale.

This was worse and worse. If someone else had seen them . . . if there was a witness to Henry's claims . . . He groaned. He didn't want to think it might be true. But the image of Lilith and Henry exploded inside his brain, too big and awful for him to contain.

Henry glanced at Marigny before going on. ''The Witch and I . . . well, we did nearly everything but the act itself. She had me under a spell, and I couldn't stop myself. When she pulled me down on that bed—''

''That's enough.'' Victor tore his gaze from Henry, feeling a coldness settle in his bones.

What did he know of Lilith anyway? She was an excellent healer. That was all he really knew. She could have seduced a hundred men, and he wouldn't have known. A few hours with her certainly didn't make him an expert on her character.

He heard Marigny dismiss Henry Jourdan, heard the sound of the door opening and closing as the overseer left, but he was too numb to react.

As soon as Jourdan was gone, Marigny turned to Victor. ''So you see, Dr. Drouet, you aren't the only man whom beautiful Lilith McCurtain has coaxed to do her bidding. Indeed, once she gets her claws in a man, she holds fast. That's why she went to Henry's house the night his daughter died. She wanted to see him again, and evidently she thought his wife wouldn't be there. Once she was there, however, she made the excuse that she'd come to help the child and—''

''How do you know she didn't?'' Victor faced Marigny, still not quite willing to believe the amazing tale.

''Because no one summoned her. Why would they? Henry sent a man to town for a doctor but none was available, and by the time the man returned with that news, Lilith had already been there and the child was dead.''

Victor remembered what Lilith had said about the voices.

He'd thought her fanciful when she'd told him about it. But now he must either believe in her fancy . . . or believe Marigny and his henchman.

Marigny went on. "When faced with the fact that Henry obviously cared for his wife, an embittered Miss McCurtain said her stupid curse over the child and left. Although I don't for a moment believe it was the curse that killed the child, I do think it was inordinately cruel of her to behave in such a manner, to play on Henry's superstitions in order to wound him for his rejection of her."

Despite himself, Victor thought of how Lilith had threatened to curse him when he'd tried to kiss her. Then again, that was different, wasn't it? She'd been trying to avoid a man's attentions, not gain them.

Marigny's voice softened a fraction. "Look here, Dr. Drouet, I know you find this hard to believe. She can put on a good face when she wants. But I've known Henry since he was a boy. His father was my overseer, and a good man, too. So is Henry. He's a little odd, but he takes his religion very seriously. He's extremely devout. Some would even say too devout. He would never have considered adultery if he hadn't been seduced. And I know he would never lie to me."

Victor shook his head. "But you haven't seen Lilith with the children. She's so patient, so compassionate—"

"I have no doubt of that." Marigny sipped his wine. "But as I said before, that isn't the issue. If I condone her work at the orphanage, I may lose a good overseer. Besides that, Father Tomas will make a nuisance of himself over the whole thing, and he'll certainly make trouble for you. Nay, 'tis better we have no more dealings with Lilith McCurtain."

"But the children—"

The sharp tap of Marigny's cane echoed in the room. "That is my final word on the subject." Marigny started toward the door, then paused. "And if you wish to remain my doctor, sir, you will respect my decision. Is that understood?"

Victor's eyes blazed, but he nodded.

"Excellent. I thought you would." Marigny opened the door, then stood waiting beside it. "Good day, Dr. Drouet."

And that was the end of the audience.

Victor headed back to town, his mind in a turmoil. He couldn't stop thinking about Henry Jourdan's claims. The man hadn't seemed a devious sort. He'd seemed far too dull-witted to make up such a story, and what reason did he have for doing so anyway?

Then there was Lilith. When she'd first appeared at the infirmary, she'd misled him by letting him believe that Father Tomas had called her. Later, when she'd told him of her night at the Jourdan house, she'd clearly felt guilt over the entire affair.

But her guilt had seemed to come solely from her feeling that she hadn't done all she could. That was what seemed curious about Jourdan's tale. He seemed to believe she'd come to his house that night to finish her seduction of him. There was a touch of absurdity in that. What woman seeks out a married man without being sure that his wife is away? And once she had discovered that Mrs. Jourdan was home, why hadn't she left at once?

He also found it hard to believe that Lilith would have been so attracted to Henry that she'd have taken enormous risks to be with him. Granted, the man was young and good-looking, but hardly the sort he could imagine Lilith desiring.

Or was he just telling himself that because he hated to think of her giving to another man what she'd refused him? Maybe Lilith preferred a coarser man, someone who'd stand in awe of her purported abilities.

It galled him to think that she might. And why hadn't she told him that Sophie Jourdan's father worked for Marigny? After he'd revealed that Marigny was his patron, why had she hidden that crucial bit of information? Why had she told him only part of the story if not to hide her illicit association with Henry Jourdan?

An hour later, after he'd left his horse at the stables and was walking back to the infirmary, he still couldn't decide what to think of her. Was she indeed the unpredictable creature that Jourdan had described, who devoured a man's will and then acted with vindictive cruelty when he spurned her? Or was she as unfairly maligned as she claimed?

He passed his lodgings and paused to look at the wooden structure. The placard in the front window read: DR. VICTOR DROUET, PHYSICIAN. Beneath his name was a list of the ailments he'd had success curing, and beneath that a statement about his Paris education. The sign had brought him few patients. It took time to build a practice, of course, but it was even harder in a small place like New Orleans. People were loath to try a stranger when they had an ancient family doctor to turn to, even if that doctor might as easily kill them as cure them.

What had brought him his patients was his association with Philippe de Marigny. People came to Victor now because he was Marigny's doctor.

He sighed. It didn't really matter whether Lilith was a seductive witch or a kind healer, did it? No matter what he thought of her, he couldn't afford to bring her back to the infirmary. If he lost Marigny's endorsement, he would be on shaky ground. He'd worked hard to pull himself out of poverty and find the kind of security Marigny offered. He'd be damned if he gave it all up for a woman of dubious reputation.

But that decision didn't make it any easier for him to walk into the infirmary and face the children. As he began feeding them the next dose of tea, the boys asked for Lilith. Their plaintive expressions rapidly changed to ones of betrayal when he told them Miss McCurtain wasn't returning. Elias took it particularly hard, refusing his tea and lapsing into a sullen silence.

Despite their disappointment, however, the children still seemed to be improving. Two more of the boys were sitting up and most of them had no more fever. But Victor could feel no pleasure in it. The crowded and now noisy infirmary seemed empty and quiet without Lilith. There was no more music, for he certainly couldn't sing, and Father Tomas was more wont to recite scripture verses than anything else.

When after three more hours, he went to the pot for more tea, he noticed it was nearly empty. They must have more, and he certainly didn't know how to make the brew. Besides, he wasn't sure how long to continue serving it to the boys. He'd have to talk to Lilith.

He groaned. The dearth of tea wasn't his real reason for wanting to speak to her, and he knew it. The truth was, he couldn't stand the priest's smug glances and the boys' accusing expressions—or his own torturous thoughts—anymore. He had to hear her side, even if he couldn't be sure how much of it to believe.

He had to go to her. Surely someone in New Orleans could tell him where the Witch lived.

"Where are you going, my son?" the priest asked as Victor scooped up his coat and headed for the door.

Victor looked the man straight in the eye. And lied. "I have to return to my lodgings to mix up more tea. The boys will be fine for an hour or two, I think."

Father Tomas grunted his approval. Though the priest had disapproved of the use of Lilith's remedy, he'd also been unable to deny its effectiveness, so he'd said nothing as Victor had dosed the children.

Victor felt a faint trace of guilt as he left the infirmary. He'd never lied to a priest before. That was a dramatic act, even for a heathen like him.

Then again, perhaps Father Tomas was right, he thought wryly as he strode through the town. Perhaps this was a sign of Victor's rapidly degenerating character. Maybe the Devil had his soul after all. At the moment, he certainly felt like he was in hell.

CHAPTER FIVE

Lilith stood over the table, crumbling bayberry and moldy bread into a piece of cloth to be bundled up and boiled in water. Victor would soon need more tea, and even though he couldn't let her help him at the infirmary, perhaps he would come here to ask her how to brew it.

Don't be foolish, she told herself. *Victor Drouet isn't likely to risk his position to come here.*

But he did seem to care for the children. Perhaps for their sake, he would risk it.

A part of her was terrified at the thought of his coming to her little shanty. Another part of her thrilled to the possibility. He had defended her so valiantly at the infirmary. And though in the end he had lost the fight, she couldn't blame him for letting Monsieur Marigny's slaves carry her off. He'd had no choice. As Monsieur Marigny's doctor, he had to abide by the man's wishes.

Monsieur Marigny. She bowed her head over the pot, tears welling in her eyes. As long as Monsieur Marigny continued to defend Henry Jourdan, she would never be treated fairly in New Orleans. Never.

A knock came at the door, and she rubbed away her tears. Perhaps that was Victor after all. He was the only one who'd ever shown any faith in her, who'd neither cowered before her nor regarded her with hatred. She could trust him at least to view her fairly.

She hastened to the door, eager to see him again. But when she released the bolt and opened the door, it wasn't Victor who stood on the threshold. It was the only man who'd ever made her afraid.

Henry Jourdan.

She tried to close the door, but he was too fast for her, thrusting his foot between the door and the frame before she could stop him. She shoved against the door as terror built in her chest, but her strength was no match for his, and with one great push, he thrust the door open, forcing her to stumble backward.

His large frame filled the doorway, and his eyes glittered with the strange, wild light that had been in them the last time she'd been alone with him, over a year ago. As he stalked into the room, she shrank back. She must get away. She couldn't let him corner her like this.

"I tried and tried to put you from my mind, Witch." Though his steps were determined, his face wore a look of confusion that she would have found pathetic if she hadn't known how strong he was. "I told myself that Sophie's dying was God's punishment on me for letting you put your spell on me."

"I didn't put a spell on you," she whispered as she came up against the table. "I didn't do anything. You did it all—"

" 'Tis a lie!" He cocked his head, staring at her with sorrowful eyes. "I tried to resist you. I did. You were the one . . . you looked at me with those eyes, and you made me want to touch you."

He took another step forward, and she felt the panic surge in her.

Not again, she told herself. *Never again. A weapon. I must have a weapon.* She groped around on the table behind her. Then her hands touched metal. Her knife, the one she used to cut up meat. Thank God.

As soon as her fingers closed around the hilt, she whipped the knife out in front of her. "Stay away from me, Henry! Don't come another step closer!"

He didn't even seem to notice it. "I have to stop you before you tempt someone else. I should have done it before, but I was afraid of your curses." His face grew hard. "I'm not afraid of you anymore. And I won't let you tempt me to fornicate again like you did. I won't let you get me into your bed."

"It was *your* bed, and I didn't want to be in it," she cried. She shook her head, the tears burning her eyes. "You forced me. I . . . didn't want you . . . to touch me. . . . Why can't you see that?"

When he stepped closer, she slashed the knife through the air in a threatening gesture, but she knew it was fruitless. She could stick him, but she couldn't kill a wild bull like him. She didn't have the strength. And if he weren't afraid of her—

"I'll curse you," she whispered, falling back on the ploy that had helped her send the angry mob from her house. "I'll put a plague upon you, Henry Jourdan, if you come another step!"

He shrugged, and the fatalistic gesture frightened her more than his advancing steps. "I'm already cursed. I think about you all the time . . . about your pretty little body . . . your breasts . . . your mouth. . . . I know it's wrong, and I try to fight it, but I can't sleep for thinking of it."

He lifted his hands, and she was reminded of how strong they were, how easily he'd held her by the throat while he'd touched her and . . . and torn her clothes and—

"It hurts my head to think about you out here all alone," he was saying. Suddenly his expression changed, and an angry red flush spread over his face. "But you're not alone anymore, are you? That doctor probably comes out here to touch you. That Dr. Drouet."

Her eyes went wide. "How do you know the doctor?"

"He came to Monsieur Marigny's today." The red flush crept down his thick neck. "But Monsieur Marigny told him all about you. He told him how you put spells on men, how you tried to get me into your bed."

"No-o-o," she whimpered. "He told Victor such lies?" Tears crammed her eyes, and it was all she could do to fight them back. Wasn't it bad enough that everyone else thought her a witch? Must they prejudice Victor against her, too?

"You put a spell on that doctor, didn't you?" Henry said. "You want *him* to fornicate with you as you wanted me to."

"No . . . no, I never put a spell on anyone. . . . I don't want to fornicate with anyone—"

"Lies." He shook his head as he took another step. "All of it is lies."

She had to do something. But her knife hand shook, and she didn't know how she'd find the strength to bury the weapon in him. "Just go home and leave me alone! Please go. . . ."

Then a new voice echoed in the room. "The lady asked you to go, Henry."

Lilith's gaze swung to the entrance. To her shock, Victor Drouet stood in the doorway, his blue eyes ablaze.

Henry turned, too, and a welter of emotion showed in his face. He pointed to her. "You see, Dr. Drouet? You see? She's tempting me again! Like she tempted you! Don't you see?"

Victor's gaze touched her for only a moment, but it was long enough for her to feel the sympathy in it. "I see only a scared young woman holding a knife."

With a bob of his head, Henry said, "Yes, she's got a knife. That's because she knows I've come to punish her for her witchery!"

A cold anger flashed over Victor's face before he masked it. Fixing his gaze on Henry, he edged into the room. "You don't need to punish her, Henry. I'm here now. Why don't you leave her . . . ah . . . punishment to me?"

"No!" With reddening face, Henry stamped his foot, and the floorboards shook. "You'll fall under her spell, too. You don't see her true character as I do. You don't see her witchery. She'll tempt you. . . . She'll—"

"She can't tempt me." Victor's voice was soothing as he edged nearer, but his eyes were hard as ice. "Father Tomas gave me protection against her before I left the infirmary."

Henry frowned. "Protection? What protection?"

Victor looked blank for a second, but he recovered quickly. "Um . . . holy water. The priest sprinkled holy water on me.

I'm safe from her." Now he was only a few steps behind Henry. "But you're not safe. You should leave and let me take care of her punishment myself. Go back to Rosemarie."

Confusion spread over Henry's face at the mention of his wife. "I don't know . . . I . . . I—"

"Rosemarie is calling you," Victor said. "Can't you hear her?"

Henry cocked his head, listening, and a chill snaked down Lilith's spine. The man was even worse than she remembered him, as impressionable as a child, though strong enough to act on his delusions.

"You hear her, don't you?" Victor prompted. "She needs you, Henry. You mustn't abandon her when she needs you."

"But the Witch will—"

"I will deal with the Witch." Clapping a hand on Henry's shoulder, Victor added, "I'll make sure she's punished for all her sins. You can count on me. But Rosemarie is calling, and you should go now. Go to her."

Lilith held her breath, her knife still at the ready. Henry was so unpredictable, there was no telling what he'd do. His face was beet-red, and his fists were clenched. If he attacked Victor, she didn't know who would win. Victor had no weapon, and Henry was the larger man. She remembered with painful clarity how strong Henry could be in his demented state.

But Victor must have realized that. He made no attempt to subdue Henry by force. He merely kept repeating that Rosemarie was calling, and that seemed finally to affect Henry. Apparently his concern for his wife was strong enough to reach through the strange labyrinth of his thoughts.

Suddenly, he went limp, like a marionette who'd lost its puppeteer. "Rosemarie," he whispered. "I . . . I should go to Rosemarie."

"Yes." A trace of relief was in Victor's voice. "I'll help you to your horse. You should hurry."

"I should hurry," Henry echoed as he let Victor lead him from the room.

She stayed frozen as they walked out, then strained to listen for the sounds of Henry mounting his horse. As soon as she heard Victor say "Gee-up!" and felt certain that Henry had ridden off, she dropped the knife and crumpled to the floor. The tears that she'd been holding back spilled wildly down her cheeks. She couldn't seem to stop them. What if Victor hadn't come along? What if Henry had put those thick hands around her neck and—

"Are you all right?" came Victor's voice from the door.

She choked back a sob. "Is he . . . is he gone?"

Victor moved into the room, shut the door, and then after glancing through the window, bolted it. "I think so. I watched until he was a good distance down the road. Pray God he doesn't return."

"He would have hurt me again. If you hadn't come, he would have hurt me." Hugging herself, she began to rock back and forth. "It would have been worse than before. I know it. He would have killed me."

He was beside her now. Kneeling down, he took her hands and murmured, "Hush, it's all right. He can't hurt you anymore. I won't let him."

"I know what Monsieur Marigny probably told you, but I didn't seduce Henry." The words spilled out of her in her urgent need to convince him. "It was Henry. He did it all. He pushed me down on his bed . . . and tore my clothes and put his hands on me." She bent over double, remembering that horrible time. "It hurt so much. It hurt when he pawed my breasts and . . . shoved his fingers in me. He would have put his man thing in me if Rosemarie hadn't come. He would have raped me—" She broke off into violent sobs.

The firelight glittered over Victor's tortured expression as he drew her into his arms. "It's all right, sweeting." His voice was hoarse, but sure. "I'm here now. You're safe. I won't let him hurt you ever again. Never."

She lost herself then in his strong arms, letting them encase her in a safe haven she'd never before had. Clinging to him, she buried her face in his coat. The tears poured forth, a constant flood she couldn't hold back. He murmured soft, soothing words as he stroked her hair with a comforting touch.

It was several minutes before she could gain control over

her emotions. When she did, she drew back and lifted her face to his. "You believe me, don't you? You don't think I . . . I wanted him to . . . to—"

"Of course I believe you," he said earnestly, his eyes full of a remorse she didn't understand. "Oh, sweeting, how could I not believe you? I have only to remember how I frightened you with my kiss to know that you speak the truth."

When she ducked her head, embarrassed to remember how she'd cursed him then, he murmured in a teasing voice, "Besides, I don't know many women who seduce a man while holding him off with a knife."

She shuddered at the thought that she might have killed Henry. If he'd attacked her, she certainly would have tried. "He scares me. He's not . . . quite sane, you know? He terrifies me."

"I know." He cupped her cheek with such gentleness that it made her ache inside. Why had she ever recoiled from him? It was easy to see that he was nothing like Henry.

He rubbed away her tears with his thumb. "After the first time, you should have told Marigny the truth and gotten him to send Henry away."

A bitter laugh escaped her lips. "Marigny send his trusted overseer away? On the word of a 'witch,' a half-breed whose mother was a 'savage'? He wouldn't have listened to me. Henry's words have the ring of truth. Of course, that's only because Henry believes they *are* the truth, but Marigny wouldn't have seen the distinction. No, if I'd gone to Marigny, he would have run me out of town for lying. He would have believed Henry—and his wife—over me."

Tears stung her eyes again. With a soothing word, he brushed her hair back from her forehead. "After it happened, why did you go to the Jourdan house to help Sophie? Surely you were afraid of Henry."

A sob caught in her throat. "I was. That's why I waited . . . too late. That's why Sophie died. If I had ignored my fears and heeded my voices . . ."

"No," he whispered. Clasping her chin, he lifted her head. "No. 'Tis not your fault. If it's anyone's, it's Henry's for forcing himself on you and making you afraid. And they didn't call for you, after all. They were willing to risk their child's death for their delusion. By going to Sophie's aid in spite of that, you did more than anyone could have expected of you."

His words lightened her heart so much, she had to smile. "I see I was wrong to accuse you of not knowing how to assess the pains of the heart. You are so kind, so fair."

"Not as kind as you think," he said ruefully. "I came here ready to condemn you tonight."

"Only because Marigny told you lies about me."

He stared at her a long moment, a troubled expression on his face. Then with a sigh, he rose and went to stand by her fireplace. "Still, I should have realized they were lies. But I let my pride stand in the way of that. My pride and my jealousy. I was angry that you would offer to Henry what you refused me. I didn't even consider the possibility that you'd refused me because Henry had taken forcibly what you hadn't offered."

She stood, too, and moved up behind him. "You couldn't have known that. And I . . . I was too ashamed of what he did to tell you."

"You had no need to be ashamed," he said softly. "I'm the one who should be ashamed. I'm as bad as Henry. I wanted you, so I took what I wished without asking, without considering your feelings in the matter—"

"No!" She laid her hand on his shoulder. "No, it wasn't like that."

"Wasn't it?" He turned his head to stare at her. "You said I 'pawed' you. I remember it very well. 'Tis the same thing you said of Henry. And you were so disturbed by my kiss that you threatened to lay a curse on me."

A blush stained her cheeks to remember her violent reaction. "But it wasn't the same with you as with Henry, truly it wasn't. I . . . I . . ." She dropped her gaze from his. "I liked your kiss. You made me feel like no man ever has. I wanted you to . . . to touch me. It's just that . . . I was afraid."

She'd been afraid of men for a long time, shying from their touch, terrified of what lay behind each handsome face. But now she was tired of being afraid, tired of being alone. And to her surprise, she realized Victor was the man whom she wanted to put an end to her loneliness. The only man.

She lifted her gaze to his once more. "I'm not afraid now, Victor. Not the least bit."

He seemed to turn to stone. All except his eyes. They blazed with life as he looked at her. "What are you saying?"

Putting her desire into words was difficult, yet she couldn't think of any other way to show how she felt. "I'm saying that . . . if you were to kiss me now . . . I would welcome it."

He swung his gaze back to the fire, clenching his hands at his sides. "I can't."

That wasn't the response she'd expected. She dragged in a ragged breath. "Why not?"

"Because I don't want to stop with kissing." A muscle jerked in his jaw. "I *am* as bad as Henry, you see. I want to lay you down on that bed over there, to take your clothes off and touch your body . . . to put my 'man thing' in you. I want to have all of you." He swallowed, his eyes looking bleak. "And I know you don't want that."

His words should have terrified her. They should have brought forth awful memories of Henry's violation. Instead, they made a warm heat erupt in her loins, spreading throughout her body like a fiery liquor.

She stepped between him and the fire, forcing him to look at her. "I didn't want it with Henry, 'tis true. I didn't want it thrust upon me against my will." Timidly, she put her hand on his chest. "But I want it with you. I want you to be the one to make it . . . beautiful for me."

His hand closed over hers. Looking down at it, he traced each of her fingers with his thumb. "I don't want to hurt you, Lilith. You may not be ready for this."

"But I am," she whispered. Her words sounded more sure than she felt, but she had to put the past behind her sometime. And she'd rather do it with Victor.

"There will be some pain, you know. There always is the first time."

"I know." It meant a great deal to her that he hadn't questioned her virginity. "But I trust you not to hurt me too much. You said before that I wouldn't trust anyone with my body, and that's true. But I trust you."

His gaze shot up to meet hers, dark, wild, intent. "Then God have mercy on both our souls." Closing his hands on her shoulders, he drew her to him, and the next thing she knew he was kissing her.

It was nothing like their first kiss. It was as if he wanted to warn her, to make her see how very much he wanted from her. He slid his hands up to bracket her face, holding her head still as he took her mouth with raw abandon. He stabbed his tongue against her lips until she opened to him and let him drive inside in hard, possessing strokes. And though fear did flicker briefly in her chest to have him kiss her so forcefully, she fought it back, determined that she would have him.

When she brought her arms up around his waist, he tore his mouth from hers, staring at her with eyes a bright, vivid blue. "You see what I want from you, sweeting? If it's too much for you, tell me now, and I will leave you. I swear I—"

She cut him off with a kiss of her own, rising up on tiptoe to press her lips to his as she tightened her arms around his waist. He hesitated, going still as her mouth played on his. Then he moaned low in his throat, and enfolded her in his arms.

After that, his kisses were long and drugging, each one more sensuous than the last. The fire of the sun and the beauty of the moon were all rolled up into his sweet kisses. . . . They held forth to her a promise she couldn't resist, and she lost herself in them without regret.

Soon his lips left her mouth to trail along her cheek and down to her neck. Throwing her head back, she groaned when she felt him kiss her neck, lower and lower until his open mouth was on her throat, his tongue tasting the hollow. Then he began to work loose the bone buttons of her jacket, and she went rigid at once.

He paused in what he was doing and lifted his face to hers. The desire in it was tempered with understanding. "I don't want to make you uncomfortable, Lilith, but I confess I want very badly to see you unclothed. Will you let me?''

That he asked her permission touched her deeply. She nodded, though she couldn't help but lower her gaze from his, a blush spreading over her cheeks.

He lifted her chin with one hand, and when she looked at him, he was smiling. ''Would it make it easier for you if I undressed first?''

She bobbed her head. She was being a coward, she knew, but she wanted to put off as long as possible the moment when she bared herself before him. When Henry had torn her clothes off, the sight of her naked body had seemed to incite him to hurt her. She still wasn't entirely certain that wouldn't happen with Victor, too.

Victor wasted no time in dispensing with his coat and shirt, and as he threw them aside, she couldn't help staring at his chest. It was well-formed and broader than she would have expected for a man who spent his days inside. A few short blond hairs whorled around his nipples and another trickle of hair led down his lean belly to his navel and beyond. For the first time in her life, she was curious about the beyond. Very curious. And terrified at the same time.

He took off his breeches, but hesitated when he brought his hands to the waistband of his drawers. ''Here,'' he said, taking her hands and placing them on his waist. ''You take them off.''

Just as he must have realized, his words took the edge off her fear. It gave her the choice of undressing him. She wasn't at his mercy at all. She could remove his drawers or turn him aside unfulfilled.

But the latter had no longer become an option, not as far as she was concerned. Swallowing hard, she unbuttoned the tiny buttons on either side, then drew his drawers off.

The sight of his erection, however, gave her pause. It had been one thing to say that she wanted him, but another thing entirely to face the reality of it. He would put this . . . this large thing inside her, and it would hurt. It would have to hurt more than a little.

Yet he'd sworn he wouldn't give her pain beyond what a

virgin must expect the first time. And she trusted him.

"My turn," he whispered, and she tore her gaze from the part of him she still half-feared.

Keeping his eyes fixed on her face, he finished unbuttoning her jacket, then reached behind her to unclasp her skirt. She felt her skirt sweep down to the floor, and moments later, her jacket followed it, leaving her wearing only her shift. He dispensed with that in a matter of seconds.

Only then did his gaze leave her face to wander over her nude form. "Sweet God in Heaven," he muttered hoarsely, his face stark and drawn with his desire. "You're the most beautiful creature I have ever seen."

She tensed, waiting for him to crush her breasts with his hands as Henry had done, to force her down on the floor and shove his fingers inside her. If he did, she would fight him. She knew she would.

But all he did was run his fingers from her neck down over the curve of her breast to her belly, a look of wonder spreading over his face. Then to her shock, he bent on one knee and kissed the underside of her breast.

All her fear dissolved into a puddle. His lips were gentle as he pressed soft kisses around her breast, so when he then opened his mouth over her nipple and began to suck, she felt nothing but pleasure, bright and wanton, coursing through her blood. He lavished attention on first one breast, then the other, melting her with his heat, making her want more and more.

But when she buried her hands in his thick, luxurious hair to clasp him closer, he groaned and stopped what he was doing. With eyes afire, he stood, then swept her up into his arms.

She caught him about the neck and stared questioningly into his face, but he was scanning the room. He fixed on whatever he was looking for, and she turned her head to see what he carried her so purposefully toward.

It was her bed.

A tremor of fear rippled over her, but it was nothing to the wild, urgent heat spreading outward from her belly. He was going to make love to her. He had said he would, and she had no doubt of it now. And she wanted him to. She was terrified of it, but she wanted it anyway.

When they reached her cane bed, he laid her on the moss-stuffed mattress, then stretched out beside her. She was trembling. He put his hand on her belly, and she knew he felt her shivers, for a spasm of anguish crossed his face.

"I know you're afraid," he whispered. "And if I could turn back the clock and erase from your memory what Henry did to you, I would. But it doesn't have to be hard and cruel, sweeting. It can be beautiful. It *will* be beautiful between us. I swear it."

He was so kind. She'd never dreamed that the doctor with the cold eyes could have such a warm heart. "I believe you," she whispered, lifting her hand to stroke his face. "I know you'll make it so."

Passion flared in his eyes, and he caught her hand to press a kiss in the palm. Then he placed her hand on his chest and lowered his mouth to hers once more.

Instantly, he made her forget she was lying naked on a bed with a man as naked as herself. His mouth clung to hers, coaxing at first, then devouring. Only when he felt her relax beneath him did his hands move over her body . . . stroking here, kneading there . . . finding all the parts of her that craved his touch. And when his fingers found the place between her legs, he explored it with tenderness, teasing her until she arched up against his hand and found herself wanting him to do more.

It was so much the opposite of what Henry had made her feel that silent tears streamed down her face. She could tell what it cost Victor to be so patient, so gentle, and no one had ever cared so much about her feelings before.

He felt the dampness of her tears against his cheeks and drew back, his hands going still. "Have I hurt you?" he asked in a husky voice.

Unable to speak for the tears that choked her throat, she shook her head, then lifted her body against him in an unconsciously seductive gesture.

After that, he didn't need to ask again. Whispering sweet

words in her ears, he worshipped her body. He caressed her breast with one hand as his other hand caressed her in more secret places. When he had her moaning and writhing beneath him, he moved between her legs. He hovered over her, his arms braced on either side of her shoulders, and his face as rigid as marble with the strain of holding back.

"Will you take me, Lilith McCurtain?" he rasped. "Will you give yourself to me freely?"

"Yes," she whispered, brushing a kiss across his taut lips. He groaned, and the next thing she knew he was easing inside her.

It was entirely different from what she'd expected, what she'd feared. He was careful and slow as he filled her, and when he broke through the barrier of her innocence, he did it so quickly, she hardly knew what had happened, for there was only the faintest twinge of pain.

After that, there was only him . . . the fullness of him inside her, claiming her . . . making it beautiful. He was all passion and moonlight, her sky warrior come to bring the moon into the heavens. But it was she he was carrying into the sky as he thrust deeper and harder, into the very soul of her. Soon she was arching up to meet his thrusts, straining to fold her body into his.

"Oh, yes, Lilith . . . yes," he whispered, his face alight as he drove into her. "You're everything I want . . . everything . . . always."

He brought her higher and higher until the stars were a blur of light whistling past her, and the sky was hers for the taking. And as he exploded inside her and the most exquisite pleasure broke over her, she realized that he was everything she wanted, too. Everything.

CHAPTER SIX

Victor awoke from a sound sleep to find himself naked and alone. As he stared up at an unfamiliar wooden ceiling, he tried to gather his bearings. He wasn't in the infirmary, that was for certain. He'd left the children for a while to come to Lilith's house at the edge of the swamp.

Ah, yes. He was at Lilith's. They'd made love. He smiled. Much as he'd enjoyed it, the hour was probably approaching when he must return to give the children their next dose of tea. Though he wished he could stay with Lilith, he knew she would understand his urgent need to go back.

Easing up on his elbows, he scanned the room, only to find it empty. Where was Lilith?

Leaving the bed, he dragged on his drawers before catching sight of the open door. For a second, he panicked. Had Henry returned to drag Lilith off? Surely not. Surely there would have been some noise to awaken him. But still . . .

He hurried onto the porch, then stopped short at the strange sight that greeted him.

Lilith stood beneath the full moon in the crisp night air, clothed in nothing but her shift. She danced on bare feet, her fine creamy arms lifted to the moon, her eyes closed. And her face rapt with joy.

He stood frozen, not wanting to bother her, feeling as if he'd somehow stumbled upon a very private ritual. She looked like something out of an exotic dream, her long hair twining about her like a Spanish veil and her lithe body undulating in the dance.

As she turned in slow circles, she began to sing. But it wasn't quite singing. It was more like chanting. He'd never heard Indian chants, but he imagined they were something like this—melodic, rhythmic . . . ancient.

A chill swept over him as she shaped words he could never understand, made sounds he could never make. What a fool he'd been to think he'd finally captured her. She was a stranger to him still, this fey creature of the night . . . a glorious, wonderful stranger who could never be wholly his, no matter how much he bound her to him with lovemaking.

As if she felt him watching her, she opened her eyes and stopped, her gaze locking with his. He wanted to apologize for interrupting her, but he seemed powerless to speak, for she looked more beautiful in the moonlight than any woman he'd ever seen. Her eyes glowed like mystical jewels and her skin shone like burnished bronze. He felt ashamed to have disturbed her, to have encroached upon her privacy.

Suddenly, a smile broke over her face. She crooked her finger, beckoning him near, and he moved off the porch in a trance, scarcely feeling the cold, damp earth beneath his bare feet. When he reached her, she lifted his arms into the air, then knit her fingers with his.

Slowly she began to turn again, her eyes never leaving his face, and he turned with her, hardly conscious of what he was doing. The chant tumbled from her lips once more, but this time he felt included in it, as if she sang it for both of them.

After a while, it was as if he understood the words. He was the sky and she was the earth, joined forever by the moonlight that fell from one to the other. Her hair swung about them as they danced, and it seemed to bind them together, closer and closer until he found he was kissing her as they turned. Her lips were cool as earth, only warming under the touch of his.

She slowed her steps, wrapping her arms around him, and he pulled her into his embrace with a groan. He kissed her as if he might never get the chance again, wanting, needing to know she was his. She seemed flesh-and-blood and yet not so

. . . a creature of light and air who might vanish if he held her too tightly.

Next thing he knew, they were sinking onto the ground, their mouths still locked in the kiss. He drew up her shift. She drew down his drawers. And then he was entering her, feeling the same exquisite thrill that had overtaken him the first time he'd driven into her sweet flesh. He lost himself in her tight warmth just as he had then, forgetting the children, Marigny . . . the torments of France. There was only her, fused to him at the mouth and the loins, taking him out of himself as no one else had ever been able to.

Unlike their first time together, however, there was no fear in her now . . . and no apparent desire to take things slowly. She urged him on in aching whispers, rising to his every furious thrust, moaning out her pleasure as she wrapped her long legs around his waist and arched her head back. A few moments later, she cried out and jerked beneath him, and he found his own release, spilling himself into her with his own hoarse cry.

He rested on her only a moment before rolling off to lie beside her on the damp, packed earth. His breath came in hard pants, taking some time to slow. Finally, he began to be aware of the cool ground beneath him and the musty smell of the nearby swamp.

She slid her small hand in his, and he clasped it tightly. When he twisted his head to look at her, the sight of her flushed face gave him a pleasure almost like pain. "Don't be angry at me for saying this," he murmured, "but I think you are indeed a witch. You're a beautiful, seductive, fascinating witch with an extraordinary power to drive me out of my mind." A smile touched his lips. "For such a witch, I don't mind being damned."

She stared at him with solemn eyes. "You won't be damned. I won't allow it." Her tone lightened, and there was a hint of shyness in her expression. "Besides, I'm not the only one with extraordinary powers. You made my fear go away when I thought it would be my bedfellow all my life. For that, I will always be grateful."

He dropped his gaze to their locked hands, a sudden inexplicable guilt overtaking him. Perhaps he *had* banished her fear, but he'd also taken her innocence. And given her nothing in return. Worse yet, he could offer her nothing, not even marriage. If Marigny would withdraw his support simply because Victor had allowed Lilith to help him with the children, he could only imagine what taking her as his wife would do. And what good would he be to her as a husband if he couldn't even provide for himself?

He released her hand and sat up, crossing his legs Indian-style. "Making your fear go away is the only thing I've done for you, I'm afraid. I was unsuccessful in helping you regain your place as a healer in town, and now I've taken from you the one thing that might at least have gotten you a good husband."

She sat up beside him but remained silent. When he glanced at her, she was staring off into the swamp, her eyes distant. He had to tell her something. He had to make it clear why he couldn't marry her.

"Lilith, I . . ." He drew in a heavy breath. "I would like nothing better than to take you as my wife. You are everything I've ever wanted in a woman and—"

"I did not ask you to offer marriage," she said evenly.

"I know. But I want to marry you. I love you." He realized as he said the words that they were more true than anything he'd ever spoken in his life. How he had fallen in love with her in less than a day, he didn't know, but he had. And it didn't change anything. "The problem is . . . Marigny made it quite clear this afternoon that if I continue to let you help the children, it will end my chances to establish a practice here. I'm sure that marrying you would have the same effect. It would do neither of us any good."

She was silent for a moment, her face rigid. "I understand," she finally said. "I didn't give myself to you because I expected anything from you, so you need not concern yourself about that."

Her aloof manner, her seemingly nonchalant reaction filled him with anger. He'd expected her to argue, to make a case

for why it could work, why they belonged together. He'd expected at least an answering profession of love. What he
hadn't expected was for her to treat their joining as if it had
been nothing more than a night's pleasure.

She turned her head sharply away, but not fast enough for
him to miss the single tear that slipped from the corner of her
eye. It suddenly dawned on him that she wasn't at all nonchalant. She was proud, too proud to let him know how his
words had hurt her. With both Choctaw and Scottish blood
running through her veins, how could she not help being
proud?

Guilt seared him. "When I made love to you, Lilith, I
wasn't thinking about the consequences. I wasn't considering—"

"Enough," she said, her voice unsteady. "I understand the
difficult situation you are in, and I certainly don't wish to
make it more difficult." She hugged her knees to her chest.
"But you must understand my situation as well. What we did
tonight . . . it cannot go on. If you were to come to me every
night, to be with me, I would soon be regarded as nothing
better than a whore among my neighbors. My life is hard
enough without that."

Her words astonished him as much as if a lead weight had
fallen on his chest from out of the moonlit sky. He didn't
know what he'd expected . . . anything but being summarily
dismissed. "So this is to be the end of anything between us?
I am never to hold you or make love to you again?"

She turned her gaze on him, her face as implacable as that
of any Indian princess. "You can't marry me, yet you expect
to bed me whenever you want? Do I understand you cor-
rectly?"

He jerked his gaze from her. "That's not what I meant."
Then he cursed himself. How absurd. What else could he have
meant? He had assumed—perhaps unconsciously—that she
would still want him with her, that she would be willing to
hide their relationship from the world to be with him. He'd
been just as presumptuous in his beliefs about her character
as all those in New Orleans who called her a witch. "Well,

yes, I suppose that *is* what I meant. But now I see it was unfair of me. You're right, of course. We should not . . . meet in this way again.''

She was silent a long moment, and when she spoke again, her voice was strained. ''I think you should leave now. It's best.''

Trying to control the violence of his emotions, he nodded and stood up. *It is indeed best,* he told himself as he headed toward her little shack to gather his clothes. But that didn't mean he liked it.

CHAPTER SEVEN

The next night, Victor stood at the door to the infirmary after dusk, watching the moon rise over the city. Had he made love to Lilith only last night? He remembered leaving her shanty, burdened with packets to be made into tea. Despite her anger at him, she'd been careful to instruct him in the continuing care of the boys. As always, she'd put the good of her patients over her own feelings. He would have done no less. In that, as in so many things, they were soul mates.

Soul mates. She wasn't his soul mate. It was true they both found their joy in healing others. It was also true that he wanted her, but that was only the effects of desire, which could turn a man into a slobbering idiot. A moment's whimsy—brought on by days of little sleep and food—had made him fancy himself in love with her. That was all.

He groaned. Whimsy wasn't part of his character. He'd never been the romantic sort, to imagine himself in love with every pretty face that crossed his path. Even in France, when he'd worked night and day through the midst of the terror, he had never imagined himself in love with any of the women who helped him.

No, this wasn't mere whimsy. What he felt for Lilith was harder, deeper . . . more painful than anything he'd felt before. Despite having known her only one brief day, he missed her as intensely as a mariner misses the sea . . . or a newly blinded man misses sight. He felt newly blinded, as if she'd opened his eyes to life, then taken that sight away from him, leaving him eternally bereft.

Turning back into the room, he caught sight of little Elias, and his sense of loss pained him even more. Victor wasn't the only one who missed Lilith. Elias had refused all sustenance ever since Victor had told him that Lilith wouldn't return. The child wouldn't even take the tea, crying that he would have it from no one but Miss McCurtain.

At first, Victor had thought Elias's stubbornness would pass once he saw that Lilith was indeed not returning. But six times now Victor had given the dose of tea to the boys and Elias had refused it. As a result, while the other boys sat up in bed, reading or tossing jokes around, Elias lay still, his little body racked with fever.

Victor dragged his fingers through his hair. Earlier in the day, he had suggested to Father Tomas that they should ask Lilith to come here, if only to get Elias to take his medicine. The priest had refused, saying that Elias would take the medicine when he was too ill to resist. But that time hadn't come yet, and Victor was now afraid he would lose Elias entirely if he didn't do something.

He went to Elias's side and smoothed back the boy's hair, wincing at the heat emanating from him. He'd long ago stopped trying to protect himself from caring for the children. He'd learned that much at least from Lilith.

But was giving the child comfort all that was left to him now? The urge to fetch Lilith was overwhelming. Indeed, he'd spent the entire day trying to work out in his head some way for them to be together. He'd considered trying to make Marigny see how falsely she'd been accused, thereby gaining the man's consent to have her at the infirmary. He felt sure if he told Marigny what he'd witnessed between her and Henry, the man would change his opinion of her.

Then again, Marigny believed Victor to be so enamored of her that he would say almost anything to protect her. And in the end, it would only be Victor's word against Henry's.

Father Tomas came up beside him, a frown spreading over his face. "The boy is exceedingly stubborn. I've never seen a child refuse the very physic that will cure him."

"His stubbornness will kill him," Victor said in a tight voice. He turned to the priest. "So will yours. You must let me bring Miss McCurtain here to give him the medicine. If you don't, I can't answer for what will happen."

The priest's chin quivered. "She still has an evil hold over you, my son. Can't you see that? You must fight her for your soul and in so doing fight the Devil himself. If you haven't the strength for it, then listen at least to the counsel of those stronger than you—Monsieur Marigny and myself."

With an inward oath, Victor turned away from the priest. Father Tomas was so damned convinced that Victor had sold his soul to the Devil by helping Lilith. Such nonsense! Victor hadn't sold his soul to anyone. His soul was his own.

Or was it? He remembered the first time he'd met Marigny, how the man had enticed him to be his doctor by promising him a horse, a substantial yearly sum, a valuable recommendation. Victor had weighed those inducements—and his own dire financial straits—against his principles, against his hatred of slavery and his dedication to serving all the public, not just the wealthy. In the end, he'd accepted Marigny's offer. At the time, he'd rationalized his decision by telling himself that a few years' service to Marigny would enable him to help a greater number of people.

But now he saw that decision for what it was—a bargain with the Devil. By the time Lilith had come along, he'd had no soul left to sell to her. It had already been sold to Marigny.

Suddenly, it was as if the scales fell away from his eyes. That had been the meaning of his dream of two nights ago, hadn't it? It had been Marigny's face he'd seen in the pit. He was standing now on the edges of that pit, and he had a choice. Join himself to Marigny forever, and thus seal his fate—a lifetime of compromises and choosing the easy way, even if there was evil in it. Or join himself to Lilith who was all that was pure and bright and good.

It was no choice at all, and he made it instantly, feeling as if he'd finally emerged from the dark cavern where he'd been wandering for many months.

He only hoped he hadn't made his choice too late.

*   *   *

It was night again, and Lilith dreaded it. Although she'd tried to drive Victor from her thoughts by spending the day in hard labor—weeding· her garden, pounding herbs into powder, making bread·—he still haunted her. Now it was time to retire to her lonely bed, and she didn't know if she could bear it.

Before he had come into her life, she had been easy in her solitude, able to accept it if not relish it. But ever since he'd shown her the delights of love, the pleasures of having a companion, her solitude had become like that torture instrument her father had told her of—the Iron Maiden. It pressed in on her, drained the life from her.

Tears welled in her eyes, and she wiped them away furiously. She wouldn't let him do this to her. She would not! If she allowed him to alter her life in this way, she would soon find herself throwing away her pride to run after him. Already, in moments of weakness, she imagined what it would be like to have him constantly in and out of her tiny cabin, by day teaching her what he knew of doctoring and by night taking her in his arms and teaching her more of love.

A hollow ache began in her chest and spread to her loins. She cursed it even as she admitted that it wouldn't soon wane. She loved him. There was no getting around it. She'd known it from the minute he'd danced with her beneath the moon. Nothing could change the fact that she loved him with all her breath, her heart, her soul. And the temptation to have his love in return was so great that she feared it would only be a matter of time before she agreed to be his mistress, to meet him in secret whenever he wished.

Only her pride stopped her from running to him, and thank heavens for it. Her father would have wept to see her grown so eager to put aside her reputation for the love of a man who would hide her away. Her mother, however, would have understood, for she had left her home and her people to be with the man she loved.

There was a sound outside the cabin, and she started, her heart leaping inside her. It couldn't be Victor, she reminded herself, for he had made it quite clear he wouldn't be returning. She could only pray that it wasn't Henry Jourdan either.

But when she peered out the window to see who it was, she was surprised to find it was neither man, but a young boy. She recognized him at once. It was Claude's older brother, who'd asked about Claude often during the day she'd tended the younger brother at the infirmary. She hurried to open the door.

"Beggin' your pardon, ma'am," the boy said, taking off his hat in a gesture of respect that she found sweet. "Dr. Drouet sent me here with his horse to ask you if you would be so good as to hasten to the orphanage. He needs you sorely, he says."

The request was so unexpected that she couldn't speak at first. Victor was asking for her? And what was the meaning of it?

The boy took her hesitation for a refusal and babbled on in an anxious voice, " 'Tis Elias, ma'am. The others are all much better, but Elias won't take his physic unless you give it to him. Now he lies near to death, and Dr. Drouet says you are the only one can save him. You must come, ma'am. You must!"

His words struck her with fear. She'd become very attached to Elias, and the thought of him dying was too much to bear. Why hadn't his "voice" called out to her? But she knew why. She'd been so sunk in her misery over Victor that she wouldn't have noticed any other pain.

"What of Father Tomas?" she asked as she gathered her shawl and the bag that contained her herbs. "I suppose he has chosen to allow this, or Dr. Drouet wouldn't have summoned me."

"Oh, no," the boy said as he led her to Victor's horse. "Father Tomas is furious. He set off to fetch Monsieur Marigny. That's another reason we must hurry. Dr. Drouet says that you must arrive before Monsieur Marigny, or there will be hell to pay."

The boy mounted the horse, and she mounted behind him. But as they started off at a quick gallop toward the city proper, she couldn't help but wonder what Victor's intention was in all this. Did he think that if he sneaked her in to give Elias

his tea, then sneaked her out before Monsieur Marigny arrived,
he would be safe from Monsieur Marigny's wrath?

If so, he was much mistaken. Marigny wouldn't care that
she wasn't there when he arrived. He would still be angry with
Victor, and that would mean the end of Victor's association
with him.

But she had little time to worry about it. Consumed as
Claude's brother was with reaching the infirmary, he gave her
a harrowing ride through the muddy streets of New Orleans,
narrowly missing colliding with the few people out at that
hour.

When they thundered into the orphanage courtyard, Victor
hurried out of the infirmary to help her down from the horse.
He looked haggard and worried, though he also seemed heart-
ened to see her. Once she was off the horse, he launched into
a terse description of Elias's condition as they strode into the
infirmary.

Her heart sank when she approached Elias's bed. The child
was worse off than he'd been the first time she'd entered the
infirmary two nights ago. He didn't even open his eyes when
she laid the back of her hand on his forehead, and his fever
was much too high, though Victor had opened the window
and the door.

"I've bathed his head, but his fever climbs higher with each
moment," Victor said at her side. "He wouldn't drink the tea
unless you gave it to him, so Father Tomas and I tried forcing
it down him. But he was so agitated, he threw it up." He laid
his hand on Elias's chest and lowered his voice. "He was
calling your name constantly until an hour ago. Now I fear
. . . I've waited too late."

His eyes were fixed on Elias, and the pain in them triggered
an answering pain in her. He cared so much for the children.
How could she ever have thought otherwise?

"I'll do what I can," she told him, "but I don't know if
he'll come out of it. Sometimes the tea takes longer to work
when you start the dose after it has been interrupted."

"I should have called you sooner." He held tight to Elias's
hand. "I was such a fool. I—"

"Miss McCurtain?" came a plaintive voice from the bed. She looked down to find that Elias's eyes had fluttered open. They were dull and listless with pain, but at least he was still conscious.

"I'm here." She took the bowl of tea that Victor handed her and held it to Elias's lips. "You must drink your physic, poppet."

"Is it really you? 'Tisn't a dream?"

"It's not a dream, I promise." She pressed the edge of the bowl to his lips and he opened them, letting her trickle a little of the tea inside his parched mouth. It was hard for him at first, for he coughed a few times, and she feared he would vomit the tea up simply because he was too far gone to do anything else.

Then he paused halfway through drinking the tea and cast her an anxious look. "If I drink it all, you won't leave, will you? You'll stay?"

"That's for Dr. Drouet to say—" she began.

"She won't leave," Victor cut in. He laid his hand on her waist as her gaze swung to him. His eyes locked with hers, dark with meaning. "She won't go away ever again, Elias. We won't let her."

She felt a leap of hope that she tamped down immediately, in case she was reading too much into his words and his look. But when she returned her attention to Elias, her heart was lightened despite her attempts to be cautious.

"Sing me a song, Miss McCurtain," Elias rasped after he drained the last of the tea. "Sing me that song about the turtle and the rabbit."

"You mean, the tortoise and the hare." She cast a quick glance at Victor, who nodded his approval, so she began to sing. With a sigh, Elias curled his small fingers around her hand and laid his head back against the pillow.

While she sang, Victor moved about the room, checking on the children and obviously trying to keep busy. But she knew he must be worried about the coming confrontation with Monsieur Marigny, for she'd never seen him look more solemn.

Unfortunately, she couldn't give him any comfort, for she

was wholly absorbed with Elias. Indeed, as soon as she'd finished her song, Elias prompted her for another and then another. After a while, she lost track of how many there were.
Elias would doze as long as she sang, but whenever she
paused, he roused to ask for another, as if only her singing
kept him on this side of death's door.

When he finally fell into a heavy sleep, she dragged the
covers up over him. She was just about to tell Victor that she
thought Elias might pull out of it after all, when they both
heard the clatter of hooves in the paved courtyard.

Monsieur Marigny had arrived.

Telling her to stay put, Victor went out into the courtyard
without waiting for Monsieur Marigny to come in. But Lilith
wasn't about to let him face the man alone. With a quick
glance at Elias to make sure he still slept, she hurried into the
courtyard behind Victor.

Monsieur Marigny was dismounting from his carriage as
she came out, and Father Tomas dismounted after him. Monsieur Marigny wore the haughty expression so typical of the
very wealthy. But he was livid. That much was painfully obvious.

She cast her gaze to Victor, wondering what he would do.
Victor looked nonchalant as he faced the older man and the
priest, but she could see what no one else could—that Victor
held his hands clenched together behind his back.

To her surprise, Monsieur Marigny addressed her first.
"Thank you for your time, Miss McCurtain, but we have no
more need of your services here. You may leave."

Though couched in polite terms, his words were no less than
an order. But before she could answer them, Victor did it for
her. "Miss McCurtain isn't leaving. She is here by my invitation, and she'll remain until Elias and the others recover. If
you would only look inside the infirmary and see what a
change she has wrought—"

Monsieur Marigny tapped his cane on the paving stones.
"As I told you before, that is immaterial. And if you insist on
allowing her to stay, you will no longer be my doctor. I can
put it no plainer than that. I warned you once, and it is only

because I respect you that I am giving you another chance to break your shameful association with this woman."

"I'm sorry to lose your patronage," Victor said, his voice surprising her with its steadiness, "but that doesn't change my decision. Lilith McCurtain stays."

Father Tomas stepped forward, his ancient face creased with anger. "You have gone too far this time, Dr. Drouet. I can no longer excuse nor condone your behavior. That you would let this . . . this evil woman come here with her spells and chants and—"

"Where is she? Where is the Witch?" came a new voice from the entrance to the courtyard, and Lilith turned in shock to find Henry Jourdan standing there, his wife at his side. Rosemarie looked as if she wanted to be anywhere but there, and Lilith felt a stab of pity for the woman.

Monsieur Marigny turned toward Henry with a scowl. "What are you doing here? I told you to stay behind. I told you I'd handle this. You have no business being here!"

"You're right about that," Victor interjected. "Monsieur Jourdan indeed has no business here, but he doesn't need a reason to pursue Miss McCurtain. All he needs is the excuse of her 'witchery,' and he can justify anything, even attempted rape."

The word *rape* stunned everyone. Rosemarie went pale. A look of confusion spread over Henry's face. Thunderous fury shone in the faces of Father Tomas and Monsieur Marigny.

And Lilith could only stare at Victor in shock. Didn't he know what a chance he was taking by making this public accusation? To her knowledge Marigny was the only one— other than Victor—who'd heard Henry's tale about her supposed seduction of him. He'd managed to suppress it quite well, out of respect for Henry. He wouldn't be happy at all to have it bandied about in this manner, before a priest of God, no less. Victor would be ruined. Ruined! And all because of her!

"You, sir, have said quite enough—" Monsieur Marigny began.

"Not yet. Tell me, Monsieur Marigny, why your reliable,

honest overseer is here when by your own account he 'has no business being here.' And while you're explaining that, also explain why he came to Lilith's house alone last night. He certainly had no business being there either.''

"What on earth are you babbling about?" Monsieur Marigny snapped.

Victor glared at him. "Monsieur Jourdan went to Lilith's house last night. I went there, too, to consult her about the children, only to find her holding Monsieur Jourdan at bay with a knife, as he threatened to punish her for bewitching him, for forcing him to desire her!"

"Lies, all lies," Father Tomas cried. "Don't you see, Monsieur Marigny? The doctor is so enchanted by her that he will say anything!"

"Ask Monsieur Jourdan if he was there," Victor said. "Or better still, ask Mrs. Jourdan if her husband left his house at any time last evening."

Lilith held her breath. She hadn't wanted to force this confrontation, because she'd known how unpredictable would be the outcome. But she was glad Victor had done so. It was time to put an end to the lies and the uncertainty.

Rosemarie was shaking now, her pretty young face distraught. But before Monsieur Marigny could ask her anything, her husband blurted out, "Aye, I went to the Witch's house! I went because the Witch called me there! She wanted to cast her spell upon me once more and force me to fornicate with her. But I knew it. I knew what she wanted, and I went there to punish her!"

Victor stepped toward Henry, his hands forming fists at his sides. "She wanted to seduce you? Is that why she held you off with a knife? Why she begged you to leave her alone?"

"She said those words," Henry protested, "but her eyes said 'come.' "

Marigny was looking upon Henry with astonishment now, and even Father Tomas's face wore something like surprise.

"Tell the truth, Henry," Victor pressed. "That day at your house when you tried to force yourself on her, did she say the words then, too? Did she beg you to stop hurting her when you put your hands on her? Did she scream and try to push you away?''

Victor whirled on poor Mrs. Jourdan, fury in his face. "And you, Mrs. Jourdan. When you came upon your husband and Miss McCurtain together, was she truly trying to seduce him? Or was he forcing her to lie down on that bed and suffer his touch? Tell the truth!''

When an anguished expression passed over Rosemarie's face, the memory of that awful night flooded Lilith. Rosemarie had looked anguished that night, too, when she'd stumbled upon her husband holding Lilith down. It had taken all the woman's strength to drag him from Lilith, and she'd muttered, "I'm sorry, so sorry," all the while she'd done it, all while Lilith had fled the place in terror.

It was only later that Rosemarie had sided with Henry's version of events. Whether Rosemarie had done so out of concern for her husband's position or out of her own inability to stand against him, Lilith didn't know, but it was clear from the remorse in her eyes that she regretted it.

"Rosemarie?" Monsieur Marigny prompted.

Rosemarie started. "Yes, sir?"

Monsieur Marigny's voice softened. "Will you answer Dr. Drouet's question?"

Rosemarie bit her lip. "Yes, sir." She hesitated, lowering her gaze. "I . . . It appeared to me then that Miss McCurtain did not . . . want Henry's advances."

Relief flooded Lilith, so overwhelming that it took all her strength to remain standing. Finally, the truth was out. They'd have to believe her now.

But Monsieur Marigny was wearing a look of incredulity. "Why didn't you say this before? After your child died, when Henry came to me to tell me why and how Miss McCurtain had killed his daughter, you should have—" He broke off, a troubled expression on his face. "No, you need not answer that. I can well understand why you wouldn't gainsay your husband's tale. No wife would willingly expose her husband to public censure. And I did wrong not to question you about it, to believe whatever Henry told me."

"You believed it because it was true!" Henry protested. "The Witch *did* try to fornicate with me! That's why she came to my house when Sophie was ill . . . to torment me! To tempt me again! And when she couldn't, she cursed the child!"

"Aye, what of that?" came Father Tomas's bitter voice.

"You can hardly blame Lilith for Sophie's death," Victor snapped. "She came too late to save the child because she was afraid to be near Henry again."

"Yes, but why did she come there at all, if not to try seducing him again?" A triumphant look passed over Father Tomas's face. "You say Henry wouldn't have gone to the Witch's home unless he had an evil purpose, but the same can be said of her for going to the Jourdan house the night their child lay dying!"

Marigny's gaze turned to Victor in question, and Victor blanched. Lilith knew what he was thinking. If he told them about her voices, they would think her a witch for certain. Yet she could give them no other answer, for that was the truth.

A long, painful silence ensued. But just as she despaired of giving them any explanation that they might understand, Rosemarie spoke up.

"*I* called Miss McCurtain to our house," she said.

Everyone's gaze went to her. The young woman trembled, but she didn't shrink from them. "I called her there when no doctor in town seemed to be coming," she went on. "But I called her too late. 'Tis that which killed my child. That and naught else."

Lilith couldn't hide the shock that spread over her face. She stared at Rosemarie. The woman was lying to save her. But why?

Rosemarie's gaze locked with Lilith's, and suddenly Lilith knew why. Lilith wasn't the only one who'd lived with guilt over Sophie's death for the past year. Perhaps Rosemarie, too, had blamed herself for not calling Lilith, for letting her jealousy of her husband stand in the way of her child's life. And perhaps the lie was also Rosemarie's way of atoning for covering up her husband's inexcusable behavior in the first place, her way of making amends to Lilith.

Something passed between her and Rosemarie then, a silent message of understanding, an acknowledgment that each had been the victim of Henry Jourdan's madness in one way or another.

Monsieur Marigny cleared his throat, and Lilith turned to see him looking far less haughty than when he'd entered. "This changes matters entirely," he murmured in a strained voice. "It seems that all of us owe Miss McCurtain a profound apology."

"An apology?" Henry shouted. "Is there to be no punishment for her misdeeds? Is she not to suffer—"

"That's enough, Henry," Monsieur Marigny bit out. He turned to Rosemarie. "Take him home, will you? I shall deal with him later."

A lost look came over Henry's face to hear his master dismiss him. But though he continued to mumble to himself about the outrage, Rosemarie succeeded at last in drawing him from the courtyard.

Monsieur Marigny turned to Lilith, his haughty expression once more in place. "Miss McCurtain, I will make certain that Henry is severely disciplined for his actions. I assure you, it was never my intention to allow behavior of this sort from my servants, and I will be more circumspect in the future in dealing with disputes of this kind."

"Is that supposed to compensate her for a year of lost income, of lost reputation, of living in fear of Henry Jourdan?" Victor came to stand beside her and took her hand in his. "All you can do is promise it won't happen again?"

Monsieur Marigny looked startled by Victor's bold words. "I suppose I could offer a small financial reparation—"

"I want no money," Lilith said, squeezing Victor's hand. No amount of money could erase the past year, and she didn't want to be indebted to Monsieur Marigny for anything ever. "I am content that you know the truth, sir."

"At least I can make sure that your name is cleared in the matter of Sophie's death," Monsieur Marigny replied. "I shall make the community aware of your work here at the orphanage and how much good it has wrought. That should help put to rights your reputation.''

Then he looked at Victor. ''As for you, Dr. Drouet, let us put this entire distasteful incident behind us. Rest assured that I will be pleased to have you continue as my doctor.''

''This 'distasteful incident.' That's all it is to you, isn't it?'' Victor's eyes narrowed as he stared at Monsieur Marigny. ''I thank you, sir, but I shall have to forgo your generous offer.''

Marigny looked dumbfounded. ''You will allow this misunderstanding to keep you from serving as my physician?''

''Nay. This 'misunderstanding,' as you put it, merely helped me to regain the perspective I had lost.'' Victor cast Marigny a sobering look. ''In the future, I will be happy to treat any of your family or slaves who need my assistance. The only change is that I wish to be paid for it as the service is rendered. No annual fee, no horse. If you are willing to wait on my leisure as every other patient does, then I will happily provide you with medical attention.''

''But I must have a private physician at my disposal at all times!'' Monsieur Marigny protested.

''Then you must find another doctor to take your fee and your horse, mustn't you?'' Victor slid his arm about Lilith's waist as he looked into her eyes. ''I am no longer for sale to the highest bidder, Monsieur Marigny. Never again.''

She gave him a dazzling smile, so proud of him she could hardly contain it. She knew what it had cost him to throw aside Monsieur Marigny's support. Victor wasn't a man used to taking chances. That he was taking one for her meant more than anything else he could have said or done.

Monsieur Marigny gave a disgruntled snort, but made no further argument. ''Very well, Dr. Drouet. If you change your mind, you know where to find me. Good day to you both. And to you, Father Tomas.'' Then he left.

The only one of her accusers who now remained was Father Tomas, but she could tell from his expression that he wouldn't easily change his opinion of her. He stared at her, eyes still filled with mistrust. ''A very pretty tale you have given them all today, Miss McCurtain. But I know what you are. I know what you are.''

Victor's arm about her waist went stiff. ''She's a healer, Father Tomas, and a very good one, too. Think what you will of her, but she will stay with these children until I'm certain they're out of danger. And I will brook no argument on that.''

For a moment, Father Tomas looked as if he would disagree. But he wasn't so foolish as to ignore the writing on the wall. Without Monsieur Marigny's support, he had no power at all. Grumbling to himself, he walked past them into the infirmary.

''I suppose that means he won't be performing our marriage ceremony,'' Victor murmured as soon as Father Tomas was gone.

She gazed up at him, eyes wide. ''Marriage ceremony?''

He looked solemn now as he drew her into his arms. ''Aye. If you will have me. If you can forgive me for being such a fool, for—''

''Shh,'' she whispered, joy leaping in her heart as she held her finger to his lips. ''You mustn't talk like that about the man I love. He gave up much for me today, and I shall never forget it.''

As he smiled at her, his eyes sparkled with that intense blue that always made her think of the sky. ''I gave up nothing of any worth. And in return I gained everything, my soul included.'' He laughed suddenly, and the sound was like music. ''Father Tomas would be quite astonished to learn that I have found my faith in God after all. It's obvious it wasn't the Devil who sent you here to the children . . . and to me. So it must have been God. And for that, I must thank Him.''

As he touched his lips to hers, she knew that the Dr. Drouet who'd scoffed at her voices and questioned anything beyond his sight was no more. And in his place was a man she knew she could love for a lifetime.

THE MONK

MEAGAN McKINNEY

*This is dedicated to
my Brother
Ross Steingrimur Goodman
and to
Nevermore Manor
from which I got the idea.*

CHAPTER ONE

The house on Washington Avenue stood forty-three paces from the cemetery. Leila Randolph knew this because that was how far they'd had to carry her mother's coffin. Forty-three steps and they were able to put Edwina Randolph next to her stillborn son, Sercy. One more trip for her father, another forty-three paces, and Leila would finally find herself irrefutably, irrevocably alone.

She looked across the Corinthian pillars of her home to stare at the crumbling city of the dead. October twilight trod softly on Lafayette Cemetery. Long pink beams of light fell like mist through the lace of live oaks, obscuring the rot and the dampness of untended graves. The Randolph vault was surrounded by an old iron fence replete with Gothic arches and trefoils. Even now Leila could see the caretaker chisel away at the marble plaque on the front of the vault, readying it for another occupant. An occupant who was not even yet dead.

She wondered, when it was her time, if they would chisel open the vault while she was still lying in a room off the veranda. In fifty years, would they whisper about the old spinster Randolph, shake their heads in pity at the run-down condition of her house and mark this day as the beginning of her sorrows?

Leila shut her eyes to the picture. If she did nothing, she might be the last Randolph to be buried in the family vault. But she swore to herself not even death and poverty could block her flight from such a fate. She was not going to become a spinster. People could think her vain and always in need of another party gown, but her father's long slope to the grave had taught her how alone she would one day be. And now that day was fast approaching.

"I had a nightmare last night, Leila." Leila's only sister, sixteen-year-old Jenny, clung to her waist. She didn't sob as the servants were wont to do these days; instead she looked up at her older sister with eyes painfully dry, her face small and pale. "I had a dream that when Papa died, we had to go live at St. Vincent's Orphanage. For we were orphans, weren't we?"

Leila ran a hand down Jenny's dark curls that were so much like her own. "I don't think it's that bad yet. Besides, I'm too old to go to the orphanage, and I certainly don't relish the thought of working there, so we'll have to find another alternative."

"Such as marry Charles Drew?" Jenny said in a sullen voice.

"He could take care of you in Papa's place. And I've done all right as a mother all these years, haven't I?" She gave her younger sister a tremulous smile. "Once I marry, you'll come and live with me, and my husband will think of you as his own."

"Charles Drew won't think of me as his own. He makes fun of my club foot and the strange way I walk. He even pinches me when you're not looking, Leila." Jenny scowled.

Leila was about to reply when a tall dark figure of a man appeared in the front door.

"He wants to see you," the man said as he walked onto the veranda. He was Aidan Lacour, James Randolph's former business partner. The ornate gaslights that flanked the front door cast him in shadow: Leila couldn't quite make out the details of his grim expression.

"Thank you," she answered coldly. In the darkness, Lacour

seemed taller and more threatening. She wanted nothing more than to avoid the man. She made to walk past him, Jenny's arm in hers, but his hand clamped on her velvet-clad arm.

Desperate, angry tears flooded her eyes. "Jenny, go on into Father's room. I'll be right behind you," Leila instructed. Her sister reluctantly left the veranda and Leila turned on the man. "How dare you be here for his final hour?"

"Where else would I be but at my dear friend's side?" he snapped.

"You walked him to his grave. Isn't that enough? Or must you see him good and cold too?"

A muscle bunched in Lacour's jaw. "Your father was my best friend. I came to New Orleans as a slater with nothing but calluses on my hands. He was the only businessman who would listen to a poor Irish lad's ideas. I will always be grateful to him."

"Then why did you ruin him?" Her cheeks heated with anger. She would never understand why her father had been made to suffer. Never. Aidan Lacour had put her father into financial ruin by buying out his half of the cotton brokerage when he did. James Randolph had no business acumen to start a new endeavor, and Lacour knew it. She blamed Lacour for not talking her father out of selling his shares, and for that she hated him and always would.

"I didn't want to buy him out," he said in unusual candor and familiarity. "But every decision your father made on his own was a bad one. He kept digging himself in deeper and deeper. You, his darling oldest daughter, wanted this gown and that school and another trip to Italy—I couldn't stop him from hurting himself. In the end, he told me he needed the money and I gave it to him."

"And you ruined him."

"No." Lacour's eyes flashed. "I gave him more than what his share was worth and he knows it."

"But you made sure he hadn't enough money to start on his own again."

Lacour seemed barely able to hold his anger in check. "He didn't have the money to start over because he spent it all on

you, Miss Randolph. How do you think he paid for that expensive ladies' school in Paris? What was it called? The
Ecole—?''

''*L'Ecole des Deux Lions d'Ors*,'' she answered woodenly.

''Ah, of course. The Two Gold Lions.'' He smirked. ''Well,
now you're down to none, Miss Randolph.'' The hand tightened imperceptibly on her arm.

She ripped it off her. ''I'll always blame you no matter how
poor his judgment. And may that rest uneasy upon your soul.''

He nodded his head toward the darkened foyer where the
physician and the various household servants talked in hushed
circles. ''He does not blame me, Leila. So your curses have
no teeth.''

A tear dribbled down her cheek. The heartache threatened
to erupt in long, torturous sobs, but she dashed the tear away.
''He was always so fond of you. I'll never understand his
generosity toward your character when by all rights you've
been nothing but calculating and selfish.''

''How many times must I say this?'' he retorted. ''I tried
to talk him out of selling but he would not think of it. He said
you were in need of new gowns and that was the end of it.
He wanted it all for you, Leila. He lived, and now he dies, for
you.''

The tears came full now, hot dripping rivulets that streamed
down her pain-tautened face. She thought of the armoire upstairs filled with costly satin gowns. She thought of the delightful trips and the carefree days at the academy. She never
thought about where those pleasures came from, nor did she
ever think their price would be exacted by such grief. ''I didn't
want the money.'' She wept softly. ''I would have done without the gowns and academy if I'd known—''

''If you'd known,'' he snorted. ''If you'd known, then I
wager you still would have required them all just the same.
He couldn't deny you. Even now he can't deny you, even
though you're leaving his only wish unfulfilled.''

''I will not marry you,'' she said, her voice choked with as
yet unshed tears. ''I've told you and him so a thousand times.
If I marry at all, Charles Drew is the man I choose.''

"He wants you and Jenny taken care of. Drew won't do it as well as I." His words grew husky. "How can you deny him that?"

She looked at him. "You mean, how can I deny *you* that?"

He seemed to bite back another retort. "I told him I would abide by his wishes."

"Even though you're so much older than me? Even though I've another beau to whom I'm much attached?"

His expression seemed to turn to stone. "I'm only thirty-five. Not so very old, especially for a spinster who's soon to turn twenty-one."

"I won't be a spinster for long." Her words were as chilly as the grave.

"Charles Drew is not the man for you. He gambles. What little money his family has left is quickly being depleted at the tables. How vainglorious of you to throw yourself at a parlor snake just because he's handsome."

Leila stared at him: studied him in the flickering gaslight. Aidan Lacour might have been a handsome man too if not for the way the corner of his mouth puckered and turned downward. The scar jagged down the side of his chin like a big fleshy bolt of lightning ending at a place hidden beneath his jaw. Her father told her Lacour had gotten it in a shantytown outside of New York when he was hardly more than a boy. He was clipped by a knife in a fight over a loaf of bread. The story should have been compelling to her, but after the agonies her father suffered once Lacour had bought him out, she no longer saw the heroism in it. To her, Lacour was nothing but a coldhearted opportunist and whether he fought over a loaf of bread or ownership of a cotton brokerage, he would win no matter what he had to do, no matter who he had to ruin. Physically, the scar did little to reinforce Lacour's good features. It gave him a permanent sneer that made him look evil, and it served as a constant reminder of his crude beginnings. Aidan Lacour was nothing but a hardscrabble shanty man and the fine midnight blue waistcoat and barrel tie he sported now would not hide it. To her, the scar was only his true self peeking out from the veneer.

"Charles Drew did not kill a man as you've done." She was only partly referring to his past. Her father had told her it was said that Lacour had killed the ruffian who'd cut him, but that was only rumor. What was happening now was fact. Her father's health had never been good, but the last two years of financial difficulties had taken their toll. He couldn't survive it.

Anger like a cold serpent slithered across his expression. He took a step back and tipped his hat. Without much more consolation, he said, "You've played the spoiled child to the end, Leila. So have your Charles Drew. Make your choices. You'll either find the character your father believes is inside you, or you will not. God save you if you don't."

"It's time, miss. He's ready for you." Sally, the parlor maid, stepped out to the veranda and curtsied. Her face was reddened with tears.

Leila tried to swallow the dread that had lodged in her throat. It didn't seem possible that the end was coming. She wasn't ready to say good-bye. She had no ability to cope on her own.

"Fare thee well, Leila," Lacour whispered to her as she walked past him into the darkened foyer.

"Don't exert yourself, Father. You must rest and stay calm. There's no need to worry about me. I will take care of myself," Leila whispered. She sat on the edge of her father's bed, her heavy velvet *tournure* tucked behind her.

"Leila. My darling girl . . ." Randolph burst into a fit of coughing that sent tears burning from his eyes. "I want you taken care of. No need to fend for yourself when there's Aidan to watch after you and little Jenny."

"Father, you mustn't worry about all this now. I'll manage with or without Aidan Lacour. Charles Drew will propose. I know it. He would have already except for out of respect for your bad health."

"I won't have you marry him. I won't!" Randolph grasped her hand in his trembling ones. "See inside his heart, Leila. There is nothing but a void. No heart at all."

She brushed back the tears that tipped over her lashes.
"Charles has more of a heart than most. *He* wouldn't stand
by while his dearest friend falls to ruin."

"A man must make his choices and live with them, Leila.
That's all Lacour did is let me make my choices. I tried to do
what was best—I tried—"

"You did do what was best," she cried out softly. "You
did everything right. He just shouldn't have let you sell out.
We would have been fine if only he'd left you alone."

"He warned me of it, daughter. He's a good man. A good
man—" The coughing fit began again.

Leila gripped his hand. "Be still, Father. He let you make
your decisions. Now you must let me make mine. Jenny and
I will be fine. You mustn't worry. Drew will watch out for us.
And even if he does have a penchant for the cards, he still has
monthly funds coming in from his mother's estate. That alone
can keep us in fine fashion. I don't need as much as everyone
thinks."

"You need and deserve the world. Let Lacour show it to
you." Randolph grew quiet. He looked up at his daughter with
morbid, rheumy eyes. "I know he's an ugly one. If it weren't
for the scar he just might seem a little more palatable. But you
have to see into his soul. Then you'll find him—"

"No, Father." She shook her head. "I see into his soul.
I'm not so flighty that I look only at a handsome face and fat
wallet. But I can never forgive the man for what he's done to
you. Don't ask me to. Don't do it. I beg you."

Randolph grew quiet. He stared at his daughter and one
trembling hand reached up to stroke a brunette curl. "But you
don't love Charles Drew. You don't love him."

Leila was loathe to answer. Finally she whispered, "I don't
love Aidan Lacour either."

Her father sighed. He leaned back against the pillows, defeated. Weakly, he gasped, "I didn't want to have to tell you
this, daughter, but I can see I've no choice. I've not left you
as destitute as you might imagine. You don't have to marry
at all if you don't want to."

"What?" she gasped.

"That's right," he said, his voice growing thin. "I've a fortune still left to you, but"—he clutched her and squeezed her arm—"but you'll have to retrieve it, daughter."

"Retrieve it? How can I retrieve it? What do you mean? Is it buried somewhere?" She stared at him, bewildered. Her father was sounding so crazy, she even wondered if it was the morphine talking.

"It's a mirror. The most valuable thing I own. A bejeweled hand mirror that was handed down on your mother's side of the family. It's very old and worth a lot of money because it once belonged to Anne Boleyn. Some . . . well, some say it has mystical powers, others say it is cursed—and now—now I don't know . . . It just might be."

She shook her head as if to clear it. "What are you talking about, Father? Where is the mirror now? Who has it?"

"I gave it to a man who lives on the other side of the cemetery. I needed money. He gave me money and as collateral, I gave him the mirror."

Heartsick, she leaned down and kissed his frail hand. "Oh, Father, I don't have any money to pay him back, so I'm afraid he'll have to keep this unlucky mirror."

"No. He doesn't want money in return. I know he'll take something else, something much worse, but if you're canny and you keep your head—" He suddenly went into a coughing spell, then he violently shook his head. "No. I . . . I . . . can't let you do it."

"I think I know what this man wants." Her expression turned to stone. "But I might try to negotiate away the mirror without losing my honor."

Randolph placed his hand over his mouth as if in horror. "Oh, child, if it were only honor we were talking about here. If it were only a momentary weakness of the flesh that could dispatch this debt, I would beg for such mercy." He grabbed her hand again. "No, you must accept Lacour's offer. See inside his heart as he tells me he sees inside yours. You'll find your companion in him, I know it. I know it."

Leila brushed aside tears. "Father. If the truth be known I would not like to marry either Drew or Lacour. I'd like to fend for myself and find love where I may. But you must give me the power to do it. So tell me the name of the man who has this mirror. I'll retrieve it like you said.''

''No.'' Randolph squeezed shut his eyes as if he were in great pain.

''Father?'' she said softly, her heart constricting. ''Tell me.''

''No,'' he whispered, his hand clutching his chest. ''The price is too high.''

''What is the price? Tell me the price,'' she begged, her tears coming full as she watched him dwindle away.

''Oh, my beloved daughter. Run to Lacour. Don't play this dark game.''

Panic coursed through her veins. Tears blinded her. Finally, in despair, she threw her head upon his chest and wept bitterly. ''I don't want to play dark games, Father, but you must tell me so that I know. Where does the man live? What's his name?''

''He lives in the old brick mansion on Plaquemines, the one facing the gates of the cemetery.''

She raised her head and stared at him, confused. ''But no one lives there, Father. No one has for years. It's abandoned.''

He took a sharp intake of breath. Then, as if he knew it was his last, he whispered, ''Don't pay the price. Don't do it.''

''But what is the price, Father?'' She wept. ''What is it?'' she begged.

''Your soul,'' he said. Then he was still.

CHAPTER TWO

Here lies James Robert Randolph
Born 23 December 1820 in Philadelphia
Died 3 October 1872 in New Orleans
Gone but not Forgotten

Leila read the marble plaque again and again as if to make it real, but somehow it wasn't. Her father had been gone weeks but it seemed as if the shock and horror of it would never truly sink in. Even now she wondered if she couldn't just sit on the veranda and wait for her father to return home as if he'd just spent the day with Aidan Lacour at the cotton brokerage.

But the truth kept baring its fangs. A steady stream of money-demanding shopkeepers was her only company, Charles had paid his respects the day of the funeral, but just that morning he'd delivered a note to the door explaining he'd gone to Natchez and wouldn't be back for weeks.

Not that they could plan for a wedding anyway, she told herself as she stared at her father's vault. Respectability required at least three months of mourning and preferably more. Still, she wished Drew had stayed around. He would distract her.

Her eyes raised to the other end of Lafayette Cemetery. The rusting gates framed the mansion across the street. Unpainted and crumbling, the house was the last remaining structure of

the old Verly plantation, and it sat on a full city block. She'd
heard talk that it was going to be razed in order to push in
more houses that were being built by the dozens now that the
war was over, but nothing ever happened with it. The house
still stood, but now it had pigeons roosting in the broken windows and weeds choking the paths. The old-fashioned batten
shutters were either missing or off their hinges and only a
vestige of the original verdigris paint remained on the pock-
marked stucco. The place looked totally abandoned and she'd
always heard that it was empty. It didn't seem possible that
someone lived there now.

"Where are you going, miss?"

Leila blinked and realized her maid was speaking to her.
"Where? Why, I'm not going anywhere." She stopped and
looked at herself. She'd been walking toward the house on
Plaquemines. Without even knowing it she'd been drawn to
the ramshackle structure as if it beckoned.

Sputtering, she said, "Do—do we need to go marketing
today, Sally? If so, I'll go with you." Anything, she thought,
to get her mind off that house, Anne Boleyn and her soul.

Sally's eyes grew wide. "We need a full larder, miss, but
you know there's no money for it, And no one's going to give
us any credit until Mr. Randolph's debts have been paid." The
maid wrung her hands in her apron. She was a large rough-
and-tumble Scotch-Irish woman with a ruddy complexion and
periwinkle eyes; unfortunately she looked much more capable
than she actually was.

Leila stared again at the house on Plaquemines Street.
Charles had left town and while it would have been unseemly
for him to support her before they were wed, a small loan
wouldn't have been refused. But she knew she was kidding
herself about him. Indeed he was handsome, and if he had one
ounce of character he might make a woman an acceptable
husband. But he didn't have that one ounce and she knew he
never would. Charles Drew thought of Charles Drew and
Charles Drew alone. If she wed him, she would always be at
the mercy of his desires and his failings.

Worse, she didn't love him.

So she'd admitted it. She didn't love him. And as bad as the situation was for her, she still didn't see how she could wed Drew when she wished for love.

Her gaze locked on the house. The mirror was tantamount to her salvation. If she could bargain with the man, she could save her home and herself. She could buy herself choices with the mirror and not be forced to wed a gambling rakehell just because he seemed better than Aidan Lacour with his frightening scar and wretched manipulations. She knew she had to at least try.

"Let's go home, Sally," she said, lifting her black silk parasol over her head. "I've got a note I want you to send to one of our neighbors. Call it intuition, but I think we'll be able to fill the larder more quickly than circumstances allow." With that she strode toward the back entrance to the cemetery and home.

Evening darkness settled over the Garden District like the wings of a bat. The lamplighter made his rounds and the only sounds on Washington Avenue were the clack of a wooden ladder and the distant rooting of pigs that had escaped their pen near the wharf. From the veranda, Leila watched the night float into her parlor. A gentle autumn breeze lifted the lace curtains and sent them fluttering into the air like escaping ghosts. The gaslights flanking the door licked and flared in a devil's dance. A heavy perfume of sweet olive filled her nostrils. Her thoughts drifted toward places that were shadowed and sensual.

She looked down at the note in her hand. Sally had delivered her penned message. The response had come only an hour earlier delivered anonymously. Sally had found the note tucked into the iron hinges of the front gate.

Midnight.
The Monk

The baby fine hairs stood up on the back of her neck. Every time she read the note another shiver of foreboding crept down her spine. It was enough to make her think that marriage to Charles Drew might not be such a bad thing after all.

"You look a thousand miles away, Miss Randolph."

Leila startled and peered down the staircase. Lacour stood there, bowler in his hands, while he gazed back up at her.

"Good evening, Mr. Lacour." She hastily stuffed the note inside her sleeve along with her handkerchief. "What brings you here at this hour?"

"Business, of course, Miss Randolph."

"What kind of business?" she asked warily. "You can't tell me father owed *you* anything."

"No. I've come to make a bargain with you." He looked at the stair rails, then lifted a dark eyebrow. "May I come up?"

She had hours more before she had to meet with the strange man who had her mirror. Sighing, she nodded and escorted Lacour to the parlor.

Sally was just lighting the sconces. Above her, neo-Greco masks on the gold window cornices looked most wicked as they stared down in the dim light. Leila had always liked the parlor. It was the height of fashion with its gold-tasseled drapery and rococo marble mantel. Tonight, however, she couldn't find anything but malevolence in it.

"Please sit down." She stared at him. He stared at her. His eyes were blue like her own, but his were darker, more secretive. She could feel his stare upon her face like an unwanted caress.

"I've heard all over town about your money problems." He waited until she was seated, then he cleared his throat. "I hope you won't find it unseemly of me as your father's friend to offer a loan—"

"I have no way to repay a loan," she answered evenly.

"The repayment terms can be negotiated." His stare was almost tangible.

"Charles may be willing to dispatch my debts but unfortunately he's in Natchez and won't be back for some time."

"A fine prospect," Lacour mumbled.

"Nonetheless," she said, "I couldn't accept any kind of

loan without him here. We're about to be engaged, you see. As soon as propriety allows a certain mourning period.''

''You don't love him.''

She stiffened.

''You'll never love him. There's nothing inside him to love.''

She met his stare. ''That's what some have said about me too, Mr. Lacour. I believe you yourself described me as 'vain' in nature. So perhaps Charles and I are well matched.''

''Your father was a good man. He couldn't have a daughter with a black heart.'' Lacour rubbed his chin. The ragged pink skin of the scar glistened in the dancing light. Tonight it looked especially mean. It transfixed her.

''His daughter does not have a black heart,'' she said softly, ''but she does want to make her own choices.''

He caught her gaze. ''Then choose me.''

She didn't move. His stare pinned her down. ''I don't love you,'' she whispered.

''I can make you.'' He looked desperately around the parlor as if searching for answers. ''I know I can.''

''How can you create feelings where there are none?''

He met her gaze once more. ''I've always been there for your father even when he was sinking into the mire of his own creation. You claim I ruined him but it's just the opposite. I've been the one to keep him going. Doesn't that merit any repayment in affection?''

''You hope to buy my affection?'' she asked incredulously.

''I've watched you grow from a little girl to a woman—a very beautiful woman. I want you, Leila. If you could just look upon this hideous face with love—if I could just find your heart—I would buy you gowns that would take your breath away. I would buy you jewels—''

''You want me?'' she interrupted, her heart nearly choking her. ''All this talk of jewels and gowns—what am I?—some kind of doll you want to dress and prop up on your mantel? I am not a possession to be owned, decorated and flaunted.''

''I don't want that—you know it,'' he snapped.

"No, I do not know it. I do not know you," she said. Slowly, she rose to her feet.

He stood, looking grim and angry. His bowler was creased where his hands gripped it.

She motioned to the parlor door. "I'm afraid you must excuse me now. I've a late appointment this evening. I must get ready for it."

"You'll regret this, Leila," he said fiercely. He gave her one last burning look and said, "If you push me to it, I swear, I will *make* you want me."

"Good night, Mr. Lacour, I bid you farewell." Her words were calm, but her heart slammed in her chest. With one last fearsome glance, he was gone.

CHAPTER THREE

She should have asked Sally to go with her. From the darkened street, Leila heard the forlorn gong of the church bells. It was midnight. The appointed hour. She had only a block to go and she wore her black walking suit of crepe. But though she blended with the night she felt conspicuous trammeling by the cemetery. The dead seemed to be watching her from their little crumbling houses. She was afraid.

The fear she was going to conquer, she told herself again and again. Sally might have made good company but Leila had too much pride to go begging with the servants. And this was what she was doing. She was going to beg for that precious mirror for she had no coin to repay the man. She could only appeal to the angel of his better nature and pray he be merciful.

She stopped in front of the old Verly place. The house looked worse at midnight when all was silent and dark. A flutter of black clouded the night sky over the roofline and she drew back in revulsion. Bats.

A man had to be crazy to live in such squalor, she thought to herself as she opened the iron gate. The gate swung back with a screech and unnervingly latched behind her.

The man was indeed crazy, she said to herself. The land his house sat on was worth a small fortune. He didn't have to live in a ruin.

Unless he wanted to, she thought. And her hands began to tremble.

She reached the front door. A black maw of mahogany. She drew back a gloved hand to knock, but as she did, she realized the door was already open. It swung wide and opened into a dank, musty foyer.

She stepped inside and paused. "It's Miss Randolph," she said to the unrelieved darkness. "Is anyone here?"

Not a sound permeated the dust-entrenched silence.

"I've come about the mirror." She looked around the foyer, allowing her eyes to grow accustomed to the darkness. To the rear was an immense mahogany staircase built in more recent times, but the cobwebs strewn upon it proved it hadn't been used in years.

"I know you received my note. You see I've yours right here." She lifted it in her gloved hand but showed it to no one. The foyer was empty.

Unnerved, she decided a retreat was in order. The whole thing had obviously been some kind of trick. No one lived in this place and she was a fool to have ventured inside it at midnight without her maid. She took a step backward toward the front door. Then another. She was ready to flee entirely when beneath the closed door to her left, a light appeared.

Her heart speeded. She held her breath. All logic told her she should simply enter the room and try to bargain with the man, but logic wasn't driving her. Fear clutched her throat. She backed away, her train trailing in the dust beside her.

Leave, she told herself again and again, but she paused. A fatal error. A great wind seemed to rush through the foyer. The huge mahogany front door slammed behind her. She stumbled toward it and yanked at the doorknob, but the door was stuck. It didn't budge.

She turned around and faced the dark foyer. The light didn't move from under the heavy door to her left. Without exit, she had no choice but to approach the lit room and confront the occupant.

She passed a cobwebbed mirror and glanced at her reflection. Her face was white as a casket lily. Her dark brown hair and black crepe bonnet only accentuated it. She suddenly found herself unprepared to face this man—or monster—that lurked in the other room. But she had to. The alternatives were either poverty and starvation, or finding herself becoming the trinket of a man who did not love her.

With renewed fortitude, she took a step forward and grasped the handle of the interior door. With one long drawn-out creak, the door opened and she stepped inside the lit room.

She gasped. What little blood was left in her cheeks bled out entirely. Beneath her corset, her heart drummed in horror.

The man sat on a Gothic-arched dais facing her. He didn't move or acknowledge her. He merely sat in his chair, still and deathlike. His body from his toes to his wrists to his head was obscured in coarse brown monk's robes. His hands were folded in his lap, and human hands they were, finely made male hands, their backs sprinkled with dark hair. But there was nothing else of him she could see. A cowl covered his head and created a deep shadow where his face should be. The black cavern in the hood terrified her. There should have been a face there and she wished fervently she had the courage to whip back the cowl and expose his humanity. But in the back of her mind, she wondered if she weren't simply too frightened of finding out he had none. That, perhaps, there was no face to be found in the merciful shadows of the cowl.

"Why have you come here?" a voice boomed out of the hood. The tone was deep and demanding.

"I . . . I . . ." She swallowed and held out the note. "I've come at the hour you specified. As I said in my letter, I hoped to discuss the mirror."

"The mirror is not for sale."

"I . . . I know that." She licked her dry lips. "I've no money to purchase it in any case. Instead I was hoping to see if you would relinquish it. You see, it's all that's left to me. My father told me to come here."

"Your father was unwise to tell you that."

She opened her mouth to retort but the words wouldn't come. The man was telling her she was on a fool's errand, and by all intelligence, she should believe him. Finally she choked out, "I had to come here. I've nothing left."

"Except this." Bitterness poisoned each word. He reached inside the fold of his robe and pulled out a small hand mirror.

Her eyes widened. Even in the light of one small sconce she saw how it glittered. The back was silver encrusted with rubies and diamonds in the shape of a *B*. Pearls entwined the front of the mirror and sapphires paved the handle. "It's beautiful," she breathed.

"Is it?" he asked. Then he held it to her face.

Even though she was ten feet away, she saw her reflection. But her face looked different than it had in the foyer. Her eyes glittered with more life. Her cheeks were flushed with color like berry stains on a tablecloth. Even her lips which seemed so dry before appeared effused with moisture and colored a deep carmine.

"Now it's beautiful," he said solemnly, his empty, cowl-hooded face staring directly at her.

She looked at him. Fear and confusion muddled her thoughts. "My father told me to come here. He said you would give me back the mirror."

The monk tilted his head; still, she couldn't see a face inside the darkness of the cowl. "I handed Randolph a fortune for his precious mirror. What have you to bargain with . . . if you have no money?"

Trembling, she said, "I have nothing."

He laughed. The sound was deep and throaty. "So you've nothing to do but beg, Miss Randolph. So do it. Beg."

The fear she felt earlier melted to anger. "I will not," she whispered harshly.

"Then get out." He stood. With one strong well-formed hand he pointed malevolently toward the door. "Do not come back until you have something to offer."

"But what do you want if not money? What have I to give you?" she cried, hating to be banished when the mirror was within arm's reach.

"You could give me your vanities. Your petty desires. Your misbegotten dreams." He stepped to her. The hand that pointed to the door reached up and caressed her cheek. She could feel each hard knuckle. The stroke frightened her, yet he was gentle. Impossibly gentle.

"How can I give you those things? I don't know how." She barely breathed.

"You only want this mirror so that you may gaze vainly at your pretty face. Why should I relinquish it for that?"

"No," she whispered. "It's not true. I really need the mirror. I must put my home up for sale if not."

"Return to me tomorrow this same time. I'll see that all I want is taken from you."

The words echoed in her mind. "P-please," she stammered, "tell me how you could take such things from me . . . and . . . and tell me why you would want them."

"Tomorrow," he whispered hotly, the cowl so close she could almost see a face in the darkness. "You'll learn more tomorrow."

He held up the mirror to her face. The hand rose again: It stroked her cheek, then her lips, then her jaw. The touch was almost pleasurable and she found it hard not to close her eyes and lose herself in it.

"Go and do not return until midnight tomorrow. I'll teach you what to do. Then, perhaps, the mirror will be yours." He stepped away and cloaked himself in the shadows.

A breeze ran past her and she suddenly felt cold and alone. The monk melted more into the darkness. Terror gave her the strength to stumble for the door. It opened easily, along with the front door. Before she could blink, she was out on the street, sobbing and gasping; clinging to the iron gates of Lafayette Cemetery.

I'll teach you. . . . Soon the mirror will be all yours. His promise was more like a warning. She turned and faced the Verly house. If she went back there tomorrow, she might learn things she'd never wanted to know. Tomorrow she must decide: Did she go the coward's route and marry a man she did not love, or did she summon her bravery and face this terrible creature who held her family prize, and demand he take whatever payment she was willing to give? She didn't know. All she did know was that suddenly she was very frightened. And her face still burned with phantom caresses.

CHAPTER FOUR

"I'm sorry but I've no funds now to pay you. You'll have to come back another day." Leila led Mr. Blum, the dressmaker, toward the front door.

"I would take a promissory note from Charles Drew if he would but write one," the man said, his expression crushed with a frown.

"I'm afraid he's in Natchez right now..." Her words drifted off. "But I'll have the money soon. Please don't worry." She added, "You were so kind to rush to my needs. I'll see that you're paid. I promise." She fingered the black lace fichu at her neck. Blum had spared no time in arranging for her mourning dress and she would pay him even if it meant selling the house.

"I wouldn't be so pressed, it's just that I've five children, you know, and the wife gets rather mad when I don't collect." He looked at her sorrowfully.

"Yes, I understand perfectly. And I *will* pay you. All I ask is some time."

He tipped his hat. "All right then. I'll come back another day." He went out the door, his expression like all the rest of her creditors: grim.

She shut the front door and walked to the parlor. Sally and two other housemaids had been busy all morning hanging the winter drapery. Now, because she couldn't stand the cheerful sunshine that streamed through the lace curtains, she released the burgundy velvet panels from the enormous tassels holding them back and threw the room in utter darkness.

The shadows were succor for her despair. Laying her head in her hands, she didn't even need to fight back her tears for she'd run dry of them. Her depression had grown so deep and black she wondered if she would ever find a way out of it.

Patting her face with a black-edged handkerchief, she stood and resolved to go out. Errands still had to be run, there were shopkeepers she still had to see in order to put off paying them; and she had to get through it. In the foyer, she gathered her gloves and black fringed parasol and went out into the noontime sun.

The day's heat had just enough of a touch of autumn in it to be bearable. She patted her forehead and unlatched the folding parasol. Sally should have accompanied her, but the way Leila felt, she wanted to be alone.

Slowly she picked her way across the new granite curbs, following her usual route to the cemetery. A visit to her father's tomb brought only tears and misery, but she found she couldn't stay away. She had no one now. No one loved her as her father had, perhaps no one ever would. Even in death, she was driven to his side like a magnet.

Row upon row of gray plastered tombs sentineled the path to the Randolph vault. Crumbling urns and bas-relief willows were the sole decoration. But atop her father's vault, a marble angel prayed to the heavens, her hands outstretched like the feathered wings on her back. When Sercy had died, her mother had placed the angel on the tomb. Now the angel watched out for all three of them. And one day, Leila thought darkly, the angel would watch out for her.

A movement from down the path caught her eye. She turned and every hair on her nape stood on end. He was staring at her. At least she thought he was staring from that black hole in his cowl. The monk stood at the end of the path, a hundred yards away, staring at her, his arms crossed over his chest, his body not moving.

The vision of him in broad daylight seemed almost supernatural. Or perhaps surreal. His dusty brown robes didn't flutter in the breeze; he stood frozen, watching. A chill ran down her back, freezing her in his vision. She wanted to call out to him, to brand him a lunatic and demand that he never cross her path again, but she was too afraid. And she still had to see him at midnight. She had to plead her case once more for Mr. Blum and all the others like him to whom she owed money.

Maybe he was the devil. The thought shocked her, frightened her. It wasn't a novel idea but it almost seemed to be the truth. If she was in a bargain with the devil, the monk just might take her soul, but she didn't know if that was so dear a price to pay when her soul was heartsick and weary. She didn't even know if she wanted a soul in the unfathomable loneliness of life without love.

"What am I to do, Father?" she whispered to the tomb. "Who do I turn to? This creature of night? Or do I marry a man I don't love like so many have done before me?" She fingered the letters carved in the plaque that sealed the vault. Her father had given her anything and everything. He'd done it solely out of his love for her. But now his generosity might have proved to be too much. She wasn't prepared for want and deprivation. She had to caution herself against doing something foolish in order to avoid them.

"Let me do the right thing, Father. Help me to do the right thing." She repeated her words like a prayer and finally found the courage to look down the path again.

The monk was gone. Until midnight.

"What do you mean the bill has been paid?" Leila stared down at the ledger. "How was it paid? Who paid it?"

M. J. Davis of Davis Emporium closed the ledger book. "I can't say, Miss Randolph. All I know is that an envelope arrived this morning and in it was the instruction that we were to clear the Randolph account. There was more than enough money to do so. Here is your change, miss." He handed her a half-dozen silver dollars.

She stared down at the coins, then shook her head and tried to hand them back. "No, I'm afraid there's some mistake. This can't be for my account. There's nothing left, you see. I don't see how this money could have materialized—''

''Perhaps it arrived from an anonymous benefactor. The Drew family I hear is quite fond of you.'' Davis placed the ledger back on the bookshelf and rubbed his hands. ''Now, may I show you something today, miss? Are you in need of any articles for your mourning?''

Numb, Leila shook her head. She thanked the shopkeeper and walked out onto Canal Street, parasol in hand.

It was inexplicable, Charles must have made provisions before he left for Natchez to have her bills taken care of, but as uncharitable as she knew it sounded, she just couldn't believe it. Charles could barely take the time to keep his own accounts current, she just couldn't imagine that he'd had the presence of mind to attend to hers.

But maybe she'd misjudged him. Perhaps there was more character and feeling in him than she'd been led to believe. She'd have to write him that very day and tell him how grateful she was; she would assure him that she would pay him back as soon as possible.

Exhausted, she decided to take the streetcar home. The side-to-side roll of the car was much like the rocking of a cradle, and she preferred that over a long, stuffy ride in a crowded omnibus. She arrived at the designated street corner just as a familiar black carriage pulled alongside.

''Good day to you, Miss Randolph.''

''Mr. Lacour,'' she answered, staring at him from beneath the black fringe of her parasol.

''May I offer my carriage?'' He alighted and held the door for her.

She hated him to do her favors when he'd caused her father so much misery, yet, on the other hand, she was tired. A carriage ride was much more acceptable to her weary feet than the streetcar.

''I'm not a vampire, Miss Randolph, I don't bite.'' He grinned, watching her hesitation.

''Of course you don't. You wouldn't dare.'' She glanced at him.

His grin widened. "Oh, but I do dare. It's just that I prefer to do other things to young women than bite them."

Taken aback, she said, "Such as?"

He again motioned to the carriage. "Why don't you allow me to help you into the carriage, and I'll show you?"

"I should refuse your hospitality, Mr. Lacour." She gripped the handle of her parasol.

"Yes, you should." He again nodded to the carriage.

Reluctantly, she gave him her hand. The carriage turned on Calliope and they were headed back to Washington Avenue.

"Tell me, Miss Randolph," he said after a few moments of silence, "I understand there's been a stream of creditors at your door. If I may be so bold, how do you plan on making them go away? Do you plan on selling the family home? If so, I may be interested in purchasing it."

She gave him a dismissive look. "My father left me a very valuable mirror which should take care of any debts as soon as I acquire it."

"Acquire it? You mean you don't have it now?"

"No," she answered gloomily.

"Where is it?"

"That's none of your business. But I plan to keep my home, so your offer to buy it—while generous—is premature."

"I thought to buy it so that we both may live there." He met her gaze. His eyes searched hers so deeply her breath stopped.

"Mr. Lacour," she said softly, "why do you persist when I've refused you time and again?"

"The human heart needs hope, Miss Randolph." A muscle bunched in his jaw. "I can't help but dream that one day you'll see beyond your father's ruin, and beyond this scarred face to see the man who sits before you now."

She looked down and ran her palm over the jet beads of her purse. "When I was in Paris at the academy, there was a small kitten who showed up in the courtyard. He was a brindle color, all battered and scarred from fighting. He was quite ugly actually, and mean too. But I couldn't watch him starve and I began to feed him."

She looked up at him. "I tried to pet him one day, and this is what I got for my effort." She pulled off her glove and showed him a long thin scratch mark on the back of her hand. "The mark has never quite gone away, though it's been months." She pulled on her glove again. "I've learned my lesson, Mr. Lacour. I no longer look beyond the obvious."

"But this ugly scarred cat, he kept the rats away, did he not?" He turned to look out the window.

She studied him. In profile, with his scar away from her, he looked almost handsome. His hair was thick and dark, but closely cropped, not easily ruffled. He possessed a strong nose and chin and when he looked at her, she remembered the deep blue of his eyes.

"He kept the rats away," she answered softly, thinking of Charles and how he'd paid her accounts. She would have to write him today and thank him for his help.

"Here we are." He nodded toward the window. The carriage pulled in front of her house.

"Thank you." She looked at him.

He met her gaze. "Would you have dinner with me tonight, Miss Randolph? Perhaps I can convince you that I tried to keep your father's best interests at heart."

A strange discomfort gripped her. She didn't want to fraternize with the enemy, especially now that she'd noticed his handsome profile. It made her feel weak and vulnerable, and she was already too much of both.

"I'm afraid I cannot, Mr. Lacour, I hope you'll forgive me, but I've another engagement." Such as a visit to the Verly plantation at midnight, she thought to herself.

"Perhaps some other time, then," he said somberly.

She looked at him. The logical answer was "Perhaps" but she couldn't quite mouth the word. Giving him hope would be almost as cruel as what he'd done to her father.

The coachman helped her disembark. In silence, she trod up the front stairs to the veranda. When she next looked down, he was still in his darkened coach, staring at her as if he could not look away.

CHAPTER FIVE

At ten minutes before midnight, Leila glanced at the parlor clock and made her decision. She would go again without Sally. Not that she wasn't afraid; in fact, she was terrified. But Sally would be even more frightened and perhaps serve as a distraction. That was the last thing she needed—to go begging before a lunatic monk and have to placate Sally at the same time.

With resolve she did not feel, Leila pinned her black chip bonnet onto her head and left through the front door.

No one was on Plaquemines Street as she followed the cemetery wall toward the Verly house. Gaslights burned in few homes. Most were dark and silent like the tombs that lined the cemetery paths like little houses.

At the gate of the old plantation house, she was half-relieved to see a light burning in a window. Perhaps the man was no longer prone to theatrics. If she could just see his face, appeal to his humanity, she might be able to deal for the mirror.

But her worst fear was that he had no face, no humanity, to appeal to.

"It's Miss Randolph," she called into the dark, empty foyer. Dust and years of cobwebs covered the old gas sconces. "I've come as you asked," she called again.

A light flared in a room to her right. She stepped through the open doorway and found herself in a library with shelves of foxing books. The smell of mildewed paper hit her nostrils at the same time as the sulphurous smell of a lit lucifer.

"You still wish to bargain?"

The voice came from behind her.

She spun around and found the man in monk's robes sitting in an oriel behind the massive mahogany library doors. He held the mirror in his lap. The jewels sparkled in polychrome splendor beneath the flames of one small candle. She could see nothing more except his hands. The same hands she remembered: strong, well-formed, their backs sprinkled with dark hair.

"I . . . I wish to bargain, but I must know the terms," she sputtered, wondering if her face had turned ashen again.

"The terms are everything in your heart which you cannot sell. I want it all. The good and the evil. Every intangible emotion you will release to me, and for that I will relinquish your precious mirror." He stared at her—she was sure—through the gaping black hole of his cowl.

"I'm not sure how to go about what you ask, and even if I were, I must tell you I have other options. My father said the mirror may be cursed. Surely it has not brought you happiness or you would not hide yourself from the world in those robes."

He released a dark laugh. "The mirror is cursed. It brought Anne Boleyn little luck."

"Then perhaps I shouldn't want it back."

"But what are your other options about which you seem so smug? Tell me and, if they are compelling, I might be forced to lower my terms."

"I've a fiancé. His name is Charles Drew. My father might have spoken about him to you. Marriage to him would surely solve my monetary woes."

"Or give you deeper sorrow instead." His hands stroked the mirror. "Tell me about him."

"He's a fine man from a good family," she answered reluctantly.

"But you don't love him, and he doesn't love you. He only thinks you a prize to be won because he likes your pretty face."

"You couldn't know that." She lifted her jaw. "He'd make an exemplary husband."

"For a porcelain doll. But you're not one, are you, Leila? Prove to me you're not and the mirror is yours."

"My name is Miss Randolph," she said, her words cold.

"Ah, Miss Randolph then. But I must tell you this is not a good beginning."

"Perhaps, but I would have your name now. You're not a true monk—most certainly you've taken no vows of silence. What is your name, sir?"

"I am from a far and away isle where I was named after a monk who lived there twelve centuries ago."

She frowned. "You make no sense. What is your name?"

"That is not part of the bargain."

"Then at least let me see your face. Whether you are friend or foe, I don't see why you would hide from me."

He grew still. "I hide myself in order to better lay bare your soul."

"Perhaps I'm the one without a soul," she murmured, her depression rushing back to her like a swift black cloud.

"Did you weep at your father's passing?"

"Yes," she said, her eyes filling with tears even now. "I loved him. And he loved me."

"What was there to love in you?"

She paused for a moment and thought. "I don't know."

"There was a pretty face. You have a lovely face, Miss Randolph—"

"But he loved more than just my face," she cried out. "He was part of me and I was part of him. Neither of us were any good with money. Both of us were lost without Mother. You see, I am the daughter of two good, wonderful people and I will be strong and good and righteous if only just to serve their memory well."

She caught her breath. Her words were more passionate than she'd wanted, and more revealing.

"You did love them, Leila," he said.

"Yes," she conceded with a whisper.

"Bravo."

She watched him. He still stroked the mirror. His handsome big-knuckled hands moved up and down along the bejeweled back with a lover's touch. The contact of his palm was feather light, and she shivered remembering how that same caress felt upon her cheek.

"Will you look into the mirror, Leila? Will you make it beautiful again?" He held the hand mirror out to her.

Gently, she took it into her grasp. It was heavy, and the sapphires that paved the handle made it awkward to hold.

"Look at your face," he commanded.

She looked into the mirror. Perhaps it was the age of the glass, or the dim lighting, but the reflection of her visage seemed to have faded. She polished the face with her sleeve, yet the reflection became no clearer. Her reflection was almost ethereal, growing more translucent with each viewing.

"This is certainly an old mirror. The silver seems to be clouded."

He nodded and held out his hand.

With extreme reluctance, she gave him back the mirror.

"You will come here every night at midnight until you've won the mirror."

Dismayed, she said, "But I don't have forever. I must decide my path now. The creditors visit my house like a flock of ravens."

He looked at his own reflection in the hand mirror. She wondered what he saw. "It won't take forever. You will make your choices. So go now. Don't come back until tomorrow."

Leila drew herself around the pillow and breathed a long sigh. Sleep proved elusive. She'd been back from the Verly place for hours but still she tossed around in her bed like a rag doll.

What did the man want from her? The question haunted her more than the vision of a tall muscular man in monk's robes. She'd expected lewd proposals, but even her father warned her that that was not what he wanted. The monk wanted more—but what? Her soul? If such a thing were for the devil's taking, her soul was not so worthy that he couldn't take a hundred more from the streets and be just as satisfied.

What she suspected he really wanted was someone with whom he could play cat and mouse. The man got his fun scaring young women and she was all set to play because of her desperate need for funds. The man probably loaned her father the money for the mirror just in order to do that. Knowing James Randolph's notoriously poor health, he was probably just waiting for her father to die so that the game could begin.

She mustn't go back, she told herself logically. It was a game she couldn't win. The man might be mad. He might hurt her. And he was bound to keep the mirror. She had no legal authority to acquire it. It was his until he should decide to give it away, and it was a costly price to pay for a few moments of perverse fun.

She rose from the bed and swatted away the mosquito netting. Lighting a candle, she took pen in hand and began to write. She sealed the note with a red wax seal, pressing the letter *R* into the hot wax. She then placed it by her bedside table in order to post it first thing in the morning.

Charles would return when he received her plea, she thought to herself. He would be compelled to return. If all went well she might find him back from Natchez by the end of next week. Surely she could hold out that long. If he was willing to pay her bills, then he should be willing to marry her quickly and in secret. Then in six months, when the mourning period was over for her, they could remarry with the blessing of his family.

She rolled on her side and heaved another sigh. Somehow, her mind told her to believe it would happen, but her heart did not.

CHAPTER SIX

"Oh, Jenny, what's to become of us?" Leila stared out the parlor window at the dreary morning. Cold gray rain dripped on the leaves of the live oaks that lined the front of the Washington Avenue house. There were seven trees, lined up like soldiers, their branches twisted and turned like skeletal fingers clawing for the sky.

Jenny rose from her chair and walked over to her sister. "It's me, isn't it? I'm a burden, aren't I? Sixteen years old and not a beau in sight. No wonder Charles ran to Natchez. He probably wasn't counting on Papa dying and leaving the cripple under your care."

"Nonsense!" Leila shook her head. "Charles knows we're together and he's paid our bills, or didn't I tell you that? Indeed I went shopping yesterday and from what I can tell, all our accounts have been cleared."

"He did that?"

"Yes. Before he 'fled' to Natchez, so no more talk about you being a burden. I don't think it, and clearly Charles doesn't think it."

"Do you love him, Leila?"

The question was quiet and respectful. Leila found she couldn't refuse an answer.

"I wasn't sure. But now that he's cleared our accounts, perhaps if I know he loves me—perhaps I can grow to love him."

"You can't. He's not worthy of your love, and you know it." Jenny sank onto the settee. "I know, I know. I certainly don't like the man, but, Leila, his character is such that—"

"His character is such that he's cleared our accounts," Leila interrupted. In dismay, she said, "You've never hid your dislike of him, Jenny, but he is the most eligible man in New Orleans. He's handsome and witty and rich."

"And he drinks too much, and he doesn't appreciate you, and his mother controls him like a puppet." Jenny shook her head. "Oh, I don't want to argue. If you want him, you must have him. No one's ever been able to deny you."

"You know I want what's best for you too, Jenny. You know you're never far from my thoughts," Leila supplicated.

Jenny looked at her sister. She smiled softly. "Some say you're cold and superficial, Leila. The gossipmongers like to say you went after Charles Drew like a mercenary just because you knew Father was dying. But you know I don't think it. You've always put my needs before your own, and, though you'd deny it, I know this controls your every action and deed."

"I love you, Jenny. I could never turn my back on you," Leila whispered, tears flooding her eyes.

"I know it," Jenny answered, tears in her own eyes, "but you mustn't marry a man you don't love in order to see me taken care of. I can't let you do it. There has to be another way."

"There is another way," Leila answered enigmatically.

"Which is?" Jenny prompted.

"Which is going to remain a mystery unless it works out." Leila looked down at her hands. They were giving her away; they were trembling. She did a lot of trembling thinking about the monk and his strange philosophical ramblings.

"You won't tell me anything?" Jenny exclaimed, her expression clearly taken aback.

"Unless it works, there's no point in you knowing. Father told me about this just before he died. It's one last avenue to pursue and I'm doing just that."

"It doesn't involve Charles Drew, does it?" Jenny seemed to be holding her breath.

Leila laughed. "Oh, how sorry you'll be when he's your brother-in-law. No, it doesn't involve Charles Drew."

Midnight came again with the sounding of twelve bells from the dining room clock. Leila stole out of the darkened house and made her way along the cemetery wall to the old Verly house. The monk seemed all too happy to ask the questions but tonight, she'd decided to ask some of her own.

"You're late," he said when she met him in the old library room full of cobwebs. His hands toyed with the light of a lone candlestick, causing grotesque shadows to dance along the cracked plaster walls.

"I came at once, but I have to warn you I cannot come here indefinitely. I've written to my fiancé to return to New Orleans. I've begged him for a quick marriage and as soon as he arrives here, I'll no longer have any desire to acquire your confounded mirror." She looked at him. He was dressed as always in the robes. The cowl still shielded a face. Tonight was the first night her courage was up, and she wondered what he would do should she trick him and pull back the hood.

"Your fiancé was a fool to have left the city and you behind. I cannot imagine he will have the intelligence to return swiftly." The monk laughed.

"He'll come and when he arrives I plan to marry him. I've discovered he cares for me more than I thought, and with him, I believe my sister and I will be in good hands." Leila lifted her chin in defiance.

"Charles Drew has done nothing for you and never will," he grumbled.

"*Au contraire*. I find he's cleared our accounts and he had to have done this before he took off for Natchez. Clearly our well-being was foremost on his mind."

"Drew's concern for your well-being is nothing but bovine excrement."

"Excuse me?" she interrupted. "I hardly think you to be a judge of me as you sit here in your ghostly quarters hiding your face from all and sundry. I don't even believe you're a real monk. You just dress in those robes to hide from the world."

"I was not always like this," he murmured.

"No?" she said. "So how is it that you've come to be like this then?"

"As other monks, I find myself banished because of a woman. She turned from this hideous face and forced me into this cloak. Would you like to see it, Miss Randolph? Would you like me to be unmasked so that your dreams will turn to nightmares upon the glance of this ghoulish face?"

Her heart drummed in her chest. She could feel the blood rush to her cheeks. A part of her wanted to see his face. She wanted to confront the devil and her fears. But her emotions quickly twisted in the grip of her imagination. There were some things not meant to be gazed upon. The Bible was full of such stories. Perhaps she should decline.

"Afraid you might turn into a pillar of salt, Leila?" he dared, obviously reading her thoughts.

"I haven't come here to gaze upon your face, gruesome though it might be. I've come for the mirror," she refuted.

He nodded. "Yes. The mirror. It's over there, by you. On the table."

She looked to her right. The hand mirror lay upon a quarter inch of dust atop an old-fashioned rosewood table. She went over to it. Her finger traced the cursive *B* along its back and she pondered the sad fate of its former owner.

"Hold it to your face," he whispered.

She did as he told her. But quickly, she brought the mirror to her side once more.

"Put it to your face," he commanded again.

"I can hardly make out my face for the light in here is too dim. The reflection is poor."

"Hold it to me then and see how crisp the reflection really is." He stared at her.

She did his bidding. She held the mirror to him and saw each fold of his cowl, but when she shifted the hand mirror to her own face, the reflection grew cloudy and indistinct. "I don't understand . . .'' she gasped. ''My face seems to be fading from it. This doesn't make sense when everything else is so clear.'' A sudden terror hit her. Her father told her the monk wanted her soul. Was he slowly taking it from her? Was that fact being revealed in the fading reflection in the mirror?

''You look pale, my dear. I bid you sit.'' He stood and towered over her. She hardly had time to catch her bearings before he led her to a dusty chair next to his.

''I think I must go and not return to this evil,'' she said, trembling all over again.

''What do you fear most? Me? Or the mirror?''

''I don't know.'' She looked at him. He was in front of the candle, but even so, she was so close she could almost make out a face in the cowl though the features were still a blank. ''Am I a fool to be afraid of an inanimate mirror when I should truly be afraid of a madman in monk's robes?''

''You'd do well to fear neither. I and the mirror only want to know your soul.''

''Or take my soul.'' She stared at him. ''Are you the devil? Are you Satan and am I to become your handmaiden? Is this the price my father feared I'd pay for my freedom?''

''Is freedom what you want above all else—?'' He grabbed her hands in his own. Hers were cold while his were warm and strong. He stroked his index finger along her palm until she shivered and tried to draw away. But he wouldn't let her. ''Or is it your precious Charles Drew you want?'' he whispered. ''You spoke of marriage before. I vow I will take your soul like the devil if only to spare you from giving it to Drew.''

She pulled away from him. His hands were too strong and too masculine for her sanity. She was beginning to like the way he ran his hard finger down her sensitive palms. ''If the truth be known, I want my freedom above all. I have my sister to care for and I can't do it without the means.''

''Tell me about your sister.''

''She is a beauty.''

''So she takes after you.''

Leila was taken aback by his compliment. Pausing, she

looked at him and wondered for the thousandth time what his terrible face looked like. "She is very beautiful, and only sixteen, but she was born with a club foot. She limps and sometimes is forced to walk with a cane. She fears no man will ever want her, and as much as I try to disabuse her of this notion, she will not abandon it. Now with Father gone, I fear her prophesy may turn out because we haven't the means for a debut, and I don't know how we're to get along in society with no funds."

"You love your sister."

"Yes," she answered. "I'll never leave her."

"Could you ever love a man with such fidelity?"

"You mean Charles?"

"I mean a man, any other man than him."

"I might love Charles that way. Now that he's—"

"What if you discovered it was not he who cleared your accounts? What if you found out it was another?"

She stood and drew back. "Who else would it be?" she asked, a new fear running through her.

He stilled. "I want you indebted to me, Leila. It will ensure that you come here every night until the mirror is yours."

Tears came to her eyes, but the shock of his words froze them. "I can't believe it. You think to make me your emotional captive? You think I believe this lie you're weaving? You couldn't have paid my accounts. It had to have been Charles."

"Your precious Charles is up at Natchez, gambling with the devil's own fever, and I'll wager he's given you and your sister nary a thought."

He voiced her worst fears, but still she had to fight it. She had to have hope. "No, I won't believe it was you."

"Write Charles. If he's truly any kind of man, he'll deny paying them."

"What do you want from me?" she said, finally unleashing her tears. She swatted at her cheeks and backed away. "I've come here in honesty, I just want you to return the mirror, I don't want more indebtedness."

"It frightens you, doesn't it?" He walked toward her. Behind them, the candle sputtered in a pool of wax, soon to extinguish in it. "This indebtedness seems such a burden, and yet, what have I asked of you? A spare visit at the midnight hour. Just a conversation, and then I set you free once more."

"But you want more. Father warned me you'd want more. So tell me what it is."

The candle hissed and dimmed. Suddenly her back met with the wall. She was trapped. He loomed before her, his tattered, dusty robe nearly enfolding her.

"What I want is a visit, a conversation, a pretty face at my knee. Is that so much to ask?" His hand reached out. She cringed but he ran his knuckles across her cheek anyway.

"Your hand should be cold as death: Instead it's warm. Traitorously warm. I think you deceive me with your costume. I think you're only too human and frail, no spirit at all." She shivered, but refused to run. Her defiant glance met with the dark void of his cowl. She was utterly brave, until the candle went out.

"You think I'm only too human? Let me show how human I am, how human and vulnerable to your pretty face." He placed his hands on either side of her cheeks. He swept back the dark hair that had fallen over her brow and he turned her so that her face was tipped toward his and in silhouette from the window that still flickered with low light from the street gas lanterns.

"Don't," she begged as his finger luxuriantly traced her lips.

"Don't touch you? I don these robes so that I will not touch you. Why else would I pick monk's robes?" he growled, his hands turning to iron.

"Please," she gasped.

"Yes, please," he whispered, the black void of his cowl drawing near her like a face.

"I beg—" she murmured before the cowl descended upon her face and his lips met with hers.

Terror and revulsion hit her. She fought to break free but arms made of iron wrapped around her and held her against him. She moaned; her hand rode up to shove him away, but before she could even find his face, his hand intertwined with her own and clamped it to her side.

. His lips moved as any other man's might have done. If there was anything sinister in his kiss it was that he refused to let her see his face; he even kept her hands to her side in an effort to dissuade her from touching him. He remained as cloaked and mysterious to her as he ever was, though their intimacy was thorough. His mouth roamed hers like a man starved. He was as ferocious as he was gentle, and the gentleness began to supplicate and win her over. Finally, when she could no longer summon the will to fight, his kiss grew more intense, and she felt his tongue explore her mouth. With every deepening movement, her resistance ebbed, until her guard came down completely, and she leaned against him wanting more.

"Now how do you beg?" he said cruelly, sensing her surrender.

Disoriented, she broke away and grabbed for the wall to steady herself. "I won't beg at all," she whispered defiantly, her tongue thick and unruly after the wine of his kiss.

"I've wanted to stay away from you. I've wanted you to come to me. Will you do that?" he asked, his voice sounding just as drugged as her own.

"No," she gasped, clinging to the wall. "I will not beg from a man who will not even show me his face. You won't even let me touch you—"

"Perhaps my face is so ghastly that I want to shield you even from the feel of it."

"But why?" She tried to gather herself, but her mind still reeled from what had transpired. Her hands trembled as she pressed her fingers to her kiss-bruised lips. "I just want to see the man behind the hood. I want to know you're real. It's less frightening that way."

"I could not bear to see the loathing on your face if I reveal myself." The words were etched with anguish.

"But I shall steel myself from the horror of it. I'm prepared to see anything now."

"But not this. Not me." He shook his head. Mournfully,

he stepped away from her. In the darkness, all she could see was the ghostly outline of his monk's robe.

"I must go. These visits are futile. . . ." She licked her lips, hating the lonely feel of them now. "Perhaps even dangerous, I think."

"You must return. Tomorrow night," he roared, his anger a presence in itself.

"Why?" she countered, backing once more against the wall.

"Because you want your freedom, and there is no freedom without this." He held up the mirror. Even in the darkness, she could see it glitter with an unearthly sheen.

"I shall return once more. You'll make your terms clear tomorrow night, or I shall take the other path given to me."

"You will not marry Charles Drew. Your life will unravel into abject misery if you do."

"There are worse men I could call husband."

"No."

"Yes," she countered. "I could marry a man in monk's robes who never shows me his inhuman face." With that, she stumbled to the door and fled.

CHAPTER SEVEN

"It's Mr. Lacour, Leila," Jenny announced as Leila was just sinking into a tub bath.

"Here now?" Sally interjected, still holding the last copper can of hot water.

"Yes." Jenny's eyes widened. "He says you agreed to go to dinner with him."

Leila rolled her eyes. "Of all the dastardly tricks. I most certainly did not agree and he knows it. Oh, how awkward he's making all of this." She shoved aside the bubbles and began to scrub with a bar of Castile soap.

"What shall I tell him?" Jenny asked anxiously.

"Tell him—oh, tell him—no, *I'll* tell him," Leila exclaimed and rose from the rub. She took the proffered dressing gown from Sally and wrapped herself in it. "I'll be down shortly, and then I'm going to give that man a wretched piece of my mind."

"Oh, Leila . . ." Jenny just stood there, a glum expression invading her face.

"Well, what is it?" Leila asked.

"I hate to even ask since you despise him so, but he told me his nephew was in the city today all the way from Ohio. And he asked if I might come to dinner also in order to keep his nephew company—with your chaperonage, of course."

Leila stared at Jenny. There was no way to say no when all

the light of excitement and wonder shone in her sister's sad eyes. "His nephew, is it?"

"Yes. He's a clerk in a law firm. He's studying to become an attorney, isn't that exciting?"

Of all the things Leila wanted to say, the word *exciting* didn't come to mind. Used, manipulated; these notions were certainly at the forefront, but when she gazed at Jenny, she couldn't summon the disposition to tell her the truth. Besides, she felt it rather self-centered of her to believe that Lacour had arranged the entire thing as a ruse to get her to have dinner with him. Perhaps he truly did have a nephew in town. Certainly it was possible he had no other eligible females to introduce the poor boy to other than she and Jenny. It was pretty obvious just from meeting Aidan Lacour that he was not a social butterfly.

"Sally, tell Mr. Lacour I'll be down as soon as I'm able." Leila looked at her sister. "Then help Jenny with her maroon velvet. That's the gown for this dinner, don't you think?"

Jenny grinned. "It's my best."

"It makes your cheeks look pink as a posy. That should charm this young law clerk." Leila glanced at herself in the mirror. She, on the other hand, would need some work to look young and fresh. The midnight hours she'd been keeping wore hard upon her; her eyes were smudged with lavender shadows and her cheeks were white and drawn. In short, she looked enough of a fright to scare even the monk himself.

"When should I tell Mr. Lacour that you'll be down to see him, miss?" Sally asked before taking her leave.

Leila sighed and had another bout with the mirror. "I don't know, Sally. In fact, don't give him a time. It'd do him good to cool his heels in the parlor. The man has more gall than anyone I've ever met."

"And more handsome nephews . . . At least that's what he told me," Jenny added, her expression giddy.

"He'd better be right about that," Leila threatened, then returned her attention to the mirror.

*   *   *

". . . and so I introduce to you, ladies, my nephew, Josiah Kelley." Lacour lifted a dark eyebrow. "And I follow this introduction with a quote from Brigham Young, saying that any man who is unmarried at the age of twenty-one is a menace to the community."

Leila smiled. Jenny giggled nervously at her side. The young man who stood next to Lacour in the Randolph foyer blushed a deep scarlet.

"You overestimate my ability for mischief, uncle," the young man said.

"Oh, do I? I thought I rather underplayed it." Lacour smiled and held out Leila's black velvet mantle. "Shall we go? I've a private room at Pierre's. It should be quite sufficient to hide two ladies in mourning."

Leila accepted the mantle. She thought Lacour's hands lingered a bit longer than they should have upon her shoulders but there was no recourse. She locked arms with Jenny and allowed the gentlemen to escort them down the veranda steps to the waiting Lacour carriage. Sally brought up the rear and sat with the driver, offering added chaperonage.

Lacour sat across from her in the carriage. Leila gave him a couple of glowering looks, but his nephew, Josiah, already seemed entranced with Jenny. The girl's club foot didn't seem to bother the boy at all. The situation seemed too good to be true, so Leila pinched herself and reminded herself that she was only along because Lacour had orchestrated the entire affair. The warning siren was still going off in her head when they arrived at the French Quarter landmark of Pierre's.

Seven octagonal gaslights flared beneath the old copper awning. Pierre himself greeted them and escorted the ladies to his own private room. There, the table was surrounded with the rich bejeweled costumes of last year's Rex, King of Carnival.

"Oh, this is quite lovely, Mr. Lacour," Jenny gushed, her hands shaking as she reached for her first sip of champagne.

Or dangerous, Leila thought, cradling her champagne stem in her fingers and mentally vowing to keep to one glass.

"I was just telling Mr. Kelley today that New Orleans is

famous for its beauties but none can rival the two Randolph girls.'' Lacour raised his champagne glass. Kelley followed.

Leila nodded uneasily. ''Mr. Lacour, I fear flattery will get you—''

''Will get me what? I'll take even your leavings, Miss Randolph. My public infatuation with you is becoming quite a spectacle.''

Kelley laughed. ''You have to watch out for us Irishers, Miss Randolph. We can talk anyone into kissing the Blarney Stone, isn't that right, Aidan?''

''Indeed. We pride ourselves on our persuasive powers. It's the Druid in us. It's quite mystical, if you can tap into it.''

''Druids. Mysticism. This is all rather over my head, I'm afraid.'' Jenny glanced sheepishly toward her sister.

''Yes. We've never even been to a séance, and as you know, they're all the rage these days.'' Leila stared at Lacour from the top of her champagne glass.

''Is there anyone in particular you'd like to speak to if you did attend a séance?'' Lacour returned the stare.

''I would like to talk to our mother.'' Leila glanced at Jenny. ''I know you think we are quite spoiled, Mr. Lacour, but our father was always showering us with gifts in order to compensate for the fact that our mother died at Jenny's birth. After that, we had no one but him.''

''He loved his two daughters more than any man I've ever known,'' Lacour said solemnly. He stared at Leila and added, ''Perhaps I can understand why he wanted them taken care of after his own passing.''

''He did want us taken care of, but without even realizing it, he gave us the best gift of all: the will to take care of ourselves.''

Lacour smiled. ''I want all the details of how you plan to manage, Miss Lacour, but in the meantime, here is Pierre. Let us enjoy our dinner without past rancor, shall we?'' He lifted his champagne glass.

She had no choice but to comply.

* * *

The party arrived back on Washington Avenue well after ten o'clock. Leila nervously glanced at the clock on the marble parlor mantel. She didn't have much time before she would be due at the Verly house.

Kelley said his good-bye to Jenny along with the invitation to take both ladies for a carriage ride the following afternoon. Lacour kissed Leila's hand and she had the definite suspicion that he would be along for Kelley's carriage ride at four. The men took their leave. Jenny seemed to float up the mahogany staircase as if she were waltzing on clouds.

Leila hoped it wasn't a mistake to have introduced Jenny to Josiah Kelley. The two seemed like the perfect couple and Kelley did seem genuinely taken with Jenny, but Leila knew to be cautious where love was concerned, especially with Jenny as vulnerable to hurt as she was.

"Is he just the most handsome, wonderful man you've ever seen?" Jenny sighed as Sally unhooked her dress.

Leila took a perch on the window seat and stared out at the street below which was quickly being covered with a midnight fog. "He did seem genuine. I hope we discover it's so."

"What do you mean?" Jenny asked dreamily.

Leila didn't know what she meant. Struggling with her words, she said, "Kelley's uncle is rather manipulative. I just hope this evening had less to do with Aidan Lacour's machinations, and more to do with the fact that you are a truly charming lady, Jenny."

"Oh, it's too good to be true. I suppose I shouldn't get my hopes up." Jenny seemed to come crashing to earth like Icarus.

"It's not that I don't want you happy, I didn't mean to cast doubts upon this evening. We both had a fine time," Leila supplicated.

"Yes," Jenny answered, throwing aside her evening gown, "we did have a fine time, but I want you to know, sister, that you don't have to worry about me. I'm not going to do anything silly like fall in love with a man who doesn't love me. I know I'm less than most women with this ugly old limp of mine, but I have my head on straight."

"Kelley couldn't find a better lady than you, Jen. In fact the young lout hardly deserves your company and if Father were still around to turn the young men away, I'd be happy to see him given a run for his money. As it is now, while we're still grappling with our future—"

"As it is now, I have the most wonderful sister in the world who I know will work things out." Jenny smiled and squeezed Leila's hand. "I just want her to not be afraid of my disappointment. I've already had more than I ever expected this evening."

Leila gave her a wavering smile. "I'm glad. I don't want to see you hurt."

"The only one who's going to get hurt is you, Leila. Especially if you pursue that odious Charles Drew."

"He's cleared our accounts—"

"Charles Drew!" Sally popped her head from the dressing room. "Oh, miss, I completely forgot. A letter came from Natchez while you were out this afternoon. It was from Drew himself. I put it on the parlor mantel and forgot about it until now."

Leila felt her heart quicken. The thrill of the letter was unexpected; again her hopes flared. "Thank you, Sally." She rose from her chair and kissed Jenny on the forehead. "Don't you worry about me, either, sister. Things may not be as bleak as they appear. I've still a few surprises left, you know."

"Yes, but where Charles Drew is concerned, they'll all be bad surprises." Jenny plopped into her feather bed and smiled.

Leila could only shrug.

25 October 1872
Natchez, Mississippi

My Dearest Miss Randolph,
How my heart grieves for your loss! At this dark hour, how I wish that mine was the shoulder you cried upon. I think of you always and I curse the cruel fate that placed me here in this den of iniquity instead of by your noble side.

*I await your letters with a still and mournful heart. I
know how vile your duties are now. In order to settle
your father's estate, it should be your husband to deal
with the attorneys and bookkeepers. We should have
married in haste. And I plan to do so, darling, upon my
imminent return to the Crescent City.*

*The only delay that keeps me here even one day
longer than necessary is financial. My dearest, I
wouldn't even ask this of you, but now that your father's
estate has surely been settled, a small loan would bring
me closer to your side than anything you can bestow
upon your beloved. Of course, I shall repay you in all
speed, but who cares for these details when soon we will
be united in love, and what's mine will be yours and
yours mine.*

*If you could but send one hundred dollars by courier
as soon as you receive this, my grateful soul will return
to your side with all the swiftness of a bird.*

Much love and tender regard,
Yours truly,
Your ever beloved,
Charles

Leila lowered the letter. Her hands shook with disappointment. Her worst fears were confirmed. The cad didn't even
have the intelligence to realize she would see through his
schemes. He sorely underestimated her.

Outside the long parlor windows a fog swirled through the
streets playing devil with the gaslights. Behind her, the mantel
clock dinged the half hour. It was eleven-thirty.

So Charles was more of a bounder than even she guessed.
By the request for funds in his letter, it was obvious he was
not the one who cleared her accounts. She thought of the letter
she had just posted to him and she smiled with wry amusement. Her thanks and gratitude were surely going to confuse
him. And he was going to be sorely disappointed when the
one hundred dollars he'd requested of her didn't arrive. Even
if she had one hundred dollars to her name, she was in no

position to be handing it over to him to settle his gaming debts.

She walked over the hearth and placed Charles's letter in the coal grate. She watched it burn to ashes in the flames. Her decision was made then and there that she had to forget Charles Drew and do without him. He was never going to amount to anything. More than that, his letter had proved a godsend. She didn't love the man. It was best now to forget him.

But she couldn't forget the monk.

Her wary gaze rested upon the parlor clock. Fifteen more minutes to midnight.

He was her last chance at salvation and survival. Even now she knew he waited for her, his monk's robes thick with dust and damnation.

Her father's warnings rang through her ears as she retrieved her evening mantle from the foyer settee. She hadn't even bothered to change from her dinner dress and she wondered if the satin evening gown, black though it was, was a bit too décolleté for a visit with a man who'd made a vow of chastity—even if that vow was with the devil.

She looked at herself in the parlor mirror. The gilded mask of Hercules stared down at her from the top of the mirror frame. He was laughing at her. Her visage was perfectly clear in the mirror this night. Once more she saw dark blue eyes shadowed in a pale face, surrounded by brunette hair. But she somehow couldn't shake the premonition that she and Hercules knew her face was destined to be much more indistinct in the Boleyn mirror.

She swallowed her feelings of doom and replaced them with a sort of reckless anger. Tonight the mirror would be hers. She was determined to do whatever it took to have it in her hands by dawn.

Even if it meant selling her soul to the devil to do it.

CHAPTER EIGHT

The fog was thick along the Lafayette Cemetery walls where Leila stole through the night. She clung to the shadows in her black velvet mantle as if afraid to be seen by the occupants of the street. Or perhaps she was more afraid of the dead seeing her. For all she knew, the monk lay among the residents of Lafayette. One night he might whip back the cowl and there would be no human face to greet her, only the vision of a smiling skull.

Her hands shaking, she opened the rusty iron gate to Verly. A candle was lit on a lower room of the mansion. A small comfort. In all probability, ghosts did not need to light candles.

She opened the front door.

The monk was there at the end of the long foyer. He was draped in his robes, the cowl successfully hiding his face once more.

"You're late." His voice was hoarse.

"I didn't realize I would receive marks for tardiness," she said with an acerbity she didn't feel.

"This isn't some little ladies' academy whereby you receive a grade if you pass." He held up the mirror. The moon shadows from the rear foyer windows gave it a surreal glow. "This meeting is about whether you win back your mother's prize, or whether you lose it to me forever."

"What will you do if I lose it to you?" she asked, still not moving from the front doorway.

"If you lose it to me, then I will have won. All the terrible things I see in your character will be exposed as the truth."

"The terrible things in my character," she mused, "such as vanity?"

He nodded.

"Selfishness?"

Again he nodded his head. The cowl bobbed up and down.

"But what will you do if I prove those things are not within my character? What will you do if I take the mirror from you and you no longer possess it?"

"Then I shall leave this place and go back to where I came from."

"And never think of me again?"

He didn't move. "I will always think of you. Whether you're vain and selfish, or an angel, I must always think of you."

"Why? I'm still not sure why you toy with me like this. I cannot bring you anything by these games."

"You can bring me company." He seemed to stare at her. "Take off your mantle and let me see you in your evening gown."

Slowly she unclasped the jet-adorned frog and allowed the mantle to slide past her shoulders.

"What do you bring me, Miss Randolph?" he whispered, staring. "You bring me pleasure."

"Where will you go if I take back my mirror and banish you?" she asked, walking toward him, her heart made brave by the darkness and his strange worship of her.

"I will return from whence I came."

"Where is that?"

He grew still. "Exactly where you came from, Leila. From the ashes and dust of a thousand moldering corpses that went before us."

"So you admit you're a man made of flesh and blood, or are you a creature of my dark imagination?"

"I am both," he answered.

She drew toward him as if he willed her to his side. "If I'm to reclaim the mirror, I need to know the truth about it, and I need to know it tonight. Why does it obscure my face?''

''You must determine that for yourself. See yourself in it now. What do you find there?'' He held up the jeweled mirror.

She looked in it and this time saw nothing but the far end of the foyer. Her face, her whole being, was gone from it entirely.

''Good God, there's nothing there,'' she gasped, her lips shaking.

''This is how Anne Boleyn saw herself the day she walked to the executioner,'' he said.

Her heart constricted with fear. ''She had no vision of herself in it either?''

''No.'' He tipped his head back and laughed. The sound echoed through the house like a cry from the grave.

''What kind of magic is this?'' she lashed out, panicked. ''What does it mean to not be able to find your face in this wretched mirror?''

''It means that you are either pure of soul or devoid of a soul.''

''Which is it for me then?'' She grabbed the mirror and looked at herself again, but she could find nothing of herself in it: only the reflection of the furnishings and walls behind her.

''You know which in your heart. Only you know the truth that lies within the mirror.''

Hating him at that moment, she lowered the mirror and looked at him. ''If I must lose my face to this mirror, then it's only right that you must show yours.'' She went to him and tried to grab the hood. He moved quickly like a cat from the jungle. Before she could utter a cry, his arms were wrapped around hers, capturing her.

''I know you have a face. I've felt your lips on mine. They were real,'' she cried.

''Your father told you I would not take your flesh when I wanted your soul. But I will have the sins of your flesh too,'' he promised.

She struggled to be free but his arms were like a vise. Claw-

ing at his hands only proved her undoing for he quickly tipped
her face to his and kissed her once more.

She moaned; she melted. His hands were warm and inviting
while the drafts from the old house were like icy fingers on
her shoulders. Leaning into him, she took his mouth on hers
like a draught from a wine jug. His taste was musky and hard,
like bourbon.

"Please, no more," she whispered when he broke his mouth
from hers.

"What is the price you're willing to pay, Leila? Your flesh
or your soul?"

"My flesh would be the easiest," she moaned, his caress
on her cheek undoing her.

"But what is the soul without the flesh to follow it? If I
wait, I might get both," he told her.

He leaned down and kissed her again. Her hands reached
up inside the cowl, searching for his face, but he clasped them
with his hands and forced them to her side.

She opened her mouth to his tongue. He filled her with
honeyed demanding strokes. Before she could get her bearings
once more, she realized his hand was on her breast, cupping
it, stroking it, his fingers toying with the neckline of her dinner
gown.

"You must stop this," she gasped, pulling away his hands.

He whispered, "Flesh to flesh, is it not right we be together?"

"But I cannot sell myself for a mirror," she cried.

"It's not just a mirror, it's a window to the Otherworld.
Don't you see? This isn't about material goods and possessions. Your spirit needs mine as mine does yours. Don't think
about your wretched house and all the bills your father left
behind. Go beyond that and you'll see the truth about which
I speak."

"I'm afraid," she sobbed as he held her.

The hands turned gentle. They stroked the pads of her
cheeks and brushed aside the dark curls that fell into her eyes.
"Don't think. Just do, and I'll be yours." Slowly, persua-
sively, he lowered his lips to hers. Her face was shadowed by
the cowl, and still his features were nothing but darkness and

obliterating shadow. But she knew his kiss well. His lips moved like velvet-covered iron over hers and begged with an eloquence she had no will to refuse.

"Kiss me this time," he whispered, outlining her lips with his thumb.

She stood on tiptoe and did as he asked. Her fingers found his own lips in the darkness of the cowl and she pressed hers luxuriantly upon them.

The kiss grew and matured. His arm went around her waist and nearly took her feet from the floor. This time, when his hard, impossibly warm hand reached beneath her neckline and captured her breast, she couldn't rebel. She wanted his touch too badly.

"Give me all your worldly desires. They will be made real in this fantasy we spin now like a web, trapping us together." His voice was low and harsh against her cheek.

"My only desire is to feel safe, as safe as I feel when strong arms are around me."

"Are my arms strong enough?" he asked, his thumb brushing her nipple.

"Yes, they're strong, but treacherous, for they haven't a man's face." Unbidden tears began to stream down her face.

Shocked, he stared down at her. What little she could make of his mouth in the darkness, now all she saw was a grim line.

He let go. She nearly fell to the dusty floor. His arms were more strong around her than she'd imagined. They were nearly holding her up.

"This is only about *things* when I would have it about souls," he cried out bitterly.

"Show me your face. Prove to me your humanity. You want and lust like any other man, but how can you take me when you have no face to show your pleasure?" She grabbed for the mirror and held it up. "Show me your face now that you've taken mine. Show me the monster or the man behind the hood."

"I cannot. If I do, all is lost . . ." he groaned, backing from her.

With resignation, she nodded. "If I must give you my soul for this mirror, it's the price I'm finally willing to pay. So either way, I will take the mirror now. Unless you have the means to stop me.''

He grew angry. Growling from his corner, he spat. "That is our bargain. But are you sure you're willing to pay so high a price as to discard your own soul for a mirror that is nothing but a piece of metal and stone?''

"I'm not discarding my soul. I'm selling it. If I must,'' she answered quietly.

"Take the mirror then. You decide if your soul was worth it.''

She clasped the hand mirror to her chest. "If I sell my soul to the devil, then I at least want to see this devil's face.'' Without warning, she stepped to him and grabbed the cowl. It fell around his neck, but he jerked his head around before she could make out his features.

"I see the devil has a head of dark hair much like a real man,'' she said to his back.

"You pretend to be more guileless than you are, Miss Randolph.''

She looked at the mirror. Reluctantly, she placed it on a dusty table near the front door. She had to be sure she was willing to pay the price, no matter how dear, and she needed one more day to think about it. If she must give up her soul, she wanted another day to ponder the loss. "That I am, sir. That is why I won't be taking the mirror with me tonight. It brought Anne Boleyn such ill-fortune, and perhaps even my mother. I don't know. All I do know is that I must first think long and hard how much I'm willing to pay for this vile thing. I shall return tomorrow night at midnight. Then I will have determined whether this mirror has cleansed my soul . . . or removed it.''

She stared at him. He looked back at her, keeping his face hidden in shadow.

"So you think to set the rules to this game now,'' he snarled.

"Let the buyer beware. I learned that well from my father.'' She flipped her mantle over her shoulders and left him to his moldering dark house and even darker thoughts.

CHAPTER NINE

"You're so quiet today, Leila. Aren't you feeling well?" Jenny walked up to her, her characteristic limp helped by the use of a cane.

"Goose! I'm feeling quite well today," Leila answered, her brow furrowed in thought.

"You seem a million miles away. What's weighing on your mind? Is it the money troubles?" Jenny placed her hand on her sister's shoulder.

Leila turned from the parlor window where she had spent all morning staring out at the empty veranda. "No, no. I don't want to even hear about you being worried with our finances. We're going to do just fine. You'll see . . ." she answered, her voice trailing off.

"Perhaps I should send Mr. Kelley a note and tell him we won't be going with him today."

"Where are we going, Jenny dear?" Leila asked.

"Remember? He asked if he could take me out in the carriage this afternoon? I just assumed you'd come along as chaperon and—"

"Oh, yes. Of course. No, don't cancel out on him. You should have some fun. It's long overdue."

Jenny looped her arm with Leila's. "But how can I have fun when you seem so preoccupied?"

Leila sighed. She looked down at their arms and shook her head. "I'm just being a ninny. I keep thinking about the cost of things and my mind starts wandering away down dark paths.''

"Please don't worry. When you worry, I worry."

Leila looked at her. "Then let's not talk about this. Let's go upstairs and pick which traveling dress would look best for your ride with Mr. Kelley. I think the black taffeta, don't you?''

Jenny smiled. "Oh, do you really think black is my color?"

Leila stopped. She looked at her sister and she began to giggle. "Yes, I'm with you all the way, dear Jen. The day we get to go into lavender half-mourning is the day I go mad with joy. Good lord, I know Father would forgive me, but I'm so very sick of black.''

Mr. Lacour was strangely absent from the carriage when Josiah Kelley arrived to take the two Randolph ladies out. Leila thought it odd, but his behavior was far from her mind as she sat silently between her sister and Mr. Kelley.

Her thoughts had been focused on the mirror all day. She hadn't slept last night because she knew she had to make a determination soon or lose her mind.

It was the price that she still didn't know if she was willing to pay. The idea of her face not showing in the mirror shocked and horrified her. She wanted to believe it was that she had been cleansed of her vanity, but the doubts assailed her. She was no angel. Perhaps she had already lost her soul to that terror cloaked in brown.

Sensing her preoccupation, Mr. Kelley made the ride short. He brought them back to the house in due time with promises of another invitation to dinner. Jenny again was nearly swooning over the gallant Mr. Kelley after he departed. She nearly ran up the stairs to her room.

Leila, on the other hand, had too much on her mind to notice her sister's happiness. She decided to take a walk to the lending library on Calliope Street. In the back of her thoughts, she wondered if perhaps the library might have something on Anne Boleyn—or even her ill-fated mirror—which might help her with her decision. All she knew was that she was going to have one more meeting at midnight with this monk, and she would either walk away with the mirror, or realize that poverty and death were preferable.

Leila left Sally at the entrance to the old Milhouer Lending Library. She decided to ask one of the librarians to help her and soon she was ensconced at a leather-topped table, surrounded by a parapet of books on mysticism, spiritual telegraph, biographies of the wives of Henry the Eighth, and catalogues on the crown jewels of England.

"Oh. I forgot. One more thing." She looked up at the harried young man who was assisting her. "Do you have any books on monks? Or Druids?"

The man lifted an eyebrow, but he returned shortly with three more volumes.

"Thank you," she said brightly, knowing she must look eccentric at best.

"My pleasure, miss." The young man bowed and left her to her studies.

Leila immersed herself in reading. The library gaslights were lit at five and still she couldn't break away from the books. Spiritualism had never captured her like the rest of the country, but she found the subject fascinating, and innately comprehensible.

"The library will be closing in thirty minutes, miss." The young man expediently took away the books she'd already gone through.

"I'll be done shortly," she promised, then turned to her books on monks. The first was a tome about the monasteries of Ireland. She flipped to the table of contents.

Then her eyes popped open.

CHAPTER TEN

The night was cold and brisk when Leila walked by the cemetery wall at midnight. A full October moon lit her way and the iron gates squeaked and rattled in the wind. By chance, she realized it was All Hallows' Eve. Tomorrow she and Jenny would go to Lafayette and adorn their father's tomb with laurels like all the good Catholics in New Orleans.

But tonight, she was paying her final visit to the monk. Her way was clear. Her mind was set. She would face the devil and play his game of magic, for finally she knew how to win.

Verly appeared tragic and run-down beneath the silver moonbeams that broke through the bramble of tree branches. The gate screamed in rebellion as she opened it, but this time a chill didn't run down her spine. Her need for flight wasn't lit aflame by every bat that flew from the eaves of Verly. She didn't need succor as before.

She was a different woman tonight.

Perhaps the mirror had taken a bit of her soul after all. Or maybe it had given her back the piece that had been missing. But now the pieces had all fallen back together. The fractured existence that she saw before had been neatly mended into a clear image. One she was going toward with open, grateful arms.

"I've come to see you," she said solemnly to the monk. He hid in the darkness of the library, and her every gesture seemed to cause him to cower from the light.

"Have you made your decision?" he demanded, his hand in front of the black void in the cowl.

"I have," she answered, walking toward him.

He seemed less terrifying tonight. Though she'd swear against it, she thought she saw him take a step backward into the room's oriel. It was almost as if he were more afraid of her than she of him. His hands seemed to itch to draw the oriel's curtains and hide himself away in the darkness.

"Anne Boleyn was deprived of the knowledge I have tonight. She met her death because she'd given her soul to the devil—her husband. That's why her face didn't show in the mirror. I know that now," she said solemnly.

"Is that what you've found out?" His voice held a sneer. "But is that the case with you? You have no husband, yet, to fear him."

"No," she said softly. "And even if I did, my soul is intact; it's my heart I've given away."

"To Charles Drew?"

"I've been thinking a lot about marriage this day. I wonder, would it be so terrible to give myself to a man who only longed to take care of me? Would it destroy my soul to tell this man his love is not in vain? I can't answer these questions."

"If it's for Drew, you waste your breath. Your end may not be what Anne Boleyn's was. But at least hers was swift and heartless—perhaps a blessing. If you hook yourself to Drew, your demise might be far more miserable for its length."

"I don't want to suffer. I've suffered for my mother, my father. Now I suffer for Jenny. I want to see her happy."

"Her happiness might be worth the price of this mirror." He held it to her.

Outside the wind blew through the shutters. They banged and scratched at the windows like lost souls begging to get inside. She knew her moment had come. The mirror would finally be hers. The truth would finally be hers. The hour had rung.

She moved toward him, her hands outstretched to take the mirror. The wind picked up, the candle flared in the draft.

She reached out to take the mirror.

He bowed his head and placed it before her.

In a flash, she lifted her hand and whipped back the cowl.

The face she'd expected was there, staring at her in horror and self-loathing.

"I knew it," she whispered, her heart pummeling, the blood rushing through her ears.

"How did you know?" he gasped, holding his hands up to his face as if to hide it once more.

"I read about the Irish monk who made his bargain with the devil. Ireland would starve no more for the soul of poor . . . *Aidan.*" She smiled, his scarred face suddenly very precious to her, not evil at all. "When I read about him, I knew it was you who was behind the robes. You yourself gave it away. You said you were from a faraway isle, and that you were named for a twelfth-century monk. I finally saw that the good St. Aidan was trying to make a bargain with the devil again. But this time for me." She looked at him. "I should hate you, you know. I should more than ever, but I don't. I think I understand why you forced this trickery upon me."

"Your father knew I wanted you. He didn't want me to play these wicked games, but you rejected my every advance. In the end I told him I might not have any other choice. And so it was."

"I didn't want to believe my beloved father created the misery he had by himself. It was easier to blame you for his money problems and refuse to see the flaws in his character. Just as it was easier to blame you for our problems and refuse to see the vanities within my own soul."

He lowered his hands from his face and stared at her as if seeing her for the first time. "I would not have caused James Randolph misery. I did everything I could to keep him in good stead. I would have moved heaven for him."

"I see that now. I understand that you cared for him. *And for me,*" she added in a whisper.

He stared at her. The candle flared again, throwing light into the crags of his expression. She wondered if there were tears glistening in his eyes as there were in hers.

"I know you must have paid off our accounts," she said. "I was a fool to think Charles had done it. I just wanted to believe the truth that was in my head, not my heart."

"I don't want to buy your love, Leila. I want it freely given."

She laughed. "So is that why you've hidden here at midnight in this wretched place and toyed with my very soul in this mirror so that I might freely give my love to you?"

"It was my last chance. The only way. I could never see you falling for this ugly scarred face, so I thought by hiding it away, you might see the man instead. But now that you know who I am and what I've done, I see I can't play these tricks any longer. I want your love freely and generously. I don't want to hide anymore. I want all your love, or I'll take nothing. I'll deserve nothing."

She took the hand mirror from him. Her face shone in it as clear as if it were a new glass. A new hope was born inside her. "My soul is cleansed by our meeting, sir monk. I've proven my worthy heart to you and to myself. Now the mirror is mine, once and for all. With it, I've all the money I need, so you're most definitely in a bind now. You've finally given me the means to not be in need of a man to take care of me."

"So take the mirror then," he said angrily. "Take it and be gone. You've won it fairly, and now you may sell it to the next unwary fool."

"Yes. I can do that, can't I?" she said, studying her reflection in it. Her face was crisp and clear. All back again.

"You can do anything you want, which is the folly of these tricks I've played." Slowly he sat down upon the dusty Gothic chair she'd seen him in that first night. He hung his head in his hands as if weary of the world.

"Yes, I can do anything. Which is why I fear I might not want to sell the mirror. I don't have to, do I?"

He looked up. Shock crossed his features and the painful gleam of hope entered his eyes. "If you were my wife there would be no need to sell it. I've no need for money. I've more money than I can spend."

"That is certainly an option. But I'd rather my fiancé dress in a morning coat and tie than monk's robes. The neighbors might not take your vows of chastity for the truth.''

He reached out and grabbed her hand. She placed the mirror on the table next to them and allowed him to pull her onto his lap.

"I've loved you even when you were nothing but a spoiled little girl pulling on your father's sleeve for a piece of licorice.'' He looked deep into her eyes as if searching for something. ''Even then you seemed to have a piece of my soul. And when you grew to womanhood, I felt I knew you. I was desperate to win your love. When your father died, I despaired because I didn't have him there to convince you.''

"You still think me spoiled?'' she asked playfully.

"You are spoiled, but as I've just seen, you've a heart that compares to none. Jenny alone proves that.''

She shivered beneath the sure stroke of his hand on her cheek. Her heart seemed to expand beneath her corset. She voiced her worst fear. ''My love, I hope Josiah Kelley really does return her affections. I'd hate to think you trumped that up as another one of your machinations to snare me. She is so alone. Sometimes I just weep thinking about how much she hates that cane of hers.''

"Josiah's mother was a beauty much like Jenny is, but she was confined to a chair for her leg was mangled at birth. I don't think Josiah has even noticed her cane, and if he did he's probably glad Jenny is not as much an invalid as his mother.''

"Oh, dare I hope this to be true?'' She locked gazes with him.

"Do you believe my love to be true? Here, let me prove it.'' His hand went around her nape. He pulled her forward and locked his mouth with hers.

The kiss was deep and strong. Her fingers ran along his jaw and she was amazed to feel how soft his scar was. The evil expression she'd always placed on him seemed gone though his face had not changed. Now all she saw was the love that flickered in his eyes even in the dim light of one candle. Her own heart filled with love also. If this was a bargain with the devil, she prayed every day to play such games.

"You must tell me one thing." She picked up the mirror and reflected both their faces in it. "How did you work this so that my face disappeared in it?"

"It was magic."

"Come now." She giggled, touching his cheek. "It can't have been."

"I'm a Celt. My ancestors were Druids. I told you the other night that strange stuff has long run in my blood."

"Even this devilish magic? I don't believe it," she gasped.

"What is love if not magic?" he whispered, taking her face in his strong hands and kissing her once more.

HERE IS AN
EXCERPT FROM
DANGEROUS TO LOVE—THE
PASSIONATE NEW ROMANCE FROM
REXANNE BECNEL:

No one had warned her that he wore an earring!

That was the first thought that shot through Lucy's head.

They'd arrived very late at the grand address on Berkeley Square. She'd thought the butler a trifle surprised and perhaps a little worried when he'd bowed them into the foyer. But she'd attributed that more to the fact that Lady Westcott had not sent word ahead that they were coming.

She'd caught the scent of tobacco in the air as she followed Lady Westcott to her suite of rooms, and had suspected, from the lights she'd seen burning, that someone was at home. When the door to the dowager countess' sitting room crashed open and this unannounced male stalked in, however, she knew at once that something was amiss. And also that he must be the new earl.

He was home all right, and he was not in the least happy to see his grandmother arrive.

Still, of all the things she might have noticed about him— his dark lean features; his glossy black hair; his tall, broad-shouldered silhouette—it was the earring that transfixed her. A gold, glinting hoop that winked back the oil-fed light, and defiantly proclaimed his gypsy heritage.

She was to protect Lady Valerie from *him?*

Her knees went weak and her mouth went dry. How had
his grandmother described him? *He is not without a certain
appeal?* Though Lucy would freely admit that her experience
with men had been limited in recent years, there was not a
doubt in her mind that this man very likely possessed more
physical appeal than half the men in London combined.

Then he opened his mouth and she discovered the reverse
side of that considerable appeal.

"Get the hell out of my house!"

Lucy gasped—or at least she assumed it was she who'd
made that shocked sound. Lady Westcott merely stared at her
coldly furious grandson without so much as blinking an eye.

"I believe we've had this conversation previously. As I told
you then, I will not be put out of my own home. You, however, are free to leave, if that is your desire."

"My desire," he snarled, glaring at the dowager countess
with eyes as frigid as the winter sky, "my desire is to never
lay eyes on you again."

Lady Westcott stiffened. It was only the tiniest of gestures,
but Lucy saw it, and her heart broke for the frail old woman.
She forced her frozen limbs to life.

"How impossibly rude you are," she snapped, moving to
stand beside her hostess. "Lady Westcott has had a long and
tiring day. The last thing she requires is to be set upon, and
in her own private quarters. Did no one ever teach you to
knock?" she finished in her sternest governess' tones.

The unconscionable rogue did not do her the decency of
even transferring his glare from his grandmother to her. Nor
did he in any other way acknowledge that he'd heard Lucy's
indignant words. "I am entertaining guests," he continued in
the same insulting tones, "none of whom are of the sort you
are wont to mingle with. Nor are you their sort," he added,
with a mocking twist to his lips.

"I have no intention of greeting your guests," Lady Westcott retorted, holding firm to her position. Still, Lucy detected
the hurt in her voice and she sprang once more into the fray.
How dare he attack an old woman this way, his own grandmother! And how dare he ignore *her* as if she did not even
exist!

This time she stepped in front of the countess, forcing him to recognize her presence. "I'll thank you to depart these apartments. Now," she added. "Right now!"

The glacial stare focused on her. The mocking smile thinned. The furious voice turned low and dangerous. "Unless you are here for some useful purpose, it would be better if you remove yourself from this discussion."

"I am here for a . . . for a very useful purpose," she sputtered. If a body could burn with outrage and yet freeze with unreasonable fear, hers did both. "I am a guest of Lady Westcott's and I—"

"This is my house, not hers. The only guests I will allow are my own." The frosty glare moved over her, head to toe, taking a swift yet alarmingly thorough appraisal of her appearance. Then those bitter blue eyes met hers again. "Dare I hope your purpose here is carnal? And that it involves me?"

She slapped him.

It came out of nowhere. Certainly she did not plan it. But in the ringing silence left in its aftermath, she was not sorry. He deserved it. It remained now only to see how he responded. There was no predicting what a man as cruel and hateful as he might do in retaliation.

He raised a hand to his offended cheek and despite Lucy's intentions to be brave, she took an involuntary step backwards.

The room shuddered with the silence. From somewhere far off in another wing of the house she heard the faint echoes of music, of a piano forte playing and a woman singing. But in this particular chamber there was no sound at all.

Then the earl took a breath and Lucy braced herself for the worst.

Instead of lunging at her, however, he bowed—a very correct though abbreviated bow. Lucy blinked in disbelief, then stared warily at him. What was he up to?

His expression told her nothing, for he'd wiped his face clean of any telltale emotion. His voice, when he spoke, was equally unemotional.

"My apologies, Madam. I more than deserved that. I only

hope you will find it in your heart to overlook my unfortunate behavior.''

It took Lucy a moment to collect her wits. An apology was the last thing she'd expected from this man, this gypsy earl who was as handsome as sin. She was certain, however, that it was just about as sincere as Stanley's and Derek's apologies to each other usually were.

She drew herself up, tugging angrily at the waist of her wrinkled traveling suit. ''I have never—never!—been so rudely treated in my entire life!''

His face remained impassive. But at least he was looking at her now instead of glowering at his exhausted grandmother. It occurred to Lucy that Lady Westcott remained uncharacteristically quiet, but she was not about to give ground by breaking eye contact with the earl. If she was to be dealing with him as often as Lady Westcott had indicated, it was critical that she establish the ground rules right now.

As their locked gazes held, his lips curved up ever so slightly. Or at least she thought they did. ''Might I inquire who it is that I have treated so rudely?'' he asked, one dark brow arched in question.

Lucy assumed the countess would introduce her. After all, it was only proper. When she did not, however, Lucy let out an exasperated breath. ''I am Miss Lucy Drysdale of Houghton Hall in Somerset.''

''Miss Lucy Drysdale,'' he echoed, emphasizing the ''Miss.'' Again his eyes flickered over her. But before she could take umbrage at his boldness, he executed another bow. ''Allow me to introduce myself, Miss Drysdale. I am Ivan Thornton, Earl of Westcott, among other things.'' He paused. ''You said you had a useful purpose for being here?''

Once again one black brow raised in question, but this time Lucy could see the arrogant purpose lurking behind the bland expression he'd adopted. He was no more sorry for insulting her than she was sorry for slapping him, the wretched man!

''I am here to act as chaperone to Lady Valerie Stanwich for the season. Your cousin, I believe? To safeguard her from inappropriate suitors—''

"Like myself, perhaps?" He grinned then, and in that one isolated moment Lucy had a terrible revelation about herself. For with that easy grin, that tiny movement of flesh over teeth—beautiful, strong, white teeth, as it happened—he deflated all her anger. Like a silly, smitten girl, she reacted to that smile, to the appeal his grandmother had alluded to. Her heart began a maddened pace, her cheeks began to heat. And all on account of a smile.

With a silent groan she ordered herself to cease such foolishness. She gave him a severe look. "If this is typical of your behavior, then yes, I would say you are entirely inappropriate for a proper young lady."

This time he laughed, though she'd certainly not meant her statement to amuse him. Before she could muster an indignant response, however, Lady Westcott finally broke her silence.

"Do not bother to argue with my grandson, Miss Drysdale, for you will get nowhere at all with him. His greatest joy in life is baiting me. Since I refuse to participate in his game, I fear you may become his next target. I advise you to ignore him," she finished.

Lucy had kept her eyes trained on the earl while his grandmother spoke and saw the quick veil of dislike that covered his face. When he responded to the countess's comments, however, his words were directed at Lucy. "My grandmother may be right, Miss Drysdale. After all, she has known me longer than anyone else. Now, if the two of you will excuse me? I have a house full of guests. If I do not return to them they may come searching for me. I suspect you would not enjoy that."

Without further excuse he left, and with him, it seemed, went all the vitality in the room. What an absurd idea, Lucy thought. And yet it was true.

Lady Westcott let out a long sigh, as if she'd been holding her breath. Lucy too exhaled, somewhat unsteadily. She looked over her shoulder at the older woman who raised a hand, forestalling anything Lucy might have to say.

"You needn't say a thing, my dear. I can see it in your face. He is not what you expected, is he?"

Lucy grimaced. "I would not state it quite so . . . so blandly as that. May I sit down?"

"By all means. I'll ring for a tray. There's nothing like a glass of cognac to calm the nerves." She gave Lucy a searching look. "Are you up to this, Miss Drysdale? Can you hold your own with my unpleasant grandson? Or would you rather beat a hasty retreat back to your quiet countryside?"

If Lucy *had* been reconsidering her reason for being in London, the countess' reference to Somerset cured her of it—and she suspected the clever old woman knew it.

"I would prefer to have been better forewarned that he . . . dislikes you so intensely," she said, deciding to be candid. "Also that he has so . . . is so . . . That he has such a presence about him," she finally said.

"That he is so damnably attractive, you mean." Lady Westcott squinted at her. "I trust you are not so unwise as to be swayed by his manly countenance."

"Of course not!" Lucy retorted. "But I cannot vouch so easily for your godchild."

"You will be able to handle Valerie; that does not worry me at all. As for his dislike for me, that is of no moment. No moment whatsoever."

So she said, Lucy thought as a maid brought in a tray of tea and biscuits, and a decanter of cognac. So she said. But it was obvious that the old woman was as drawn to her brooding grandson as were all the other ladies of the *ton*. Lucy suspected the old woman wanted his affection. She wanted his familial love.

Whether she would ever get it was highly debatable, and quite beyond Lucy's sphere of influence. All she could do was make sure the Lady Westcott got what she said she wanted: Lady Valerie Stanwich safely wed to an acceptable gentleman. And safely out of Ivan Thornton's clutches. Beyond that she would not concern herself with the gypsy earl's personal affairs.

Later, however, once Lucy was settled in her bed, in a very pretty room across the hall from the countess' suite, she found her mind wrestling with the most inappropriate thoughts.

He really was a gypsy, with his coal black hair waving over his collar and that hedonistic earring. But he was an earl, too, and Lucy understood fully the magnetic pull he would have on any young woman's senses. To even think of those enigmatic eyes gazing into hers, of those strong tanned hands touching her—

She let out a decidedly unladylike oath and turned angrily to her other side. She would *not* think of such things. She could not allow herself to do so. Her role was simple and easily defined: keep Lady Valerie out of Ivan Thornton's clutches.

Still, she couldn't help wondering what female would ultimately fall *into* his clutches. And whether her lot would be awful—or wonderful. . . .

DANGEROUS TO LOVE
BY REXANNE BECNEL—
LOOK FOR IT IN OCTOBER
FROM ST. MARTIN'S
PAPERBACKS!

If you crave romance and can't resist chocolate, you'll adore this tantalizing assortment of unexpected encounters, witty flirtation, forbidden love, and tender rediscovered passion...

MARGARET BROWNLEY's straight-laced gray-suited insurance detective is a bull in a whimsical Los Angeles chocolate shop and its beautiful, nutty owner wants him out—until she discovers his surprisingly soft center.

RAINE CANTRELL carries you back to the Old West, where men were men and candy was scarce...and a cowboy with the devil's own good looks succumbs to a sassy and sensual lady's special confectionary.

In **NADINE CRENSHAW**'s London of 1660, a reckless Puritan maid's life is changed forever by a decadent brew of frothy hot chocolate and the dashing owner of a sweetshop.

SANDRA KITT follows a Chicago child's search for a box of Sweet Dreams that brings together a tall, handsome engineer and a tough single mother with eyes like chocolate drops.

For The Love of Chocolate

YOU CAN'T RESIST IT!